Brett Battles lives in Los Angeles, where he is currently at work on the third book in the Jonathan Quinn series. His website is www.brettbattles.com.

THE DECEIVED

Jonathan Quinn is a professional 'cleaner': he disposes of bodies and ties up loose ends; he doesn't get his hands dirty; he doesn't ask questions. But when Quinn is hired to vanish all traces of Steven Markoff, a rare friend in his line of work, all that has to change. Determined to avenge Markoff, Quinn embarks on a trail that snakes from the corridors of power in Washington to the bustling streets of Singapore, along with his quick-witted apprentice Nate, and the brilliant, beautiful Orlando. But events spiral dangerously out of control. The pace quickens as the bullets get closer . . . and to trust is to be deceived . . .

Books by Brett Battles
Published by The House of Ulverscroft:

THE CLEANER

BRETT BATTLES

THE DECEIVED

Complete and Unabridged

CHARNWOOD
Leicester

First published in Great Britain in 2008 by
Preface
The Random House Group Limited
London

First Charnwood Edition
published 2009
by arrangement with
The Random House Group Limited
London

The moral right of the author has been asserted

British Library CIP Data

Battles, Brett.
  The deceived
  1. Intelligence officers- -Fiction.
  2. Suspense fiction.
  3. Large type books.
  I. Title
  813.6–dc22

  ISBN 978–1–84782–761–6

Published by
F. A. Thorpe (Publishing)
Anstey, Leicestershire

Set by Words & Graphics Ltd.
Anstey, Leicestershire
Printed and bound in Great Britain by
T. J. International Ltd., Padstow, Cornwall

This book is printed on acid-free paper

For Ronan, Fiona, and Keira

1

The stench of rotting food and diesel fuel hung over the dock like it had been there forever. Even inside the small warehouse, the foulness overpowered everything. That was until the man in the light gray coveralls opened the door of the shipping container. Suddenly death was all Jonathan Quinn could smell.

Unflinching, he scanned the interior of the container. With the exception of a bloated body crumpled against the wall to the right, it was empty.

'Shut the door,' Quinn said.

'But Mr. Albina wanted you to see what was — '

'I've seen it. Shut the door.'

The man — he'd said his name was Stafford — swung the door shut, locking the handle into place.

'Why is this still here?' Quinn asked.

Stafford took a few steps toward Quinn, then stopped. 'Look, I got a dock to run, okay? I got a ship out there that's only half unloaded.' He sucked in a tense, nervous breath. 'I got customs people all over the place, you know? It's like they knew something like this was coming in today.'

Quinn raised an eyebrow. 'Did you know it was coming in today?'

'Hell, no,' Stafford said, voice rising. 'Do you think I'd be here if I did? I'd've called in sick.

Mr. Albina's got people who should take care of this kind of crap.'

Quinn glanced at the man, then turned his attention back to the container. He began walking around it, scanning it up and down, taking it all in. After a slight hesitation, Stafford followed a few paces behind.

Quinn had seen thousands of shipping containers over the years: on boats, on trains, being pulled behind big rigs. They were large, bulky rectangular boxes that moved goods between countries and continents. They came in black and red and green and gray.

This one, with the exception of where the paint had chipped away and rust had started to take hold, was a faded dark blue. On each of the long sides, tall white letters spelled out BARON & BARON LTD. Quinn didn't recognize the name, but that wasn't surprising. At times it seemed as if there were nearly as many shipping companies scattered around the globe as there were containers.

When Quinn reached the point where he had begun his inspection, he stopped, his eyes still on the box.

'You're going to get rid of this, right?' Stafford asked. 'I mean . . . that's what Mr. Albina told me. He said he was sending someone to get rid of it. That's you, right?'

'Manifest?' Quinn asked.

The man took a second to react, then nodded and picked up the clipboard he'd put on the ground when he'd opened the container's doors.

'What's supposed to be inside?' Quinn asked.

With the trade imbalance the way it was, nothing came into the States empty anymore. Any container that did would be suspicious.

Stafford flipped through several pages, then stopped. 'Tennis shoes,' he said, looking up.

Quinn glanced over at the man. 'One pair?'

'That's really funny,' the man said, not laughing.

'Who found it?' Quinn asked.

Stafford seemed unsure what to say. When he did speak, his words didn't match the evasiveness in his eyes. 'One of the dockhands. Said he smelled something when the crane set it down on the pier.'

'From that ship out there?' Quinn asked, motioning toward the door that led outside. 'The *Riegle 3*?'

Stafford nodded his head. 'Yeah. It was one of the first ones offloaded.'

'So this dockhand, he just brought the container in here and called you?'

'Yes.'

'You didn't call the police?'

'I run everything by Mr. Albina. He said to wait for you.' When Quinn didn't reply right away, Stafford added, 'That's the way it happened, okay?'

Quinn continued to stare at the man for a moment, then he turned and started walking toward the exit.

'Hey! Where are you going?' Stafford asked.

'Home,' Quinn said without stopping.

'Wait. What am I supposed to do?'

Quinn paused a few feet from the door and

looked back. Stafford was still standing near the container.

'Where did the crate come from? Who found it? And why did they let you know?' Quinn asked.

'I already told you that.' This time there was even less conviction in Stafford's words.

Quinn smiled, then shook his head. There was no reason to blame the man. It was obvious he was only saying what he'd been told to say. Still, Quinn didn't like being jerked around.

'Good luck with your problem.'

He pushed open the door and left.

★ ★ ★

'That was quick,' Nate said.

Quinn climbed into the passenger seat of his BMW M3. Nate, his apprentice, was sitting behind the wheel, a copy of *The Basics of Instrumental Flight* in his lap. Just a week earlier, Nate had begun small-aircraft flying lessons. It was just one of many outside training courses he'd be taking during his apprenticeship.

While his boss had been inside, he'd also rolled down the windows to let the cool ocean breeze pass through the interior while he waited. His iPod was plugged into the stereo playing KT Tunstall low in the background — a live cover of the old Jackson 5 hit 'I Want You Back.'

'Turns out they didn't need us,' Quinn said.

'No body?' Nate asked, surprised.

'There was a body. I just decided it might be better if they take care of it themselves.'

4

Nate let out a short laugh. 'Right. Better for who? Them or us?'

Quinn allowed a smile to touch his lips. 'Let's go.'

Nate looked at Quinn for a moment longer, seeming to be expecting more. When that didn't happen, he tossed his book in the back and started the engine. 'Where to?'

Quinn glanced at his watch. It was 11 a.m. The drive back from Long Beach to his house in the Hollywood Hills would take them over an hour. 'Home. But I'm hungry. Let's stop someplace first.'

'How about Pink's?'

Quinn smiled. 'That'll work.'

They drove in silence for several minutes as Nate maneuvered the car through the city and onto the freeway.

Once they were up to cruising speed, Nate said, 'So what exactly happened?'

Quinn gazed out the window at nothing in particular. 'They didn't tell me all I needed to know.'

'So you just walked?'

'I had to,' Quinn said. He turned to his apprentice. 'We don't need to know everything. That's not our job. But to do it right, sometimes there are things we have to know.'

He started to tell Nate about his meeting with Stafford. When he reached the point where he questioned the man about the discovery of the body, his cell phone rang. He pulled it out, looked at the display, then frowned. He knew the call would come, but it didn't make him happy.

'This is Quinn.'

'I understand you're not interested in helping us out.' The high pitch of his voice was unmistakable. Jorge Albina.

Based out of San Francisco, Albina was an expert at getting things in and out of the country. Money, people, guns, and apparently now bodies, too. His services didn't come cheap, but his success rate was one of the best in the business.

'We can pretend that's the reason if it helps,' Quinn said.

'It doesn't help if it's not the truth.'

'That's exactly where you and I agree.'

There was silence.

'Stafford told me you just left. No reason,' Albina said.

'He was mistaken.'

'That's not an answer.'

Quinn took a deep breath. 'Jorge, what's the most important part of my job?'

There was a hesitation. 'Whatever I say is going to be the wrong answer.'

'Not if you really thought about it,' Quinn said. 'But I'll tell you. Trust.'

'Trust,' Albina said as if he was trying out the word for the first time.

'Yes. See, you're trusting me with the knowledge of what happened, aren't you? You're trusting me to get rid of a problem so that it won't surface later, right? And you're trusting me that I'll never use what I've learned against you. Seems pretty important to me.'

'A little dramatic, don't you think?' Albina

said, irritation creeping into his voice. 'You're a cleaner. Your job is simple. Just get rid of the body.'

The muscles around Quinn's mouth tensed. 'You know, you're right. It's the simplest job in the world. So I'm sure you can find someone else to help you from now on.'

'Wait,' Albina said. 'Okay. I'm sorry. I know what you do isn't easy. And I trust you, all right? I trust you.'

Quinn took a deep breath. 'I have to trust *you*, too. I don't need to know a lot. Sometimes I don't need to know more than where the problem is. But when I do ask a question, there's a reason. I have to think about who else might know about the situation, and if they need to be steered in a different direction. I have to concern myself with where potential problems might come from while I'm working. I won't take on a job if I don't trust the information I've been given.'

He could hear Albina take a long, low breath on the other end. 'So where was the issue?'

'I asked your man how the container got there, who discovered the body, and why they called him. He lied.'

Albina sighed. 'Look, two days ago I received a phone call, okay? I was told a package was on its way to me. Something for me personally. I was given the name of the ship, the *Riegle 3*, and the container number. My people were already scheduled to unload it, so controlling it wasn't difficult.'

'Who was the call from?' Quinn asked.

'I don't know. It was ID'd as a Hawaiian number, but that was a dead end. Who knows where it really came from?'

'Man or woman?'

'Man.'

'But you didn't recognize the voice,' Quinn said.

'No. I didn't.'

Quinn contemplated for a moment. This explanation made a hell of a lot more sense than what he'd been told at the warehouse. But Albina was a smoother operator than Stafford, better at lying, so Quinn wasn't ready to trust the information yet.

'Is your decision not to help a final one?' Albina asked.

'Who's the dead guy?' Quinn asked. 'One of your people?'

He had seen the body for only a few moments, and even then it had been bloated and discolored.

'Is that really something you need to know?' Albina said.

'It is now.'

Albina was silent for several seconds. 'Not one of mine,' he finally said. 'The man on the phone told me the dead guy's name was Steven Markoff. I've never heard of him.'

Quinn tensed, his eyes frozen on the road ahead, but his voice remained neutral. 'Markoff?'

'Yeah. He spelled it for me. M-A-R-K-O-F-F. You know him?'

'Name's not familiar.'

'Whoever the hell he is, I just need to get rid

8

of him.' Albina hesitated a moment. 'It's my fault Stafford lied to you. My orders. I just didn't want to get dragged into this more than necessary.' Another pause. 'I need your help.'

Quinn knew Albina was holding something back. Only now it didn't matter.

'Quinn?' Albina asked.

'If I do this, you need to follow my instructions exactly,' Quinn said. 'No questions, no deviations.'

'Of course.'

Quinn tapped Nate on the shoulder, then pointed to the next exit. Immediately Nate began moving the BMW to the right.

'First you need to get the container away from the port,' Quinn said. 'You can get it past the customs people, right?'

'I can do that.'

'The trailer you put it on should be untraceable. You won't be getting it back. And make sure the truck you use doesn't have any tracking devices. If it does, I'll know it, and you won't hear back from me. If everything goes right, I'll leave the truck someplace where you can pick it up when I'm done.'

'Okay. No problem.'

'There's a truck stop along the I–15 east of L.A., toward Corona,' Quinn said, then gave him the name of the exit. 'Have your driver park the rig there and leave the keys under the seat. You should have someone follow him in a car so they can leave together. But that's it. No one else, understand? If I pick up even a hint that I'm being followed by anyone, the deal's off.'

'Done.'

'Call me once they've left the port.'

Quinn hung up without waiting for a response.

'So,' Nate said, 'does this mean we're back on?'

2

They made a few stops on the way out of town, picking up some items they'd need.

'Park over there,' Quinn said when they reached the truck stop. He pointed toward a group of big rigs parked just behind a row of cars. Albina had called only five minutes before to tell him the container had just left the port, so he knew it hadn't arrived yet. Still, he did a quick scan of the trucks to be sure Jorge wasn't playing any games. The container wasn't there.

After they parked, Quinn got out and had Nate pop the trunk. The storage space was covered by a dark gray carpet Quinn had installed himself. On the left side, on top of the carpet, were the items they'd purchased on the way.

Quinn ignored those and lifted up a section of the carpet on the right. Underneath was what anyone would expect, the metal bottom of the trunk. The only exception was a small black square mounted at the junction where the floor met the rear of the car.

Quinn placed the pad of his left thumb on the square. A moment later, the base of the trunk hinged up an inch, exposing a custom-built compartment below. He reached into the gap and released the catch, freeing the panel to open all the way.

The space below held his standard kit, things

he might need at a moment's notice. There were several cases, most made of hard plastic, and a few simple leather pouches. He ran his fingers over the cases until he found the one he wanted. After pulling it out, he grabbed one of the leather pouches, then shut the panel and put the carpet back into place.

He walked up to the open driver's window. 'You watch from here,' he told his apprentice.

'Got it,' Nate said.

Quinn opened the leather pouch and removed one set of communication gear. He inserted the earpiece into his right ear, its small size making it all but invisible, then attached the tiny transmitter inside his collar.

'Let me know if you spot anything I should know about,' he said, handing Nate the bag with a second set of radio gear still inside.

The interior of the truck stop was a familiar one — restaurant, gift shop, restrooms. Quinn wandered around looking at the postcards, the T-shirts, and the discount CDs as he checked out the other people inside. No one registered as a threat.

He bought a cup of coffee, found a stool near the window, and sat watching the action outside as trucks came and went. It was another forty-five minutes before a black Peterbilt semi arrived pulling a trailer that carried the familiar Baron & Baron, Ltd. shipping container. Following right behind it was a dark green Toyota Land Cruiser.

Quinn watched the driver park the truck, climb out of the cab, and walk over to the

12

waiting SUV. His door was barely closed when the Toyota sped off back down the road.

'Follow them,' Quinn said quietly, so as not to draw the attention of anyone nearby. 'Make sure they get back on the freeway. Then do an area check. See if anyone else might be hanging around waiting for us.'

'No problem,' Nate said over the radio.

Quinn watched his BMW pull out of the lot and disappear down the road. Cars and trucks continued to pull in and out while Nate was gone, but none paid any attention to the waiting truck.

Twenty minutes later, Nate returned. 'All clear,' he said.

Quinn exited the restaurant and walked across the asphalt to where the semi was parked. Learning to drive trucks had been just another part of his own training when he'd been an apprentice. As a cleaner, he had to be ready to use anything at his disposal.

Quinn's old mentor, Durrie, had enrolled Quinn in a three-month-long truck-driving class. Quinn had complained at the time, but in the years since, he'd realized it had turned out to be a very useful skill. Nate would be going through the same training the following year.

Quinn removed a thin rectangular metal box from the case he was still carrying, then flipped a switch near the top. He could feel a slight vibration as the detector came to life in his palm. Taking his time, he worked his way around the truck. The detector remained silent, picking up no evidence of any tracking devices. True to his word, Albina had left the truck clean.

Quinn returned the scanner to its case, then walked around to the rear of the container. A part of him wanted to make sure Albina hadn't pulled a bait-and-switch and put something else in the box, but the real reason for the check was that Quinn needed to confirm for himself that the dead man inside was indeed who Jorge had said he was.

He did a quick scan to make sure no one was near, then opened the door.

Again the stench. Bad, but not as bad as it had been in the confines of the warehouse. He climbed inside and pulled the door closed behind him.

He pinched his nose closed with one hand, forcing himself to breathe through his mouth. With the other hand, he pulled a small flashlight out of his pocket and turned it on.

The corpse was in pretty much the same place it had been when he'd seen it last — still against the wall, halfway back on the right side. He walked over and gently used his foot to roll the body onto its back.

For a couple of seconds, he all but forgot where he was. He stared down at the bloated face. Even with the disfigurement and the low light, there was no mistaking the features. It was Markoff.

'Everything all right?' Nate asked over the radio.

Quinn blinked. *No*, he thought. *Everything isn't all right.*

'Time to go,' Quinn said.

★ ★ ★

Quinn drove the rig east through San Bernardino and over the Cajon Pass toward Las Vegas. He exited a few miles later at Highway 395 and headed north into the Mojave Desert. Nate followed a half-mile behind in the BMW, watching for tails.

The desert had once been hundreds of square miles of nothing but sagebrush and dirt. Both were still there, but over the years the occasional town had popped up, creating pockets of forced green in the endless brown landscape. It was by no means a full-scale human invasion. There were parts where you could drive for nearly fifty miles without seeing anything more man-made than the distant high-power lines or some out-of-date billboards or the occasional abandoned car rusted to a deep brown and half buried in the sand by a flash flood.

There were roads, though. Dirt ones, branching off from the highway and winding miles into the nothingness. Some were well worn by traffic, perhaps indicating a home in the distance. Others looked as though they'd been abandoned for dozens of years.

It was easy to lose things out here, things that wouldn't be found for a long time. And if you did the job right, things that would never be found.

Because he rarely took work so close to home, Quinn seldom had a need to come out this way. Of course, that didn't mean he was unfamiliar with the terrain. One always had to be prepared.

About twenty miles before Randsburg, there was a little-used dirt road that led off to the southeast. Quinn made sure the only other car in sight was his own BMW, then turned the rig down the road, slowing to navigate the uneven terrain.

It took thirty minutes to reach a suitable spot. The road first went past several hills before dipping into the deep ravine. Not far beyond where Quinn stopped, the road seemed to disappear, as though its destination had been washed away by one of the spring storms, giving it no reason to continue.

By the time he got out of the cab, Nate had caught up to him in the BMW. Quinn motioned for his apprentice to park behind the truck. He then walked around to the container's doors.

In the distance, the sun was approaching the horizon. Night was less than an hour away.

Quinn reached up, hesitated for only a second, then flung both doors open all the way. He almost didn't notice the smell this time.

Behind him, he heard the door to the BMW open and shut, then footsteps approaching the truck.

'Coveralls, gloves, and plastic sheeting,' Quinn called out without looking around.

'What about the gasoline?'

'Not yet.'

As Nate returned to the car, Quinn climbed inside and walked over to the body. He couldn't imagine what had led to Markoff being entombed in a shipping container. Sure, Markoff had once been CIA, but he'd taken an early

16

retirement the previous winter, bored stiff by the desk job at Langley he'd taken only months before.

So what happened? Quinn silently asked his dead friend.

The only answer was the sound of Nate's footsteps outside the back door.

'Here,' his apprentice called out.

Quinn turned toward the back. Nate was standing on the ground, only the upper third of his body showing above the lip of the container. In one hand he held up a pair of coveralls and gloves.

Quinn looked down at Markoff one more time, then headed toward the opening to get changed.

★　★　★

They worked quickly and efficiently. Nate, more times than not, seemed to anticipate Quinn's next request, helping to keep conversation to a minimum.

Dealing with Markoff was first. They wrapped his body in the sheeting, then placed him across the hood of the BMW, securing him in place with several lengths of rope. Next, Nate donned a breathing mask, and used a portable paint sprayer to douse the interior of the container with gasoline.

'Quinn?' Nate called out. He'd finished half of the inside, but had stopped and was staring at the wall. 'Did you see this?'

Quinn pulled on his mask and joined his

17

apprentice. After his eyes began to adjust to the dimness inside the box, small marks began to appear on the wall.

'Grab some paper and a pen,' Quinn said.

While Nate was gone, Quinn knelt down to get a better look. He adjusted his face mask, but the stink of gasoline and death still seeped in around the edges. He forced himself to ignore it, focusing his concentration on the marks on the wall.

They were crude, like something a child would have written. *Or maybe by someone writing in the dark*, he thought. *Someone already weak, about to die.*

As Nate climbed back in, Quinn pulled out his flashlight and turned it on. The beam exposed walls dripping with gasoline. He pointed the light at the marks on the wall.

Numbers. Letters. Seventeen of them. Repeated twice.

45kLD9D8NTY63779V

'Looks like a VIN number,' Nate said, meaning a vehicle identification number.

'It's not.'

Though the sequence had been written twice, there was something different about the second time around. At the very end, separated by a small space, were an additional two characters.

lP

They were only there the one time. Perhaps they were part of the long sequence and they had just been forgotten the first time through, or perhaps they were something else entirely.

Quinn handed the flashlight to Nate, then took the pen and paper and wrote down the sequence. He included the last two characters, though kept them apart from the others, just like they had been on the wall. The one thing he wasn't sure about was whether it was the letter *L* or the numeral *1*. Either way, none of it meant anything to him.

'Is that blood?' Nate asked.

Quinn nodded. Markoff must have used the only ink he had available.

'Okay,' he said, rising back to his feet. 'Finish up. We don't have much time.'

As soon as Quinn was out of the container, Nate sprayed the rest of the inside with the fuel, giving the message a double douse. Before he started on the outside, they unhooked the semi from the trailer, and Quinn drove it back to the point where the road climbed out of the ravine, parking it.

By the time Nate finished the exterior, there were about three quarts left of the five gallons of gas they'd brought. He unhooked the paint reservoir that contained the remaining fuel and placed it on the ground, then tossed the rest of the paint sprayer and the empty gas cans into the back of the shipping container.

'Done,' Nate said.

Quinn nodded, then climbed behind the wheel of the BMW. He eased the vehicle back down the wash, putting a good one hundred and fifty feet between the car and the container.

19

'All right,' he said.

Nate acknowledged the go-ahead by lighting a couple of pieces of dried sagebrush on fire. Through the receiver in his ear, Quinn could hear a whoosh as his apprentice flung one of the branches deep inside the container.

A torrent of flames began swirling through Markoff's former tomb, and once Nate lit the outside, the entire box became engulfed in a roiling inferno.

Their timing was good. Any later and their makeshift bonfire might have been seen for miles in the desert night. But the sun was just touching the western skyline, so even though day was passing, the darkness had yet to descend in full force. In fact, the fading daylight did double duty, hiding the temporary illumination while masking the smoke against the dimming sky.

The scent of the remaining gasoline in the container he carried preceded Nate as he rejoined Quinn. Without being told, he hopped up on the trunk.

'I'll ride here,' he said.

Quinn slowly drove the BMW farther into the wilderness, away from the road. A couple miles later, they found another dry riverbed. At some point, the two empty waterways probably met, but it wouldn't be an issue. Not here, where it might not rain significantly for years.

As soon as they'd stopped, Nate retrieved two shovels from the trunk.

Even baked by the desert sun, the sand in the wash was soft and easy to dig up. The darkness of the desert night had finally descended, so they worked by the headlights of the BMW. In less than fifteen minutes, they dug a body-length hole three feet deep. Perhaps in a year or two, the spring rains might root up what was left of Markoff, but by then there would only be bones. Still, the thought bothered Quinn. He contemplated digging the hole deeper, but he pushed the idea out of his mind and kept to his script.

They slipped Markoff into the hole, unrolling him from the plastic as they did.

'You want me to check his pockets?' Nate asked.

Quinn stared down at the body. 'No. I'll do it.'

He leaned down and searched each pocket with his gloved hands. No wallet. No money. No receipts or papers that might have given a clue to where Markoff had been. Just a photo. It was folded and worn, and had been hidden in the collar of the dead man's shirt. Quinn almost missed it because the paper had gone soft. But the image on it was still clear. A woman.

There was a red smear along the bottom. More blood. Markoff had evidently pulled it out at one point to try and look at it. But in the darkness, it was doubtful he would have seen her image.

'Shit,' Quinn said to himself.

He looked at it a moment longer, then unzipped the front of his coveralls and slipped the photo into his shirt pocket.

Nate doused the body with most of the remaining fuel. When he was done, he removed a small box of wooden matches. As he was about to strike one, Quinn reached out and stopped him.

'Let me.'

Nate glanced at his boss, surprised, then nodded and handed over the box.

Quinn removed one of the sticks, but didn't strike it. Instead, he looked down at his old friend's body lying in the hole. He felt like he should say something, anything. But he didn't know what. Then, as he swiped the match against the side of the box, he said, without thinking, 'I'm sorry.'

After they burned and buried the body, they removed their coveralls and gloves, adding them to the pile of plastic sheeting in a smaller hole thirty feet away. They used the rest of the fuel to set the pile on fire. Once that was complete, the only thing left to do was to drop the truck someplace where Albina's people could get it.

'Who's the woman?' Nate said as he drove them back toward the semi.

'What?' Quinn asked. He'd been lost in thought.

'The picture. Do you know the woman?'

Nate pointed toward Quinn's hand. Held tightly between his thumb and his forefinger was the picture that had been in Markoff's collar. It surprised Quinn because he didn't remember pulling it back out.

The woman in the picture was smiling into the camera, her light brown hair flowing to the side, caught in the wind. A hand was on her shoulder close to her neck, a spot only someone very close would touch. Markoff's hand. Though not in the picture, the Del Coronado Hotel in San Diego would have been just off to the right.

It had been a Saturday, just after lunch. Nearly a year earlier.

The woman's name was Jenny Fuentes.

The person who'd taken the picture was Quinn.

3

Quinn stood in the shower, arms outstretched, palms pressed against the wall holding him in place. For thirty minutes, he didn't move. Instead, he let the water spray against his shoulders, splashing onto his head and running down his torso toward the tiled floor of the stall. He had hoped it would make him feel normal again, snap him out of the temporary spiral he felt himself sliding into.

He gave up near 1 a.m., knowing the anger and questions weren't going to go away. He took his time toweling off, like someone whose every muscle ached from a day of intensive labor. But there was nothing wrong with his muscles. The work he and Nate had done hadn't been overly strenuous. He'd handled more physical assignments with no problem. In his business, he had to keep himself lean and in good shape, like a distance runner ready to run a marathon at a moment's notice.

It wasn't even the image of Markoff's deformed corpse burning in a shallow grave that slowed Quinn down. Rather, it was the memory of Markoff himself, always with a quick smile and a disarming laugh. An insider who'd actually become a friend outside the realm of their secret world. A good friend.

'You've got to relax,' Markoff had kidded Quinn. 'Enjoy things a little.'

'What do you think I'm doing?' Quinn had said. They were in the Bahamas that time, sprawled out on two lounge chairs by the pool at their hotel.

'You're doing what you always do,' Markoff said.

'Which is what exactly?'

'It ain't relaxing, that's for sure.'

'I don't know what you're talking about. I'm relaxed twenty-four/seven. So screw yourself.' Quinn took a drink from his rum and Coke, then leaned back in the lounge chair.

His friend laughed. 'What you do has nothing to do with being relaxed. You're talking about patience. That, you've got more of than anyone I know.'

'They're the same thing,' Quinn said.

'Not even close. Being relaxed means you don't care. Being patient means you're waiting.'

'Right,' Quinn said. 'Whatever you want to believe.'

They were silent for a few moments.

'Let me ask you something,' Markoff said.

'Okay.'

'There're two girls off to my right. What are they wearing?'

Quinn started to turn his head.

'Don't look,' Markoff said.

'Fine. Bikinis, both of them. The blonde's got a baby-blue one on, while her friend went with black. So what?'

'All right, and the guy at the bar behind us?'

'The older one or the teenager?'

'Just proved my point, I think,' Markoff said.

25

'What?'

'You're always on, always waiting, always observing. That's not relaxed. That's waiting for something to happen.'

Though Quinn didn't want to admit it, Markoff had been dead-on. A person could never be relaxed if he was always waiting. And for Quinn, waiting was a constant state.

The annoying part was that Quinn knew Markoff had done his own share of waiting, too. As a field op, there could have been no escaping it. But somehow Markoff always knew how to turn it off. How to go from waiting to relaxing without any notice. It was a trait Quinn wished he possessed.

Of course, now Markoff would never have to wait again.

The thought took Quinn back to the body in the desert. It wasn't the way it should have been. At the very least, he should have given his friend a proper burial. Maybe even taken him back home. Not D.C., he lived there because that's where he worked. Michigan or Wisconsin, Quinn seemed to remember. Somewhere in the upper Midwest.

But that wasn't an option. Not just because of the condition of the body. It was Quinn's role in dealing with it. He'd been hired to dispose of a corpse, and in his business that meant getting rid of it so it wouldn't be found. There could be no personal considerations.

Quinn stared at himself in the mirror, wondering what the hell could have happened, but no answer came.

After a while, he gave up. From his walk-in closet, he grabbed a pair of boxer briefs and a black T-shirt, pulled them on, then went into the bedroom.

There was only one light on in the room, a reading lamp on the nightstand next to his bed. It illuminated a space that was large but underfurnished. It was just the way Quinn wanted it; it gave him a sense of freedom.

The few pieces of bedroom furniture he owned were all dark, made of teak and built to last. A king-size bed rested against the far wall. Next to it a single nightstand with the lamp, a clock, and his current read — *The Archivist's Story* by Travis Holland — on top. The only other piece of furniture was a low, wide dresser that did double duty as a stand for the seldom-used television. Reading was Quinn's vice. The evidence was several stacks of books piled against the wall where the second nightstand should have been — a to-be-read pile nearly a hundred volumes strong.

A bead of sweat formed just above his brow. Unconsciously he reached up and wiped it away. It was September, and in Los Angeles that meant hot during the day and warm at night. Even up in the Hollywood Hills where Quinn lived, there was no escape from the late summer heat.

At the far end of the room was a sliding glass door that led out onto a balcony overlooking the back of his property, and beyond it the city. He walked over, unlatched the special lock that held the door in place, then slid it open.

A gentle breeze drifted into the room, lowering

the temperature several degrees. He was tempted to grab a beer and stand outside on the deck, watching the lights on the Sunset Strip for a while, but in the end he opted for stretching out on the bed.

It was late, and he knew he should get some sleep. But after he shut his eyes, it wasn't long before he knew that wasn't going to happen.

Markoff's death had been like a vicious punch to the gut. And while Quinn couldn't let it go, it wasn't the main thing keeping him awake. That honor fell to his other problem. The one he'd been avoiding all day.

Someone had to tell Jenny.

No, not *someone*. He had to tell Jenny.

He glanced over at his clock on the nightstand: 1:19 a.m. Middle of the night, even on the East Coast.

Of course, if he called her, there was an excellent chance she'd be home. Only one problem, he didn't have her phone number. He had only talked to her when Markoff was around. He had Markoff's number, but unless they had gotten married in the last six months and moved in together, Quinn assumed they still had separate places.

But it was worth a shot. He retrieved his cell phone, and selected Markoff's home number from his list of contacts, then pressed send.

It rang four times before an answering machine kicked in.

'I'm not home. Leave a message.'

Markoff's voice. Short and sweet.

And singular.

Quinn hung up. If they had been living together, they hadn't been advertising the fact. Or, Quinn realized, there was the possibility they weren't even together at all anymore. The picture Markoff had been carrying notwithstanding, anything could have happened in the six months since Quinn had last spoken to his friend.

He dialed D.C. information, requesting a number for either a Jennifer Fuentes or a J. Fuentes. There were over fifteen listings. All J's, no Jennifers.

What now? Call each number and see if he recognized her voice? That seemed stupid. And given the hour, he couldn't rationalize waking up fifteen different people with the very real potential none were even her. Hell, she might not even live in the city. There were dozens of bedroom communities within a sixty-mile radius of the district.

There were better ways to track her down, faster ways. And, he knew, ways that could wait until morning.

He lay back down, knowing he'd be awake most of the night, but he was wrong. Sleep did come, only it wasn't deep or restful. And when he dreamt, he dreamt only of one thing: a body burning in a hole in the desert. And every time he knelt down to look at the corpse, it stared back at him.

Only the face that looked up wasn't Markoff's. It was his own.

★ ★ ★

The phone woke Quinn five hours later. Memories of his dream lingered for a moment, then disappeared, leaving him with only the vague sense of discontented sleep. He rolled onto his back, sat up, and stretched, letting whoever was calling go to voice mail.

As he stood, there was a chirp informing him that the caller had left a message. Quinn picked up his phone and headed toward the bathroom. After he set it on the counter, he switched it to speaker mode and hit speed dial for his voice mail. He then stared at himself in the mirror. It had been two days since he'd last shaved, and he was beginning to get scruffy. He knew he should do something about it, but he just didn't feel up to it.

'You have one unheard message,' an automated voice said through his speaker.

There was a half-second of dead air, then, in a different mechanical voice, 'Tuesday. 6.43 a.m.'

'Quinn. It's Jorge. Please call me. I . . . ah . . . just call me.'

Albina.

Quinn disconnected the call, switched the phone back to normal mode, then dialed Albina.

'May I help you?' The voice that answered was deep, not Albina's.

'I need to speak to Jorge,' Quinn said.

'Mr. Albina is still asleep. Please call back later,' the man said as if dismissing Quinn.

'Yeah, I don't think so. Just tell him Quinn called and I'd like him to lose my number.'

'Mr. Quinn?' The man's tone changed

abruptly. Now he sounded helpful, even concerned. 'Hold on.'

A moment later, Albina came on the line. 'Sorry if I woke you,' he said.

'Was there a problem with the truck?' Quinn asked. He'd dropped the Peterbilt off near an industrial park in Sylmar, and couldn't imagine anything had gone wrong.

'No,' Albina said. 'We got it. Thanks.'

'Then what do you want?'

'I just wanted to make sure everything went all right.'

'You would have heard if it hadn't.'

'And the body? No problems?'

'The body was the job, Jorge. Why are you calling me?' Jorge was fishing for information, but Quinn didn't feel like playing.

'I have another job for you.'

'Really? And this couldn't have waited until a little later?'

'I haven't slept, okay? I wanted to call you hours ago.'

'So what happened?' Quinn asked. 'Somebody ship you another body?'

'Don't even fucking joke about that,' Albina said. 'Not a body. So you don't have to worry about that.'

'I'm not *worried* about anything. I'm just not sure I'm available.'

'I'd pay you a new fee.'

Quinn's jaw tensed. Paying a new fee for a new project wasn't even a question. That's the way it worked. He wasn't cheap. His price was thirty thousand a week with a two-week minimum. Per job. And, as all his clients should have known, there were no carryovers from one project to another. Ever.

'I don't think I'm interested,' Quinn said.

'I haven't even told you what it is.'

'Still not interested.'

'Please just listen for a second. It's not that big of a deal. I only want you to find out who sent me the package.'

'You mean body,' Quinn said.

'Yes,' Albina said, his voice controlled. 'The body. I don't like living with unknowns, okay? But this situation, you know, it's tricky. I don't want to bring a lot of people in on it. You know about the body already. Finding out who put it in that container would probably be a snap for you. You're a cleaner, so I'm asking you to clean up a few loose ends for me.'

'I don't do that kind of cleaning.'

'Why don't you think about it?'

'No.'

'Come on, Quinn. I've heard you've been branching out. Taking on a little more. Do this for me and I'll — '

Quinn hung up.

★　★　★

Quinn's house was in the Hollywood Hills, overlooking the Los Angeles basin. There was a downward slope to his property, but his home wasn't one of those that cantilevered out from the edge perched on stilts. Instead, his had been built along the slope, using the hill to create two

32

separate levels, with a third storage level at the very bottom. All the bedrooms were downstairs, a floor below street level. Upstairs was a semi-open space that served as living room, dining room, and kitchen.

After a shower, Quinn made his way up to the kitchen, stopping first to grab his laptop off the coffee table. While he contemplated breakfast, he set the computer on the counter and turned it on. Food was soon forgotten as he connected to the Internet and began searching for information about Jenny.

It didn't take long. According to several sources, she was still working for the same Texas congressman that Markoff had told Quinn about — a guy named James Guerrero. He was a friend of Markoff's. They had both been Marines, though not at the same time. When Guerrero was on the Intelligence Committee, Markoff had once briefed him on a particular situation. The congressman had been impressed, and, as Markoff told Quinn later, he had been surprised and impressed by Guerrero as well.

The way he explained it to Quinn, he and the congressman had started meeting up for a drink or even dinner whenever Markoff was in town. In a town where politics was everything, they were very useful to each other. That was the way things worked in the District — it was all relationships and deals. But according to Markoff, they were more than just professional connections for each other.

'You've got to be kidding,' Quinn had said after Markoff had told him about his friendship with the congressman.

'I know, I know. He's a politician,' Markoff said. 'But he's different.'

'They all say they're different,' Quinn countered.

Markoff smiled. 'You're right about that. Don't get me wrong. I'd never trust him one hundred percent. But he's not afraid to speak his mind. Even gets in trouble with his own party sometimes. That makes him okay by me. Till he proves me wrong, anyway.'

So when Markoff's new girlfriend was looking for a job on Capitol Hill, it was Guerrero who Markoff called.

Only Representative Guerrero was no longer just the Texas congressman Markoff had briefed years earlier. He was now the Majority Whip, one of the most powerful people in the House of Representatives. And, according to his website, he was the first politician to announce his intention to run for President, doing so a year and a half earlier. And now, as of the month before, Guerrero had made it official, and joined a growing field of candidates for his party's nomination. And though Quinn knew that none of their chances were very good — they were running against a popular incumbent who was heavily favored to win reelection — the national exposure for the future would be extremely valuable.

'Lucky girl,' Quinn said to himself as he continued to scan the congressman's website. Jenny had really picked a winner when she hooked up with Markoff. Without him, who knows where she would have ended up working. But because of her boyfriend, her career was on the rise. Even if her boss didn't win the election — most news outlets put Guerrero in the middle of the pack at best — the campaign would make him a national figure. Perhaps in four years he would be leading the pack, instead of being mired in it.

Quinn began searching for old news stories. Not surprisingly, they all seemed to support Markoff's idea that Guerrero was a bit of a maverick. Ascending to the position of Majority Whip didn't seem to stop him from publicly disagreeing with other high-ranking members of his party. His approach was apparently blunt and direct — a lawmaker who knew how to cut through the BS. And if some of the latest stories were to be believed, it was starting to gain him the reputation of being a man of the people.

How a maverick like Guerrero had achieved such a high-level leadership position confused Quinn. That was until he found a profile piece on the congressman in the *Washington Post*.

It turned out Guerrero's wife was none other than noted conservative spokesperson Jody Goodman. That was a name Quinn definitely knew. He'd seen her quoted dozens of times in news articles and had even caught her act on some of the political talk shows. According to the article, she was the former CEO of Taylor-Goodman, a large defense contractor based in Texas. Now her time was spent being an influential member of a well-known Washington-based think tank. Apparently this was enough to allow her husband more freedom within the party than others who might have started working their way up at the same time he had.

An article in the *New York Post* described their marriage as more of a partnership than a relationship. It cited a source close to the couple claiming, 'They use each other's positions to strengthen their own. More a power match than a love one.'

Returning to Guerrero's website, Quinn found listings for two office addresses: one in Washington, D.C., and one in his home district of Houston, Texas. Quinn called the one in D.C.

'Congressman James Guerrero's office. How may I help you?' The voice of the woman who answered had the perfect balance of helpfulness and efficiency. Quinn guessed she must field hundreds of calls each day.

'Jennifer Fuentes, please,' Quinn said.

There was a slight pause. 'I'm sorry, Ms. Fuentes is not in the office at this time. Is there someone else who can help you?'

'Do you know when she'll be back?'

This time the pause was longer. Almost a full three seconds. 'Can you hold for a moment, please?'

She didn't wait for Quinn to answer. There was a click, then music, the soft jazz kind that turned popular rock songs into bland background noise that would offend no one except people with taste.

All of a sudden the music cut out, and a man's voice came on the line. 'May I help you?'

'Yes, thank you,' Quinn said. 'I'm trying to get

ahold of Jennifer Fuentes.'

'This is regarding . . . ?'

'Nothing that important,' Quinn said, keeping his voice light and unassuming. 'I was just going to be in Washington, and thought maybe we could get together for dinner.'

'You're a friend, then.'

'Yeah. We went to college together. She told me to call any time I was in town.' Quinn paused. 'Is everything all right?'

The man hesitated a moment, then said, 'She's not in the office this week.'

'Oh. Okay. Well, do you know if she'll be back next week?'

'That I couldn't tell you. She's . . . away for a few weeks. A personal matter, I believe. I'm not sure when she's due back.'

'Personal? Is she okay?'

The man hesitated. 'I wouldn't know.'

'I'll try calling her at home, then,' Quinn said.

'Yes. Why don't you do that? Sorry I couldn't have been more help.'

The line went dead.

The back of Quinn's neck tingled as he disconnected the call. *What the hell was that all about?*

He set the phone on the counter next to his laptop and replayed the conversation in his mind. Jenny out on a leave of absence? At the same time Markoff turns up dead? Granted, there was no direct connection between her personal leave and the end of Markoff's life, but Quinn didn't like the timing.

He heard a car pulling up in front of his

37

house. It had to be Nate. No one else could get through the security gate without being buzzed in. A few moments later, the front door opened. Quinn walked over to where the kitchen transitioned into the living room as Nate entered from the foyer.

'Come in here,' Quinn said. 'I need you.'

'Good morning,' Nate said.

Quinn gave his apprentice a half smile. 'Morning. Now, come in here.'

He turned and walked back into the kitchen. Once Nate had joined him, Quinn explained what he wanted, then handed over his cell phone. He had already punched in the number for Guerrero's Houston office, so all Nate had to do was hit Send.

There was a brief delay while the call connected and someone answered. After a moment, Nate said, 'Yes, good morning. This is Dan Riley from Overnight Advantage Delivery. I'm not sure if I have the right number or not, but I'm hoping you can help me.' Nate listened, then smiled. As he spoke, his voice took on the tone of a confiding friend. 'Here's my problem. Some people just shouldn't be allowed to fill out shipping information by hand. I tell ya, the packing slip I'm looking at right now is a mess. About the only thing I can make out is the name of the addressee and most of the phone number. You're the third person I've tried.' Again he waited while the person on the other end spoke. 'Let me see. The name on the package is . . . Jennifer Funtes or Fentes.' Pause. 'Fuentes? Yes. That's it. So I do have the right number.

38

Great. The most annoying part is it's person-to-person. I had no idea what I was going to do if I didn't find her. Is she in today?' This time, the person spoke for several seconds. Nate let out a few grunts of subdued surprise, then understanding. 'That's too bad. Do you know when she'll be back?' The look on Nate's face foreshadowed his words. 'So you have no idea, then.' A pause. 'I wish I could. But she's got to be the one to sign. I guess we'll try to track down the sender and see what he wants to do.'

Quinn looked at Nate, waiting. His apprentice set the phone on the counter. 'The lady said Jennifer Fuentes mainly works out of the D.C. office, but that according to the staff schedule, she's on a leave of absence. The lady wasn't sure when she was coming back. I guess I could have pushed more.'

'No,' Quinn said. 'You did fine. Pressing more could have drawn attention.'

'Is Jennifer the girl in the photo?' Nate asked.

Quinn had started to turn away, but paused, the question taking him by surprise. 'What?'

'The photo you took off the body yesterday. Was it Jennifer Fuentes?'

Quinn stared at his apprentice for a moment. It wasn't like what Nate was asking was such a mental stretch. Still, it wasn't something Quinn was eager to discuss.

'You knew the guy, too, didn't you?' Nate asked. 'Markoff, right?'

'Drop it.'

'I'm just trying to understand what we're doing.'

39

'This isn't a job,' Quinn said.

Nate shrugged, then opened the refrigerator and pulled out a carton of orange juice. 'Seems a little like a job.'

'We don't have any clients right now.'

Nate retrieved a glass from the cabinet, then filled it with juice. 'Wouldn't be the first time we've taken on a job without a client.' He lifted the glass and took a drink.

Quinn drew in a slow breath, checking his emotions. 'First, *we* don't take jobs,' he said. '*I* take them.' He started to say something more, then stopped.

After a moment of silence, Nate said, 'And second?'

Quinn looked away. He had planned on saying that second, he decided what information Nate got and what he didn't. But Nate didn't deserve that. Quinn knew sometimes he kicked into harsh instructor mode too readily.

'Second,' he said, 'yes. She's the girl in the picture. She goes by Jenny, not Jennifer. And you're right about the body, too. It belonged to . . . someone I knew. A guy named Steven Markoff.'

Quinn expected Nate to probe more, but his apprentice just smiled and downed the rest of his OJ. When he was through, he asked, 'What next?'

Quinn shook his head and started walking toward the living room. Then, more to himself than to Nate, he said, 'I wish I knew.'

4

Quinn knew he should just forget about his dead friend, buried now in the desert. Forget about finding Jenny and telling her. She could live in her ignorance. In time, she would realize something had happened anyway. Quinn didn't need to be the messenger.

So easy. So simple.

But not possible.

'We're only part of the big plan,' his old mentor, Durrie, had said in one form or another on nearly every project they worked on together. 'A small part. We'll never see everything. We'll never know everything. And it's better that way. When you're done, you're done. Walk away and forget. You won't last long if you don't.'

Quinn couldn't help hearing Durrie's voice in his head. The son of a bitch's teachings had been solid. He'd given Quinn all the knowledge needed to get a good start in the business. So it was only natural that Quinn, even all these years later, measured much of what he did against what he'd been taught.

But Durrie himself had been a troubled man who had spiraled into a dark place he was never able to pull himself out of, a place that eventually led him into a direct confrontation with Quinn. When Quinn had been forced to kill him in Berlin the previous winter, it had silenced Durrie's voice for a time. But the advice, both

41

good and bad, was back now, and Quinn was oddly comforted by it.

This particular piece of advice fell into the bad category. At least with Quinn's current problem.

Quinn had to find Jenny. He owed Markoff that much.

In truth, he owed Markoff so much more.

★　★　★

Finland. A decade before.

'Are you still with us, Mr. Quinn?' It was the voice of Andrei Kranz — flat, uninterested, and speaking English with a heavy accent. The rumor was he'd been born in Warsaw, but to Quinn his accent seemed more German than Polish.

Quinn opened his eyes and looked up at his tormentor. Kranz stood in front of him, his face only a foot away from Quinn's own. What passed for a smile grew on Kranz's thin-lipped mouth.

'Good,' Kranz said. He reached over and patted Quinn on the cheek. 'Have a good night, okay? We'll see you in the morning.'

Kranz stood up and laughed. Behind him, two other men, no more than shadows, laughed also.

A moment later, Quinn was alone.

For a while, he could hear them walking away through the forest. Then their steps grew faint until there was only the sound of the breeze passing through the trees, gusting above him one moment, then slowing to nothing the next.

The post-midnight air was bone chilling. A few degrees colder and it would have been numbing. But numbing would have been a relief.

42

The night sky, what he could see of it through the trees, was cloudless. The stars that packed the void seemed to be piled one on top of the other, unhindered by any interference from nearby civilization. It reminded him of the sky of his youth, where millions of stars filled the northern Minnesota night. Looking around, he also realized there was little difference between the land he'd grown up in and the Finnish countryside he would apparently die in.

The closest real city was Helsinki, but it was over a hundred kilometers away. It could have been a thousand kilometers away or even a thousand miles for all it mattered to Quinn. He knew no help would come from that direction. And though he tried not to think about it, the truth was no help would come from *any* direction.

If he had any doubt, he just needed to look down at the lifeless body of Pete Paras — Double-P to his friends. But Double-P would have a hard time answering to that nickname anymore. His head lay on a dark stain in the sand, the only remnant of the pool of blood that had flowed out of the gash in his neck.

Kranz had made sure Quinn watched as he sliced Paras's throat himself, having one of his men hold Quinn down while another held Quinn's head still and eyes open.

'I'm not doing this because I want to,' Kranz had said as he grabbed a handful of hair and pulled Paras's unconscious head upward. 'I don't like to do this, eh?' He ran the knife just above the skin covering Paras's throat without touching it. It was like he was deciding what would be the best line to take. 'I mean, it's not like this is something I go out of the way for. Sometimes, though, it's part of the job.' He took another swipe, this time the blade slicing deep into the flesh.

Kranz had to jump back to avoid getting splattered by any of the blood. As it was, his knife hand was covered with it. He walked up to Quinn and wiped the blood off on the cleaner's T-shirt.

The message was clear. Unless Quinn talked, his throat would be next. But he didn't know the answers to Kranz's questions. He'd been hired for a very specific assignment, and only knew the details he needed to know. Unfortunately, the Pole didn't believe him. After the initial questions garnered nothing, Kranz decided to let Quinn have some alone time.

They had left Quinn kneeling in the dirt, wearing just his T-shirt and boxer briefs. His wrists were bound together behind him by a short rope that was then tied around his ankles. It pulled his wrists backward, hog-tying him so that his outstretched fingers could almost touch his heels. If he could've sat back on his legs, he would've been able to relieve some of the pressure, but there were two additional ropes, one looped under each of his arms and tied to tree branches ten feet above him, preventing any backward movement. The ropes were rigged just long enough so that only Quinn's knees were able to rest on the ground — any shorter and he would have been hanging in the air.

They hadn't killed him, but he knew that was only a temporary stay of execution. Kranz and his men would be back in the morning. If he was still alive, they'd see if a night of tenderizing had done anything to jog his memory. But when they realized they'd get nothing more out of him than they already had, he'd join Double-P on the ground.

As the hours passed, Quinn fought the urge to shiver from the cold. Each time he did, his body would jerk against the unforgiving ropes and make it feel like his arms were about to be ripped from his shoulders and out of his skin.

He tried to figure out a way to get free. But the more he tried to concentrate, the more his mind fogged up. Maybe if it hadn't been so cold, he would have been able to think more clearly. That's what he told himself, at least. That's how he rationalized his failure.

What did pass through his mind, giving him at least a few minutes' respite from his hopeless situation, was the image of what he would do to Kranz if he were to somehow escape. Quinn wouldn't make the same mistake Kranz did. Quinn would walk up to him and kill him. A single shot to the head, point-blank range. A straight-out execution. Never mind that Quinn had never done anything like that before, or that his chances of being in a position to carry it out were nonexistent. For those brief moments, he was happy.

He heard things during the night: the wind, a small animal in the trees above him, the occasional car on the distant road. And there had been the voice of Durrie, too. His mentor talking to him in a voice so low Quinn couldn't make out the words, but the meaning was clear.

Disappointment. Displeasure. Disgust.

But the worst sound came two hours before dawn, when he heard steps approaching in the distance. They could only mean the return of Kranz and his men. And that could only mean death.

As the steps grew closer, he realized it wasn't the group returning, but just one person. Perhaps Kranz had decided there was little he could learn from Quinn after all, so he had sent back a solo executioner to finish the job. In Quinn's exhausted and incapacitated state, a three-year-old with a plastic hanger could have killed him, so one man would be more than enough.

When the new arrival appeared before him, Quinn's guess was confirmed. It was one of Kranz's men. The one who had held Quinn's head during Paras's execution. A Caucasian, perhaps ten years older than Quinn. He was an inch or two below six feet, with a mop of curly dark hair that drooped over his ears and provided natural insulation from the cold.

He knelt in front of Quinn, looked him in the eyes, then nodded at Paras's body. 'Your buddy there was a son of a bitch, you know that?' the man said, his accent American.

Quinn tried to spit in the man's face, but his mouth was too dry. 'Fuck off,' he managed to whisper.

The man smiled. 'Attitude,' he said. 'That's a good sign.'

The man stood back up and pulled out a large pocketknife. As he opened it, Quinn braced himself for the worst, knowing soon his head would be lying in its own puddle of blood. But instead of slashing him across the neck, the man moved around behind him, out of sight.

Quinn waited for the blade to cut into his skin. Maybe the executioner would go for an artery, or perhaps he'd start with the soft spot just below Quinn's ribs. If he was really sadistic, he could even go for Quinn's spinal cord, crippling Quinn before killing him.

As the seconds passed, Quinn continued to tense, almost willing the knife to find its mark. Then, without warning, he was on the ground, the pressure on his wrists and shoulders gone. The ropes that had bound him in place for the last several hours lay near his feet.

'Can you walk?' the man asked.

Quinn opened his eyes. The man was leaning over him.

It could still be a trick. Some game the man was playing. Not wanting to take any chances, Quinn kicked out, aiming for the man's shin. But his muscles betrayed him, and his leg moved only a foot, then stopped, coming into contact with nothing but air.

'If you really want to hit me,' the man said, 'why don't you save your strength and wait until we get out of here. I'll give you a free shot when we're safe.'

Quinn didn't remember many details from the

next few hours. At some point, the man had gotten him to his feet. Then there had been what seemed like an endless barefoot walk along a cold and rocky path. He remembered mumbling a question to the man, but couldn't recall what it had been or if there had been an answer.

At some point, he found himself no longer walking, but sitting in the passenger seat of a car. The man was behind the wheel, eyes forward. Quinn looked out the window. There seemed to be trees everywhere, illuminated by the splash of the car's headlights as they cruised down the road.

He wanted to ask who'd planted all the trees. He wanted to know why it was so dark. And just before his body completely shut down, he wanted to ask where they were going. But the only question that he was able to ask was, 'What's your name?'

The driver laughed for a moment good-naturedly, then said, 'Call me Steven.'

★　★　★

That had been the first time Quinn met Markoff.

The CIA man had been working undercover in Andrei Kranz's organization. Kranz had been into trafficking Soviet-era weapons — both conventional, biological, and, he claimed, nuclear — to anyone buying in the West. Double-P had been one of the man's dealers, but had decided he should be the big boss. Without even realizing it, Quinn had stumbled into a turf war.

Why Markoff had decided to save him, Quinn never knew for sure. Markoff said his job was done anyway, so giving Quinn a hand on the way out was no big deal. Quinn didn't believe him. By all reports, Kranz had gotten away. If Markoff had finished the job, Kranz would have been dead.

But whatever the reason, Quinn knew then what he still knew now — he would forever owe Markoff for his life.

★ ★ ★

'I got two addresses,' the voice on the other end of the phone said. It was one of Quinn's contacts, a guy named Steiner who worked out of a mailbox and shipping store on the Venice Beach boardwalk. Quinn had called him a couple of hours ago to see if he could find out where Jenny lived.

Steiner's main gig wasn't information. He was a documents man who could assemble a set of IDs that would stand up to almost any inspection. Because of his talents, he also had a lot of contacts. Which made him a good person to know if you needed to find out something quick.

'Give them to me,' Quinn said.

'The D.C. one's the most recent.' Steiner read off an address in Georgetown. It had a unit number, so it wasn't a single-family residence.

'And the other?'

'In Houston. The information is a little old, but as far as I can tell, still valid.' He gave Quinn the Texas address.

49

'Thanks,' Quinn said, then hung up.

The back wall of his living room was all window, floor-to-ceiling. He stood in front of it and stared out into the distance. The day was one of those hazy, hot, early September ones Quinn hated. He could barely make anything out beyond Beverly Hills.

He wished it was fall, and the air had cooled, and the winds had blown away the haze. Or even winter just after a rainstorm, when the sky was crisp and clean, and the city shone at night like a bundle of white Christmas lights. But he'd gladly take the hazy day if someone could have granted the wish that he had been out of the country working a job when Albina called about the body at the port.

He should have just said no when Albina called him the previous day.

But he hadn't.

He took a deep breath, then walked across the living room into the foyer and opened the front door. Nate was lying on the hood of his ten-year-old Accord, reading his flight instruction manual and soaking up a little sun.

'Don't get too comfortable,' Quinn said.

Nate looked over. 'We get a job?'

'Maybe.'

'It's the kind we don't get paid for, isn't it?'

'Just get my car out of the garage and be ready to go in ten minutes.'

'Where are we going?' Nate said as he swung his legs off the hood and stood up.

'You're driving me to the airport,' Quinn said.

5

Stepping out of the terminal at Bush Intercontinental Airport in Houston was like walking into a wall of gelatin. The air was so thick with humidity it felt like it was pushing Quinn back, daring him to take another step forward.

He glanced at his watch: 3:15 p.m. But that was L.A. time. Here in Texas, it was already two hours later, 5:15. End of the workday, for some anyway.

Houston seemed as good a place as any to start looking for Jenny. It wasn't just Congressman Guerrero's hometown, it was hers, too. If she was on personal leave, then perhaps she had gone home.

Quinn picked up a Lexus sedan from the rental agency, then headed toward the city. When he reached Loop 610, he took it west for a while, then south as the big looping freeway circumnavigated the metropolitan area. He got off near Memorial Park and headed west again, this time along Woodway Drive.

He'd done a MapQuest search before he'd left Los Angeles, and had printed out directions to the address Steiner had given him.

Not far from the freeway, he turned right and found himself in an upscale neighborhood. Quinn guessed a mix of middle class and upper middle class. No question the homes were more expensive than your typical government

51

employee could afford. Of course, this was Texas, not L.A. Everything was cheaper here. And, as many were fond of saying, bigger. Few of the houses looked like they were less than two thousand square feet, while many looked to be more than three. Many were multilevel, with BMWs, Mercedeses, and large SUVs in the driveways.

These were people on the rise. Future company presidents and board members who would one day be trading up to even bigger homes with larger lots and more square footage and maybe even a guesthouse in back. Some would suffer heart attacks before they reached sixty, while others would become strangers to their own families as they spent more and more time at the office, if they hadn't fallen into that trap already.

Quinn found the address he was looking for tucked back in an area where all the roads sounded like names of old blues songs: Lazy River Lane, Old Bayou Drive, Sweet Jasmine Street. The house was a sprawling one-story on White Magnolia Lane. Like many of the homes in the neighborhood, it was made of brick, with white wooden doors and window frames.

An asphalt driveway curved up to the house, then back to the street again seventy feet farther up the road. There were no sidewalks, so Quinn pulled the Lexus onto the grass shoulder and parked. As he got out he heard the buzz of what sounded like an army of insects. He expected to be attacked at any second, but for the moment the bugs seemed content to keep their distance.

As he started walking up the driveway, he realized that if this had been Jenny's place, she wasn't here any longer. There were bikes on the grass. Kids' bikes, preteen size. A portable basketball hoop and backboard were set up in a wide spot of the drive near the garage. Though he hadn't seen Jenny in at least eight months, she had been childless then. And if the toys weren't enough to convince him a family now lived here, there was the car that was parked in the driveway. A minivan, dark green and well maintained. A soccer mom car. It had the look of a vehicle that got a lot of use.

He continued walking toward the front door. As he did he saw a young girl standing at the living room window, looking out at him. He put her age at around eight. She had blond hair pulled back in a ponytail and was dressed in jeans and a lavender T-shirt with a cartoon squirrel on the front. She stared at him for a moment, then turned and ran away.

By the time Quinn reached the doorstep, the front door was already open. A woman stood just inside beyond the threshold, a utilitarian smile on her face. She couldn't have been more than forty, and had the same blond hair as the girl in the window. No ponytail for Mom, though. Her hair was down, stopping an inch above her shoulders.

'Can I help you?' she said, a trace of suspicion in her voice.

'Probably not,' Quinn said. He smiled as if embarrassed, in an attempt to set her at ease. 'I was actually looking for the woman I thought lived here. Apparently either I got my addresses mixed up or she moved.'

The woman looked at him for a second, impassive, then her face relaxed. 'Must be a mix-up. We've been here over ten years.'

Wrong answer.

Steiner had said the address might be old, but not that old.

Quinn nodded. 'That's what I was afraid of,' he said.

'What's her name?' she asked. 'Maybe she's one of my neighbors.'

'Tracy,' he said, heeding the warning that flashed in his mind, and making up a name on the spot. 'Tracy Jennings. Do you know her?'

The woman's eyes widened just enough for Quinn to notice. The name was not the one she'd been expecting. But she recovered quickly. 'Sorry. I don't know who that is.'

'It's all right. I shouldn't have bothered you. Thanks for your time.'

'No problem,' the woman said.

Quinn turned and headed back to his car. As he walked down the driveway, he glanced at the house one final time. The girl was in the window again, waving at him, and in the shadows behind her, he could see the mother watching him leave. He waved at the girl, then turned away.

Once he reached his car, he got in, started the engine, and shifted into drive. He had only gone half a block when he noticed a sedan pull away from the curb in his rearview mirror. A newer model Volvo. Silver. Two men in front. One in back.

It hadn't been there when Quinn had arrived. He was sure of it. He had also not seen anyone walking up to it while he was getting back into his rental. The men had already been inside the car, like they were waiting.

Quinn kept an eye on his rearview mirror as he made his way back to the main road. The Volvo continued to follow. That in itself wasn't unusual. Quinn was taking the main route out of the neighborhood. But he wasn't buying the coincidence.

He turned east onto Woodway Drive, heading toward downtown. Behind him the Volvo turned in the same direction, then slowed a bit, putting a few cars between them.

Three men in a car going a couple miles an hour *under* the speed limit?

No coincidence at all.

★ ★ ★

For fifteen minutes, Quinn kept an even pace, turning every once in a while in what seemed like unhurried, planned moves. Each time, the Volvo followed. Whatever minute percentage of doubt Quinn might have had disappeared. They were trailing him.

Ahead, the light was turning yellow. Instead of stopping, Quinn went through. Not rushing, but just fast enough to make the light. The Volvo was stuck a couple cars back and had no chance. Even with the advantage, Quinn didn't speed away. He drove on like he had no idea they were there.

Two streets down, he took a right. As soon as the Volvo was out of sight, he jammed down on the accelerator. At the next big street, he took a left, then another right, then left, stair-stepping his way away from the Volvo.

Five minutes later, he saw a Mobile gas station and pulled in, stopping at the pumps. Though the rental's tank was still almost full, he removed his gas cap and slipped the gas nozzle into the opening. What he didn't do was start the pump. Instead, he moved around to the back of the car and opened the trunk. He unzipped the side compartment on his travel bag and pulled out a small plastic device that to anyone else would look like a battery charger. But it wasn't a charger at all. It was a less powerful version of the detector he'd used on the truck the day before.

Only this time when he circled his vehicle, the detector emitted a soft beep. It was on the passenger side, near the back fender. He knelt down, pretending to check his tire, then reached up under the fender. When he removed his hand, he was holding a small metal disk.

'Smooth,' he said under his breath, admiring the stealth that had been employed to plant the device. He'd only been out of sight of his car for the minute or two he'd talked to the woman up at the house.

Quinn set the transponder on top of the gas pump, then did a second pass. No more beeps.

He returned to the pump and leaned back against the Lexus, pretending to wait for his tank to fill. A minute and a half later, the Volvo drove by.

Quinn paid it no attention, watching it only in his peripheral vision. The car turned right at the corner, then continued down the block until it was out of sight.

The moment it disappeared, Quinn removed the nozzle and recapped the gas tank. He grabbed the transponder off the top of the pump and attached it next to the nozzle mount where it would be hard to find.

Not wasting any time, he climbed back into his car and started the engine. Instead of pulling forward, he backed out so that there was no chance the Volvo would see him. When he exited the gas station, he raced across the oncoming lanes and turned left.

But he didn't go far.

A block away, he found a busy strip mall and pulled into the lot, parking in front of a nail salon away from the street. It was starting to get dark as Quinn got out of the rental and stepped onto the sidewalk in front of the shops. From there he had a clear view back down the street. At the Mobile station, it seemed like business as usual. Someone else had already pulled up to the pump where Quinn had been.

He glanced at his watch. Five minutes passed since the Volvo had spotted him at the station. By now they would be thinking he should be almost done, if they weren't already wondering why he was still there. Soon they would feel compelled to check again. Quinn guessed it would be seven minutes total.

It was eight by the time the Volvo returned.

The distance was too great for Quinn to see the men inside, but he knew they had to be surprised not to find the Lexus still sitting there. After all, their tracker was telling them the car should not have moved.

They made a quick turn into the station and pulled up on the other side of the pump Quinn had been at. The driver stayed at the wheel while the other two men got out. They tried to look natural, one man even removing the nozzle from the pump, but their movements were forced.

It took them a little over a minute to find the transponder, and when they did, they didn't look happy. One of the men pulled out a phone, hit a couple buttons, then put it to his ear. The other quickly replaced the gas hose and climbed back into the car.

Quinn took that as his cue to get back in the Lexus. He pulled out of his spot, but didn't exit the lot immediately. Several moments later, the man on the phone got back into the Volvo, and the car pulled out, heading in the opposite direction of the strip mall.

It didn't take long for Quinn to catch them.

★   ★   ★

The darkness played in Quinn's favor. A big city meant roads jammed with cars, and lots of headlights moving in and out of the flow of traffic. It made it easy to hide among the pack and remain unseen.

After a while, it became obvious the Volvo was

58

headed back to the house on White Magnolia Lane. As they neared the neighborhood, instead of continuing the chase, Quinn turned down one of the side streets. He knew now where they were going, and while the night was great at disguising his presence on the busy main roads, he would stand out on the less traveled residential streets if he continued to tail them.

Unfortunately, the neighborhood was not set up in any logical pattern, so finding an alternate route wasn't as simple as he would have hoped. The roads twisted and turned, some making large arcs and returning to the same road they started from, while others wound away to dead ends. Everywhere the landscape was green and lush. Where the lots hadn't been carved out for homes, there were trees and bushes. Not quite wilderness, but not quite tame either. What it wasn't suited for was shortcuts.

Quinn cursed to himself as he made two wrong turns before finding his way back to White Magnolia Lane. He came at it from the opposite direction he had earlier, stopping when he was about a block away from the house. He grabbed a pair of thin leather gloves, and a compact flashlight from his bag in the trunk. He felt a momentary annoyance that he didn't have a gun. He never flew with one, so his habit was to pick up one at his destination if he felt it necessary. But things had happened so fast once he'd arrived in Houston, he hadn't had time to track down a source.

He made his final approach on foot, using the cars parked along the street as cover. As he expected, the Volvo was already there, sitting in the driveway near the garage.

What was more surprising was that the house was lit up both inside and out. It seemed as if every switch in the place had been turned on. Even the two floodlights mounted above the garage door were on.

The minivan that had been parked in front was still there, but now all its doors were open. Quinn could see several suitcases piled in the back. The bicycles that had been on the lawn were stacked on the roof of the van and tied to the luggage rack.

As Quinn watched, a man came out of the house carrying a large cardboard box. Behind him trailed the woman Quinn had talked to. She was carrying another suitcase. Following her were two children. One was the girl he'd seen in the window. The other was a boy, maybe a few years older. Husband, wife, and kids? It seemed so.

Quinn pulled out his cell phone, switching it to camera mode. His wasn't the normal, off-the-shelf model. It had only come available in the last few months, and even then you had to have connections and be willing to pay the price. But it was worth it. The camera alone was invaluable. Six megapixels and a zoom that provided sharp, clear images few consumer cameras could match.

As he took pictures of the man and the woman loading their stuff into the back of the van, the woman said something to the kids. Though Quinn couldn't hear the exact words, he picked up the tone — impatient, even urgent.

When the kids didn't move quick enough, the man barked, 'Now.'

That got more than just the kids moving. One of the suits who had been in the Volvo earlier emerged from the house and walked briskly over to the van.

Quinn raised the lens again, snapping off another shot as the new man grabbed the father by the arm, whipping him around so they were face-to-face. There was a quick, one-sided exchange, then the suit let the man go and returned to the house.

The man hesitated a moment, his eyes on the front door as if he expected someone else to emerge. After a few seconds, he climbed into the van with the rest of the family and started the engine.

They pulled out of the driveway and headed down the street, right past Quinn's position. As they passed, Quinn caught a glimpse of the little girl looking out the window. For a second, it seemed as though she had seen him, but if she did, her attention was soon drawn to something else.

With the van gone, Quinn moved closer to the house, finding a spot directly across the street, next to a Jeep Cherokee.

At first there was nothing new to see, all activity apparently taking place deeper inside the house. Quinn looked from window to window. The only one with its drapes still open was the one in the living room. But even that didn't last long. Soon one of the suits walked up to one end of the window, and a moment later the curtain moved across the glass, cutting off Quinn's only view of the inside.

Quinn continued his vigil. Twenty minutes passed, then thirty, then forty.

After almost an hour, lights began switching off all over the house until only the porch light and the floods in front of the garage remained on.

Two of the suits stepped out the front door and headed over to the Volvo. Quinn raised the lens of his camera and took several shots. He got good close-ups of each man, recognizing the shorter suit as one of the guys searching the gas station. He couldn't be sure about the taller one, but when the man climbed into the driver's seat, Quinn assumed he must have been the one behind the wheel earlier, too.

The garage floods went out, then a few seconds later so did the porch light. Quinn could barely make out the front door as it opened. Two shadowy forms emerged. One had to be the other suit who'd been following him, but he didn't recognize the other one. His hair was light, blond probably. And he carried himself in a way that made Quinn surmise he was the one in charge. Like his friends, though, he was also wearing a suit.

When the doors to the Volvo opened, an interior light came on, illuminating the two men as they climbed in.

Quinn was ready. He took two quick pictures before they closed the door and the light went out. The impression Quinn got from all of them

was the same. Cool, confident, in shape.
Ex-military. Maybe even elite.
And definitely trouble.

★   ★   ★

Quinn contemplated following the Volvo again.
But he decided the house was more important.

What had been going on inside? And the
family, what were they all about? The whole
situation was more than just bizarre.

After sending the photos he'd taken to Nate's
e-mail address, he remained in position for an
hour, watching and waiting to make sure no one
had stayed behind. The neighborhood was even
quieter than it had been when he first arrived.
Lights inside several of the nearby homes had
gone out, though many still had various forms of
exterior illumination on. Only two cars had
driven by the entire time he waited, neither
noticing him.

Go or no go? Quinn thought.

Again, Durrie's voice, 'Get the fuck out of
there. Just walk back down the street, get into
your car, and go back to the airport. You should
have never come here in the first place.'

He knew it was too late to make the last flight
back to L.A., but he could catch an early plane
and be back by late morning. Tomorrow he
could try to find Jenny through other channels.
But he didn't move.

His hunch was that Steiner had been right.
The home belonged to Jenny. And something
very odd had been going on there.

He looked up and down White Magnolia Lane. The street was quiet.

He slid from behind the Jeep and crossed the road at a spot where the glow of the streetlight had dropped off to darkness. At the base of the driveway, he paused long enough to make sure he was still unobserved. For a brief second, he thought he sensed someone nearby, but it quickly passed. Perhaps it had just been an animal. Maybe a possum out on its evening prowl. Still, he gave it an extra minute before moving forward.

Once he reached the front door, he placed an ear against the wooden surface, straining to hear even the faintest of sounds. As he expected, only silence. He pulled the pair of leather gloves out of his back pocket, donned them, then tried the knob. It was locked. He cursed under his breath, annoyed that he'd left his set of lock picks in his bag back in the rental's trunk. He considered retrieving them, but that seemed needlessly risky.

Perhaps there was another way in.

He left the porch and started making his way around the house, inspecting each window he passed. His hope was that one would be unlocked, but everything was shut tight.

When he reached the side of the house, he was greeted by a six-foot-high wooden fence. If there was a gate, he couldn't see it. He put his hands on top, then jumped up, extending his elbows so that he was suspended halfway above the barrier.

Like the front yard, the ground on the other side was also grass. Quinn swung his right leg up, catching his foot on top. From there, it was

64

easy to swing the rest of his body up and over the fence.

Though he could only see a portion of the backyard, he could tell it was large and lush. Directly ahead of him, along the side fence, was an old wooden gardening shed. Since the bushes and trees appeared to be well maintained, he guessed the shed was put to a lot of use.

For several seconds, he waited, half expecting someone to appear around the corner of the house, but there was no one. He turned his attention back to the house.

Unlike out front, not all of the curtains were closed here. He peered through the first few windows he passed. Though dark, he could still make out the interior. Bedrooms. Perhaps used for guests or as an office. But in their current state, it was impossible to tell. Each was a disaster — papers and clothing scattered across the floor, pieces of furniture dragged haphazardly from their original locations, pictures pulled from where they'd hung. It even looked like holes had been punched into the walls.

Before he could move to the next window, his phone vibrated in his pocket. The pattern was distinctive, letting him know it was Nate on the other end. He was about to let it go to voice mail when he realized why his apprentice was calling.

'Yes?' he said, answering the phone and keeping his voice as low as possible.

'You missed your check-in,' Nate said.

'Sorry,' Quinn said. They had prearranged a time for him to call, but he'd been focused on the house and had forgotten. 'Everything's fine.'

'Are you sure?'

Nate was looking for the specific phrase that would let him know Quinn was okay.

'No issues,' Quinn said.

'You had me worried there,' Nate said. 'I was seconds away from calling in backup.'

'Sorry,' Quinn told him. 'Things are a little more complicated here than I expected.'

He worked his way up to the back corner of the house and peeked around. More yard. He almost expected to see a gazebo in the center, but there was none.

'Quinn?'

'I'm in the middle of something right now,' Quinn said.

'Then call me back when you have a minute,' Nate said. 'I've got something.'

'Hold on.' Quinn eased around the corner and approached the next window.

The room beyond looked like it was the master bedroom. He chanced turning on his flashlight, twisting the beam into a tight spotlight to cut down on the chances light might spill through to the front of the house.

'You figure out the code from the container?' he asked as he looked inside.

'No,' Nate said. 'I haven't a clue.'

'You've gotten nowhere?'

'It doesn't fit into any of the standard codes.'

Quinn played the light across the back wall. There were three exits to the room. One to the hallway, another to what looked to be a bathroom. The third was closed. *Closet?*

'So?' Quinn asked. 'Try a little harder.'

In the room was a bed, queen size with an ornate white wooden frame. An armoire was across the room, also white but simpler in construction. It had been twisted away from the wall and sat at an odd angle. Next to it was a matching makeup table, also moved from its logical home. Quinn couldn't see a dresser, but there was something under the window below him that could very well be it.

This room had also been tossed — clothes and books and makeup and shoes thrown around randomly. The mattress was stripped bare and had been sliced open, the gaping wound spewing coils and cotton batting. The walls had also been attacked. It looked as though someone had taken a crowbar every few feet and torn holes into the surface.

'I was thinking maybe I could call a little help in on this one,' Nate said.

'You shouldn't need any help.'

Even with all the chaos, it was evident this had been a woman's room. There was no trace of a man anywhere. No men's clothes, no men's shoes. Nothing that would have pointed to a husband and wife sharing the space.

Quinn knew that wasn't proof the house was Jenny's, but it did reinforce what he was thinking. The family he'd met earlier had been a decoy, meant to confuse anyone coming to look for whoever lived there, and to cover the destruction that was going on inside.

'You know,' Nate said, 'Orlando could probably figure this out in seconds.'

Quinn turned off the flashlight. 'Orlando's not

67

the one I asked to figure it out, is she?'

'Yeah, but I could call her. She won't mind.'

'No,' Quinn said.

There was a back door leading to the kitchen and a sliding glass door that opened onto what appeared to be a family room. Both were locked.

'Did you get a port of origin on the ship?' Quinn asked.

'I did.' A bit of confidence returned to Nate's voice. 'Shanghai.'

'Interesting.'

'Not what you were expecting?'

'I wasn't expecting any place in particular,' Quinn said. Actually, Shanghai made sense. Most West Coast shipping came from Asia, and Shanghai was one of the busiest ports not only on the Pacific Ocean but in the entire world.

There was a smaller window just beyond the sliding glass door. Frosted. A bathroom. And it was open. The gap was only a few inches, no doubt to equalize the moisture buildup anytime someone took a shower, but even if it was locked in place, Quinn would be able to force it open.

'I sent some photos to your e-mail,' Quinn said as he peeked through the window into the empty room beyond. 'See if you can get a good image of each subject. You remember how to run the enhancement software, right?'

'You ask me that every single time.'

'Well, do you?'

'Yes. I remember how to use it.'

With one hand, Quinn popped the screen out. 'Good. After you get that going, I need you to run a plate for me. You have a pen?'

'Yes.'

Quinn recited the license-plate number from the Volvo. He doubted it would net anything useful. With people this detailed, if the car wasn't stolen, the plates were.

'That it?' Nate said.

'No,' Quinn said, then gave Nate Jenny's address. 'I want a comprehensive ownership history. You'll probably have to dig a little.'

'Got it,' Nate said. 'I take it you haven't found your friend yet.'

Quinn's jaw tensed. 'Not yet,' he said.

As his hand began pushing the window open, there was a sudden movement behind him in the bushes near the back fence. Just as he started to turn toward the noise, he felt a click from under the window frame, like it had just run over some sort of . . . *switch*.

He took three quick steps away from the window, but that was as far as he got before the house behind him exploded.

6

Quinn found himself flat on the ground, his chest aching from the impact. His cell phone had flown out of his hand and lay smashed in several pieces a few feet away.

He glanced over his shoulder. The house was filled with smoke. Whatever had exploded had been toward the middle of the structure, large enough to cause a lot of damage, but small enough not to bring the whole thing down. Through the now glassless windows he could see the flicker of flames. There would be little time before fire crews and police arrived on scene. He needed to get out of there, fast.

He pulled himself to his feet, then paused.

The noise at the back of the yard. The shock of the explosion had almost made him forget. He looked toward the rear fence but there was nothing.

Forget it, he willed himself. He had to get out of there. That was priority one.

Only which way? By now people from the neighborhood would have started gathering on the street out front. If he left the same way he'd arrived, he'd be spotted for sure. The immediate assumption would be that he caused the blast. He couldn't risk that delay.

As he began scanning the backyard for an alternate exit, the bushes moved again. No possum, he realized, unless it was at least five

70

feet tall. It was a person; he could just make out its shadowy form between the branches.

Quinn ducked down, reaching for a gun he wasn't carrying, then swore silently to himself. Staying low, he ran quickly over to the garden shed, putting it between him and whoever it was sharing the yard with him. He chanced a look around the side. Nothing, except the vague forms of plants and grass almost indistinguishable in the half-light of the growing fire.

From the distance came the first faint sounds of sirens. Quinn started to pull back behind the shed when suddenly two hands shot up above the plants, grabbing for the top of the fence.

Quinn didn't even think. He rushed toward the movement.

The person who'd been hiding was almost over the top by the time Quinn got there.

A woman, he realized. She was thin, agile, and had her hair pulled back in a ponytail. Like Quinn, she was dressed in dark clothing.

Jenny? he thought, pausing for a split second.

He lunged forward, his hand grasping at her foot. But his hesitation had cost him. His fingers brushed the sole of her shoe, unable to grab hold.

There was a thud on the other side of the fence, followed a second later by a groan.

Quinn pulled himself up and over the barrier, landing on his feet.

The woman was already heading across the yard toward a house that could have been a clone of the one that had just been destroyed. There were no lights on inside. Either no one was home, or the place was empty. The explosion would have drawn the attention of any occupants.

The woman was favoring one leg, slowing her progress.

'Jenny?' he called out. But the woman didn't stop.

Quinn sprinted across the lawn. In the distance, the wail of emergency sirens was nearing.

When he was only a few feet away, he said in a low voice, 'Stop.'

The woman did just the opposite, moving faster toward the house. Quinn closed the remaining distance and grabbed her just below the shoulders, pulling them both to a halt.

She flailed against him, trying to break free, but he held tight. As he turned her to face him, he realized he was wrong. She wasn't Jenny. The height had been right, and the hair was close enough to his memory of Jenny's, but the face belonged to someone else.

'Please,' she said. 'Let me go. I didn't see anything, okay?' She winced in pain, but she didn't cry out.

'What were you doing back there?' Quinn asked.

She shook her head. 'Nothing.'

'Maybe watching to make sure the bomb got me?'

'No. Please, just let me go.'

'You were trying to kill me, weren't you?' Quinn said.

'Please. I just want to leave.'

'Who are you?'

As she started to speak, a jolt of pain crossed her face. She began to lean down, but Quinn's grip held her in place.

'I twisted my ankle,' she said. 'Just let me check it.'

'Slow and easy,' he said.

As he released his grip, he moved behind her, keeping a hand on her back just below her neck. The sirens were closer now. Perhaps a minute away, no more.

The woman rubbed her ankle for a moment, then one of her hands slipped under the cuff of her pants. Quinn reached down and grabbed her wrist just as her hand reemerged. She was holding a small pistol. By the looks of it, a .22. Not a lot of firepower, but at close range enough to kill.

Quinn wrenched the weapon from her grasp.

'Give that back,' she said.

He slipped the gun into his pocket.

'Fine. Keep it. I don't care,' she said. She turned her head toward the sound of the sirens, then looked back at Quinn. 'Can I go now?'

Quinn knew they had very little time before they'd be discovered, but he didn't move. 'Who are you?'

'Does it matter?' she said. 'Look, they're going to arrest both of us if they find us here. I didn't have anything to do with the explosion, and I know you didn't either or you wouldn't have been standing so close when it went off. Right?'

Quinn didn't reply.

'Can we just get out of here?' she asked.

'Who are you?'

'It doesn't matter.'

'Actually, it does.'

He grabbed her by the arm and started pushing her across the yard toward the front gate.

★　★　★

Quinn found an old Ford Bronco parked on the street with its doors unlocked.

'Get in,' he said to the woman.

She looked at him for a second, then climbed across to the passenger seat.

'Don't think about getting out and running, because I will catch you,' Quinn said.

The look on her face told him she understood.

It took him less than a minute to hot-wire the ignition. As the engine roared to life, he sat up and jammed the Bronco into drive.

'Who are you?' he asked again.

She hesitated, then said, 'Tasha. Tasha . . . Laver.'

Quinn drove carefully, keeping his speed down so as not to draw unwanted attention. 'What were you doing in that backyard?'

'I . . . I was looking for someone.'

'Really? Who?'

Ahead was a stop sign. Quinn slowed, then rolled through it when he saw the coast was clear.

'A friend. The house belongs to her. But . . . ' She paused, then looked at Quinn. 'Who are *you?* What were *you* doing there?'

Quinn said nothing.

'I know you weren't with them, or you wouldn't have been trying to get into the house.'

'*Them?*' he asked as he took the next right.

'The people in the house. That family. The others. I've never seen any of them before. And I've known Jenny for . . . ' She stopped herself. 'You haven't told me who you are.'

'You're right. I haven't,' he said, beginning to feel he might be able to get a little more information out of the woman, but that it might not be worth the time.

Woodway Avenue was a couple blocks away. Quinn could see dozens of cars passing by on the busier road. Just before they reached it, he pulled the Bronco to the curb and turned to the woman. 'One last time: what were you doing back there?'

She hesitated, then said, 'I was looking for Jenny. Jenny Fuentes. That was her house, but I think you probably know that.' She paused. 'You . . . called me Jenny when you were chasing me.'

'Why were you looking for her?'

Again a pause. 'She's a friend. We've been friends for a long time.'

'Good for you. But that still doesn't tell me why.'

The woman seemed to think for a moment, considering her words before she spoke. 'We kept in pretty good touch. Then a few weeks ago, it was like she disappeared. I called her work but they said she was on a leave of absence.' She looked at Quinn. 'Jenny would let me know if something was wrong. She

75

wouldn't just go away without a word.'

'You're that important to her?'

'Important enough,' she said defensively.

'How do you know her?'

'Why do you need to know that? Who the hell are *you*? And why are *you* looking for her?'

'How do you know her?' he repeated, his voice impatient.

Silence.

'College,' she said, as if mad she had even opened her mouth. 'Same major. Your turn now.'

Quinn wasn't sure if her story was true or not, but she had given him enough to check her out.

'Get out,' he said.

'What?'

'Get out of the car. You can catch a ride here. Or call a taxi. I don't care.'

'No.'

'Now,' he said.

'I'm not leaving until you tell me who you are and why you're looking for Jenny.' Her tone was defiant, challenging.

Quinn stared at her for a moment. 'Fine.'

He opened his door and started to climb out.

'Where are you going?'

He didn't answer.

★   ★   ★

He walked back to the rented Lexus. The woman had followed him for a block, then stopped. As he glanced back over his shoulder, he could see her walking toward Woodway Avenue. Whether she was really a friend of Jenny's or not, he

76

wasn't sure. But her fear had seemed genuine. Still, she was a loose end. Once he found a secure phone, he'd have Nate check her out.

When he reached the Lexus, he saw that the street up toward Jenny's house was filled with police cars and fire trucks. Bright lights on portable poles were erected in the driveway, lighting up the smoldering house like a Monday night football game. Firemen were fighting what was left of the flames, while most of the cops worked crowd detail.

Quinn slipped quietly into his car. He kept his eyes forward as he started the engine, watchful in case anyone looked in his direction.

He waited a full minute before pulling away from the curb, lights off. He made a quick U-turn, then headed back toward Woodway Avenue.

If he'd been only mildly worried about Jenny before he came to Houston, he was now full-on concerned. And until proven otherwise, he had to assume that Markoff's death and the disappearance of his girlfriend were connected.

He could feel the tension building in his shoulders.

Nate had been right. This was one of those jobs they didn't get paid for. Until Quinn knew Jenny was all right, he wasn't going to be able to stop looking for her. The last thing he wanted was for what had happened to Markoff to happen to her, too.

He only hoped he wasn't too late.

7

From the scant information he had, the last place Jenny had been seen was in D.C. So a return to L.A. was going to have to wait. D.C. would have to come first.

The fastest way there would have been to head back to Bush Intercontinental and catch a plane. Hobby Airport was also an option. But both posed potential risks. The men who had been following him in the Volvo couldn't have known he was at the house when it exploded. They might still be trying to find him. Which meant there was a good chance watchers were stationed at the airports, looking for him. There was no way to know for sure, so it was best to play it safe.

Quinn took the I-10 heading east toward Louisiana. The after-midnight crowd was mainly big rigs hauling God knows what into the heart of the South. Scattered among them were the occasional sedans, almost all solo drivers.

The night was dark, moonless. Quinn could make out some vegetation along the side of the road, but it was all silhouettes, no real definition to anything.

Just before Beaumont, he exited the interstate and stopped at a twenty-four-hour gas station. He filled up the Lexus and grabbed a large cup of coffee inside.

'Pay phone?' he asked the attendant.

The man looked at him a little funny at first. 'Oh . . . um . . . outside, I think. Back near the bathrooms. If it's still there.'

'Thanks,' Quinn said.

He walked back to his car, then pulled around to where the phone was supposed to be. Turned out the attendant's memory was pretty good. The phone was there, though it didn't look as if it had been used in a while.

Quinn donned the leather gloves again, then grabbed one of the napkins he'd picked up with the coffee and got out of his car. He gave the phone a quick wipe-down, removing a layer of dust, before he put it to his ear. He then used a calling card he kept in his wallet for just such emergencies to call Nate.

'Hello?' Nate's voice was quick, abrupt.

'It's me,' Quinn said.

'How are you?'

'Decent enough.' The code again, only this time telling Nate he was okay, but on an unsecured line.

He could hear Nate exhale on the other end. 'Thank God. It sounded . . . ' He paused, obviously trying to choose the correct word. 'Abrupt.'

'It was,' Quinn said. 'I'll tell you about it later.'

'Are you coming back?'

'No. Not yet. I'll check in tomorrow. No specific time. If you have anything for me, e-mail is best for now.'

'Wait,' Nate said, no doubt sensing Quinn was about to hang up. 'Orlando called.'

'What? Why?' Quinn asked.

'She's visiting her aunt and wants to talk to you.'

Quinn was silent for a moment. Visiting her aunt would mean she was in San Francisco. Odd that she hadn't mentioned coming to California the last time they talked. That wasn't like her. Even though they both worked in the world of secrets, they had few between them. Orlando lived in Ho Chi Minh City, Vietnam, with her son Garrett, so a trip to the States was not something she would have done on a whim.

'Did she say what she wanted?' Quinn asked.

'No. Just to call her. She sounded . . . distracted.'

'Distracted?'

'I don't know. Just not herself. Maybe she's jetlagged and just wants to say hi.'

'That's it?'

'That's it.'

Quinn frowned, then said, 'I can't call her right now.'

'What if she calls again?'

'Tell her I'll get ahold of her as soon as I can,' Quinn said.

⋆   ⋆   ⋆

Quinn was able to get on an early morning plane out of Baton Rouge, Louisiana. It wasn't a direct flight, so when he arrived at Reagan National Airport it was just after 11:30 a.m. eastern time. He made a quick local phone call, then walked across the skyway toward baggage claim and caught the Metro Blue Line north one stop to

80

Crystal City. There he walked down the tunnel to the Crystal City Marriott and checked in to a room. Once he'd taken a quick shower and dressed in jeans and a green short-sleeve shirt, he went back downstairs and caught a taxi into the city.

After Houston, the temperature and humidity in Washington were almost bearable. Quinn guessed it was taking a whole minute longer for his shirt to soak through with sweat.

As his cab was passing the Jefferson Memorial, Quinn leaned forward. 'Drop me off at the Department of Agriculture,' he said.

'Not the convention center?' the cabby asked. It was the destination Quinn had given him when he got in.

'Agriculture. South Building.'

The cabby huffed a little at the shorter distance and grumbled to himself for the rest of the trip. But a few minutes later, when Quinn double-tipped him as he got out, the man's frown disappeared.

Quinn took a few steps toward the entrance, casually looking around as he did so. He knew he was being overcautious, but after the near miss in Houston, he wasn't going to take anything for granted. Once he was satisfied that he was alone, he turned again and made his way across Independence Avenue.

Ahead was the Mall. Monument Row, Durrie had once called it. Even the old son of a bitch had a certain amount of respect for the place.

It stretched almost two miles east and west, with the domed Capitol building at the east end and the memorial to Abraham Lincoln at the west. Between were fields of grass and paths of dirt and memorials of stone.

Even in his focused state, Quinn couldn't help but feel the importance of what surrounded him. It was enough to make even the most jaded person crack a little.

As usual, the Mall was packed with visitors. Most were wearing shorts and T-shirts. The smart ones also had on hats. The crowd's pace was slow, lethargic — the heat and humidity draining whatever excess energy they'd had when the day began. Several people were holding ice cream cones, kids mostly, but some adults, too. All seemed to be in a constant battle to lick up as much as possible before it melted onto their hands. Few were winning.

Quinn worked his way through the throngs, making sure his own pace was not much faster than that of those around him. He was just another tourist soaking up the history.

Just before Madison Drive, he turned right down one of the wide dirt paths traversing the Mall. Two minutes later, he spotted a man and a woman walking away from him. The man was holding a fancy, twine-handled paper bag like those found in a gift shop, while the woman carried a large purse. They stood out from the rest of the crowd because they were dressed for work, not a day of exploring.

The man was shorter than Quinn by several inches, no taller than five foot six. The woman's heels raised her an inch above the man's bald pate.

Quinn had never seen her before, but he knew the man. Though they'd only met in person once, Quinn recognized Peter immediately. He reminded Quinn of a hair- and height-challenged Charles Bronson. Maybe it was the mustache, dark like Bronson's, or perhaps it was his permanent squint, as if he was constantly sizing everyone up. Maybe it was both.

Peter was the head of an organization known as the Office. For years, the Office had been Quinn's sole client. Though Peter had made attempts to hire him full-time, Quinn always refused, preferring the independence of his perceived freelance status. But after the incident in Berlin the previous January, things had changed. Peter had been less than forthcoming then, holding back information that would have aided Quinn. Thankfully, despite Peter's reluctance, Quinn had been able to stop Durrie and that psycho Borko before they had been able to complete their plan. But Quinn knew things would have gone considerably easier if Peter had been up-front with him.

Because of that, he decided it was time he diversified his clientele. Besides, relying on a single income source had been profitable but foolish for the long run. He'd decided to remove himself from Peter's active roster. The head of the Office hadn't been happy about it, but he had also done nothing to stop Quinn.

So it wasn't without a bit of irony that Quinn approached his former employer in search of help.

'You couldn't have picked a place a little more

. . . I don't know, *inside?*' Peter said as soon as he noticed Quinn walking next to him. 'Where it might be cool?'

'Sweat's good for your skin,' Quinn said. 'It'll help smooth out some of those wrinkles.'

'I'll keep that in mind.'

'Who's your date?' Quinn asked.

'Ida? Can you give us a moment?'

The woman gave Quinn a half smile, then slowed to let them walk ahead of her.

Quinn and Peter continued down the path. In the distance, the white dome of the Capitol building shimmered in the afternoon heat.

'Is that for me?' Quinn asked, pointing down at the bag.

'These things aren't cheap.'

'Don't worry. I said I'd pay you back.'

'Yeah. Well, you'd better. It's the end of our fiscal year. We're starting to close out this year's budget, and haven't finalized next year's yet, and damn if they don't want me to cut back again. I can't afford to have gifts like this on my books.'

Peter had been complaining about budgets for years. Quinn wasn't sure if he believed him. The truth was, Quinn wasn't even sure the Office answered to anyone other than whoever hired them for a particular project. Quinn had always presumed Peter's organization was an off-the-books operation of some government agency, but he didn't know that for a fact.

'Can I have it?'

Peter hesitated a moment longer, then handed the bag over. Quinn looked inside. At the bottom was a phone very much like the one that had been destroyed in Houston. To most people, it would look like a regular cell phone, but just like his old one it was a hell of a lot more powerful than your standard, off-the-shelf Nokia or Samsung. Multi-encrypted, touch-screen interface, thumbprint recognition security system, eight megapixel camera — an upgrade from the previous version — with normal, infrared, and advanced heat-sensing capabilities, and both cell- and satellite-ready depending on signal strength.

'Thanks,' he said. 'But I asked for two things.'

The left side of Peter's mouth raised slightly in annoyance. 'I'm not your supplier.'

'Do you have it or not?'

'You promise not to do anything stupid with it?'

Now it was Quinn's turn to be annoyed. 'Just give it to me.'

Peter stared at Quinn a moment longer, then looked over his shoulder. 'Ida,' he said.

The woman picked up her pace and rejoined them.

'Give it to him,' Peter said.

She slipped her purse around so she had easy access, then zipped it open. From inside, she removed a three-inch-thick gray plastic box. Like the bag the phone had been in, it had the feel of an upscale present. Quinn guessed it was about nine inches by twelve, and seemed to have taken up almost all the room inside the purse.

'For you,' Ida said, handing Quinn the box.

'Thanks.'

Inside Quinn knew he'd find a SIG Sauer

P226, a few mags, extra ammo, and a suppressor. In Houston, he hadn't had time to get a gun, but he wasn't going to make the same mistake in D.C.

Without even being told, Ida fell back again, giving the two men privacy.

'You said you wanted to talk,' Peter said. 'You looking for work?'

'Would you give it to me if I asked?'

Peter looked over, his squint more pronounced than usual. 'Of course I would. Nobody else I hire is as good as you. You know that.'

Quinn smiled. 'I'm not looking for work right now. But I'll let you know.'

Peter snorted, but said nothing.

'I need something,' Quinn said.

'I already gave you something,' Peter replied, motioning to the bag.

'Information. I'm trying to find someone, and I think you can help.'

Peter stopped and turned to Quinn. 'Hold on. Are you asking *me* to do some work for *you*?'

'Just a quick check. That's all. You have resources you can get to quicker than I can at the moment.'

'I don't know, Quinn. I'm not sure how to handle this.' Peter was obviously relishing the moment.

'It's a favor. That's all. Don't get all worked up.'

'Aren't you the one who once told me you didn't do favors?' Peter said. 'So what would motivate me to do one for you?'

'I seem to recall I did the favor anyway. I also

seem to remember saving your ass in Berlin. If I hadn't been there, you would have taken the fall for that one.' It was true to a point. But in reality, if Quinn hadn't been there, it wouldn't have mattered who took the fall.

'I'll tell you what,' Peter said. 'I'll do your favor. But next time I need you for a job, you say yes.'

'That's not a favor, Peter. That's a trade.'

'Whatever. That's my deal.'

'I'm not even on your active list anymore.'

'Actually,' Peter said, 'I never took you off.'

Why doesn't that surprise me? Quinn thought.

He looked over Peter's shoulder toward the Smithsonian Castle across the Mall. It wasn't like Peter was asking a lot. Quinn's plan had never been to stop working for the Office entirely. But suggesting a tit-for-tat bothered Quinn. It was almost enough for Quinn to just walk away.

Almost.

'Fine,' Quinn said.

Peter smiled. 'What can I do for you?'

★   ★   ★

Back at the Marriott, Quinn connected his new phone to his computer. Before uploading his address book and other vital information, he used a program Orlando had created to erase all unnecessary information from the phone's memory, then replace it with his personal settings and thumbprint identification. It was a safety precaution in case Peter had installed any

87

hidden tracking or monitoring software. Next he programmed the phone with his number, then transferred the backup of his contact list. Once done, he called Nate.

'I'm up and running again,' he said.

'What the hell's going on?' Nate asked. 'I assume it has something to do with that house fire in Houston.'

'Been doing a little checking, have you?'

'Just the Internet. Since it's the same address as the one you wanted me to check out, I took a wild guess. One of the news reports says it was a gas leak.'

'Is that what they think?'

'Not gas, then?'

'No,' Quinn said.

'Intentional?'

'I tripped a switch,' Quinn said, recalling the click as he'd been opening the bathroom window. 'My guess is it was on a timer anyway. The booby trap was a backup in case someone tried to get in the house.' Quinn knew there was no way the suits in the Volvo would have left the house intact. They needed to destroy it and cover their tracks. 'What did you find out?'

'Jennifer Fuentes is listed as the current owner of the house.'

'What about the history?'

'That was a bit more difficult. The files had been flagged, which meant a higher level of security was added to them.'

'Really?' Quinn said, interested.

'Nothing too drastic. I used a few of the tricks Orlando taught me, and got in.'

'Did you trigger any tracers?'

'I *found* a trace program, but I bypassed it. Too risky to figure out who it was set to notify, but I could tell it wasn't anyone at the county records office.'

'What did you find?' Quinn asked.

'The previous owners were Bradley and Gabriella Fuentes. Jennifer got the house four and a half years ago. Title transfer only, not a sale.'

'Her parents?' Quinn asked.

'I checked her medical records. Again, added security and a tracer.'

'And?' Quinn asked.

'Her parents are listed as Miguel and Cecilia Fuentes.'

'Not Bradley and Gabriella.'

'No. They're her grandparents,' Nate said. 'Bradley passed away eight years ago. Gabriella followed three years later.'

Quinn nodded to himself. Now the house made sense. Jenny had inherited it. 'Good work. What about the car?'

'Stolen plates. Came off a Camry.'

No surprise there. 'I need you to check someone out for me.'

'Okay.'

'A woman named Tasha Laver.'

'You got anything else on her?'

'Early thirties at most. About five-six, in decent shape. Might live in Houston, but that's not a for sure.'

'That's it?'

'She claims to have gone to college with Jenny.

Says they're old friends.'

'I'll see what I can come up with,' Nate said.

'Anything else for me? The message? The photos I sent you?'

'The photos are running through the system. And I'm still nowhere with the message.'

'You're just full of useful information, aren't you?'

'I'm doing this by myself, you know,' Nate said. 'I *did* ask for help, but if you recall, you said no.'

'Relax, Nate. Do the check on Tasha Laver first, then go back to decoding.'

'Sure. Fine. Whatever.'

Quinn called Orlando next, but was routed straight to her voice mail. He left a quick message, then hung up.

He rubbed his hands across his face, pulling the skin tight against his cheeks and jaw, then slipped his fingers up to his temples and began rubbing up and down. A low-grade headache had settled in like a cloud, hovering just below his skull but focused in no particular place.

Part of it was due to his lack of sleep, he knew that. The hour-and-a-half nap he'd been able to grab on the plane had not been enough. But the bigger part, the thrust that was pounding hardest, was due to Markoff and Jenny. The uncertainty, the anger, the wanting to be able to do more.

He stretched out on the bed, thinking at first that if he just closed his eyes for a few moments he might be able to recharge a little. But before a minute had passed, he was deep asleep.

8

A shrill ring jolted Quinn awake. He opened his eyes and pushed himself up. The room was dark, lit only by faint light filtering in through the window. Outside, night had descended over the city.

He looked to his left. His new phone was on the bed next to him, its ring not one he was accustomed to. He picked it up and thumbed the screen to disable the security lock.

'Hello?' he said.

'Quinn?'

Still a little disoriented, it took Quinn an extra second to recognize Peter's voice.

'Are you there?' Peter asked.

'I'm here. Sorry.'

'Is this a bad time?'

'Hold on, okay?' Quinn said. 'Just give me a second.'

Quinn set the phone back on the bed, then walked into the bathroom to splash some cold water on his face.

He looked at his watch — 9:23 p.m. It had been over six hours since he had returned to the room that afternoon. Sleeping that long had not been part of his plan. He frowned in self-annoyance as he walked back into the bedroom and picked up the phone.

'I'm back.'

'You all right?' Peter asked.

'I'm fine,' Quinn said. 'You have something for me?'

'Something, yes. But not an answer.'

Quinn nodded to himself. He'd figured as much. His request of Peter was to see if he could find out what Markoff had been up to. Since Markoff had once been CIA, it was possible Peter could pull a few strings and see if anyone at the agency knew anything about their former employee's recent activities. What he hadn't told Peter was that Markoff was dead. No sense setting that alarm off yet. 'What did you get?'

'Word is no one's talked to Markoff in weeks. He just kind of disappeared. No one seems worried, though. He's retired. Maybe he went on a vacation.'

Quinn frowned. 'Disappeared and no one knows where?'

'Maybe he has other friends he's told.'

With the exception of Jenny, Quinn didn't think Markoff had any other friends outside of the business. 'You think he's taken a freelance job?'

'Perhaps, but I couldn't turn anything up,' Peter said. 'What makes you think he's not sitting on a beach somewhere relaxing?'

'Okay,' Quinn said, making no attempt to answer the question. 'Thanks.'

'Don't forget our deal,' Peter said.

Quinn hung up.

★   ★   ★

The taxi followed the Potomac River north, staying on the Virginia side until the Key Bridge took them into Georgetown. The address Steiner had given Quinn for Jenny's D.C. home was on one of the numbered streets that ran north and south throughout the city. Quinn had the driver drop him off two blocks away on M Street.

The night was pleasant, no real need for a jacket, but Quinn wore one anyway. It was thin, more a windbreaker really, but what was most important was the built-in holster on the inside, under his left arm. His gun and suppressor fit snuggly into the customized space.

As usual, there were plenty of people out on M enjoying the warm late summer night in the bars and restaurants. Quinn weaved his way through a group of college-aged kids. Two were wearing Georgetown sweatshirts, and all looked like they'd been drinking for a while.

Instead of turning down Jenny's street, Quinn kept walking, taking only a quick glance down the cobblestone road.

It was one-way with the exit at M Street. Compared to the main road, it was a morgue. The only cars on it were parked, and no one was on the sidewalks. Like elsewhere in Georgetown, it was lined with brick townhouses — some painted white, some yellow, some gray, and some left in natural brick red.

He continued to the next intersection, then turned right. He found himself on a street very similar to the one Jenny supposedly lived on. He walked down the empty brick sidewalk a half block, then turned onto the walkway of a darkened townhouse. He took the three steps up to the door, paused like he was pulling his keys out of his pocket, then checked back the way he had just come.

The road was empty. He was alone.

He descended the stairs and continued down the street, away from M. He had checked a map online before leaving the hotel, so when he reached the end of the block, he was not surprised to find that instead of an intersecting street there was a canal.

It was the Chesapeake & Ohio Canal, more commonly known as the C & O. In the 1800s, it had been used to move goods from northern Maryland to D.C. and back. Now its sole purpose was to add to the area's historical character.

The canal cut a wide east-west swath through Georgetown. Not only was there the rock-walled waterway, but there was also the old towpath that ran parallel to the water. Beside the path was a narrow park, with trees and grass and benches.

Quinn turned right onto the walkway and followed the canal back toward Jenny's street. If the map was right, Jenny's building would be the one butted up against the canal on the east side of the street.

Quinn glanced ahead. The building was taller than the two-story, single-family townhouses that made up most of the neighborhood. It looked five stories high, though not much wider than the other buildings. That made sense. Jenny's address had indicated she was in unit number 4, which would mean she was in a multi-residence building.

A building that size, it seemed a reasonable guess it was only one apartment per floor. Unit 4, fourth floor.

When his gaze reached what he assumed was Jenny's apartment, he stopped and stared. Each of the apartments had two windows looking out over the canal. But the apartment on the fourth floor was different. Where the windows had once been, there were now large sheets of plywood. Even in the dim light of the streetlamps, he could tell the bricks around the sheets were dark, almost black.

He looked at the apartments on the fifth and the third floors. No curtains in these windows, not even knickknacks on the windowsill. Only darkness and the sense of abandonment. And though there were curtains drawn across the windows of the first and second floors, Quinn got the distinct feeling no one was home.

A fire, Quinn thought. There was no mistaking the signs. And the fourth-floor apartment had taken the brunt.

What the hell? he thought.

He willed himself to continue moving forward along the path. In the distance, he could hear the traffic on M Street, but here next to Jenny's building there was an eerie quiet. Even the water in the canal seemed hushed as it moved through the old locks and tumbled from one level to the next.

When he reached the sidewalk running in front of the small apartment complex, he

95

stopped again. The light above the main doorway was out, but the darkness didn't hide the strip of caution tape strung across the top of the steps. As Quinn suspected, the building had been evacuated.

He checked the street, then walked up the steps and ducked under the tape. From the pocket of his leather jacket, he removed a pair of latex surgical gloves and pulled them on.

He tried the doorknob. Locked, but the door itself felt loose, like the deadbolt hadn't been engaged. He tried the knob again, leaning against the door to see if it might be weak. The lock in the knob held for a moment, then gave way with a muffled pop. Quinn wasted no time crossing the threshold and closing the door behind him.

He found himself in a small community entry. The first thing he noticed was the smell. Smoke. But not as strong as he'd expected. It made him wonder how long it had been since the fire had occurred.

To the right was a set of metal mailboxes. There were five in total. To the left was the door to the first-floor apartment, and straight ahead was a staircase.

Quinn walked over to the mailboxes. There was enough illumination filtering in through a large window above the main door for him to read the labels on each without pulling out his flashlight. The boxes were all numbered 1 through 5, but there were no names.

Quinn forced the lock on the one labeled '4.' The box was stuffed full, like whomever it belonged to hadn't been home for at least a week before the fire occurred. No mail would have been delivered after the blaze. Quinn pulled out several items. They were all addressed to the same person.

Jennifer Fuentes.

He put everything back, then pushed the box closed.

He turned to the stairs and headed upward. Except for the number on the apartments, the second and third floors were identical to each other: a simple landing, a door, and the stairs.

Quinn climbed to the fourth floor, this time stopping just short of the landing so he could take in the space before him. Perhaps it had once looked like the lower floors, but not anymore. The walls were black with smoke damage, and the door to apartment 4 lay in a heap off to the side. It looked as though fire crews had hacked their way into the apartment so that they would have a shot at saving the building.

Testing the floor first, Quinn stepped onto the landing and approached the threshold of the apartment but did not enter. The darkness inside was almost complete, the plywood over the windows blocking any outside light. Quinn pulled out his flashlight and turned it on.

The firemen may have saved the rest of the building, but they hadn't been able to do anything for Jenny's place. The destruction was total. The fire had been so all-encompassing it had left nothing untouched.

All of Jenny's possessions, all of them, were gone.

Quinn left the building as quietly as he had entered. He started walking toward M Street, where he would be able to catch a cab back to the hotel. As he headed up the sidewalk, he heard an engine start up somewhere along the block behind him.

He kept facing forward, like he hadn't noticed it. Perhaps it was nothing. A lot of people lived within a block or two of where he was walking. Any one of them could have been heading out on a late-night errand.

He continued on his way, waiting for the car to pass by, but it didn't. The engine noise was still there, a low rumble thirty yards back. He focused on the sound, gauging its location with every step. It remained steady, constant, as if it was moving with him, at his pace.

His hand moved to the grip of his gun, ready to pull it out the moment he felt it was necessary.

He was almost to M Street, its lights and activity a complete contrast to his current surroundings. If this was some kind of snatch-and-grab, those in the car would be coming after him at any second. He might be able to take them out, then again, he might not.

Not worth the chance, he thought as he removed his hand from his gun.

Without warning, he sprinted to the corner and turned right on M. Seeing a gap in the traffic, he raced into the street. A car heading west on the other side honked at him, but he ignored it as he ran to the far sidewalk.

When he reached it, he glanced over his shoulder back at Jenny's street. He expected to see the car that had been following him, but it wasn't there. Quinn moved into the darkened entrance of a closed gift shop and watched the corner.

It was a full half-minute before a Honda Accord appeared at the end of the street. The car was surprisingly empty. There was no team of men readying to take up the chase. There was only a single occupant — the driver.

The Honda sat at the curb for several minutes, passing up multiple opportunities to go. Quinn could see the driver looking back and forth as if expecting to find something.

Finally the car turned right onto M Street, and drove past Quinn's position. Though it was on the opposite side of the street, the driver was now close enough for Quinn to make an ID.

Son of a bitch, he thought.

Tasha Laver.

9

Quinn rose early the next morning with the echo of his old mentor Durrie's voice in his head.

'Things in our world are different, Johnny. You've got to worry about yourself, no one else.' It was a refrain Durrie had often preached. 'There's no room for anyone else. Others make things messy.'

Once again, his old mentor's message was clear. It was the same sermon Quinn had been hearing in his head since he'd decided to find Jenny. *Get the hell out of there and go home.* It's what Durrie would have done.

Except for one thing, Quinn thought. *Durrie would have never come looking for Jenny in the first place.*

Of course, that was because Quinn wasn't like him. He never had been.

Quinn actually cared about other people. He felt responsibility. He felt loyalty. None of those were Durrie's strong points. In fact, Durrie would have undoubtedly said those qualities were incompatible with being a cleaner.

When Quinn had been a cop in Phoenix, and had nearly gotten himself killed because he'd nosed around a murder investigation he wasn't officially involved in, Durrie, seeing potential in the young kid's abilities, had interceded. He had offered Quinn the chance at something more, a life that suited Quinn better than either of them had realized at the time.

Growing up, Quinn had been smarter than almost everyone else around him. But he was self-aware enough to know not to advertise the fact. Warroad, Minnesota, was a nice place, with good people, but they wouldn't tolerate a know-it-all, especially one who felt trapped and stifled in the place they called home.

So he blended in, joking and playing and laughing with the other kids, being polite and helpful and respectful to the adults, while all the time improving his attention to detail, exercising his memory, and reading everything he could. Because he kept his real self private, he unintentionally learned the art of secrets, of play-acting, of fitting in.

In his early teens, he developed a love of puzzles and real-life mysteries, enhancing his personal education with books on crimes and investigational procedures. That's when he decided he wanted to be in the police. Not a beat cop, but a detective.

Looking back, it wasn't law enforcement he had been preparing himself for. It was a life in the secret world.

That's what Durrie had seen in him, a cleaner in the making. All Quinn's mentor had to do was finish the education.

He taught Quinn the intricacies of the job, pointing out obstacles and ways around them, helping him to improve certain skills that were lacking, and to hone those that were already developed. Then, when the apprenticeship was over, he did all he could to help Quinn get up and running on his own.

Of course, that was all before Durrie went off the deep end and his truer nature took hold, ultimately putting him at the wrong end of a bullet from Quinn's own gun.

No. Durrie would have never come in search of Jenny.

But for Quinn, finding her was something he *had* to do.

For Markoff.

There was no choice.

The debt to someone who saved your life can never be repaid in full.

Not a Durrie rule. Durrie would have scoffed at such sentiment. Or, more likely, would have called you an asshole and never taken anything you said seriously again.

It was Orlando's mentor, Abraham Delger, who had said it to Quinn. Unlike Quinn's former boss, Delger wasn't afraid to show a softer side now and then.

An old Chinese proverb said that the one who saved the life was responsible for the one who had been saved. Not a debt, per se, but an acknowledgment that if a person lived when they should have died, all that they did after was due to the actions of the one who stayed death's hand.

But Quinn could never accept that way of thinking. Delger's idea that the debt was owed by the person who had been saved instead of the one who had done the saving rang truer.

And ever since that night in the Finnish countryside, Quinn owed his life to Markoff. It

102

was something he knew he'd never stop trying to pay off. Even now, after his friend had turned up dead.

Once he was showered and dressed, Quinn pulled his laptop out of his bag and set it up on the desk. Using his wireless connection, he hacked into the hotel Wi-Fi system, bypassing the pay-by-the-day page.

First he did a quick web search, verifying the address of Congressman Guerrero's office. In his gut, he knew there were answers there. But the only way to be sure was to go in person. The website not only confirmed the congressman's location, it also confirmed Guerrero's grander goal. Across the top of the site was a banner ad:

AMERICA FIRST
GUERRERO FOR PRESIDENT

Quinn smiled to himself as a way into the congressman's office formulated in his mind.

He closed the browser and opened his e-mail.

There were several messages. He ignored all but the two from Nate. As Quinn had taught him, the subject line was just the day's date — year first, then month, then day. Easy for sorting and no hint of the contents.

Quinn clicked open the first one sent.

Was working late and figured you might be asleep. I can give you more details on the phone in the morning if you want.

I ran a check on Tasha Laver. So far I've found only 3 people with that name in the entire country. It's not a common combination apparently. Unfortunately, two are in their seventies, and the other one's dead.

I'd say it's a pretty good guess none of them are your 30-year-old woman.

I'll continue to check, but doubtful about any relevant hits.

Have you called Orlando yet?

N.

No luck on Tasha. *Why doesn't that surprise me?* Quinn thought.

The second e-mail was sent a few hours after the first. Quinn opened it.

The pictures you took in Houston just finished processing through the system. Nothing.

I've started them through some of the secondary sources, and should have more info in the morning. I was thinking maybe they're not from here, so I'm also trying some of the foreign databases, but those are going to take longer to get any results from.

Do you think they might be ghosts?

Ghosts were those who eluded the system, often actively searching and removing any information about themselves that might be floating around. There was a damn good chance Nate was right. After all, Quinn was a ghost, and he was in the process of turning Nate into one, too.

Quinn clicked on Reply.

Let me know as soon as you get anything new.

On Tasha Laver, leave it for now. Name is probably a dead end.

Good job.

Q

He hit Send.

The House Majority Whip's office was in the Longworth Office Building on Independence Avenue. It was the second, and smallest, of three buildings specifically designed and constructed for the members of the House of Representatives. It was the same building where the Majority Leader had his office, so it was convenient for party matters. The minority party leaders were next door in the Rayburn Building, a massive structure that housed the bulk of the congressmen.

Each of the three buildings — Rayburn, Longworth, and Cannon — sat in a row just to the south of the Capitol building.

Quinn had never had a reason to enter any of them. In fact, he had never been inside the Capitol either. Though he'd made many trips to D.C., they'd all been on business, and usually involved meetings in generic-looking buildings far from the tourist areas.

One time, he had spent fifteen minutes at the Lincoln Memorial, then had walked over and taken in the Vietnam Veterans Memorial. Both had been more powerful than he'd expected. He had finally pulled himself away from the black granite wall when he found himself staring at names he didn't know, but realized could have belonged to his father or his uncles or any of a thousand men he'd met over the years if luck had broken differently.

After he had finished with his e-mail that morning, he'd called Congressman Guerrero's office, pretending to be a reporter doing a feature piece on the congressman. It had been easy. Part of Quinn's play-acting past. He could quickly fall into most any role. It was the one talent Durrie had admired in Quinn from the beginning.

His old mentor hated role-playing, and came more and more to rely on Quinn's abilities as the need arose. 'You're a natural liar,' Durrie had said. 'Keep it up and you'll do all right.'

Quinn wasn't sure he liked the compliment, but he couldn't deny that putting on the identity of someone else was almost as simple for him as getting out of bed.

The person at Guerrero's office had told him

he'd be happy to set up a meeting with someone from the press office.

'I actually met one of your staffers when I was in town several months ago, and wonder if she might be available,' Quinn had said.

'I can check. Who was it?'

'Her name is . . . ' Quinn paused like he was reading his notes. 'Jennifer Fuentes.'

'Oh, I'm sorry,' the woman said, not missing a beat. 'Ms. Fuentes is not in the office this week. But you're in luck, the assistant press secretary, Dylan Ray, has an opening at two-thirty. Would that work?'

'That'll be fine,' Quinn said.

At precisely 2:20, Quinn climbed the steps in front of the Longworth Building, then passed under a narrow archway into an alcove lined with several metal-framed glass doors. Quinn pulled one of the doors open and entered.

Security in the twenty-first century was not like that of Quinn's childhood. Now everywhere you went, security guards and detection machines and pat-downs and bag searches and background checks were the norm. The innocence was gone and humanity had no one to blame but itself.

The Longworth Building was no exception. As Quinn expected, the first thing to greet him upon entry was a metal detector and X-ray machine. Hence the reason he'd left the SIG back at the hotel.

'Purpose of your visit, Mr. Drake?' one of the officers asked after Quinn had handed him the ID he was using as cover.

'I have a meeting with someone on Congressman Guerrero's staff at two-thirty.'

'Who would that be?'

'Dylan Ray.'

The officer checked a computer screen, then nodded and returned the ID. 'Have a good day, Mr. Drake.'

Quinn took an elevator to Guerrero's floor, then made his way through the building, passing the offices of several other House of Representative members. Some of the names were familiar to him, from stories he'd read in the paper or reports he'd seen on TV.

After several minutes, he arrived at Guerrero's office. Even from a distance, it was apparent the congressman's suite was different from the others Quinn had been passing. Its entrance was more ornate. The dark wood façade was larger than those of the surrounding offices and shone like something out of a Pledge furniture polish commercial.

Two flags flanked the door. On the left was the Stars and Stripes, and on the right the state flag of Texas. The door between them was open.

Quinn put a smile on his face and walked through the doorway into a small lobby.

The room was designed to make people feel like important things happened there. In the center was a desk, modern and sleek, with a large multiline phone and a flat-screen computer terminal sitting on top. Behind the desk was a woman, blond and smiling and attractive. To either side of her were closed doors, no doubt leading deeper into the suite.

'May I help you?' she asked, her Texas accent evident.

'Yes, please. I'm here to see Dylan Ray,' Quinn said.

'Your name?'

'Richard Drake. I have an appointment for two-thirty.'

The woman glanced at her computer, then smiled again, apparently finding his name on the list.

'Please have a seat,' she said. 'I'll let Mr. Ray know you are here.'

All the furniture in the room was well crafted, expensive — certainly not government issue. Quinn sat down on one of the soft leather chairs that lined the walls on either side of the main entrance. In front of him was a low table stocked with the latest issues of news and political magazines the congressman must have thought his visitors should read.

Quinn took in the rest of the room, making a more thorough examination than he had when he first entered. A dark wood wainscoting ringed the room. Above it, the walls were painted off-white and curved at the top, easing into the ceiling.

On one wall hung a photograph of Congressman Guerrero. Quinn recognized him from a similar photo on the congressman's website. On the wall opposite was a collage of several photos, each framed in black metal, and all featuring Guerrero with different political figures and celebrities. Prominent among them were a few shots with the former President, the last man from the congressman's party to hold the nation's highest office.

In each of the photos, Guerrero exuded an intensity that gave the impression he was completely focused on whatever he was doing at that moment. It made him seem intelligent and concerned. His salt-and-pepper hair didn't hurt either — old enough to know a thing or two, and young enough to do something about it. Quinn put his age around fifty. It reinforced Quinn's suspicion that if the congressman lost this current attempt at the presidency, he could try again in four years, or even in eight.

The door to the right of the receptionist opened, and out stepped a man, perhaps five foot five. He was well dressed and appeared to be no more than thirty years old. And as if it was some unwritten policy, the man's sandy brown hair was cut in a similar style to the one the congressman sported in the photos that lined the room.

The man walked over to the receptionist and exchanged a few hushed words. When he looked up, he began walking toward Quinn. He looked a little tired, and the smile on his face seemed to say he'd rather be doing something else.

'Mr. Drake?' the man said, holding out his right hand. 'I'm Dylan Ray.'

Quinn stood and shook Ray's hand. 'Thank you for seeing me,' Quinn said.

'Well, as you can imagine, things are always busy here,' Ray said, then added quickly, 'But I'm happy to squeeze you in. Please, follow me. We'll go to my office.'

Quinn smiled and indicated for Ray to lead the way.

Using the same door Ray had used moments before, they passed into the heart of the congressman's suite. There was a central bullpen surrounded by several individual offices. Dozens of people were busy doing the congressman's work: typing, making calls, talking to each other.

'Which one's Congressman Guerrero's?' Quinn asked, playing up the part of curious journalist.

Ray stopped and turned. 'Over there,' he said, pointing in the opposite direction. 'See that hallway? He's down that.'

Quinn nodded as if it was one of the most interesting things he'd learned that week.

A few moments later, Ray led him into a small, windowless office. A desk, two visitors' chairs, and a couple of bookcases with pristine sets of leather-bound books on the shelves.

On the walls were more pictures of the congressman. Action shots again. Guerrero smiling, or shaking hands, or visiting a factory, or listening to citizens. Only this time there were no notable celebrities or political figures. This was the wall of the *real* congressman, or at least that's what Quinn assumed they expected people to think.

'You keep a pretty clean office,' Quinn said as he sat in one of the visitor chairs. Except for a phone, a dark blotter, and a blank legal pad, the desk was clean. No computer, no in/out trays, no files.

Ray let out a quick, embarrassed laugh. 'Truthfully, I'm at one of those desks we passed

111

by out there. Assistant Press Secretary doesn't rate an office. Besides, we're a little cramped for space. This was the congressman's idea, actually. An office anyone can use when necessary.'

'The paper has me in a cubicle next to the bathroom,' Quinn said. 'That's why I prefer fieldwork.'

'I know exactly what you mean,' Ray said. 'I love it when we have an event outside the office. Nothing like stretching your legs and mingling with the people.'

'Very true.' Quinn sensed a shift in the staffer's demeanor, a relaxing as if Ray had detected some sort of common connection. *Perfect.*

'How can I help you, Mr. Drake?'

'It's Richard. I'm hoping you can give me a little more background information. Fill in a few holes I still have in the story.'

'Of course,' Ray said. 'This is a profile piece on the congressman, right?'

'Exactly. We've seen an increase in his poll numbers back home in Colorado,' Quinn said, using some of the information he'd dug up that morning. 'Looks like he might be starting to get noticed. My editors thought it would be good to be ahead of the curve instead of following the story. So they sent me out here.'

Ray beamed. 'We've seen those numbers, too. And Colorado isn't the only place we're trending up. I can't tell you how good it is to see the congressman's message is getting out.'

'I can understand that.' Quinn gave Ray a knowing smile. 'My guess is this time next year, you may be close to moving out of that cube and into a real office down the Mall from here.'

'That's still a long way away,' Ray said, unable to hide the hope from his voice. 'A lot could happen between now and then.' He raised a hand off the desk. 'But if you want to talk about the election, I could put you in touch with someone on his campaign staff. Technically, I can only deal with things directly related to the congressman's current job.'

'Of course, I understand,' Quinn said. 'And that's why I've come to you.'

For fifteen minutes, Quinn asked questions that sounded important, but were really softballs Ray would be able to answer at length. As Ray spoke Quinn wrote in the pocket notebook he'd brought along, acting interested and intrigued by the man's answers.

After a lengthy recounting of the congressman's most recent trip back to Texas, Quinn said, 'Certainly sounds like he cares about the people he represents.'

'Absolutely.'

'When I met Jennifer Fuentes on my last trip out, she mentioned the congressman was not someone who blindly followed party lines. Do you think that's going to be a problem for him in the election?'

'Again, I'd have to direct you to his campaign press person. Her name is Nicole Blanc. Let me give you her number.' Ray began writing on the legal pad. 'Someone had mentioned you'd initially talked to Jennifer. Odd she didn't have you go through the press secretary or myself.'

He ripped the piece of paper off the pad and

113

handed it to Quinn.

Quinn smiled. 'Not so odd. Jennifer and I have a friend in common. A guy I knew back in college. He connected us.'

'Okay.' Ray gave an exaggerated nod, understanding. 'That makes sense. Still, we'd rather handle press requests through our office. Someone in her position, we'd rather not bother her unless we really need to.'

'I did get the impression she keeps pretty busy.'

'Her position is very demanding,' Ray said.

'Well,' Quinn said, 'I think I've got everything I need. I appreciate you giving me the time.'

They both stood up. 'My pleasure,' Ray said. 'Before you leave, I have something for you.'

He leaned back down and opened one of the drawers on the desk. From inside, he pulled out a canvas tote bag. It was dark blue, and printed in white on the front was *Compliments of Congressman James Guerrero*. He handed the bag to Quinn.

'Thanks,' Quinn said.

'What you'll find most interesting inside is the copy of *Houston Living*. It has a wonderful article about the congressman. They even put him on the cover.'

'I'll take a look at it.' As Ray came around the desk, Quinn said, 'I was wondering if I could say hi to Jennifer since I'm here.'

'I'm sorry,' Ray said. 'She's currently not in D.C.'

'Business trip?' Quinn kept his question light, like he didn't even expect an answer.

'Family emergency, I'm afraid.'

'I hope everything's all right.'

Ray gave Quinn a concerned smile as he motioned him toward the door. 'We all do.'

They walked back through the bullpen, Quinn casually scanning the room. The activity level seemed to have picked up some since they'd last passed through.

As they were near the exit, Ray said in a low voice, 'There's the congressman.'

Quinn followed the aide's gaze across the room toward the offices on the opposite side. Guerrero had just emerged with an older woman walking beside him taking notes.

The congressman was wearing an expensive-looking dark gray suit and was carrying a black leather notebook. From the pictures, Quinn had guessed he was tall, and he'd been right. Guerrero looked to be around six foot three.

Ray hesitated as if considering something, then said, 'Wait here for a moment.'

The assistant press secretary headed across the room and stopped a few feet away from Guerrero. When he got his chance, he said a few words to the congressman, then looked in Quinn's direction. With a nod, Guerrero followed Ray back across the bullpen.

'Congressman Guerrero,' Ray said after they reached Quinn, 'I'd like to introduce you to Richard Drake. He's doing an article for the *Denver Post*. A profile piece on you.'

Guerrero smiled and held out his hand. Quinn returned the gesture. 'Very glad to meet you, Mr. Drake. Colorado is one of the most beautiful states in the nation. You're a lucky man.'

'Thank you, sir,' Quinn said. 'Our readers will be glad to know you feel that way.'

'What part of Denver do you live in?'

'Actually just west of the city. In Golden.'

'Very nice,' Guerrero said. 'You're basically in the mountains at that point.'

'You've been there?'

'A few times, yes.' He smiled good-naturedly. Not a politician's smile, but a natural one, like he meant it. 'Went on a few road trips to Vail when I was in college. We'd stop in Golden to tour the Coors plant and get a free beer.'

They all shared a laugh.

'Mr. Drake is a friend of Jennifer Fuentes,' Ray said, simplifying the lie Quinn had told him, and hitting closer to the truth than he realized.

For a millisecond, a look of concern passed over the congressman's face. 'You're a friend of hers?'

'Not very close,' Quinn said. 'I actually just met her a few months ago. Mr. Ray tells me she's away on personal leave.'

The congressman stared at Quinn for a moment, a put-on smile frozen on his face. 'Yes. Well, too bad you missed her,' the congressman finally said. 'If you'll excuse me, I have to get over to the Capitol.'

'Of course,' Quinn said. There was something the congressman wasn't telling him, but now was not the time to press. 'Thank you for taking a moment to speak with me.'

'The pleasure was all mine.'

116

They shook again, then the congressman was off.

'You're lucky,' Ray said.

'Why?'

'If you'd have come next week, you would have missed him.'

Quinn looked at the aide, his brow creased in a question.

Ray smiled. 'He's going overseas with several other members of the Intelligence Committee.'

'Really? Where's he headed?'

'Singapore.'

'Anything interesting?'

'A fact-gathering trip,' Ray said. 'Pacific Rim security. These days you can't afford to be uninformed.'

'One of the main rules I live by,' Quinn said.

10

Quinn exited the Longworth building and took the steps down to the sidewalk. As he walked west down the Mall, he pulled out his phone and made a call.

'I need another favor,' he said once Peter answered.

'Of course,' Peter said. There was an underlying sense of greed in his voice. Just one more thing he would use in future job negotiations, Quinn knew.

'There's someone I need to talk to, but I don't want him to realize that.'

'An accidental meeting?'

Quinn paused. For a brief second, he'd had the sensation someone was watching him. He stopped and casually looked back the way he had come. 'Yes,' he said into the phone. 'The more public, the better.'

Several people were walking up and down the sidewalks on either side of Independence Avenue. But no one seemed to be paying him any attention. He began walking again.

'Tell me one more time. You're not involved in something stupid, right? Like a hit?' Peter said.

'A hit?' Quinn asked, surprised.

'Look, we haven't worked together for over six months, so God knows what you're into now. And I can't be connected with anything like that. Not here.'

'That's not my thing, Peter. Nothing's changed,' Quinn said. 'I just want to talk with him.'

'I have your word on that?'

'I've never lied to you.'

'But you have withheld information.'

'You're right,' Quinn said. 'I have.'

There was a moment of silence.

'Okay. I'll see what I can find out,' Peter said. 'Who is it?'

'Congressman James Guerrero of Texas.'

'The presidential candidate?'

'You know him, then.'

'I know who he is.' A pause, then Peter said, 'Let me see what I can find out.'

Quinn thought if he could get the congressman out of his office, someplace Guerrero couldn't make a quick escape, maybe he'd be able to see if the wannabe President truly knew more than he was letting on.

'Thanks,' Quinn said.

Next, he tried Orlando again. He was surprised she hadn't returned his call. After all, she'd attempted to get ahold of him first. But it had been over twenty-four hours since he'd called her back. At the very least, she should have sent him a text message. It wasn't like her.

Four rings, then 'Please leave a message after the tone.' It was the same generic, prerecorded voice as before.

'Orlando, it's me,' Quinn said. 'What's going on? Where are you? Call me. Doesn't matter what time.'

Once he hung up, he held the phone in his

hand for a few moments, staring at the display. He was thinking — hoping — she'd just been slow to answer and was already in the process of calling him back.

But the phone remained silent.

As he was slipping it back in his pocket, the feeling he was being watched returned. He looked around again. There seemed to be more people on the sidewalks now as some of the government employees got an early start to their evening.

Quinn slowly scanned both sides of the street, taking in every face. Even then he almost missed her. She was standing on the other side of the road, tucked up against one of the trees in front of the Hirshhorn Museum. Not exactly hiding, but close enough.

As Quinn stepped onto the street and began walking toward her, he expected her to run. But she held steady, her eyes never leaving him.

'Hello, Tasha,' he said as he reached her.

'You *are* looking for her, aren't you?' she said.

Quinn stepped in close, a smile on his face. 'Who are you?' His voice was calm and low, but the stare he gave her was anything but friendly.

'I . . . I already — '

'You're not Tasha Laver. I checked.'

'How? I mean — '

'Who are you?' he repeated.

She hesitated. 'My name really is Tasha,' she said 'But . . . but Douglas, not Laver. I . . . panicked in Houston. I didn't know who you were.'

'You don't know who I am now.'

120

Her eyes looked into his for a moment. 'Are you looking for Jenny? Please tell me that's what you're doing. Tell me that you're trying to help her.'

Quinn started to say something, but stopped. They were in the middle of a busy sidewalk, having a conversation anyone could hear. He looked out at the street. Several cabs were heading in their direction. He waved one down.

'Where are you going?' she asked.

He answered by putting a hand on her upper arm, squeezing tight, then pulling her toward the cab with him.

'FDR Memorial,' he said once both he and Tasha were in the back seat.

Tasha gave him a bewildered look, but said nothing, obviously getting the message that this wasn't the time for conversation.

In the late afternoon traffic, the ride to the Franklin Delano Roosevelt Memorial took nearly twenty minutes. When they arrived, Quinn paid the driver, then pushed Tasha out the door.

'What are we doing here?' she asked.

He squeezed her arm again, letting her know it wasn't time yet, then led her into the memorial.

Unlike most of the other monuments in D.C., the FDR was low-lying and sprawling. Statues and red granite walls and waterfalls weaved in and out of the memorial, creating distinct areas that represented different eras of the Roosevelt administration. To most people, it was probably beautiful and inspiring. To Quinn it was useful.

He led her past the life-size images of FDR and quotes etched in granite until they reached the very end of the monument. There they found the last and the largest of the waterfalls. Rivers of water cascaded down from the top of the wall onto granite blocks, creating a hypnotic and, more importantly, loud display. Quinn moved in as close as he could.

'Why did you bring me here?' Tasha asked, raising her voice to fight the crashing of the waterfall.

He leaned into her so he wouldn't have to yell, too. 'Are you wearing a wire?'

'What?'

'A bug. A transmitter. Are you wearing one?'

'No. Why would I do that?'

He pulled his phone out of his pocket and accessed the camera function. He selected the heat-sensing mode, then began scanning Tasha up and down.

'What are you doing?' she asked.

'Turn around,' he said. When she didn't move right away, he added, 'Now.'

While the phone was multifunctional, a built-in bug detector was not one of its options. Still, using the heat-sensing mode, he'd be able to identify any energy sources that might be powering a transmitter. Nothing on her body, but he did get a hit from her purse.

'Open it up,' he said, pointing to the bag.

As soon as she did, he stuck his hand in and started feeling around.

'Hey,' she said. 'Those are my things.'

He pulled out a cell phone, then scanned the bag again. The heat source was gone. As he suspected, it was her cell.

He slipped his own phone back in his pocket, then spent several seconds examining Tasha's. It looked all right. Cheap. One of those models cell phone companies gave away to increase sales. He popped open the cover and did a quick check for anything that shouldn't have been there. It was clean as far as he could tell. But to be safe, he popped out the battery, then put the cover back on. He put the phone and the battery into the back pocket of his pants.

'That's mine,' she said.

'Why are you following me?' he asked.

She glared at him. 'Give me back my phone.'

'We'll see. Answer my question first.'

She was silent for several moments. 'What's your name?' she asked.

'None of your business. Why were you following me?'

'You know mine,' she said.

'Do I?' he said.

'I just told you. I'm Tasha Douglas.'

'And last time you told me you were Tasha Laver.'

'I'm not lying now.'

'There's no way I'm going to believe that until I check it out.'

'Okay,' she said. 'I understand. Can you at least give me something I can call you?'

His eyes narrowed. 'Jonathan.'

'Jonathan,' she repeated.

'Tell me why you're following me,' Quinn said.

'I haven't been following you.'

'Really? So you just happened to be standing on Independence Boulevard when I walked by?'

Her eyes darted away.

'And last night, in Georgetown? It was just chance we both ended up there at the same time?'

She tensed. 'You saw me?'

Quinn just looked at her, waiting.

'I was already there when you got there,' she said. 'I just didn't know how to get inside. Breaking and entering isn't something I usually do.'

'Then why were you there?'

'I was there because of Jenny.' It almost looked like she was going to cry. She covered her face with her hands as she took a deep breath.

'Because this Jenny was your college buddy?' Quinn said.

'No,' she said. 'More than that. Jenny's one of my best friends.'

'Really? That's sweet,' he said, his voice flat. 'Still doesn't explain why you're following me.'

'I told you, I wasn't following you,' she insisted. 'Don't you see? We're doing the same thing. We're both trying to find Jenny.'

'Is that what you think?'

'I'm right, aren't I?'

'Why are you following me?'

'Don't you get it? Everywhere you go is another potential clue to Jenny's whereabouts. And since I'm looking for her, too, those would be the same places I'd go.'

Quinn laughed. 'That's one of the most convenient answers I've ever heard.'

Her cheeks started to turn red, and her sudden anger spilled over into her voice. 'So fucking what? Talking to someone Jenny works with seemed like a logical thing to do, to me. Unfortunately, when I went into the congress-man's building, they wouldn't let me go up without an appointment. I was trying to figure out what to do when suddenly you came out.'

Quinn took a step back, preparing to leave. This was getting him nowhere except more annoyed. 'If I see you again,' he said, 'I won't be as nice. Understand?'

'Please.' She took a step toward him. 'I . . . I don't have anyone left to turn to. No one else can help me.' She stopped for a moment and took in a nervous breath. 'I tried to find her boyfriend, but he's missing, too.'

Quinn paused and turned back toward her. 'Maybe they ran off together and just didn't tell anyone.'

'I know that's not true. Jenny and Steven would never do that.'

Steven. Steven Markoff.

Quinn took a deep breath. 'If you're really Jenny's friend, I suggest you drop it.'

'What?' she asked.

'You saw what they did to her house in Houston, and what happened to her apartment. These people aren't just playing. They will kill you. Go home. You can't do anything for her.'

For the first time, she started to smile. 'You *are* trying to find her. If you were one of them, you wouldn't have warned me.'

'Think what you want, just get the hell out of here,' he said again. 'You're only going to get yourself in trouble.'

'I can't just let this go,' she said. 'Jenny *asked* me to help her.'

Quinn stared at her for a second. 'What are you talking about?'

She looked at him, her face serious. 'Three weeks ago she called me. Said that she was in trouble and needed to leave town.'

'You didn't mention this before,' he said. 'You just told me she suddenly dropped out of communication.'

'I didn't know if I could trust you.'

'And you can trust me now?' Quinn asked, his eyebrows lifting in disbelief. 'You don't even know who I am.'

'I'm not sure I do trust you, but I don't know what else to do.' She looked down for a moment, then tilted her head back up. 'When she called, I asked her if there was anything I could do. She said no at first, but then she changed her mind, and said she'd call me every two days to let me know she was all right.'

'And?'

'She kept to her word. For a while anyway,' Tasha said. 'The last call I got from her was six days ago.'

'Was there something you were supposed to do if she didn't call?' Quinn said, still skeptical.

'She said I should find Steven. Tell him what happened.' She paused. 'But he's gone, too.'

'So you're trying to figure out where she is on your own?' Quinn asked.

'What else was I supposed to do?'

Quinn looked at the waterfall for a moment. Was she telling him the truth or just feeding him

126

some bullshit? He was trained to think the worst, so there was no way he was going to believe her on the spot. But if she was lying, she was putting on a pretty damn good act.

'How did you contact each other? Did she give you a phone number?' he asked, looking for holes in her story.

'No. She always called me.'

'What about caller ID?'

Tasha shook her head. 'The numbers always came up blocked.'

Quinn frowned, annoyed. 'Fine,' he said.

'Fine? Fine *what?*'

He leaned toward her, his face stopping only six inches in front of hers. 'Fine, we're done. And this time I'm not suggesting it, I'm telling you. Go home.' Whether what she was saying was the truth or not, it seemed pretty clear she was going to keep getting in his way. It was a complication he didn't need.

'Only if you tell me you're trying to help Jenny. That you're going to find her,' she said.

He knew he should just remain silent and walk away. But if he did that, she'd continue to be a problem.

He pulled Tasha's cell phone and battery out of his back pocket and handed them to her. 'I'll find her,' he said. 'Now don't let me see you again.'

★ ★ ★

'There's a reception tonight. 8 p.m. An art gallery opening in Georgetown.'

'An art gallery?' Quinn said into his phone. Peter had called him as he was riding in a cab back to his hotel.

'In Washington, even a gallery opening is a political event.'

'You're sure he's going to be there?'

'He RSVP'd.'

'Everybody RSVPs,' Quinn said.

'True,' Peter said.

'Give me the address.' It might turn out to be a bust, but it was Quinn's best chance.

'You'll need to get on the list,' Peter said.

'I'm sure you can arrange that.'

Quinn could almost hear the smile in Peter's voice when he said, 'Of course I can.'

11

With the right amount of cash, a good hotel can get you anything in a hurry. The Crystal City Marriott was no exception. After tipping the concierge a hundred dollars, the man seemed to take a personal interest in making sure Quinn had exactly what he needed.

By a quarter to eight, Quinn was dressed in a dark blue Brooks Brothers suit, white shirt, and a tie that was just nice enough to say he might have money, but not so garish as to stand out in a crowd. His overall look was conservative, successful, and confident. In a room full of politicians and D.C. insiders, he would blend in and barely be noticed.

Instead of a cab, Quinn had the concierge rent him a car for the night. He needed to be flexible. He wasn't sure if he was going to be able to get a moment with the congressman at the gallery or would have to follow him afterward — all, of course, depending on whether the congressman showed up in the first place.

Quinn drove the Lexus sedan north from the hotel, following the same path he'd taken in the cab to Georgetown the night before. He was armed again — the gun which he'd left at the hotel that afternoon was safely stowed under the passenger seat beside him.

He spotted the gallery a half block north of M Street, toward the eastern end of Georgetown, and less than a mile from Jenny's burnt-out apartment.

There were over a dozen people standing outside the gallery's front door talking and smoking. Some even held wineglasses. Several cars were stopped next to the curb, waiting to be helped by the blue-coated valets stationed nearby.

As Quinn pulled into the line behind a late-model Cadillac, he could see into the main entrance. Just inside was the familiar arc of a metal detector. The gun would have to stay in the car.

'Good evening, sir,' a valet said as he opened Quinn's door. He handed Quinn a ticket as they switched places.

The front of the gallery was a series of floor-to-ceiling windows. Light from inside spilled through them onto the brick sidewalk beyond. Like most of the other structures in Georgetown, the rest of the building was made of the same red brick as the sidewalks.

Above the windows was a sign: *The Delaney Gallery*. And in smaller letters below it: *Fine Art*.

There was a woman at the door, college aged and dressed in all white. It was an unfortunate choice. Her skin was almost as pale as her dress. In contrast, her hair was dark, almost blue-black. A dye job. No doubt about it. She was holding a clipboard, and beside her on a small table sat a stack of cards.

'May I have your invitation?'

'I was told you'd have my name on a list,' he said.

She nodded, not smiling. Quinn guessed it was part of her act.

'Name?' she said.

'Richard Drake.'

She consulted the top sheet on her clipboard, moving her finger down it until she almost reached the bottom.

'Yes. Of course. Mr. Drake.' She looked up, her face still neutral. 'Please, enjoy the exhibit.'

Quinn entered the gallery and passed through the metal detector. There was a large man standing just past the device. He was wearing a dark blue suit and a smile. Security, no doubt, but more dressed-up rent-a-cop than serious muscle, Quinn guessed.

There was already quite a crowd inside. It wasn't elbow to elbow, but it was enough to raise the volume to a loud buzz. Most of the men were dressed like Quinn in conservative, expensive suits, while the majority of the women wore the standard black cocktail dress. Quinn did note a few spots of color, but none of the dresses were too bold or too revealing. This wasn't Hollywood, after all.

He checked for the congressman, but unless he was in some other room, he had yet to arrive.

Not far from the front door, a refreshments table with hors d'oeuvres and empty glasses for wine had been set up. Behind the table were two men, both dressed in all white like the girl at the door. They hovered next to bottles of Rutherford Hill wine, filling the glasses as guests came up and asked for a drink.

'May I pour you a glass?' one of the men asked.

'Please,' Quinn said.

'Cabernet sauvignon or chardonnay?'

'Chardonnay. Thanks.'

Once he had wine in hand, Quinn turned and surveyed the room again, this time ignoring the people and taking in the layout and exhibit.

The space seemed to consist of one main room with one or two smaller offshoots near the back. Those could have been offices or restrooms, Quinn couldn't tell yet.

The front room was large, around sixty feet wide and half again as long. It was broken up in an almost mazelike way by canvases that hung in curving rows on wires attached to the ceiling. Even the paintings that lined the periphery of the room had been hung several inches from the walls in the same manner.

The effect was an interesting one. It gave the illusion of both space and confinement.

A closer look at the paintings showed the theme didn't stop with the gallery décor. The images were stark — grays and blacks and whites blending together to form buildings and streets and homes. There were people, too, in the same tones, almost receding into the background as if they were ghosts. But on each canvas there was something in color. Bright, vibrant color. A child's ball in reds and yellows and pinks, left alone on an abandoned sidewalk. A jacket in a deep, glowing blue, hanging from the back of a door. A kite, lying alone on a park bench, in all those colors and more.

There was a sadness in each piece. A deep, lonely sadness. Quinn was surprised to find himself drawn in by the work. He had to consciously tear himself away to finish his examination.

He began walking toward the back of the room. He stopped every few moments and pretended to examine a new painting. As he did he noticed a second refreshment table set up at the back of the room, between the doorways Quinn had spotted earlier.

As he neared the closest doorway, he realized it didn't lead to another room, but to a hallway. At the far end was a metal door. It was propped open, and there was another metal detector and security man stationed just inside the doorway. There was no smile on this guy's face. He just looked bored. Beyond the exit, Quinn could see several people standing outside talking and smoking. Halfway down the hall, three people stood in a loose line near a door marked *Restroom*.

Quinn moved to the next doorway. This one did lead to another room, though much smaller than the main gallery. He peeked in. More paintings, only smaller than the ones out front. A few people were examining the artwork, while several others stood in the middle of the room talking.

As Quinn turned away, it seemed to him that the crowd in the main room had grown larger than it had been a few minutes before. He even thought he recognized a few faces here and there. Not people he'd met before, but ones he'd seen on TV or in the newspaper — other lawmakers, a national news reporter or two.

But still no Guerrero.

Quinn glanced at his watch; it was 9:05 p.m. Part of being a politician, particularly one with higher aspirations, meant mixing with the people. And a smart politician would come when the crowd was at its height. So if Guerrero was coming, it had to be soon.

Quinn thought about getting an hors d'oeuvre, when his eyes were drawn to a new arrival at the front of the gallery.

'Son of a bitch,' he said to himself.

Tasha.

She hadn't listened to him at all. She must have found out the congressman was going to be there, and was going to try to talk to him. She was becoming more than just a problem; she was becoming dangerous. He decided to wait until she moved further into the room before taking any action.

One thing he noticed as he watched her was that she seemed more confident than she had at either of their previous meetings. It was like she was willing herself to be a person who was in control, steeling herself so that she wouldn't back down when the moment came to talk to the congressman. Quinn had seen other civilians do the same in similar situations. An appearance of toughness to do things Quinn could do without thinking.

As she squeezed past the other guests, her eyes moved across the room. She was doing a good job at looking like she was just interested in the exhibit while she checked out those around her. As her eyes moved toward Quinn's position, he took a step to his left, effectively hiding behind one of the paintings.

Several moments later, she stopped at the refreshment table near the hallway. While she waited for her glass of wine, Quinn walked up behind her.

'Maybe you should wait on that,' he said.

Tasha turned. Quinn had seen her scared, nervous, even confident, but this was the first time he'd seen her surprised.

'What are you doing here?' she finally managed.

'Come on,' he said. He put a hand on her arm and pulled her toward the hallway.

'Wait. Where are we going?'

Quinn didn't answer; instead he relied on the fact she wouldn't want to make a scene. He led her down the hallway, through the metal detector, and out into a small alley.

'You're hurting me,' she whispered. 'Let me go.'

Without releasing his grip, he walked with her along the alley until they were out of listening range of the people who'd stepped outside for a smoke.

'How did you get in?'

She looked unsure for a moment, then said, 'A friend back in Houston . . . works at a gallery. She was able to make a few calls and get me an invitation.'

'Are you *trying* to get yourself killed?'

'I'm not going to stop looking for Jenny just

because you told me to. I asked for your help, but you refused. So that means I'm on my own. The congressman is supposed to be here. I'm going to talk to him.'

'You really think he's going to tell you anything?' Quinn said. 'You probably won't be able to get within five feet of him. I told you before, go home.'

'No.'

His fingers dug into her biceps as Quinn felt his anger rising.

'Stop it,' Tasha said, looking at his hand.

He loosened his grip. He wanted to scare her away, not hurt her. 'Look, I'm not sure the congressman even knows anything. So please, just leave.'

'I have to tr— '

'You won't get anywhere with him,' Quinn said, cutting her off. He took a breath, then added in a calmer voice, 'But I might.'

She looked at him, skeptical at first. 'You just want me to get out of your way, don't you?'

'Yes.'

'Fine,' she said, after a moment's consideration. 'I'll do that, but only if you tell me what you learn.'

Quinn started to say no, but stopped. The look on her face told him it wasn't an answer she would accept. 'If I do, then you need to promise me you'll forget about all of this and go home.'

'Are you really trying to help Jenny?' she asked.

'Yes.'

She searched his face, as if she was trying to determine whether he was telling her the truth or not.

'Deal,' she finally said.

12

'Pull out your phone,' Quinn told Tasha. 'Pretend you're texting someone.'

She looked at him as if she didn't understand what he meant.

Quinn looked over at one of the groups of smokers, then back at her. 'If you're doing something, no one will pay you any attention.'

'You promise to come back?' she asked.

'I'll come back.'

She nodded reluctantly, then pulled out her phone as he headed back into the building.

The crowd in the gallery had grown even larger since Quinn and Tasha had left. Quinn had to push his way through several groups until he found a spot where he was able to survey the entire room.

Once he did, it didn't take long to spot the congressman.

Guerrero must have just arrived, for he hadn't made it very far into the room yet. He seemed to know almost everyone, sharing a few quick words or a laugh, and shaking every hand that was thrust at him. A politician who could actually talk to the voters and appear to immediately relate to them. If his campaign ever caught fire, that would be the reason why.

Quinn recognized the woman with him immediately. It was the congressman's wife. The TV-friendly Jody Goodman of the Texas

Goodmans. Quinn had seen her picture in several of the news reports he'd read earlier. He'd even watched clips of her appearances on CNN and MSNBC on You Tube.

She was probably around the same age as the congressman. Caucasian, shoulder-length blond hair, and wearing a vibrant blue dress that accented her thin frame. But whereas her husband gave off the aura of being a man of the people, Ms. Goodman seemed more distant, more above the fray. Even across the room, Quinn got the impression she thought she was smarter than anyone else around. And that included the congressman.

Glancing back toward the front door, Quinn realized Guerrero and his wife hadn't come alone. There was a man stationed near the entrance who hadn't been there before. He was standing about five feet away from the man working the metal detector. He had the distinct look of personal security, his eyes constantly checking the room, but always coming back to the congressman. This one was a professional, not a rent-a-cop. But probably not Secret Service. Even though the congressman was running for President, he wouldn't have rated that kind of protection yet. No, this guy was private and expensive.

Guerrero and his wife slowly moved further into the gallery, eventually stopping near the center of the room. Instantly a small crowd began congregating around them.

Quinn checked the man at the door again. He was still in position, his attention more on a new group of arrivals than those already in the room.

Good, Quinn thought. It was time to make his move.

He walked toward the congressman, angling his approach so that most of the crowd was between him and the muscle at the front door. He weaved his way through the crowd until he was standing just a few feet away from Guerrero.

The congressman laughed at something a man standing in front of him said. As he finished, he swung his head around, taking in the crowd. When he noticed Quinn, he stopped for a second, a question crossing his face.

'We've met recently, haven't we?' Guerrero said.

'This afternoon at your office.'

The question cleared from the congressman's brow. 'Of course. You're the reporter. Mr. Drake, right?'

'That's right. Richard Drake.'

'From . . . Denver.'

'Right again.'

'I'm surprised to see you here,' Guerrero said.

Quinn shrugged. 'A friend recommended I come. He had an invitation he couldn't use, and I had a free night.'

'Your friend was right. Marta is a tremendous artist.'

Quinn had seen the name on a sign near the door. Marta Harmon. This was her exhibit.

Guerrero's wife looked around her husband at Quinn. 'Hello. Mr. Drake, is it? I'm Jody.' She held out a hand. Her handshake was quick and firm, and her smile was forced and plastic.

'My wife,' Guerrero said.

'It's a pleasure to meet you Mrs . . . ' Quinn paused. 'Do you go by Guerrero or Goodman?'

'I see someone's been doing their homework,' she said. 'Did I hear James correctly? You're a reporter.'

'Yes, but strictly profile pieces.'

'Not a troublemaker, then?' Again with the fake smile.

'No. I leave that to others.'

She gave him a small courtesy laugh as she looked him up and down. 'In social situations, it's Mrs. Guerrero. But you can call me Jody. I save 'Goodman' for business.'

'Nice to meet you, Jody,' Quinn said.

'Are you enjoying the exhibit?' the congressman's wife asked.

'The work is certainly unique.' Quinn glanced at one of the paintings. 'It's very sad, isn't it?'

'Sad?' the congressman said. 'I have to disagree with you there. I think there's hope in every picture.'

'No,' Jody said. 'I think Mr. Drake might be right.'

'Hope is lost, or almost,' Quinn said.

Jody tilted her head and smiled, only this time it wasn't plastic, it was more intrigued.

'What do you think?' Quinn asked her.

'I'm still trying to figure that out,' she said. 'But I'm impressed. It's obvious you know your art.'

'I know a little bit about everything,' Quinn said. 'You never know when it might come in useful.'

'That's a very smart approach to life,' Guerrero said. 'In my job, I have to do pretty much the same thing.'

The congressman's wife looked across the room. 'I could use another glass of wine.'

'I'll get it for you,' her husband said, then looked at Quinn. 'Mr. Drake, if you'll excuse us.'

As Guerrero started to turn away, Quinn said, 'Actually, since we're both here, I did have one thing I wanted to talk to you about.'

Guerrero and his wife looked back at Quinn.

'Just a quick follow-up for the article. Shouldn't take more than a minute or two.'

Guerrero was somehow able to combine a sigh with a welcoming smile. 'It would be best if you set up an appointment. Come see me at my office tomorrow.'

'Unfortunately, I have to be in New York tomorrow,' Quinn said.

'Perhaps next week, then.'

'We'll be out of town next week,' Jody said.

'You're right. I'd forgotten,' the congressman said, though it was obvious he hadn't forgotten and was annoyed she had mentioned it.

His wife smiled. 'Why don't I get my own drink, and you two have your little chat.'

'It won't take that long,' Quinn said.

'Fine,' Guerrero said. 'But if it goes more than a few minutes, we'll have to schedule a follow-up for later. I'm not here to do interviews. I'm here to support Marta and her art.'

'I understand,' Quinn said. 'I won't keep you long.'

By unspoken agreement, Quinn and Guerrero

left the center of the room and found a quieter spot near the back. Quinn positioned himself so he could keep an eye on the man at the front door. The security man was watching them, but he didn't appear to be alarmed.

'So what can I answer for you?' Guerrero asked.

'It's about Jennifer Fuentes.'

Guerrero looked surprised. 'Jennifer? What about her?'

'I'm trying to find her, and I think you might be able to help me.'

At the front door, the bodyguard had turned to talk with two new arrivals, men who didn't look like they were here for the art. The conversation looked more business than casual. Colleagues, perhaps?

'She's on a leave of absence.'

'Where did she go?'

'That's none of your business, Mr. Drake.'

'Actually, it is,' Quinn said. 'I need you to — ' He stopped.

The two new security men had finished their conversation and had turned to look across the room. Quinn nearly froze. He had seen these men before.

In Houston. Riding in the Volvo that had followed him.

If they're part of the congressman's security detail, then that means . . .

He suddenly missed the feel of his SIG against his side.

'You need me to what?' Guerrero asked.

'I need you to tell me where she is.'

143

Guerrero raised his chin a couple of inches so that he was almost looking down at Quinn. 'I think we're done here.'

'No. We're not.'

Quinn put a hand on the congressman's arm, stopping Guerrero from leaving. He moved to his left so that the congressman hid him from view of the new arrivals.

'You aren't the least bit worried about her, are you?' Quinn asked. 'You know her apartment was destroyed. You also know the same thing happened to her home in Houston, don't you?'

'Who are you?' Guerrero said. 'You're not a reporter.'

'Where is she? What have you done with her?'

'I haven't done anything — ' Guerrero stopped himself. 'I don't like what you're insinuating. Let go of me, Mr. Drake. Right now!'

Quinn leaned forward and said in a low voice, 'I'll make this very clear. I think you do know where she is. I think you have something to do with her disappearance. And if it turns out I'm right, I'm going to come back here. I promise you, you don't want that.'

'Are you threatening me?'

'No,' Quinn said. 'I don't threaten people.'

This time when the congressman tried to pull his arm from Quinn's grasp, Quinn didn't fight him. There was little more Quinn was going to be able to get out of him. But he'd learned enough to know something was definitely wrong, and Guerrero was involved.

As the congressman walked away, his security

team started walking toward him. Quinn tried to melt into the crowd and get out of sight, but he wasn't quick enough. One of the men from Houston got a good look at his face, then said something to his partner.

Instantly they both began pushing their way through the crowd.

Quinn moved toward the rear exit. Just before he disappeared into the hallway, he glanced over his shoulder. His pursuers were closer now, but the crowd was hindering their progress. At best, Quinn figured he had a thirty-second lead.

Before he was even two steps into the passage, he was running.

'Out of my way,' he yelled at two women who were standing near the bathroom entrance.

They moved against the wall just in time.

As Quinn neared the exit, the guy working the metal detector stepped into the opening, blocking the way. Maybe he thought Quinn had stolen something. Maybe he thought this was his chance to be a hero. But whatever he thought was soon forgotten as Quinn smashed into him, knocking him into the metal detector with a loud 'Oomph.'

A couple of the people standing just beyond the doorway yelled out in surprise when Quinn raced outside.

Tasha had moved across the alley and was standing alone. Quinn raced over to her, grabbed her arm, and began pulling her down the alley to the left.

'What's going on?' she said.

'We have to get out of here now!'

'What happened?'

'Come on,' he said. 'Just run.'

She looked confused, but instead of asking another question, she pulled off her high heels and began running barefoot beside him.

They sprinted toward the street at the end of the alley. When they were only a few feet away, Quinn heard more shouts behind them. He looked back and confirmed what he already knew he'd find. It was the men from inside. They appeared to hesitate for a moment. Thrown off, Quinn thought, by the fact that there were two people running from them. Not just Quinn.

'Go right,' Quinn said as they came to the street.

They ran down the sidewalk.

'Who are those guys?' Tasha asked.

'Two of the congressman's security team,' Quinn said. 'They were in Houston, too. At the house.'

'What?' she said, surprised.

Quinn angled between two parked cars, then ran across the street. Tasha was right behind him. At the intersection, they shot to the left down the new road.

For a moment, they were alone. They still had at least a thirty-second lead. Forty, tops.

'Go across the street,' he said. 'Hide behind those cars. I'll get them to follow me.'

'What if they catch you?'

'They won't. Once they're gone, head up to M Street and I'll meet you there.'

She didn't look confident, but she did as he said.

Alone now, he made sure to run heavy so that his steps would be loud and traceable. At the same time, he scanned the road ahead of him looking for someplace to hide. A few seconds later, he spotted it, another alley. This one off to his left.

He hesitated at the opening just long enough so that the first of his pursuers turning onto the street saw him. Then he continued forward.

The alley turned out to be another dead end. Its only purpose seemed to be to provide access to several private garages along the right. About three-quarters of the doors were closed. Those with open doors were empty, but hiding in any of them would be suicide. Guerrero's men would flush him out in a hurry. The left side of the alley provided even less opportunity. The only thing there was a ten-foot-high brick wall.

He processed all his choices in the first second of his arrival and came up with only one viable option. The garage at the far end abutted the corner of the building the alley deadended against. It also had its door open.

Quinn rushed forward and, grabbing the side of the open doorway, climbed up the wall, using the V formed by the meeting of the two buildings like a staircase.

As he pulled himself up and onto the roof, he could hear the men again, this time nearing the alley. Quinn scrambled up the slope of the roof, slipping over the apex seconds before the others arrived. Gravity wanted to pull him down the slope and into the small backyard of the townhouse behind him, but he held on, and tried to remain as quiet as possible.

'Where the fuck is he?' a voice said from the alley.

'He's not in any of these,' another called out.

'Check the closed ones.'

Quinn could hear metal rattling, and wood groaning in protest.

'They're all padlocked,' the second voice said.

'He must have hopped the wall.'

Quinn could hear hands slap against brick. Then a grunt of exertion, followed by a strained voice. 'There's another alleyway. He's got to be back there somewhere.'

'Come on. It'll be faster if we go around.'

Quinn listened as their footsteps echoed down the alley.

Knowing there was no time to waste, he crawled back over the top and eased himself down in front of the garages.

Two minutes later, he was back on M Street. Tasha was standing near the entrance to a bar, blending in with the small crowd outside.

Good, he thought. *She's learning.*

She looked relieved when she saw him. 'Are you okay?' she asked.

'Fine.'

'Where are they?'

'Still looking for me,' he said.

He told her to wait where she was while he returned to the gallery to retrieve his car. A twenty to the valet got his rental brought over in a hurry, and he was able to leave without anyone else noticing him.

'Did you talk to the congressman?' Tasha

asked, after he'd picked her up and they were heading out of Georgetown.

'Yes,' he said.

'And?'

'And he didn't have much to say.'

'He must have said something.'

'The only thing he said was that Jenny was on a leave of absence,' Quinn told her. Though it was more what the congressman hadn't said that had got Quinn's attention. 'But I didn't have all that much time before our friends saw me.'

Tasha was silent for several moments.

'Those men,' she finally said. 'What do you think they would have done if they caught us?'

'Taken us for a ride. Asked us a few questions,' Quinn said. 'Then killed us.'

Tasha grew noticeably quiet.

13

Tasha told Quinn she was staying at a small motel about twenty minutes south of the District, in Virginia. Quinn's plan was to dump her there. What she did after that was her problem. He was going to head back to Los Angeles and use other methods to figure out where Jenny might have gone. There was, though, one person he wanted to talk to before he left the area.

About halfway to Tasha's motel, Quinn pulled out his phone and called Nate.

'I need you to get me an address,' he told his apprentice.

'Sure. Name?'

'Derek Blackmoore.'

'Anything else you can give me?'

'He should be in the D.C. area. At least he was last time I heard.'

'Okay. I'll see what I can do.'

'Nate, he's not going to be listed in any phone book.'

'I didn't expect he would be.'

'And I need you to text the address to me in the next thirty minutes.'

'Of course you do,' Nate said.

Tasha guided Quinn toward the motel. As they approached it, Quinn could see it was one of those holdovers from the seventies. An ugly box of a place, forty rooms stuffed into a single two-story building. It was called the Lambert Motor Hotel, and surprisingly seemed to be a pretty busy place. Most of the parking spots surrounding it were full.

'I'm on the ground floor,' she said. 'Room eighteen, near the back.'

Quinn turned into the lot and drove slowly toward the rear.

'You can just drop me off he — '

Quinn glanced over at her. She was staring across him toward the building. The look on her face was both confused and scared. He turned to see what she was looking at.

The door to room 18 was wide open.

Tasha started to open the passenger door.

'No,' he said. 'Get down.'

'What?'

'Just get down. Don't let anyone see you.'

Tasha slumped down in her seat as Quinn drove past her room, then made a slow U-turn and headed back out to the street. Half a block down, he pulled the rental to the curb and turned off the engine.

'Does anyone else know where you're staying?'

'No,' she said. 'I . . . Oh my God.'

'What?'

'When I called my friend in Houston to get me into the show, he gave me a number to call to set up the details.' She looked at Quinn. 'I used the phone in my room to make the call.'

'So someone at the exhibit could have figured out where you were staying.'

'That was stupid,' she said, rubbing a hand over her face. She then glanced back toward the

151

motel. 'Do you think it's them?'

'Maybe the maid just forgot to close the door.'

'You don't really believe that, do you?'

Quinn leaned over in her direction, then reached down toward her legs.

'What are you doing?' she asked, pulling back slightly.

He said nothing as he slipped his hand under the seat, then pulled out the SIG.

Tasha's eyes grew wide, but she said nothing.

Quinn opened his door and climbed out. 'Stay here. I'll be right back.'

Instead of heading straight for her room, Quinn made his way along the back of the motel using a small service walkway. There were windows along the wall, but most had their curtains closed, including the window to Tasha's room.

As he neared the end of the building, his phone emitted two short vibrations, telling him he'd received a text message. He pulled it out and took a look.

It was from Nate. An address.

He slipped the phone back into his pocket.

Emerging from the service walkway, he found himself at the back end of the motel parking lot. Holding his gun at his side, he walked around the short end of the building to the sidewalk that ran in front of the first-floor rooms.

Room 18 was three doors down from where he stood. Quinn did a quick check of the cars parked nearby. They were all empty. He could hear TVs in several of the rooms, but outside he was alone.

He walked down the sidewalk slowly, trying to look like someone heading to his room. The TVs were on in both rooms 20 and 19, but the drapes on the windows were closed.

He raised his gun as he neared the entrance to room 18, stopping just short of the open door. He listened for a moment, but all was silent. Slowly he eased himself around the jamb and looked in.

The room was dark, lit only by whatever passed through the doorway from the parking lot. Still, it was more than enough for Quinn to see inside.

The room was deserted, but someone had definitely been there and had done nothing to hide their visit.

They had tossed the room. Not a robbery, though. The TV was still there, as were the phone and the clock radio. But the bed had been stripped and the mattress pushed haphazardly against the wall. There was a suitcase on the ground near the door. It was empty, its sides sliced open. Its contents were scattered all around the room. Clothes, mostly. Women's.

Just like he'd seen at Jenny's house in Houston, it looked like someone had been searching for something. But whoever had done it was gone.

Quinn lowered the SIG and kept walking down the path. There was no need to go inside. He wasn't investigating a crime. Knowing what had happened in the room was enough.

As he returned to the car, he carefully checked

to make sure he wasn't being followed or watched.

'Well?' Tasha asked once he had climbed into the sedan and closed the door. 'Did you go inside?'

Quinn started the engine and pulled away from the curb. 'You can't go back there.'

'But my suitcase . . . my clothes.'

'You can replace them.'

'What happened?'

'Did Jenny give you something?' he asked. 'Something other people would be looking for?'

Tasha shook her head. 'No.'

'Are you sure?'

'Nothing.'

'Do you know if she had anything that would force her to hide?'

'Is that what this is about? She has something they want?'

'Do you know if she has something she shouldn't have?'

Again, she shook her head. 'I have no idea.'

Quinn turned the car left onto the road that would take them back to the interstate.

'Where are we going?'

'You need to get someplace safe. Do you have any friends nearby? Relatives?'

'Here? I don't know anyone but Jenny.'

He knew he should just stick to his plan and let her fend for herself. But someone was directly after her now, and if she really was Jenny's friend, he couldn't bring himself to abandon her. Markoff was already dead. Jenny might be, also. He didn't need to add Tasha's

154

death on top of that.

'I'll find you someplace safe,' he said. 'In a few days, maybe a week, you can go home.'

'Hide out?' she said, as if the words were foreign to her.

'They were in your room, Tasha. They know who you are. You have to lay low.'

'What about Jenny?' she asked.

'Let me worry about Jenny.'

He could feel her looking over at him, but he kept his eyes on the road.

'Okay,' she said.

'Okay, you've heard what I've said, but you're still going to look for her? Or okay, you'll let me do it?'

She hesitated. 'Okay, I'll let you do it.' Now that they knew who she was, she was scared. He could hear it in her voice.

'Good.'

He'd take her back to his hotel and figure out what to do with her then. He reached into his pocket and pulled out his cell phone, accessing Nate's message again.

First, they had a stop to make.

* * *

Derek Blackmoore lived nearly an hour south of the District on the outskirts of Fredericksburg, Virginia. It was a neighborhood of scattered houses built among the trees of the receding forest.

It wouldn't be long before the majority of the trees were gone as the bedroom community of

155

Fredericksburg continued to expand. The signs were there — a handful of new homes in various stages of construction.

The houses that were already established were a mix of one- and two-stories. Each house was set on a large lot, but unlike the West Coast, no one in this part of the world seemed to believe in fences. There was no way to know where one property ended and another began.

Quinn turned down Blackmoore's street. There were mailboxes at the end of each driveway, their addresses prominently displayed. It didn't take long before he found Blackmoore's.

He drove past the driveway, then pulled onto the grassy shoulder a couple of lots away.

'What are we doing here?' Tasha asked.

'I need to talk to someone.'

'Derek Blackmoore?'

Quinn shot her a surprised look.

'You said his name on the phone,' she said.

He nodded once, remembering. 'Just stay here,' he said.

'Is he someone who can help find Jenny?'

'I'll be back in a little bit.'

He quickly got out of the car to avoid any further conversation, then slipped his gun under his waistband at the small of his back.

Derek Blackmoore had been a spy runner for the Agency. Quinn had never met the man himself, but he had heard plenty of stories from Markoff. Blackmoore had been Markoff's handler more times than not. This was before the older man had been forced into retirement as a scapegoat for intelligence gaffes during the second Gulf War.

'He had nothing to do with it,' Markoff had told Quinn later. 'He was all buttoned up. It was some asshole above him who hadn't listened to Blackmoore's warnings, then the guy turned around and pointed the finger at him.'

Markoff had once said Blackmoore was the only person in the business other than Quinn he trusted completely. There was no bullshit between them, no hidden agendas.

So if Markoff had trusted him when they'd worked together, maybe he'd trusted him enough to let him know what was going on now. It was a long shot, but at the moment, every move Quinn made was a long shot.

Blackmoore's house was set back from the road down a long driveway. It was on a gentle slope that dropped away from the road for about a hundred yards before it rose again on the other side of the small vale. Quinn could hear running water down where the two hills met. A brook, probably barely deep enough to get your feet wet.

Lights were on in Blackmoore's house. Quinn took that for a good sign. He would have hated to wake the old man up.

He walked slowly down the driveway, making sure he was in sight of the front window at all times. If he wanted any chance of getting help out of Blackmoore, then sneaking up on the old spook would not be a great idea.

He climbed the three steps up to a wide porch that wrapped around the front of the house, then approached the front door. But before he could knock, he heard a voice behind him.

'What do you want?'

Quinn turned quickly, expecting to find someone standing there, but there was no one.

'I said, what do you want?'

This time the voice came from his right. Quinn looked over, but he was still alone.

He searched the shadows in the direction the voice had come from, then saw it. A tiny speaker hidden in the eaves of the porch overhang. The voice had been crystal clear, so it had to be top-of-the-line.

'Answer the question or get the hell out of here.'

This one was from the left, but Quinn didn't look this time. Instead, he approached the front door, stopping only a foot away.

'Mr. Blackmoore, I need to talk with you.'

'I'm not interested in conversations. Get your ass off my property before I call the police.' This speaker was just above the door.

'Steven Markoff sent me.'

Silence.

'You're lying.'

'I'm not,' Quinn said.

'Who are you?'

'My name's Jonathan Quinn.'

Silence again.

'Prove it.'

'And how am I supposed to do that?'

'Tell me how you met Steven.'

Quinn tensed. The only person he had ever told the story to was Orlando, and they hadn't talked about it since. 'Finland,' he said. 'Markoff was undercover and he saved my life.'

'How, exactly?'

'By cutting the ropes that suspended me from the trees,' Quinn said, his teeth clenched. 'By walking me out of the forest. By driving me all the way to Turku, and taking me on the ferry to Stockholm. Is that enough? Or do you want more?'

Blackmoore said nothing for several seconds, then, 'You're armed.'

'I am.'

'Put it on the ground.'

Quinn held both hands out in front of him, then slowly moved his right hand around to the small of his back. He pulled out the gun, then set it on the porch, and slid it gently toward the door before standing back up.

For several seconds, nothing happened. Then the door opened. Standing there was a small gray-haired man. His face was lined with creases and wrinkles. Liver spots dotted his receding hairline. Over his eyes, he wore a pair of metal-framed glasses with thick lenses. He was dressed in a gray Baltimore Orioles sweatshirt and dark blue sweatpants. But the most important part of his outfit was the Smith and Wesson pistol in his right hand.

'So you're the cleaner,' he said, his voice surprisingly strong for his body.

'And you're the spy runner,' Quinn said.

'Past life. What do you want?'

Quinn said, 'Markoff's dead.'

Silence hung between them for several

159

seconds. With a sigh of resignation, Blackmoore stepped across the threshold and picked up Quinn's gun, then motioned for the cleaner to follow him back inside.

'Tell me,' he said.

★ ★ ★

They sat in Blackmoore's living room, Quinn on the worn couch and Blackmoore on a cloth-covered recliner. The SIG sat on the side table within easy reach of Markoff's old boss.

The room was an interior decorator's nightmare. A mess of converging styles, none done particularly well. Bad seventies-era furniture, next to worse eighties-era lamps. And everywhere stacks of magazines and papers and books. On the coffee table were plates that hadn't been washed for days, maybe weeks.

Quinn made no judgments as he recounted a condensed version of the events from the past few days. He left out Tasha, wanting to limit her liability as much as possible. It wasn't that he didn't trust Blackmoore. Markoff trusted him, so that was good enough for Quinn. It just didn't seem necessary.

'Son of a bitch,' Blackmoore said when Quinn finished. 'You're sure it was him?'

'I'm sure,' Quinn said.

'Did you check the DNA?'

'I didn't need to check the DNA. I made a positive ID.'

'These things can be faked, you know. The fuckers have ways of doing it. You said the body

160

was in bad shape. That would make it easy.'

'It was him, all right,' Quinn said. 'He's dead. He's not coming back.'

'Son of a bitch.'

'What I'm worried about now is Jenny. I don't have any physical proof, but my gut tells me his death is connected to what's happened to her.'

'Of course it's connected.'

Quinn paused. 'You say that like you know something.'

'Forget it. Doesn't matter, he's dead.'

'What about Jenny? She's not dead yet.'

'She might be.'

'I'd rather assume she isn't,' Quinn said.

'Doesn't matter. She's not important.'

Quinn decided to try a different tack. 'What about finding out who killed Markoff?'

Blackmoore let out a single derisive laugh. 'You really think you can do that?'

'I'm going to try.'

'You're just a cleaner.'

'And you're just a paranoid old man.'

Blackmoore stared at Quinn. After a moment, he pushed himself out of his chair.

'Whoever killed Markoff,' he said, 'they'll get theirs eventually. They always do.' He started walking toward the foyer. 'I'm tired. It's time for you to go.'

Quinn remained seated. When the old man realized he wasn't being followed, he stopped and turned back.

'It's late and I don't want to talk about this anymore.'

Quinn didn't move.

Blackmoore took a few steps back. 'Get the hell out of my house.'

'You said of course they're connected. What did you mean?'

The old man's eyes bored into Quinn again, but Quinn didn't budge. Finally Blackmoore said, 'Fuck.' He returned to his chair but didn't sit down. 'If they were able to kill Markoff, do you really think they'll let you live once they know you're looking for them?'

'I guess we'll find out.'

'Don't be so blind,' Blackmoore said. 'Drop it.'

'Look,' Quinn said, unable to contain his anger any longer. 'I have to do this. I have no choice. I owe him.'

'Owe him? You mean Markoff?' The old man nearly laughed. 'Markoff's dead. You don't owe him shit.'

Quinn tried to keep his voice calm and even. 'What did you mean when you said they were connected?'

'Jesus. You're not going to stop, are you?'

'What did you mean?' Quinn repeated.

'I'm surprised you've lasted this long, cleaner. Do you always get this wrapped up?'

Quinn started to repeat his question, but Blackmoore held up a hand to stop him.

'I know it's connected because the reason he was out of the country was due to her.'

'How do you know that?'

'How do you think? He told me.' He sighed, then sat back down. 'They were having

162

problems, okay? Don't ask me details. What the fuck do I know about relationships? I've been alone for over forty years. Just problems.' Blackmoore frowned. 'She had some kind of emergency. Left town without even telling Markoff where she was going. When he located her, he went to see if he could help.'

'Where was she?'

'I have no idea.'

'None?'

Blackmoore looked down for a moment, then sighed.

'Goddamn it,' he said. 'Follow me.'

14

Blackmoore took Quinn into one of the rooms at the back of the house. Though it had been designed to be a bedroom, it was now part office, part technical workspace.

There were no windows in the room. If they had been there once, they were now covered by a wall. There was also no closet. Either it, too, had been boarded over, or there never had been one in the first place.

Lining three of the walls was a two-foot-wide workbench covered with tools and bits and pieces of electronic gear. And against the wall next to the door was a desk, complete with computer monitor and keyboard. Above the desk and mounted just below the ceiling were five television monitors. Each displayed a view of Blackmoore's property. Live shots from cameras placed strategically so that no one would get near the house without being seen.

On one of the monitors was a shot of the empty driveway. The same monitor Blackmoore must have been watching when Quinn approached the house.

The former spy sat down in front of one of the computer terminals and began typing on the keyboard. Quinn watched as Blackmoore navigated through a website to the groups section. The old man signed in, then selected one of the groups from his list of member areas. Sandy Side Yacht Club.

'There,' Blackmoore said. 'It's the best I can do.'

'There what?' Quinn asked.

Blackmoore turned, then looked at him like he was an idiot. 'What do you think?'

Quinn looked at the computer again and realized what Blackmoore meant. 'This is your backup, isn't it?'

'Maybe you're not so dumb,' Blackmoore said.

In the field, there were always emergency contact systems. You'd never know when the primary route to your handler might not be available. There were fewer options in the pre — Internet days, but now an agent could have dozens of different backups if he really wanted them.

Blackmoore clicked on one of the links and accessed a message board. 'We'd post here. Use a simple location code.'

'Key letters?' Quinn asked.

'No. Place, number. Easier to sniff out, but also easier to use on the fly.'

Blackmoore accessed the archives, pulling up the messages from two weeks previous. He clicked on one from somebody called SailorXsuper9393.

'This is the last message Markoff posted to me.'

Quinn leaned in. It had been posted to the message board sixteen days previously. He then glanced at the message itself.

Place/number was a simple code. Which,

Quinn realized, would have been the reason Markoff had chosen it. The code was perfect for someone who wasn't used to operating in the world of secrets to grasp quickly and understand. Someone like Jenny.

In the first sentence was the name of a location, Jamaica. That would be the key. Since Jamaica had seven letters, it was every seventh word *after* Jamaica that was important. Once those words were extracted from the post, reversing them gave you the real message. Quick, clean, and easy.

Before Quinn had a chance to decipher it, Blackmoore said, 'He was letting me know that he'd found her. Apparently she'd heard something she wasn't supposed to hear, and had gone into hiding before anyone could get to her. He wrote he was going to help her out, and that he might be contacting me again in case he needed me to look into anything for him.'

'But he never did,' Quinn said.

'No.'

Blackmoore located a message sent two days later. The sender's ID was not Markoff's.

'From you?' Quinn asked.

'Not me.'

Blackmoore opened the message. Again there was a place name. Miami this time. The message itself was short.

''All safe,'' Blackmoore deciphered on the fly. ''I wish you were still here. Hurry. Be careful. Love.''

The old man scrolled down. There was a

response to the message. It was from SailorXsuper9393.

'Markoff,' Quinn said.

The response was also short: 'Everything's okay. I'll fix this. Love back.'

Quinn pulled back slightly. 'The first message is from Jenny.'

'So it would seem.'

'Are there any others?' Quinn asked.

'Yes,' Blackmoore said, obviously pleased with the question. He searched through the message board until he came upon one that had been sent ten days ago from Jenny's address. 'There are actually three messages. This is the oldest, then one from last Friday, and the latest from this morning. The first two are basically the same. 'Where are you?' But no response from Markoff.'

'What about the message this morning?'

Blackmoore found the message. The code key was Cape Cod. Quinn decoded the message himself this time.

''I'm coming to find you. Love,'' Quinn said out loud.

'Yes,' Blackmoore said.

'You never replied to any of her messages?'

'Why should I? They weren't meant for me.'

'But Markoff's dead.'

'And I didn't know that until you just told me.'

'Bullshit,' Quinn said. 'Maybe you didn't have any proof, but you had to believe it was probably true. You worked in the business too long to be that stupid.'

'What did you want me to tell her? I think

your boyfriend is dead, good luck?'

'You could have tried to help her.'

'How?'

'Used your contacts. Done something.'

'I think you're overestimating my current state of influence.'

Quinn could feel frustration building inside his chest. But after a deep breath, he was able to push it back down. Blackmoore was showing him a way to contact Jenny, after all. That was the important thing.

'Do you know what she was running from?'

'No idea.'

'Something to do with her boss, maybe?'

'That congressman?' Blackmoore asked.

'Yes.'

'Maybe. I don't know. Markoff didn't tell me. And I'm glad, because I don't care.'

Quinn thought for a moment, then said, 'I need to send her a reply.'

'Not from my screen name.'

'I'll create my own.'

'And not from my computer. I don't want the message to be traced back to me.'

Quinn stared at the old man. 'I find it hard to believe anything could get traced back here.'

There was a hint of a smile on Blackmoore's face. Finally he pushed back from the desk and relinquished his chair.

'A new ID,' he said. 'I'm not giving you the password to mine. And no more than five minutes.'

Quinn quickly composed what he wanted to say, then replied to Jenny's last message with his new screen name. Hiding within a note about sailing off the coast of California was his true message:

It's Quinn. Please, I need to talk to you. Respond earliest.

The place key he used was Coronado, the island where he had taken the picture of Jenny he had found on Markoff. He hoped it would make her realize it was really him.

'Touching,' Blackmoore said, looking over his shoulder. 'And if she responds?'

'Then I help her.'

'I guess you'll be joining Markoff soon enough.'

He tapped Quinn on the shoulder with the barrel of his gun. Quinn got the message and stood, then the old man started leading him toward the door.

'There's something else I wanted to ask you,' Quinn said.

Blackmoore stopped just before the hallway and stared back at Quinn. 'I'm done talking.'

Quinn reached into his pocket. As he did, Blackmoore tensed, raising the gun in his hand a few inches.

'Markoff left a message,' Quinn said as he pulled out his wallet.

The air grew still.

'You said he was dead.'

'He was still alive when he was locked in the container. At least long enough to scrawl something on the wall.'

'What?'

Quinn opened the wallet and removed a piece of paper with a copy of the message on it. He held it out to Blackmoore.

The old man hesitated several seconds, then walked back over and grabbed the note. Quinn watched as Blackmoore stared down at the characters.

'Some sort of code perhaps?' Blackmoore said without taking his eyes off the paper.

'You don't recognize it?' Quinn asked.

'No. But that doesn't mean anything.' Blackmoore moved the paper slightly closer to his face. 'What are these two characters? Are they part of the string?'

He was looking at the 'lp.'

'I'm not sure. He repeated the sequence twice, but these two were only after the second go-round. And they were set off by themselves.'

'What is that? A one?'

'Either a one or an *L*,' Quinn said.

'*L?*' Blackmoore said, trying it out. '*L . . . P?*' Suddenly his face clouded over. 'You need to get out of here now.'

'Why? What is it?'

Blackmoore began pulling on Quinn's arm. 'Jesus, I hope it's not too late,' Blackmoore mumbled to himself. 'Get the hell out of my house!'

He was rushing Quinn down the hall toward the front door.

'What is it?' Quinn asked. 'LP? Is that it? What's it mean?'

'No. I'm too old for this shit.'

170

As they neared the door, Quinn put on the brakes. 'I'm not leaving without my gun.'

The old man dropped his hand from Quinn's arm and hurried into the living room. A moment later, he returned with Quinn's SIG.

'Here,' he said, thrusting it at Quinn. 'Take it.'

Quinn took the gun, then said, 'And I'm not leaving until you tell me what LP means.'

Blackmoore raised his own gun and pointed it at Quinn. 'Get out. Now.'

* * *

Quinn returned to the car, his head spinning from the encounter with Blackmoore. Something had scared the old spy, something to do with the letters *LP*. But what?

He wanted to run the entire conversation through his mind again, see if there was something he'd missed. Unfortunately, Tasha had a different plan.

'Thank God,' Tasha said. 'Thank God.'

She seemed agitated, almost hysterical.

'What is it?' he asked as he slipped his gun under his seat.

She held her cell phone in her hand and was staring down at it. 'My . . . my brother called. From Houston. Someone broke into my apartment. Went through everything I have.' She put a shaking hand to her brow. 'The place is a disaster, he said.' She looked at Quinn. 'They know where I live. I can't even go home now. What am I going to do?'

He got her calmed down, then drove her back

to the Marriott in Crystal City.

Once inside his room, he pointed toward the bathroom. 'If you want to get freshened up.'

She raised a hand to her face self-consciously, then, without a word, she turned and walked to the bathroom.

Quinn wasted no time collecting his bag and setting it on the bed. He did two passes through the room, making sure he had everything, then a third pass wiping down any surface he may have touched.

Tasha reemerged from the bathroom a couple moments after he'd finished. 'Are you leaving?' she asked.

'Yes.'

'What about me?'

Quinn hesitated before answering. The best thing for her would be to go someplace where she knew no one. A big city, far away from the East Coast, where she could become one of the anonymous. St. Louis, Minneapolis, Detroit, any of those would work. He was tempted to give her the keys to the rental and say, 'Drive west.' And, 'Good luck.' But he couldn't do that. He still wasn't ready to trust her completely, but she might very well hold the key to contacting Jenny. So keeping her near seemed a more secure option than letting her fend for herself.

'I'm going back to Los Angeles,' Quinn said. 'You'll come with me. It'll be safer there.'

He could see her relief as her whole body seemed to relax. 'Okay,' she said. 'Thank you.'

Traveling under her own name, though, was out of the question. He would have to dummy up an ID for her, but he had the gear to do that with him. Nothing too fancy but it would work in the short run. And they'd have to get her some other clothes. Again not impossible either, even at the late hour.

He excused himself and walked into the bathroom, closing the door behind him. After he splashed some warm water on his face, he put the top down on the toilet and took a seat. From his pocket, he pulled out his phone and called Nate.

'I'm heading home,' Quinn said. 'Things have gotten a little complicated here. I'm also bringing someone with me. I'll call you back when I know our arrival time so you can pick us up.'

'Quinn, wait,' Nate said.

'What?'

'I talked to Orlando.'

There was something in Nate's voice that made Quinn pause. 'When?'

'About an hour ago.'

'I've left her a couple messages, but she hasn't called back.'

'She's . . . not herself. I think she thought she was calling your cell.'

'What's going on?'

There was a long silence. 'Her aunt died.'

Whatever strength Quinn had left drained away. 'No.'

'It happened when you were in Houston.'

Quinn put an elbow on his knee and rested his forehead in his open palm. 'What was it?'

'Cancer. I guess she was diagnosed a couple of

months ago, but only told Orlando last week.'

No wonder he hadn't received a call back. 'How did Orlando sound?'

'Dazed. Like she couldn't believe it.' Nate paused. 'The funeral's tomorrow afternoon.'

Quinn sat up. 'Are you kidding?'

'No.'

Quinn stared at the tile near his feet, his mind thousands of miles away to the west.

'Quinn?' Nate asked. 'Still there?'

'I'll . . . call you back.'

Quinn disconnected the call.

For the next ten minutes, he didn't move.

15

San Francisco bay rose on both sides of the plane. For a moment, it seemed as if they were going to land on the water. Then all at once there was runway beneath them.

After the phone call with Nate, Quinn forgot about his planned return to Los Angeles. Orlando had lost her aunt. With the exception of her son Garrett, her aunt had been the only close member of her family left. Quinn needed to be there for her.

It wasn't until he and Tasha were in the air heading west that he remembered there was someone else he could pay a visit to while he was in town. Jorge Albina, the son of a bitch who hired him to get rid of Markoff's body, was based out of San Francisco.

At the airport, Quinn rented a sedan, and soon he and Tasha were driving north into the city.

'After we check into the hotel, maybe you can get a little rest,' he said.

'Sure,' she replied, sounding like she needed it.

Using one of his aliases, Quinn had reserved two adjoining rooms at the Marriott on Fourth Street before they left D.C. Quinn had stayed there before, and knew the hotel was always packed with guests attending conferences and conventions at the nearby Moscone Center. It was the perfect blend of comfort and size, providing them whatever they might need, including anonymity.

When they pulled up out front, he told the valet to keep the car close as he would be leaving soon.

Tasha shot him a questioning look.

'I have something to do,' he told her. He could see the uncertainty in her eyes. He smiled and put a reassuring hand on her arm. 'You'll be fine. No one knows you're here.'

'I don't want to be alone. Maybe I should go with you.'

'You won't be alone. Someone will be in my room next door.'

She pulled away. 'Who?'

'A friend.'

She looked at him, obviously not pleased. But she said, 'Okay. I trust you.'

Once inside, they bypassed the reception desk and made their way directly to the elevators. There were two choices: High Rise or Mid Rise.

Quinn pulled out his phone and punched in a speed-dial number.

'We're here,' he said.

'Rooms twenty-seven-forty-six and -forty-seven,' Nate said.

*   *   *

It didn't take Tasha long to fall asleep. Quinn had introduced her to Nate, then showed her that their rooms were connected on the inside. He could tell she still wasn't happy with the situation, but she didn't say anything more.

Once Quinn was sure she was out, he closed the door between the rooms so she'd have some privacy.

'Suit?' he asked Nate.

'In the closet.'

Quinn found a garment bag hanging inside. He removed a black suit and started to change.

'Protection?' Quinn asked.

'One for each of us. In there,' Nate said, nodding toward the suitcase at the end of one of the beds.

Inside would be a replacement for the SIG Quinn had had to leave in D.C. and a Glock for his apprentice.

'Do you want it?' Nate asked.

Quinn thought for a second, then shook his head. Though Orlando probably wouldn't be upset if he was armed, it seemed wrong to go to her aunt's funeral with a gun. 'When I get back. I should be all right for now.'

'I feel bad that I can't go,' Nate said.

Quinn gave him a half smile. 'She'll understand.'

'You'll tell her I'm sorry, right?'

'I'll tell her.'

They fell into silence as Quinn continued dressing.

As he was tying his tie, Nate looked toward the adjacent room. 'What if your friend wakes up?'

'Get her something to eat. Let her watch TV. But don't let her leave.'

Nate nodded, then as Quinn headed to the door he said, 'Don't forget to tell Orlando.'

'I won't.'

Orlando's Aunt Jeong had lived in one of those Edwardian shotgun houses built not long after the famous 1906 San Francisco earthquake. A two-story with a basement. But unlike most of the other homes in the neighborhood, the building had not been subdivided into separate upstairs and downstairs apartments. Somehow Aunt Jeong had resisted the urge to mutilate her home for the quick cash.

It was the second time in the last five years Quinn had been to her house, and neither time had been a happy one. In fact, his previous visit had marked the beginning of a four-year stretch during which he and Orlando had lost contact with each other.

'Lost' wasn't the right word, Quinn knew. More like 'broke off.' But he preferred 'lost'; it smoothed over the pain. That first time had been after a job he and Durrie had been on. But instead of bringing Durrie to her alive, Quinn had brought her an urn filled with ashes they both thought belonged to her boyfriend. That later it turned out not to be true didn't change the fact it had been the worst day of Quinn's life. And, he guessed, of Orlando's, too.

There were five steps leading up to the front of the house. Quinn hesitated for several seconds at the bottom, then willed himself up the stairs. He knocked, waited half a minute, then knocked again. There was no response.

Orlando had told Nate the funeral was that afternoon, but she hadn't mentioned exactly

178

when. Quinn had tried calling her several times since arriving in the city, but she hadn't answered.

He tried knocking again. Still no answer. He turned back to the street, looking first right, then left.

God knew where the service was being held.

All of a sudden, he felt very weary. Markoff dead. Jenny missing. The responsibility he was beginning to feel for Tasha. And now this, his best friend losing the aunt she had loved so much.

He sat down on the stoop. There was nothing he could do now but wait.

And if there was one thing he was good at, it was waiting.

★ ★ ★

'Let's see. The first time you broke the law,' Orlando whispered.

Quinn thought about it for a moment. 'I was twelve. Shoplifted a candy bar on a dare from a friend.' His voice also low.

'Get caught?'

'Sort of.'

She cocked her head, wanting more.

Quinn moved his legs a few inches to the left, trying to get comfortable. It was tough to do in the utility closet they were crammed in. Most of the space was taken up by a switching system for the company computer network.

Orlando was sitting closest to the door, while Quinn was shoved back in the corner, giving her as much room as possible.

'I actually took two,' he said. 'It was the local grocery store. One of the managers stopped me on the way out and made me give one back.'

'Not both of them?'

'He didn't know about the other one. But he did let me go. I think he thought he'd scared me enough.'

Again the questioning look.

'Yeah,' Quinn said. 'He did. I didn't shoplift again until . . . well, until I started working for Durrie. How about you?'

'Stole fifty bucks from the principal's office in sixth grade.'

'Holy shit,' Quinn said. 'What'd he do when he found out?'

'Expelled a kid in another class.'

'He didn't know it was you?'

'They found the other kid's fingerprints on everything,' she said. 'And it helped that he'd dropped his lunch card under the desk.'

Quinn smirked. He wanted to believe her, but he didn't know her well enough to trust her yet. Besides, maybe she was just trying to impress him. Though they were both still apprentices — he with Durrie, and she with Durrie's occasional partner Abraham Delger — Quinn was the veteran. He'd been at it almost four years, while Orlando had only begun her training nine months earlier.

'I think I hear someone,' she said, looking toward the door.

Quinn moved his head so that his ear was facing the door, then focused all his attention on the hallway beyond the door. A half-second later, he heard the steps. They were light but rhythmic and unhurried. No sense of urgency, no panic that might suggest knowledge of any security breech at the Net/Gyro facility. Though for the last thirty minutes, that had been exactly the case.

Quinn and Orlando listened as the steps drew nearer, walked past the door, then receded in the opposite direction. Not once was there a pause in the person's gait.

'Your turn,' Orlando said once it was quiet.

'Why'd you decide to get into this?' he asked.

She shook her head. 'Work's off-limits. As is anything too personal.'

'Breaking the law's not personal?'

She tilted her head, looking at him with dark smiling eyes. 'Okay,' she said. 'I got in because nothing else seemed as exciting.'

'That's a job-interview answer.'

'Really? So tell me a better one.'

He smiled. 'How about, I got in because if I'd said no, they would have killed me.'

Her eyes narrowed. 'Is that true?'

'You just asked for a better answer, not a true one,' Quinn said, though his answer was essentially correct.

'I took Abraham's offer because if I didn't, I'd have ended up sitting in a cubicle in Silicon Valley, programming crap so some idiot could spell-check his document a little faster. Bullshit work. At least this way, I get out sometimes.'

She moved a finger to her mouth and touched it to her lips, letting him know she'd heard something else. This time he didn't turn his head, but instead looked toward the door. Which, of course, meant he had to look directly at her, too.

He'd met Orlando several times over the previous nine months, but before, Durrie and Delger were always around. This was the first time they had spent any time alone together.

For some reason, their bosses decided today's mission would be best conducted by the two rookies. The task wasn't that difficult. No cleanup involved. It was an info-gathering job. Get in, plant some bugs, then get out. It was a mission more aimed at Orlando's specialties than Quinn's, but Durrie had deemed it a good exercise for his apprentice.

The building was the research facility for Net/Gyro Inc., one of those overnight technology wonders that seem to have sucked in a lot of cash but had yet to turn a real profit. Someplace Orlando might have ended up working at if she had taken the safer path.

Quinn's function on this mission was guide and bodyguard, while Orlando was tasked with inserting the bugs into the phone system so that specific lines could be monitored. Who would be making those calls, and what they would be concerning, neither of them had any idea. It was just another one of those 'you don't need to know' situations.

They'd gotten into the facility fine. They'd even planted the bugs without any trouble. It was the getting out that had been a problem. Their exit route, one planned by Durrie, had proved to be unusable. Building construction had sealed off an entire wing of the structure, removing it from play.

Exiting the same way they'd come in also wouldn't work. The automated video loops of empty corridors that covered their arrival would have stopped working at least fifteen minutes earlier.

So Quinn had contacted Durrie, who told them to find someplace to hole up while he tried to figure out an alternate exit.

It should have been annoying, but Quinn didn't mind. In fact, for the moment, he didn't care how long they had to wait.

As Orlando glanced over at him, he raised a questioning eyebrow, hoping to hide the fact he had been staring at her. She pointed to the right, indicating the noise was coming from that direction of the hallway. Quinn had already heard it, but he pretended to listen, then gave her a nod as the footsteps grew nearer.

When she looked away again, he couldn't help but let his gaze return to her — the curve of her neck, her pale brown skin, the ponytail of dark hair that reached just below her shoulders. He didn't want to care. He didn't want to be interested. But he didn't know how not to be. She'd captured him, and she didn't even know it.

Outside, the footsteps began to slow. They were close now, almost to the door. Quinn could feel Orlando tense. He cursed himself for not letting her enter the closet first so he would have been between her and the door.

One step.

A second.

Then a hand on the door.

Quinn pulled out the only weapon he'd been allowed to bring along. It was a handheld Taser. He leaned forward, across Orlando's lap, ready to strike the moment the door opened.

He could hear the knob turn, then the latch release. He expected the door to ease away from the jamb slowly, but it didn't.

With a jerk, it flew wide.

Quinn lunged forward, the Taser aimed straight in front of him. But the man on the other side seemed to expect the move. He was standing several feet away from the threshold, well out of Quinn's initial range. Quinn started to push himself up for a second attempt, but the man's words stopped him.

'Nice try,' Durrie said, a knowing glint in his eyes. He was wearing the uniform of a Net/Gyro security officer. 'Get to know each other better in there, did you? Well, teatime's over. Let's go.'

*   *   *

It had been a test. Durrie had known all along the way out he had given them wouldn't work. What he wanted to see was if they'd keep calm when things went wrong. It was an exam they both passed.

And though Durrie couldn't have cared less, he had been right. Quinn and Orlando had gotten to know each other better, enough to establish a friendship that continued to grow stronger over the years. Only never in the direction Quinn had hoped. Instead, somehow that honor had fallen to Durrie. Orlando had been too good for Quinn's old mentor, but there was no way he could tell her that. She had loved Durrie and taken care of him.

Quinn would have considered it a waste if not for Garrett — the son Durrie would never even acknowledge as his own.

16

An older couple walked up the steps to Orlando's aunt's house at three-thirty. They were dressed in black, and they appeared to be Korean, like the mother Orlando had lost when she was just a child and like her recently deceased aunt Jeong. The woman stared at Quinn as she walked by, careful to keep as much distance between them as possible. The man gave Quinn a nod, then paid him no more attention.

The couple had a key to the front door and soon disappeared inside, not bothering to see if Quinn wanted to come in also.

A few minutes later, more people started arriving, all Koreans. Some looked at Quinn as if they were asking, 'Should I know you?' But most just ignored him.

At three forty-five, a black limo pulled up to the curb. An elderly couple emerged from the back. Quinn guessed the woman was at least eighty, and the man a few years older. Once they were on the sidewalk, a third person climbed from the car. A woman, much younger.

She was wearing a black calf-length dress, conservative but stylish. Her hair was pinned back from her face, and she had on a pair of simple, wire-framed glasses. Despite the fact that she was also wearing heels, she stood no more than five foot two. But unlike the other arrivals, she was only half Korean. Her father was a mix of Thai and American Irish, making his daughter Orlando a true American blend.

As she stepped up onto the sidewalk to join the couple, she glanced toward the front door of the house. When she caught sight of Quinn, she stopped, her eyes locking on him. Then, perhaps only noticeable to him, she seemed to relax, her shoulders lowering, her mouth easing open in what could almost be a smile.

Quinn pushed himself off the stoop and walked over to her. There were tears in Orlando's eyes as she closed the gap and fell into his embrace. The older couple she had arrived with walked toward the house, their eyes straight ahead, pretending not to notice the sudden public display.

Quinn placed one hand in the middle of Orlando's back, then rubbed the other across her shoulder.

'You came,' she said, not looking up.

'Always the queen of the obvious,' he said.

He could feel her smile against his chest, then her left hand moved away and punched him in the arm.

When she finally pulled away, he said, 'I'm sorry I didn't make the service.'

'It's okay. I got your messages. I was just . . . too busy.'

She looked toward the door of her aunt's home. A woman was there, the one who'd arrived first, looking down at Orlando. She motioned for her to come inside.

'Come on,' Orlando said to Quinn.

187

★ ★ ★

The woman said something to Orlando in Korean as they entered. After Orlando answered her, the woman looked at Quinn, then turned and walked away.

'Aunt Jay's sister-in-law,' Orlando said. Jay was Aunt Jeong's nickname. 'She seems to think she owns all this now.'

'Does she?'

'No,' Orlando said. 'I do.'

'You could always give it to her.'

'Not a chance.'

As was the nature of a shotgun-style house, Aunt Jeong's place was much longer than it was wide, with room after room from front to back. Just beyond the entrance was a small living room overcrowded with old furniture. The walls were covered with pictures: a painting of Christ, some landscapes, and several photos. Several guests had already staked out positions on the tan couch and the two ratty-looking recliners.

Orlando led him into a hallway that ran along the left side of the house. They passed the stairs to the second floor, a small bathroom, a guest bedroom, and a formal dining area before coming to the end of the hall and entering the kitchen.

This was where most of the crowd was. Over a dozen people were crammed into the room. Quinn had heard them talking in Korean as he and Orlando approached, but as soon as he entered the kitchen all conversation stopped.

Orlando said something to them. The only

word Quinn could pick out was 'Jonathan.' He got a couple nods from the men, but no more than blank stares from the women.

Orlando turned to him. 'More of my aunt's in-laws.' She whispered, 'They think maybe you're my white boyfriend.'

'What if I were Korean?'

'They'd be pulling out chairs for you and stuffing food in your face.'

Quinn smiled. The truth was, he had relatives who would have treated Orlando pretty much the same way if their roles had been reversed.

Orlando grabbed two plastic cups off the kitchen table and handed one to Quinn. 'Here,' she said. 'Lemonade.'

They stood in the kitchen for a while, Orlando talking first with one guest, then another, and Quinn just trying to be the caring friend.

After about forty-five minutes, Orlando held up her empty cup and said, 'I think I need something a little stronger than this. Coming?'

'Whatever you want,' Quinn said.

⋆　⋆　⋆

Orlando's definition of something stronger turned out to be a double espresso at the Starbucks stand in the Safeway grocery store on Market Street. Once they had their drinks, she led him back outside.

'Walk?' she asked.

'Sure,' he said.

They headed north along Market, their pace slow.

'How are you doing?' Quinn said. It was a stupid question, but he didn't know what else to ask.

'Okay, I guess,' she said. She sighed, then tried to smile. 'I knew my aunt was sick. That's why I came out to visit. I just didn't realize how close she was to the end.' She raised her espresso to her lips and took a drink. 'If I'd known, I would have brought Garrett with me. She really wanted to see him.'

'You left Garrett at home?' The boy was only six years old.

She nodded. 'Mr. Vo and his wife are watching him. He's fine.'

Mr. Vo worked for Orlando at the Tri-Continent Relief Agency she ran in Ho Chi Minh City. He was a good man, and was devoted to helping Orlando.

'You did the best you could for your aunt. You know that, right?' he said.

Her half smile turned to one of regret. 'I don't want to talk about it. That's all I've done for the last three days.'

'Sure.' Silence for a couple of moments, then he said, 'We can talk about football.'

She almost laughed. 'Why were you in D.C.?' she said.

'Nate tell you that?'

She said nothing, skilled at protecting her sources.

'Just work. Not important,' he told her.

'Sounded like it was more than just work.'

Quinn paused as he was about to take a drink. 'What did he tell you?'

190

'Relax,' she said. 'He didn't tell me anything. Just that you were away on business, but I could tell there was something more. I *did* ask him. But he didn't give you up.'

Quinn took a sip of his coffee, then said, 'Markoff's dead.'

Orlando stopped walking, surprised. 'When?'

'Sometime in the last week or two.'

'I'm sorry,' she said. Other than Markoff himself, and apparently Derek Blackmoore, Orlando was the only one who knew about Quinn's connection to his old friend, about Finland, and about the debt Quinn had felt since then. 'How did it happen?'

'That's what I'm trying to figure out,' Quinn said.

As they started walking again, Quinn told her what had been happening. He told her how he'd had to dispose of his friend's body, about his search for Jenny, about Houston and D.C., and the congressman and Tasha and Blackmoore.

'Do the initials 'LP' mean anything to you?' he asked, once he'd finished his story.

She concentrated for a moment, her eyes staring off into the distance. 'I don't know. Doesn't immediately ring any bells.'

'Yeah. Means nothing to me, either. But it sure seemed to scare the hell out of Blackmoore.'

Neither said anything for a moment. Then Orlando asked, 'What about Jenny? You have no idea where she is?'

Quinn shook his head. 'I can tell you where she's not. That's wherever Markoff had left her. I think she's gone in search of him.'

'But where would that be?'

'Nate said the ship he came in on had sailed out of Shanghai.'

Orlando looked unconvinced. 'Give me your phone,' she said.

He handed it to her, activating it first so she could use it. He then watched as she accessed the Internet and navigated through the web until she arrived at some sort of database.

'Name of the ship?'

'The *Riegle 3*,' he said.

She punched in the name, then stared at the screen for several seconds. 'It's out of Shanghai, but that's not the last port it visited before coming to L.A.'

'Are you sure?'

'Don't go getting all mad at Nate,' she said. 'Do you know what databases he used?'

'He didn't say. Probably DSIT. I've shown him that one before.' DSIT was the Daily Shipping Information and Tracking. One of a bundled package of databases available for a very expensive yearly fee.

'That explains it.' She found her way to the DSIT site, using her own password to get on. After a moment, she held the screen out to Quinn. 'There. See?'

He looked at the displayed information. It was for the *Riegle 3*. The date was the date Quinn had been hired to bury Markoff.

'Origin: Shanghai,' he said. 'Dammit.'

It was an easy mistake. Origin did not mean what port the ship had last sailed from, but what port the ship called home. In this case, Shanghai.

He tried to remember if he'd explained that part clearly to Nate, but he didn't know.

Orlando scrolled over, then stopped. There, in a column labeled PP for Previous Port, was the location the *Riegle 3* had stopped in just prior to sailing to Los Angeles.

Quinn could feel a tingling at the back of his neck. Singapore.

'What?' Orlando asked.

'That guy I met with at the congressman's office,' Quinn said. 'Dylan Ray. He said Guerrero was going to be in Singapore next week.'

'Why?'

Quinn closed his eyes, remembering the conversation. 'Some sort of information-gathering trip. Fact-finding, I think he called it. About security.'

'Is he going alone or with a congressional committee?'

'I don't know.'

'So you're convinced the congressman has something to do with Jenny's disappearance?'

Quinn frowned. 'He has to be involved. The same men who were with him in Georgetown were the ones I saw in Houston. And when I talked to him, I could tell he was hiding something. I can't put it all together yet, but either he's responsible for what's happened to her, or at least he knows.'

She nodded her head. 'I could . . . you know . . . I could look into it.'

'You've got other things to worry about. I'll have Nate do it.'

He tried to take his cell from her, but she

wouldn't let go. 'I need something to distract me,' she said, her eyes dead serious. 'I can . . . even poke around on that LP thing, too.'

They stared at each other for a moment, then he said, 'All right.'

'Good,' she said. She held out his phone. 'You can have it back now.'

He took it from her and slipped it into his pocket.

They started walking again, both quietly sipping their drinks and saying nothing. At the next intersection, they stopped at the corner, waiting for the light to change.

'Before I go digging too much, are you sure this is something you want to get involved in?' Orlando asked. 'I know Markoff was your friend. And I know you are trying to do the right thing by telling Jenny what happened. But this looks like it's getting deep. You could be getting yourself into something that's not worth the trouble.'

Quinn's jaw tensed. 'Wouldn't be the first time.'

'That's kind of why I'm bringing it up. Last time was a riot. You sure you can handle that kind of fun again?'

You can never fully repay someone who has saved your life.

'I can handle it.'

'This isn't your game. You can just walk away.'

'You know I can't do that,' he said with a finality he hoped would get her to change the subject.

'Because of Markoff?' she said.

194

Quinn took a deep breath. There were only a handful of people in the world Quinn would drop everything for, and do whatever he could to help them. Even posthumously. Markoff was number two on that list. Quinn was talking with number one.

'I don't really have a choice,' he said. 'I owe him.'

The look she gave him surprised Quinn. It was almost as if he had said anything else, she would have been disappointed.

'Then neither do I.'

'You know, you're right. This could be a lot of trouble. You don't need to help me out. I'll take care of it.'

She laughed. 'Like you could stop me now.'

'Orlando,' he said, 'this is personal for me. Not for you. You don't need to get involved.'

She laid a hand on his arm, and her eyes locked on his. 'Last winter, when everything seemed lost, when . . . Durrie had taken my son. That was personal, too. But you were there for me.'

There was more she didn't have to say. He knew she felt as he did. That whatever the problem either of them had, this is what they did for each other. They were there for the other one. Always.

The light changed and they began walking again.

When they reached the other side, he said, 'Thanks.'

She looked up at him for a moment, then

leaned against him. He put his arm around her shoulder.

'Maybe we should go back,' he said.

He could feel her shaking her head. 'Not yet.'

17

Durrie had been a son of a bitch. That was a fact no one would have ever argued. Even on his good days, it seemed like the simple act of waking pissed him off. The few friends he'd had learned early on to walk out on him if he was in one of his moods. But as Durrie's apprentice, Quinn didn't have that option. He'd had to stay until dismissed, acting the part of whipping boy more often than not.

For a long time, Quinn wasn't sure if the bad moods were real or just a put-on. In the end, he decided they were a little bit of both. It bothered him for the first year or so, but after that, he realized it didn't matter. He was there for one thing only: to learn how to be a cleaner. And while Quinn tuned out most of Durrie's philosophical and life-coaching bullshit, his old mentor had been excellent at teaching him the nuts and bolts of the job.

Perhaps the bastard's most valuable trait had been the ability to see the strengths of his student. He would use these as focal points, helping Quinn expand on his abilities. And as for any weaknesses, he'd push Quinn even harder on those, showing his apprentice ways to negate them.

In the strengths department, Quinn had many. Durrie had often called Quinn's acting abilities his strongest quality, but they both knew it was

Quinn's observational skills and attention to detail that were really what topped the list.

Quinn saw things others missed, picking out the small details that made jobs go that much smoother. It was this skill, though raw at first, that had brought Quinn to Durrie's attention in the first place. And it was this skill, honed sharp, that had carried him through his apprenticeship and allowed him to become a full-fledged cleaner.

'You've got to be aware of everything,' Durrie had said. 'It's what'll set you apart from the competition.'

'From you?' Quinn said, the hint of a smile on his face.

'Never from me,' Durrie said, all business. 'You'll never reach my level.'

Durrie may have actually believed that, but there was no way Quinn was going to let that be true. He worked harder than he ever had in his life, studying late and sleeping little. All in an attempt to be the best he could possibly be. To be able to perform, one day, at an even higher level than his mentor.

Proof that Quinn's training was paying off came during a job in Neuchâtel, Switzerland. It had been in an apartment above an antique shop. The building was within the walls of the old medieval city, in a crowded touristy area.

There were two bodies, a man and a woman. They were lying on their backs in bed; a duvet covered them from the waist down. The woman's eyes were closed, but the man's were open, cloudy and unfocused.

It was obvious they were dead, but there was no blood or visible wounds. Of course if they were still alive, Quinn and Durrie wouldn't be there. They'd have still been waiting for word back at their hotel.

'Piece it together for me,' Durrie said.

They were standing just inside the bedroom doorway, neither having ventured further into the room. Quinn scanned from left to right, taking in everything.

'This is her place, not his,' Quinn said.

'Good. Why?'

'The curtains. The perfumes on the dresser. The color of the walls. None of it says male. She lives alone.'

'Okay. What else?'

'I'd say he was more excited about being here than she was.'

Durrie said nothing, waiting.

'He was in a hurry to get his clothes off,' Quinn continued, pointing to the pile of men's clothes on the floor next to the bed. He then looked across the room at a chair near the entrance to the bathroom. The woman's things lay on the seat, neatly folded. 'She took her time.'

'How were they killed?'

'Suffocation,' Quinn said without a pause.

'You're sure?'

Quinn took a second look. There were no wounds he could see, and it was doubtful the duvet was covering anything life ending. Even if it had, he would have expected blood to seep through, staining the cover. There was no stain.

But most telling was the lack of the tangy smell of blood.

'Absolutely.'

'No struggle?'

'Drugged,' Quinn said. 'Something recreational, easily obtained. It would look like an accidental overdose if they'd been discovered before we could get here.'

'Then why suffocate them at all?' Durrie said.

'Whoever killed them didn't want to leave a calling card behind.' He was talking about a bullet, but he didn't need to tell Durrie that.

Quinn's mentor nodded to himself. 'All right, smart guy. Tell me how.'

Quinn scanned the room again, not to see if there was anything he missed, only to make sure his thoughts were in order. 'I'd say the assassin used that pillow over there.' He pointed to a pillow sitting on top of a blanket chest under the window. 'It's convenient, and it's out of place.'

'Really? Where's it supposed to be?'

'It goes on the bed when no one's in it. There're three others on the floor next to the man's clothes. The fourth one should be there, too. The killers were sloppy.'

'There was more than one?' Durrie asked.

'If there was only one, he would have shot them between the eyes, and not worried about the bullet. He wouldn't have been able to suffocate one without chancing that the other would put up a fight. So there had to be two. One for each victim.'

Durrie was silent for a moment as he stared into the room. Finally he turned to Quinn.

'Right,' he said, sounding as if he'd expected Quinn's answers. 'Let's clean it up.'

As it turned out, that was the last job Quinn went on as Durrie's apprentice. He had just turned twenty-six, completing his training in four years. And though they did work the next several projects together, it was as colleagues, not as teacher/student, Quinn getting a full cut of the fee.

It was ironic that one of the most valuable lessons Quinn learned was on the jobs after his apprenticeship was over. Two or three times, Durrie had been forced to take on substandard help to fill out their team. A sloppy mistake had lost one man his life, and on another job, one man's incompetence nearly got Quinn and Durrie arrested.

'It's the people you surround yourself with that really make you look either good or bad,' Durrie had said as they shared a drink after the near miss with the law. 'If the client finds out what happened today, I might not get work for months. Remember that, Johnny.'

Quinn did. That's why he loved working with Orlando. He had no doubt that when it came to her specialties of information and technology, there were few in the business smarter. But it wasn't just the areas she was trained in that made her valuable. She had a keen mind for all aspects of a job. Quinn often found himself running things by her to see what she thought. He trusted her implicitly. That wasn't something he could say about anyone else. Nate someday, maybe. But he still had a ways to go.

If a job required more personnel than the three of them, Quinn would hire only those he knew would do it right and could improvise when necessary. If he couldn't get the team he needed, he wouldn't take on the project. It was the reason he had reached the level he had — a level higher than Durrie had ever reached. His clients knew the high-quality work they would get from him. There would be no problems, no accidental body discoveries, no unwanted attention from local authorities.

And when things got messy like they had in Berlin the previous winter, and now seemed to be getting with Jenny, he and his core team could deal with that, too.

★　★　★

'She's up,' Nate said when Quinn returned to the hotel. 'I heard her in the shower a few minutes ago.'

Quinn raised an eyebrow.

'Hey,' Nate said. 'I didn't go in and check. I just heard the water, all right?'

'Whatever makes you happy, Nate.'

'Why don't you go check?' Nate said. 'I'm pretty sure she wouldn't mind.'

'What the hell does that mean?'

Nate smiled, then plopped back down on one of the beds. 'Never mind.'

Quinn pulled off his suit jacket and hung it in the closet. Whatever garbage Nate was pushing, Quinn didn't have time for it. He removed his

202

tie, shoes, and slacks, and changed into his street clothes.

Nate, a sucker for vintage shows, was watching TV. A rerun of *The Rockford Files*.

'Don't get too comfortable,' Quinn said. 'We're leaving soon.'

'How was the funeral?' Nate asked.

'I was too late.'

'Then where have you been all afternoon?'

Quinn stared at his apprentice. 'A, none of your business. But B, I said I was late to the funeral. I didn't say I didn't see Orlando.'

'Sorry,' Nate said. 'How is she?'

'Ask her yourself. We're meeting her in a little while.'

Quinn walked over to the door that separated the rooms. He knocked, but got no response. He pulled the door open and peeked in. No one was in the room, but the sound of water was coming from behind the closed bathroom door. He walked over and tapped on the door.

'Tasha?'

The water shut off.

'Is someone there?'

'It's me,' Quinn said. 'I need to talk to you when you're done.'

'Hold on,' she said.

He could hear her moving around, then the door opened just enough to reveal her head and her bare left shoulder.

'Sorry,' she said. 'I couldn't hear you.'

'When you're done, come into our room.'

'Okay,' she said. 'What's going on?'

'We just need to talk.'

'Give me ten minutes.'

Quinn nodded and started to turn away.

'Jonathan?' she said.

He stopped and looked back at her.

She smiled. 'Thanks.'

⋆ ⋆ ⋆

Back in his room, *The Rockford Files* was just ending.

'I hope wherever we're meeting her is someplace I can get something to eat,' Nate said. He hefted his suitcase onto the bed and unzipped it. From inside he removed two pistols. 'You want this now?' he asked, holding up the SIG.

'Yeah.'

Nate pulled out a suppressor from the bag, and handed it and the weapon over to Quinn.

'Extra mags?' Quinn asked.

'I could only get one.' He grabbed the SIG's magazine and tossed it over.

Quinn donned his modified windbreaker and stowed his gun. He then pulled out his computer and got onto the Internet. Within moments, he was on the Sandy Side Yacht Club message board. He found the original message from Jenny, with his posted reply. There was now a third message.

Quinn clicked it open. It was from Jenny. Code word: Los Angeles. The message was an eleven-digit number, followed by a time and day.

4:00 p.m. GMT Saturday

Quinn quickly calculated the time difference between Greenwich Mean and the west coast of North America: 9:00 a.m. Tomorrow. The eleven-digit number before it had to be a phone number. Quinn wrote everything down on a piece of hotel stationery, then folded it and put it in his pocket.

As he was shutting down his computer, Tasha came through the door. She was dressed in the same sweatpants and T-shirt they'd picked up for her the night before. Her hair, still damp from the shower, was pulled back in a ponytail.

'Good sleep?' Nate asked.

'Fine,' she said. She looked at Quinn. 'What did you want to talk about?'

'I've arranged for a place where you can stay,' Quinn said. Orlando had used one of her local contacts to find an out-of-the-way location for Tasha to lie low. It was in the mountains on the way to Lake Tahoe to the east, someplace no one would ever think to look.

'What?' Tasha asked, surprised.

'They won't be able to find you. It'll be safe.' Quinn walked over to the closet. From the inside pocket of the suit he'd been wearing earlier, he removed a map, a house key, and a valet ticket.

'I thought I was staying . . . with you. Help you find Jenny.'

He walked over to her. 'There's a car downstairs,' he said, handing her the ticket, then the map and key. 'The route is traced out on here. You won't have any problems. It's a safe house. Stocked with food. You won't have to leave. It'll only be you.'

She looked at him for several seconds, her brow furrowed like she didn't completely understand. 'Why can't I stay?'

'It's out of the question.'

She looked at Quinn, then Nate, then at the front door, then back again. She seemed almost panicked. 'I'm staying,' she said. 'You need me.'

'You'll get in the way and get one of us killed.'

'I won't!'

'This is not a negotiation,' he said. 'You're leaving. We'll drive you there ourselves if we have to.'

She stared at him, her eyes pleading with him to reconsider. But when he said nothing, the desperation on her face began to wane.

'How . . . how long?'

Quinn sighed inwardly, relieved. 'A couple weeks would be best. It should be okay by then.'

'A couple of *weeks*?' She had a pained look on her face again, only this time it seemed more for show than anything else. She knew she'd already lost the battle. Quinn could see that, too.

'You know what these people can do. So, yeah. Two weeks.'

Her gaze moved from his face to a point on the floor near his feet. He let her absorb the new reality for a moment, then said, 'It's time to go.'

'What about Jenny?' she asked, obviously stalling.

'I'll find her.' He paused, then added, 'I'm already in contact with her.'

Her eyes grew wide. 'You've talked to her? You know where she is?'

'You don't have to worry about her anymore.

Go lay low. This will all be over soon.'

'But . . . I — '

'This isn't a choice,' Quinn said. 'Get your purse and let's go.'

She hesitated, looking like she wanted to push back one more time, but after a few seconds, she turned and walked back into the bedroom.

Nate had sat unmoving through the entire conversation, his eyes glued to a rerun of *Three's Company*. As soon as Tasha left the room, he held up the remote and changed the channel.

'Don't get comfortable,' Quinn said.

'Oh, I'm not comfortable,' Nate told him. 'You could have given me a heads-up you were going to do that.'

'I'm going to take her down to the car. Wait ten minutes, then meet me in the lobby.'

As soon as he finished speaking, Tasha came back into the room.

'How will I get ahold of you if there's a problem?'

'There's not going to be a problem,' Quinn said.

'How do you know that?'

Quinn hesitated, then walked over to the desk and tore a corner off one of the remaining pieces of stationery. On it he wrote one of his many dummy phone numbers. Calls to any of the numbers would be rerouted to his cell phone.

'Here,' he said, handing the paper to her. 'But only if you have no choice.'

She put the scrap into her purse.

'Wait,' she said. 'I'll give you mine, too.'

She walked over to the desk and ripped off

207

another strip of paper. She wrote something on it and handed it to Quinn.

'Promise me you'll call me every few days to let me know what's going on,' she said.

'I can't do that,' he said.

Her lips pressed together for a moment, and her eyes narrowed. 'All right. Then here's the deal. If I don't hear from you every . . . seventy-two hours, I'll start looking for her again,' she said. 'That *I* promise you.'

Quinn tensed, but he sensed this was not an argument she would give up on. 'Fine,' he said as he jammed the paper into his pocket. 'Let's go.'

He headed for the front door.

'Hold on,' she said. 'I want to hear you promise me.'

He looked back at her, annoyed.

'Well?'

'I promise,' he said.

18

Quinn and Nate took a cab to an Italian restaurant a few miles away, in Richmond. There was better Italian food in North Beach, but the quality of the meal wasn't as important as the privacy of the location. And there was no place better for a meeting than a restaurant that served mediocre food.

Richmond was a mix of the new and the old. Family businesses that had been in the neighborhood for years, next to boarded-up buildings awaiting renewal. On some blocks, the gentrification had already begun. But that wasn't true for the block Angie's Fine Italian Restaurante was located on. It was part of a 1970s-era strip mall. Its neighbors were an insurance broker to the left and a defunct tanning salon to the right. The sign for Easy Tan was still mounted above the front window, but the space itself was empty.

The front window of Angie's was unadorned except for a layer of grunge that had gathered on the inside over years of disinterest, blurring the view. The only thing that could be made out was the neon 'Open' sign, but even that had a hazy, ethereal cast to it.

As Quinn opened the front door, they were assaulted by the odor of garlic and tomato sauce — but cheap, like out of a can.

'I think I lost my appetite,' Nate said.

The promise of a less than stellar experience conveyed by the exterior continued inside. Almost all expense had been spared on the décor. A row of high-backed booths lined the walls on both sides, with an additional set running down the center of the room. The seats and backrests appeared to be covered in brown vinyl that was no doubt some amateur designer's idea of faux leather.

The main dining room was empty. No customers. No employees.

Quinn pointed to a booth halfway down the left side. They walked over and sat, Quinn taking the side with the view of the front door.

Almost a full minute passed before they heard footsteps approaching from the back of the restaurant. Soon a woman wearing a flower pattern dress and a red apron was standing at the end of their table. She was at least in her mid-sixties, Quinn guessed. And the smile she wore looked like it came more from habit than from pleasure.

'Thought I heard someone come in,' she said. 'Did you get menus?'

'No,' Nate said.

'Two seconds,' the woman said.

She walked over to a small counter next to the front door and picked up two menus off a large stack.

Once she had handed them out, she asked, 'Can I get you something to drink first?'

'You have Moretti?' Quinn asked.

'Should have a few bottles left.'

'Same for me,' Nate said.

'I'll be right back.' She left the way she had come.

Quinn moved his menu to the side without even looking at it.

'I guess I could get the spaghetti Bolognese,' Nate said, studying his menu. 'They can't mess that up too much, can they?'

The sound of the traffic outside increased briefly as the front door opened. Quinn shot a glance over, then stood a moment later when Orlando reached the table. Nate jumped up as soon as he realized who it was and gave her a hug.

'I'm sorry about your aunt,' he said.

'Thank you,' she said.

'I wish I could have been there this afternoon, but I was put on babysitting duty.'

'It's okay. Don't worry about it.' She looked at Quinn. 'You send her off?'

'All done.'

'Any problems?'

'No.'

Quinn moved out of the way so she could sit on his side of the booth.

'You're going to make me sit on the inside?' she asked.

'Yes, I am,' Quinn said.

She rolled her eyes, then slipped in.

Before anyone could say anything else, the waitress returned. She was holding a tray with the beers. Only one was a bottle of Moretti. The other was a Red Stripe.

'Three of you now, huh?' the waitress said. 'Only had the one Moretti.'

Quinn reached up, grabbed the Red Stripe,

then handed it to Nate.

'So I guess this is yours,' she said, setting the Moretti in front of Quinn. She turned to Orlando. 'Something for you, hon?'

'Pellegrino?' Orlando said.

'The only water I got comes with or without ice,' the woman said.

'I'll take tea,' Orlando said. 'Hot.'

The waitress lost a little bit of her fake smile as she sighed. 'It'll be a minute.'

'Take your time,' Orlando said.

When they were alone again, Quinn said, 'I got a response.'

'From the message board?' Orlando asked.

'Yes.'

'Wait a minute,' Nate said. 'I — '

'Genuine?' Orlando said, ignoring Nate.

'Seems to be. The code word was Los Angeles. When I worked it out, this is what I got.' Quinn pulled the piece of paper he'd written the message on and handed it to Orlando — the series of numbers followed by '4:00 p.m. GMT Saturday.'

'Excuse me,' Nate said. 'What the hell are you talking about?'

'What are these numbers at the top?' Orlando asked. 'A phone number?'

Quinn nodded. 'That would be my guess.'

She set the paper on the table and pointed at the first few numbers. 'Brazil?'

Quinn shook his head. He had tried the number on the ride over just to check it. 'I thought so at first, but the number doesn't work.'

'Maybe you screwed up one of the digits.'

'Thanks for the confidence.' Quinn turned the paper around. 'Anyone have a pen?'

Orlando didn't, but Nate pulled one out of his pocket and held it out. 'I'll let you use this if you tell me what's going on.'

Quinn snatched the pen from him, then set to work on the numbers. He applied the Los Angeles code — eleven digits, including the space — to the number Jenny had sent him one more time. This time, instead of skipping words, he increased each digit by eleven, starting again at zero once he reached the number nine.

'She double-encoded it,' Orlando said.

As soon as he finished, he turned the paper around so Orlando could see it.

'Six-six-eight,' she said. 'Bangkok cell phone.'

'Yes,' Quinn said.

'Hold on,' Nate said. 'Can one of you please — '

This time Nate cut himself off as the waitress reappeared. When she reached their table, she set an empty cup on the table in front of Orlando and placed a small teapot next to it.

She looked around the table. 'You all going to order now?'

'Not yet,' Quinn said.

'You are going to eat, aren't you?' she asked.

'Maybe,' Quinn told her. 'We're not sure yet.'

This time the woman's smile vanished completely. She turned without another word and headed back to the kitchen.

Nate leaned forward. 'What message are you talking about?'

Quinn finally looked at his apprentice. 'Jenny contacted me.'

'What?' Nate said, surprised.

Quinn gave him a quick description of how he'd used the message board to contact her, and of how he had just received her response.

'So she wants you to call tomorrow afternoon?' Nate said.

'GMT,' Orlando said.

'Right,' Nate said. He paused a moment. 'So, nine in the morning for us.'

'Yes,' Quinn said.

'That's great,' Nate said, a smile on his face. 'Make sure she's all right, tell her about Markoff, then you're all done.'

'Do you really think she's going to be all right?' Orlando asked. 'Someone is obviously after her. Are you saying we should just let her hang out there on her own?'

The smile slipped from Nate's face. 'No,' he said. 'Not really. I was just . . . just being a little hopeful.'

Quinn looked over at Orlando. 'I want to record the call and see if we can trace it. You have what you need to do that?'

'Yes,' she said. 'I have something that will work.'

'Then come over to the hotel around seven-thirty,' he said. 'That should give you enough time to set up, right?'

As Orlando was about to answer, the front door to the restaurant opened again. Moving only his eyes, Quinn glanced at the new arrival. A man, six feet tall, in shape, no more than thirty-five years old, with hair trimmed short and neat. He wore a dark suit that looked just a little too nice for this part of town.

'Keep your eyes open. I'm going to check him out,' Quinn whispered. Maybe this guy was a customer, but there was no sense in taking a chance.

As he started to rise, Orlando put a hand on his thigh. 'I'm the unknown,' she said. 'I'll do it.'

It was the right move. If the man was looking for anyone, it would be Quinn. He wouldn't recognize Orlando. The solution didn't make Quinn happy, but he nodded.

'I'm going out for a smoke,' Orlando said just loud enough to be heard across the room. 'Any of you want to join me?'

Reluctantly Quinn slid out of the booth so she could get up.

'Careful,' he whispered to her as she passed him.

Her quick smile told him to shut up.

He gingerly slipped his gun out from inside his jacket and placed it on his lap. From the corner of his eye, he watched the new arrival take several steps into the restaurant. The man picked up a menu off the counter and opened it. Unfortunately, he didn't appear to have any interest in what was written inside. Instead, he used the menu as a prop so that he could scan the room unobserved. At least, Quinn thought, that's what the guy believed.

Orlando worked her way around the center aisle of the booths, then headed toward the front door. She was playing it cool, her focus on the

215

exit, never on the man. The new arrival watched her for a moment, then moved his attention back to the restaurant, scanning the empty booths.

A slight alteration in Orlando's path put the man between her and the door. Just before she reached him, his gaze fell on Quinn and Nate. His eyes started to narrow, and a hand moved up a few inches toward the opening in his coat.

'Excuse me,' Orlando said.

'Huh?' the man said, glancing down at her. 'Oh. Sorry.'

He moved to the side.

'Thanks,' she said, then slammed the palm of her hand into the bottom of his chin.

19

The man went down hard.

Orlando drove a knee into his chest, then hit him again in his face. He twisted violently, throwing her onto the floor near the front door.

Quinn was already out of the booth, racing toward them, his gun ready. But he had no clear shot.

The man slipped his hand under his jacket and pulled out a pistol. As he brought it around to aim at Orlando, Quinn did the only thing he could do. He dove forward, pushing the man's arm back against the floor. There was a loud bang as the gun discharged, the bullet flying harmlessly into the counter a few feet away.

Orlando tried to hold him down again, but the man twisted his body, throwing her off balance and into Quinn. The jolt sent Quinn's SIG clattering to the floor, where it slid under a nearby table.

'What's going on?' It was the waitress calling out from the back of the restaurant. 'Stop it! Stop it! I'm calling the police!'

Quinn shot a glance back at Nate. His apprentice had climbed out of the booth and was holding his Glock, but he seemed torn between whether to help Quinn and Orlando or go after the waitress.

'Stop her!' Quinn yelled at him.

The words broke Nate's indecision. He ran

through the restaurant toward the kitchen.

The man tried to bring the barrel of his gun around to get a line on Quinn, but he'd only moved it a few inches when his body suddenly jerked. Orlando had pushed herself to her feet and was kicking him hard in the kidney.

Another kick. Another jerk. All Quinn could do was hold on so that their would-be attacker couldn't put up any defense. The fourth time she brought her foot into the man's back, it wasn't just his torso that moved, his trigger finger also twitched. The gun went off with a deafening roar only inches from Quinn's ear. He could feel the heat radiating off the barrel.

Orlando reached down and slammed her fist into the man's face. Once, twice. By the third punch, he had gone slack.

Finally able to move again, Quinn ripped the gun from the man's fingers, turning the barrel on its previous owner, then pushed himself up off the floor, watching for any sign of movement. Orlando held a couple of fingers against the man's neck.

'Son of a bitch,' she said. 'He's still alive.'

Quinn knelt down and made a quick visual survey of the man.

He tapped Orlando on the shoulder. As she looked up, he put a finger to his mouth, then pointed to the man's collar. On the knot of the man's dark blue tie was a small disk. It was black and blended in with the fabric.

A transmitter.

Quinn then motioned to a bulge under the collar just below the man's left ear. He carefully moved it so he could slip a couple fingers underneath. When he pulled them back out, he was holding a skin-tone earpiece attached to a wire leading beneath the man's shirt.

He looked at Orlando. Her eyes were hard, all business.

Quinn pointed toward the rear of the restaurant. She nodded, then immediately got up and headed in the same direction Nate had gone moments before.

Quinn searched the man's body, but the guy had nothing on him. No ID. No cash. No keys. His pockets were empty, not even a scrap of paper.

Who the hell are you? Quinn asked silently.

He scooted across the floor and retrieved his SIG. Carefully he rose into a crouch, then began running toward the kitchen, his back bent low.

Before he had even gone five feet, the glass covering the front door shattered. As he ducked back to the floor, he heard something crash into the wall not far from the booth he had shared with the others. Bullets.

Apparently, the unconscious man had friends, and they seemed to be armed and pissed.

Quinn turned his head, listening. There were footsteps running toward the restaurant. Two, maybe three people.

He pushed himself back to his feet and began sprinting. The kitchen door was still twenty feet away. He wasn't going to make it in time.

Thup-thup. Bullets passing through a suppressor. Almost simultaneously, Quinn could feel the air change as the projectiles passed by only

219

inches from him. He dove forward, pushing the swinging door open as another bullet smashed into the doorframe.

He rolled forward, then shoved the door closed with his feet. He took two quick breaths, then jumped back on his feet and glanced around.

The kitchen was about half the size of the dining area. Along one wall were two ovens, a large blackened grill, and several burners. On the wall opposite was a prep table, much of it covered by boxes and bags of ingredients. It wasn't the cleanest kitchen Quinn had ever seen, not even close.

Orlando and Nate were at the far end of the room, near the back door. The waitress and an older man — Quinn guessed perhaps the cook — were huddled on the floor under the prep table.

Quinn moved over to them.

'Do you have a pantry or a restroom or something?' he asked. 'Someplace you can hide in?'

'What's going on?' the man asked.

Quinn looked at the waitress, repeating his question without saying a word.

'Yes,' she said. She pointed toward a door just beyond the grill.

'Get in there now. After it gets quiet, wait at least thirty minutes, then come out.'

They didn't move.

'Now,' Quinn ordered.

The woman nodded and pulled the man up with her. Within moments, they had disappeared into a small storage closet.

Quinn joined the others at the back door. 'Everyone okay?' he asked.

Nods all around.

Quinn handed the weapon he'd acquired from the man out front to Orlando. Now they were all armed.

'No suppressor on that,' he told her. 'So be judicious.' He looked at the back door. 'This and the front are the only exits?'

'One-story building, shops on each side,' Orlando said. 'So just the two as far as I've seen.'

Suddenly they heard someone running through the dining room.

'Keep an eye on this,' Quinn said to Nate, pointing at the back door.

He didn't have to tell Orlando anything. She followed him without hesitation.

'How many do you think?' she whispered as they neared the front of the kitchen.

'Counting your friend on the floor out there, three or four total,' he said. More than that would have drawn too much attention.

She nodded in agreement.

Quinn motioned for her to take cover behind the central prep table, then he tucked himself in next to a storage cabinet. From beyond the door, he could hear breathing. Not labored, but deep nonetheless.

Quinn gripped his gun in both hands, then concentrated all his attention on the people beyond the door.

A footstep, so light it was almost nothing. Then two steps, simultaneous. Two people.

The door inched open, its old hinges emitting a low creak.

Quinn waited, hidden from view by the cabinet. He could hear two people quietly enter the kitchen. The door began to close behind them.

Quinn took a deep breath.

'Drop them,' he said as he pushed himself out, gun leveled at the new arrivals. Men, dressed much like their friend had been.

The man nearest the entrance moved the hand holding a gun quickly toward Quinn, while his partner ran to his left. Quinn fired first, catching the man square in the chest. He then turned his SIG toward the partner. But the man had crouched out of sight behind the far end of the prep table.

'Don't be stupid,' Quinn said. 'Put down the gun and step out.'

Quinn caught a glimpse of the barrel of a gun turning toward him. He dove to the floor just as the man's weapon went off.

'Throw it down. Now!' the man said.

He stood up, his gun pointed at Quinn. That was unfortunate for him. He was paying so much attention to Quinn, he didn't see the heavy skillet in Orlando's hand rushing toward his head.

The pan connected solidly against his temple, staggering him.

As Quinn jumped up, the man tried to raise his gun. This time when the skillet connected with his skull, he dropped to the floor.

'You could have just shot him,' Quinn whispered to her.

'You said to be judicious.'

Quinn smirked. 'Check him.'

While she bent over the man, Quinn moved to the dining area door. The two men in the kitchen and the one on the floor near the front entrance, that was three. If there was a fourth person on the team, he would most likely be in back, watching the alley. But best not to take any chances.

Quinn eased into the dining room, keeping low. He did a quick sweep, but with the exception of unconscious man number one, the room was still empty. It wouldn't be for long, though. Quinn could hear the wailing of at least two approaching police cars. They were still several blocks away, but they would be here soon.

He ran back into the kitchen.

'We're going out the back,' he said as he moved quickly through the room to the rear door.

Orlando was already there, standing next to Nate.

'What if there's someone else out there?' Nate said.

Quinn moved a finger to his mouth, quieting his apprentice. The sirens from the police cars were very near now. Any moment they would be entering the parking lot out front.

'Cover me,' he said to Orlando.

She nodded. Quinn counted to five, then pulled the door open.

Nothing happened.

Holding his gun in front of him, he walked

223

quickly into the alley and did a 360 sweep. Again, nothing. If there had been another one of the team waiting to stop their escape, the sirens must have scared him off.

'Let's go,' Quinn said.

★   ★   ★

At the Marriott, Quinn and Orlando kept watch while Nate went up to the room and quickly gathered their things. After that, they went to Aunt Jay's house. By then, it was almost 11 p.m.

'There're two bedrooms upstairs, you guys can take those,' Orlando said as they entered the living room.

'What about you?' Nate asked.

'I've been using the guest bedroom down here.'

That was all Nate needed. He grabbed his bag and headed up the stairs.

'Do you have any of that lemonade left?' Quinn asked.

'I can do better than that,' she said.

She led him into the kitchen and opened the refrigerator. There was a six-pack of Kirin beer sitting on the top shelf.

'Picked it up after everyone left this afternoon,' she said. 'Bottle opener's in the drawer over there.'

Quinn retrieved it while she pulled out two bottles.

'Come on,' she said.

She headed toward the back door, opened it, and stepped outside. Quinn followed.

The door let out onto a short flight of steps that led down to a tiny backyard, perhaps twenty feet wide by fifteen deep. They descended the steps, and Orlando sat in one of two ratty-looking lawn chairs in the middle of the yard.

'Are you sure those things won't break?' Quinn asked as he stepped onto the grass.

'Not the one I'm in,' she said.

He handed Orlando the bottle opener, then carefully lowered his weight into the empty chair, ready to jump up if it seemed like it was about to collapse. The chair held.

Orlando popped off the caps, then handed him one of the bottles.

'Skoal,' he said, holding out his bottle.

She smiled, then tapped her bottle against his. Without another word, they both took deep drinks.

'They must have figured out who I was, and followed me out here from D.C.,' Quinn said.

'Then what?' Orlando asked. 'Tracked you down at the Marriott, then followed you to the restaurant?'

He shrugged. 'How else?'

She didn't look convinced, but it was the only thing that made sense.

'If that's true, they could have followed you here earlier today,' she said.

He shook his head. 'I don't think so. Someone would have been waiting here for us if they had.'

She took another sip of her beer. 'This is the first time they've actively come after you, right?

225

Until now, they've only been reacting to your presence.'

She was right. At the house in Houston, at the gallery in D.C., it had been Quinn who'd made the initial contact.

'They must think I know something,' he said. 'Probably something to do with whatever it is they've been looking for.'

'Or maybe they just think you know where Jenny is.'

'That could be it, too.'

They were silent for a few minutes.

'So what now?' she asked.

He took another drink, then said, 'We call Jenny in the morning.'

'And then?'

This time his pause was even longer. Finally, instead of saying anything, he merely shrugged his shoulders. *And then I'll do whatever Jenny needs me to do*, he thought, but didn't say.

They sat in silence for another ten minutes finishing their beers, then Orlando pushed herself up and stepped over to him. Moving in close, she kissed him on the cheek.

'What's that for?' he asked.

'For you.'

He looked at her, not sure what she meant.

She smiled, then said, 'You're being a good friend. Markoff would appreciate it. You just need to relax a little. Don't let this one wind you up.'

The hand she had set on his shoulder lifted as she turned and walked back up to the house.

He knew she was right. The whole thing was making him tense.

But he also knew what Markoff had told him so many years before was right, too. What Quinn did wasn't relaxing. It was waiting. And that was exactly what he was still doing.

Waiting.

For Jenny.

For justice for Markoff.

And though he didn't want to admit it, for Orlando.

20

Quinn rose before dawn. He dressed quietly, then slipped out of the house and through the backyard. For the next two hours, he checked the streets within a four-block radius of Aunt Jay's house, making sure that no one was lying in wait. He kept a low profile, staying in the shadows and pausing for long periods just to watch. By seven-thirty, he was as sure as he ever was going to be that the house wasn't being watched.

He stopped at the same market he and Orlando had gone to the day before and picked up some coffees and several muffins. When he returned, he found Orlando in the kitchen.

'Read my mind,' she said as he handed her a cup of coffee. 'Aunt Jay only kept instant. I forgot to go out and get anything else.'

Quinn set the bag of muffins on the counter. When he turned back, he noticed Orlando's eyes growing moist.

'I'm sorry,' he said. 'I should have never dragged you into this. You've got your own things to deal with. Nate and I will get out of here. Let you do what you have to do.'

She scowled at him. 'Like I really want to sit here and sulk with all my aunt's in-laws. You will *not* do that to me.'

'I'm sure you have a lot to take care of.'

'What do you think I've been doing? Just

sitting around watching her die?'

Quinn was silent for a moment. 'But we're in your way here.'

'Are you *not* hearing me?' she asked. 'Just drop it. All right?'

'Okay,' Quinn said. He held up his hands and smiled. 'I get the message.'

'Good,' she said. She walked over and grabbed a blueberry muffin out of the bag. 'Now stay out of my way while I get things ready.'

Nate strolled in as she was finishing up. Quinn glanced at his watch. It was 8:55.

'Thanks for joining us,' he said.

'Is that coffee?' Nate asked.

'It's probably a little cold,' Orlando said.

'No problem. I'm good with cold coffee.' He walked over to the counter. 'Oh. Muffins, too. Nice.' He took his coffee and a muffin over to the kitchen table. 'It's all right if I sit here, right?'

On the table were Quinn's cell phone, Orlando's laptop, and a set of Bose speakers.

Orlando pointed at the chair on the opposite side of the table from the computer. 'You can sit there,' she said. 'Just don't spill anything.'

He gave her a do-I-look-like-an-idiot look, then sat down.

Jenny's number was already entered on Quinn's phone. He only needed to push Send. Once a connection was made, both sides of the conversation would be played through the speakers while it was being recorded on the computer.

The computer also had another, even more important task. Using a secure, satellite Internet

229

connection, Orlando had accessed a program that could pinpoint the location of any cell phone in the world once the phone was activated.

The software was a copy of something created by a joint venture between Japan's Public Security Intelligence Agency and the NSA in America. There were others she could have used, but Quinn knew she considered this one the best. She had hidden it on a server owned by NHK TV in Tokyo.

Orlando took her place in front of the computer, while Quinn chose to stand.

'Okay,' he said. 'It's time.'

He picked up the phone and punched the Send button.

Through both the phone at his ear and the speakers attached to the computer, he could hear the call begin to ring.

Orlando and Nate watched him, waiting.

Ten seconds passed. Then twenty. Then a half a minute.

'That's a long ring,' Nate said. 'Shouldn't there be voice mail?'

'Doesn't sound like it,' Orlando said.

'Maybe she's not there,' Nate said.

Quinn continued to let it ring, giving Jenny as much time to answer as possible.

Twenty seconds later, he heard a click as someone answered. 'Yes?' the voice said.

'Jenny, it's Quinn,' he said.

Silence.

'Jenny?'

Still nothing. He looked at the phone to make

230

sure the call hadn't been disconnected.

'Are you there? Please. It's Quinn.'

'I don't believe you,' she said, her voice a near whisper.

'You got my message. You know it's me.'

'You're just trying to trick me. You're not Quinn. Quinn has no reason to get ahold of me.'

Quinn closed his eyes, wishing she were right. 'San Diego,' he said. 'A year ago. Markoff rented a sailboat. We spent a lot of time at the Del Coronado. I took a picture of you and Markoff on the beach, only it was more of you than of him.'

He could hear her suck in a breath. 'No. Someone told you all that,' she said, not sounding convinced.

'I helped him pick out a necklace for you,' Quinn said. 'It was in La Jolla. A gold disk with the heart cut out of the center. You said you loved it. He said he knew you probably would rather have a diamond, but you told him no, it was perfect.'

Dead silence, then, 'Quinn?'

'Yes.'

'Wha . . . why are . . . '

'Tell me you're all right,' Quinn said.

'I don't understand. Why are you trying to find me?'

'I know you're in danger. I want to help.'

A pause. 'How? How do you know?'

'Jenny, I think — '

'Steven? Where's Steven?'

He realized he couldn't hide the truth from her. 'He's . . . dead.'

231

Her breathing became shallow, ragged.

'Forget about me,' she said. Then the phone went dead.

Quinn hit Redial, but was greeted with a prerecorded message in Thai telling him the subscriber was currently out of range. There was no option to leave a voice message. He tried two more times with the same result, then set the phone back down on the table.

'Did you get anything?' he asked Orlando.

'Give me a minute,' Orlando said.

Quinn leaned over and looked at the laptop's screen.

Orlando was scrolling through a list of data. It was all numbers and letters, no coherent words. Without warning, she stopped the scroll, and used the cursor to highlight a row of alphanumeric text. She copied it, then minimized the window, making it disappear. Underneath was a second window, all black with the exception of two empty white boxes stacked in the center.

Orlando clicked on the upper box, activating it. Inside, she pasted the information she'd copied, deleting the last five characters. Those she put in the bottom box, then hit Enter.

For a moment, the entire screen went full black.

'Maybe it didn't work,' Nate said. He'd come around the table and was leaning in over Quinn's shoulder.

After several more seconds, the black screen was replaced by a dark gray background. Superimposed over the background was a series of bright yellow lines depicting Asia from a point south of Indonesia to a point north of Mongolia. East and west, it took in Japan, all of China, and most of India. The only other color on the screen was a tiny blue pinprick in the upper right quadrant.

Quinn smiled. 'You got it.'

'Maybe,' Orlando said, not looking happy.

She worked the keys for a moment, blowing up the area around the blue dot. As the image zoomed in, more lines appeared, denoting country borders, then major roads and cities.

The dot was in northeast China.

'Beijing?' Nate asked.

Quinn shook his head. 'Farther north.'

'It's in Shenyang,' Orlando told them.

'You don't sound convinced,' Quinn said.

She frowned but said nothing. The image on the screen continued to zoom in, getting closer and closer to street level. Suddenly the blue dot started flashing yellow.

'Son of a bitch,' Orlando said.

Quinn tensed.

'What?' Nate asked.

Orlando opened a smaller window on the screen and began rapidly scrolling through a list of data.

'What is it?' Nate asked again.

'False signal,' Quinn said. Jenny's phone call had been rerouted to look like she'd been calling from northern China.

'You think you can pin it down?' Quinn asked Orlando.

'I'll get it. Just give me a minute.' Though she

sounded annoyed, Quinn could tell she actually was enjoying the challenge.

'How did she fake her location?' Nate asked. 'She's not a pro.'

'Markoff,' Quinn said. 'He must have given her one of his phones and instructions on how to remain hidden. It's something he would have done.'

After two more bogus locations, Orlando said, 'Got it.'

'Where?' Quinn asked.

On the screen was the outline of a peninsula caught between the South China Sea and the Strait of Malacca. On the left side of the peninsula, not quite on the coast, was the shape of a city. The blue dot was within the city limits.

'Kuala Lumpur,' Quinn said. 'You're sure this time?'

Orlando nodded. 'I'm sure.' She continued the zoom, moving in as far as she could. 'Somewhere near the towers.'

She was referring to the Petronas Towers, at one time the tallest buildings in the world, but moving further down the list every few years.

'Is that as close as you can get?' Nate asked.

Orlando looked up at him, annoyed. 'No, not at all. I could go in a lot closer. It's just a lot more fun if we have to guess exactly where she is.'

'Right,' Nate said. 'That's as close as you can get. I was just checking.'

'I'll put a tracer on the number,' Orlando said to Quinn. 'Since we know basically the part of the world she's in, it'll be easier. Next time she turns on her phone, we'll have a record of it.'

'Real time?' Quinn asked.

'Close. But not as if we were tracking her on the ground.'

As Orlando began typing on her keyboard, Quinn's eyes remained on the screen. They weren't focused on the current image; instead, they were remembering an earlier screen, the one Orlando had entered the data on. There was something there that felt familiar.

He stretched his arms back, then rolled his head trying to clear his mind. It wasn't until he was walking toward the bathroom that it came to him.

The numbers on the entry screen. He remembered now why they seemed familiar.

He rushed back to the kitchen. Orlando was the only one there.

'Where's Nate?' Quinn asked.

Orlando looked up. 'He went outside.'

Quinn ran over to the rear door and pulled it open. Nate was sitting on the back steps, holding his cup of cold coffee. He looked up as Quinn stuck his head out.

'What?' Nate asked.

★   ★   ★

Two minutes later, they were gathered in the kitchen again. Nate had retrieved a piece of paper from his bag upstairs and had given it to Quinn. Quinn compared it to the copy he had in his wallet, just to be sure he hadn't gotten anything wrong.

Written on each piece was the same line of numbers and letters. It was the sequence that had been on the wall of the shipping container Markoff had died in.

45kL09Q8NTY63779V IP

To Quinn, they looked very much like the line of data Orlando had used to locate Jenny's cell phone.

'Punch this in,' Quinn said.

He handed the original to Orlando. She looked at it, then looked back up at him.

'Is this . . . ?'

'Yes.'

'I'll be damned,' she said. 'It's a phone identity module.'

'SIM card?' Nate asked.

'Something like that.'

She turned back to her computer and brought up the black screen with the two empty data boxes. She filled the first box, then typed the remaining characters into the second one. But this time, instead of having only five digits for the second box, there were nine.

'These last two,' she said. 'That's where you got the 'LP' from, isn't it?'

'Yes. I showed the paper to Blackmoore, and that's the only thing that meant anything to him.'

'Well, I can officially tell you they have nothing to do with the other numbers,' she said. 'They're extraneous.'

'You're sure?' Quinn asked.

'Absolutely.'

So whatever the 'LP' meant, the two letters were a message unto themselves.

'You know,' Orlando said, holding up the piece of paper, 'if you'd shown me this earlier, I could have told you what it was.'

Nate snorted. 'I believe I made that very suggestion.'

'Just show me where it points,' Quinn said.

Orlando hit Enter. Again the screen went all black for a moment. When the map appeared, it was a familiar one. Asia again.

'The good news is the chip is still active,' Orlando said.

She started zooming in before Quinn saw where the blue dot was. Once more, the image closed in on the Malay Peninsula jutting south from Thailand. Only this time, it bypassed Kuala Lumpur, going further south down the peninsula before stopping above an island off the tip.

'How about that?' Quinn said. 'Singapore.'

Orlando continued letting the map zoom in. Yellow lines started to outline the bay, then the Singapore River. Quinn began identifying the different quays: Boat, Clarke, Robertson. The map continued to zoom in, going further in than it had when tracking the cell phone. Streets began appearing, then the outlines of buildings.

When the program could get no closer, the zoom stopped. There in the center of the screen was a single building on the edge of the river. And in the center of the building, the blue dot — now as big as a bottle cap — pulsed on and off.

21

'I'm getting out,' Markoff said.

'Right,' Quinn told him.

They were on a twenty-one-foot Luger sailboat on Mission Bay in California. Markoff had rented the sloop for the entire week, but this had been the first day they'd taken it out.

They were sitting near the stern, Markoff steering the boat while Quinn sat nearby, drinking a rum and Coke from a plastic cup.

'I mean it,' Markoff said. 'Not everything. But out of the field. They've offered me a desk job.'

Quinn was having a hard time imagining Markoff stuck in some office, going to policy meetings and shuffling paperwork all day.

He looked toward the opening that led down into the small galley where Jenny was changing into her swimsuit. 'It's her, isn't it?' he asked.

Markoff smiled. 'What do you think?'

'I think you've crossed over into a world I'm not familiar with,' Quinn said, then took a drink.

'It's not as bad as it sounds. You might want to try it someday.'

'Doubtful.'

They both laughed.

'What's so funny?' Jenny stood on the steps leading out of the galley. She was wearing a white one-piece swimsuit that showed every curve and contrasted nicely with her brown skin. On her head was a large floppy hat, also white.

The conversation turned to the weather, to the ocean, to the beautiful day. Quinn watched as his friend interacted with Jenny. There was a change in Markoff, a mellowing. It surprised Quinn, and though he didn't want to admit it, it also made him a bit jealous. For the afternoon, he wanted what they had.

But he knew that was one thing that would never happen.

★   ★   ★

'11 a.m.,' Peter said.

'And he was okay with the location?' Quinn asked. He was sitting on one of the benches in Union Square, near the Financial District in San Francisco. Nate was standing nearby, keeping an eye on the morning crowd.

'He wasn't happy, but he'll be there.'

'What did you tell him?'

'That I had a deep cover guy who needed his help.'

'A lie,' Quinn said, acting impressed. 'You're not afraid of ruining your name?'

'Fuck him. Albina's a jackass. What do I care what he thinks?'

'He's got a lot of contacts.'

'So do I.'

★   ★   ★

Quinn's instructions had been precise. Albina was to get on the first outbound MUNI 'N Judah' train arriving at the Embarcadero station

239

after 11 a.m. He was to take the train two stops to Powell station. Peter had instructed him to get off the train, exit the station, and get in line for the cable car at street level. He was told he would be contacted at that point.

The first part was right, but Quinn had a different plan for after Albina boarded the train.

Since Albina knew Quinn by sight, Nate drew Embarcadero duty. He took up his position a full thirty minutes before Albina was due, and had a bag of groceries as a prop.

While most of the inbound trains terminated at Embarcadero, the N train continued around the northeastern corner of the peninsula, taking riders all the way to the baseball stadium if they desired. So when it returned to the station on its outbound trip, more often than not there were already people onboard.

Quinn waited one stop north of Embarcadero, timing it so he got on the train that would arrive closest to, but not before, the appointed time. It was a two-car train, so Quinn chose a seat near the rear of the first car. He was wearing a black San Francisco Giants baseball hat and a lightweight black jacket. He'd ripped open the lining of one of the pockets so he could hide his SIG inside. To further conceal his identity, he sat with his back against the window, facing away from the platform, his nose stuck in a copy of the *San Francisco Chronicle*.

As the train pulled into Embarcadero, he moved the paper down a few inches, giving him a view of the window on the opposite side of the car. He could see the reflections of around twenty people on the platform behind him waiting to get on. It only took a few seconds to pick out Nate.

Quinn had given his apprentice Albina's description. Once Nate made the ID, he'd been instructed to see who Albina was traveling with. He would then stand behind them as Quinn's train pulled into the station. Hands at his sides meant Albina was alone. A yawn, and there was one person with him. A yawn with his hand in front of his mouth meant there were two others. More than that and Nate would stand to the side alone. If the latter was the case, Quinn would exit, and they'd call the meet off.

Nate was yawning, but there was no hand in front of his mouth.

One extra, Quinn thought. Albina's trust for Peter didn't appear to be one hundred percent, but he hadn't been suspicious enough to get serious about it either.

Quinn's hope had been that the train would stop at a point where Albina would get into the same car as he was in. But no such luck. As soon as the doors opened, Albina and his man got onto the second car. Nate followed.

Within moments, the doors shut and the train was on its way again.

At the next stop, Montgomery Street, Quinn quickly exited and worked his way down the platform toward the second car. As much as possible, he kept other commuters between him and the windows. He was still able to catch a glimpse of Albina's man. The bodyguard was standing near the center of the car, checking out the people getting on and off.

Quinn moved to the last door of the car, slipping on board just before the doors shut again. Keeping his back to Albina's man, he opened his paper and began reading again. For a few moments, he could sense he was being watched, but as the train started to move out of the station the feeling went away.

It wasn't long before a prerecorded voice announced, 'Powell Station,' and the train began to slow again. Quinn shifted his weight casually, naturally, turning enough so that he could see the others through the corner of his eye.

Albina was sitting on one of the yellow benches near the front of the car. His bodyguard stood a few feet away in the aisle, facing forward. Nate was also standing, but nearer the front exit. As the train pulled into the station, Albina stood. With his man in the lead, they made their way toward the still-closed door.

Quinn let a few other people get up before he began walking down the aisle. He kept his face lowered so that the angle of his cap covered most of his features. By the time the train came to a complete stop, he was standing directly behind Albina.

There was a pause, then the doors slid open.

As they did, Nate stepped forward like he was about to get out, the rest of those waiting surging forward behind him. Just as he was crossing onto the platform, the bottom of his grocery bag split open — the product of a well-placed cut and a hand that had been under the bag until the critical moment.

A jar of pickles, several apples, a carton of milk, and a bag of rice crashed onto the floor right in the threshold of the door. While the jar of pickles had stayed intact, the milk carton and the bag of rice had not.

Everyone pulled back, both in surprise and in an attempt to keep from being hit.

'Ah, hell,' Nate said. 'Sorry.'

Outside the door, those waiting to get on moved rapidly down the platform to another entrance, while two of those on the inside jumped over the mess so as not to miss their stop.

The bodyguard glanced back at Albina, who nodded for him to do the same.

'I'm really sorry,' Nate said to the guard.

'Just get out of the way,' the man said.

'Sure, no problem.'

A tone went off, indicating the doors were about to close again.

'Now,' the bodyguard said.

Nate moved to the side.

As the guard passed him, Nate reached up, put two hands on the man's back, and shoved him as far onto the platform as possible. The man stumbled out of the train and fell to the ground.

'What the hell?' Albina said.

He started to move to the door, throwing out a hand to keep it from sliding shut.

'Relax, Jorge,' Quinn said, poking the end of his concealed gun against Albina's ribs.

As Albina froze, the doors closed. On the other side, his bodyguard was pushing himself up, but it was too late. The train had already begun pulling away from the station.

'Have a seat,' Quinn said.

Making no sudden movements, Albina turned around.

'Quinn?'

Quinn nodded at the nearest bench seat. 'Right there is fine.'

Albina sat, then slid over against the window. Quinn glanced at the other passengers in their car. Only one man was looking in their direction, and he seemed more curious than anything else. Quinn signaled for Nate to keep a watch out, then sat down next to Albina.

'You know you could have just stopped by my office,' Albina said. 'You didn't have to get all secret agent on me.' He glanced down at the bulge in Quinn's pocket where the gun was. 'And you definitely don't need that.'

'Yeah, but it got your attention, didn't it?' Quinn asked.

'Why didn't Peter just tell me it was you?'

'Because I told him not to. Thought maybe you wouldn't be so interested in seeing me.'

'Why would you think that? We're friends.'

'We've never been friends.'

'You didn't have to say that so fast,' Albina said. 'Okay, to you we're business associates, then. I still consider us friends. Besides, I've been waiting for you to show up for a couple days now. What the hell took you so long?'

Quinn paused. 'You were waiting for me?'

'Figured you'd want to talk to me at some point.'

'And why would that be?'

'Come on, Quinn. I know Markoff was your friend. I mean real friend. Not like me, I guess.'

'You knew Markoff and I were friends?'

'Why the hell do you think you were hired?'

'You *hired* me because the body in the container was Markoff?' Quinn said, trying to make all the dots connect.

'Well, it wasn't my idea.'

Again, Quinn paused before speaking. 'Whose idea was it?'

'My client's.'

'And who was your client?' Quinn said.

'Do we have to talk here?' Albina asked. 'I could use a cup of coffee.'

★ ★ ★

They found a small café just off Market Street. No waitresses, just a counter and a condiments table. After they each got a cup of coffee, Quinn told Nate to have a seat on one of the chairs outside, then directed Albina to a table along the wall.

'Markoff and me, we did work on and off over the years,' Albina said. 'He always treated me fairly, so I did the same for him. I'd feed him a little information, and for me, he'd look the other direction when it was convenient. Okay, so maybe we weren't buddies, but I respected him. He was a good client.'

'He told you we were friends?' Quinn asked.

'He may have mentioned it.'

Not a real answer, but Quinn let it drop for

245

the moment. 'That doesn't tell me how you ended up with his corpse on your dock.'

Albina ripped the tops off a couple of packets of sugar, then dumped the contents into his coffee. As he stirred the liquid, he looked up. 'It was sent to me. By my client.'

'And who is your client?'

'Come on, Quinn. You know I can't share that kind of information.'

Quinn leaned forward. 'On the train you acted like you've been waiting to tell me everything. So who the hell is your client?'

They stared at each other for a minute.

'You found the message Markoff left, right?' Albina asked.

'I found it.'

'Did you figure out what it means yet?'

'Why? Do you know what it means?'

Albina shook his head. 'Nah. I was just curious, that's all.'

'Client, Jorge. Who is it?'

More coffee stirring, then a sip, then, 'I can tell you this much. He knows you, and respects you.'

'He respects me?' Quinn said. 'I could care less what he thinks about me. He kills my friend, then ships him here for me to bury. Who is he?'

'I told you. I can't.'

'Okay. We're done.'

Quinn started to get up, but Albina reached out and put a hand on Quinn's wrist.

'Don't get confused here,' Albina said. 'I believe my client was trying to do the right thing. He told me the dead should be with friends, not lost overboard somewhere.'

'This is just bullshit. Who the fuck is he?'

The café went quiet. Several people turned to look in their direction.

'Relax,' Albina said. 'Don't get so worked up.'

Quinn settled back in his chair, his eyes narrowing. 'Who sent you the container?'

Albina paused for a moment, then shook his head. 'No. But there's a reason why.'

'I don't care why.' Quinn leaned further back.

'Yes, you do. You think whoever sent the container to me is the one who killed Markoff. But I happen to know that's not the truth. But here's the problem. Only two people know who that container came from. The person who sent it and me. If word got out, it could get ugly for him. Know what I mean?'

'Who?' Quinn asked.

'Were you not just listening to me?'

'I was. I just don't care,' Quinn said.

'That's up to you. I can only tell you what I know.'

'You can tell me the truth.'

Albina raised his hands off the table, palms out to Quinn. 'You don't want to believe me, you won't believe me.' He paused. 'Look, there *is* something I can tell you. The container, it didn't come in on a ship. It was flown in.'

'Flown in?'

'From my understanding, that particular container hadn't been on a ship in at least three weeks.'

Quinn processed this new information quickly, realizing almost instantly what it meant.

Markoff's body hadn't become bloated and discolored by a week at sea, but rather it had happened on land while the container just sat there, waiting. Someplace hot, where the warmth of the sun would have turned the metal tomb into an oven, slowly cooking him to death. Quinn was sure his friend had been alive when he'd been put inside the box; the message on the wall was proof of that. Sure, it could have been written by someone else, but Quinn's instincts told him it was Markoff.

And ultimately what Albina's revelation meant was that the whole time while Markoff lay dying, he was likely less than a mile from people who could have rescued him.

'Why take it to the port?'

'You would have asked a lot of questions if it had been anywhere else.'

'I'm asking the questions now.'

'Sure, but you've also already been on the job for a few days, haven't you?'

The implication of Albina's words surprised Quinn. 'Your client wanted me to investigate Markoff's death?'

'I don't know about want, but he was giving you the option.'

'So the fact that the *Riegle 3*'s last port of call was Singapore means nothing?'

'I never said that.'

Quinn tried to read Albina's face. 'You tell me that your client had nothing to do with Markoff's death. That the container was flown in. That Singapore is actually still in play. But you won't tell me who your client is?'

Albina finished a sip of his coffee, then set his cup down on the table. 'Now you're catching on.'

★ ★ ★

'We need to get out of town tonight,' Quinn said.

He and Nate had just arrived back at Aunt Jay's house. Orlando was hunched over the computer in the same position she'd been in when they'd left.

'I'm way ahead of you,' she said.

'You've already got the tickets?'

'Done,' she said.

'But I haven't told you where.'

'I'm not that stupid.'

'How many?'

Orlando looked at Nate, then back at Quinn. 'Three,' she said as if it was obvious.

'You don't have to come with us.'

'Shut up.'

'I'm serious,' he said.

'So am I.' She looked back down at the computer, discussion closed.

Quinn poured himself a glass of cold water and took a drink. 'We shouldn't leave from San Francisco,' he said.

'We're not.'

'Or Oakland.'

'We're not.'

'Okay, then,' he said. He looked over at Nate, who was standing near the kitchen entrance. 'Let's get packed.'

'So,' Nate said, his brow furrowed, 'where exactly are we going?'

22

It was raining when they arrived in Singapore, the remnants of a storm whose main thrust had struck Indonesia to the south. Outside the window of the airplane, the tarmac was soaked and the day was gray, but Quinn knew in no time the clouds would move on, giving way to a blue tropical sky.

Orlando had made the decision to break up the trip into legs, making it harder for them to be followed. It was a good strategy in principle but was hell in practice.

They had flown out of Sacramento, taking Air Alaska to Vancouver, B.C., via Seattle. From there, it was Cathay Pacific to Hong Kong, Thai Air to Bangkok, and finally AirAsia to Singapore.

The only good thing was Quinn was able to sleep through most of it. Flying first-class was a definite advantage for international travel.

Singapore's Changi Airport was one of Quinn's favorite in the entire world. Clean, efficient, fast in, fast out. In no time, he, Orlando, and Nate had passed through passport control and customs.

Bags in hand, Quinn led them through the green X — nothing to declare — exit, and over to the doors leading outside.

The system for getting a cab at Changi was efficient to say the least. Just prior to the door leading outside, there was a series of ropes herding people into a line like they were waiting to get a ride at an amusement park. Even if there weren't a lot of people trying to get a cab, skipping the ropes was not allowed. It was the system, and everyone was expected to follow it.

They joined a line of several others.

Outside was a row of parking spaces numbered one to ten. A man standing next to the door stopped everyone, then said something into a walkie-talkie.

Almost instantly, ten taxis came zooming up the road, each parking in one of the numbered spots. Most were the sky blue Toyota Crowns operated by Comfort Cab, the sides of their cars turned into rolling billboards that pushed, among other things, cell phones and Tiger beer and Milo chocolate-milk mix.

Once the cabs were all parked, the man with the walkie-talkie gave the go-ahead for the line of people to start moving. As each group passed, he counted them off.

'One . . . two . . . three . . . four . . . five . . . six . . . seven . . . eight . . . nine . . . ten.'

The numbers corresponded to which cab would be theirs.

'Okay, that was just weird,' Nate said once they were seated in the back of their cab. They had been number eight.

'Not weird,' Orlando said. 'Practical.'

Nate raised an eyebrow. 'All right. Weirdly practical, then. Better?'

She rolled her eyes but said nothing.

The cab took them along the tree-lined East Coast Parkway toward the city. The rain had let up, and, in the distance, Quinn could see blue sky peeking through the layer of gray. The island nation usually felt like an open-air sauna as far as Quinn was concerned. But the storm had temporarily cooled the otherwise constant hyper-humid 85-degree temperature to a more bearable level.

Through the trees to the left, he caught glimpses of the Singapore Strait. At its narrowest, it was ten miles across to Indonesia. And yet, it was one of the most crowded waterways in the world. An unending fleet of cargo ships passed through it every day, heading west toward India or the distant Suez Canal and all ports European, or northeast to Japan or China or the Americas.

It all made Singapore one of the busiest ports in the world, where cargo was loaded and unloaded at a breathtaking speed, much of the merchandise just passing through on its way to somewhere else. The island was a vital piece of the world economic machine, but seldom the destination in and of itself.

As they neared Marina Bay, the Singapore skyline came into view. Though a constant work in progress, the high-rises lining the west side of the bay were still an impressive sight. Not just typical skyscrapers, either. The architecture in Singapore was more daring than you saw in most big cities. Asymmetrical designs Quinn had noticed in few other places, and curves and lines that made several of the buildings look more like art pieces than places of business — every building a monument, a showpiece, letting the world know Singapore was important.

The cab continued around the bay and into the city proper. It wasn't long before the driver turned off the highway, weaved through the traffic, and pulled up in front of the Pan Pacific Hotel.

A doorman opened Quinn's door the minute the cab came to a stop.

'Welcome to the Pan Pacific Hotel,' the man said. 'Checking in?'

'Yes,' Quinn said.

★   ★   ★

Orlando had arranged for them to stay in three adjacent rooms, but unlike the Marriott in San Francisco, there were no doors between each connecting them. Nate had a single room, while Quinn and Orlando had one-bedroom suites.

'Thirty minutes,' Quinn told them. 'Then meet back in my room.'

Quinn took a quick shower and pulled on his clothes, finishing ten minutes early. Taking advantage of the time, he removed his computer from his bag, carried it to the desk in the living room, and turned it on.

While it was booting up, he pulled out his cell phone. Though he never turned it off while he was flying, the phone did have a sleep mode that made it look to anyone checking like it had been shut down. He activated the display screen and was immediately greeted with a signal that he had a message.

He accessed his voice mail and found there

were actually three messages. An automated voice told him the first had come in ten hours earlier.

'Jonathan, I made it to the house.' It was Tasha. 'I thought I should let you know. Please don't forget to call me . . . I mean . . . if you find her. I have to know she's okay. Please.'

He pushed 7 to erase the call, then went to the next message. It had come in six hours before.

'I really would like to talk to you.' Tasha again. 'I really think maybe I should come back. I know I can help you. I'm going to go crazy just sitting here. Can you call me?'

He erased it. The last call had come through only two hours earlier.

He was not surprised to find it was from Tasha again. 'Why aren't you calling me back? I need to talk to you. I know I can help you. Please, call me. Please.'

After he erased the final message, he set the phone on the table, intending to turn his attention to his computer. But he paused, his hand hovering a few inches above the phone. He was going to have to call her back, if nothing else than to at least calm her down.

Wait? Or call?

'Dammit,' he said, then picked up the phone and dialed Tasha's number.

With the international dateline, it was still the previous night back in California. The phone rang four times, then mercifully went to voice mail.

'Hi.' The voice was Tasha's. 'You've reached my

254

cell. Leave me a message and I'll get back to you.'

'It's Jonathan,' Quinn said, relieved he didn't actually have to talk to her. 'Nothing new on this end. But I'm still working on it. I'm glad you made it to the house. You'll be safe there. I'll call again within three days. But don't worry. Just lay low.'

He hung up and turned his attention back to the computer. Within thirty seconds, he was connected to the Internet.

Before they left, Orlando had set the tracking software she was using to keep tabs on Jenny's phone to run on automatic. It would then send periodic e-mails to both her and Quinn's accounts detailing any activity. The first two messages were the same:

Data check complete.
No activity.

The third, though, was different:

Data check complete.
Signal active: Kuala Lumpur, Sector 7.
Signal Acquired: 23:59:49. Local.
Signal Loss: 00:01:14. Local.

Interesting, he thought. Jenny had turned her phone on the previous evening right at midnight. That corresponded to the same window of time she had had Quinn call her the night before.

He used a bookmark in his web browser to bring up the Sandy Side Yacht Club message board.

He perused the list of recent messages, concentrating on anything sent in the last thirty hours. The group was an active one, so even in that short span there were several hundred posts.

Quinn paid attention only to the ID of each message. Forty-two messages in, he stopped. There was a message from Jenny.

Just got back from Mexico. The Yucatán.

We'd spend all day on the water. At night, one club after another.
The music plus the girls — very cool. I'd call it one helluva vacation.

As he started to work out the message, there was a knock at his door.

'It's Orlando,' a muffled voice called from the other side.

Quinn got up and let her in.

'Jenny went active again,' he said as he crossed back to his computer.

Orlando followed him. 'Yeah. I got the e-mail, too.'

Quinn sat, then turned his computer so she could see the screen. 'You didn't get this, though.'

'What?' Orlando asked.

'She sent a message on the group board.'

Quinn sat back down in the chair, and Orlando leaned in.

Mexico was the key word. Six letters, meaning only every sixth word after 'Mexico' was relevant.

DAY ONE PLUS CALL.

Then the final piece of the code. Reverse the order.

'Call plus one day,' he said.

'So that's why she went active last night,' she said. 'Jenny thought we were going to call her again.'

Quinn spent several minutes working out his reply. When he was done, he entered it on the website, and clicked the button to post it.

Haven't tried where you went yet. I've only been to Nicaragua, but your trip sounded great. Will spend time tonight on Internet checking it out. Have some vacation time next month but have no firm plans yet. Same old story, no time to plan anything!

Yeah. Poor old me. HAHAHA.

But sounds like you had a good time. Sailing, partying. What could be better? Sing me up!! Do you have recommendations for hotels in Cozumel? Also would be interested in other insights. Am always up for a good time.

Thanks!

'Sing me up?' Orlando asked

'Typo,' Quinn said with a shrug. 'Happens all the time.'

'Weak.'

The real message read:

AM IN SING A POOR SAME TIME TONIGHT

257

★ ★ ★

The cab from the Pan Pacific dropped Quinn and Nate on the north side of the Singapore River along Clarke Quay. Their destination was still another quarter mile up the river, but taking the sidewalk that lined the shore would be an easy and inconspicuous way to get there. Plenty of tourists used the walkway. Who would notice two more?

Clarke Quay had once been the place merchants would bring their ships in and sell their goods directly to the shop-houses that lined the river. But that was another century, long removed from the present. Now business was conducted at the huge port a few miles away on ships that would fill the river side-to-side and then some. Ships that were stuffed with cargo emptied by giant cranes instead of the shop owners' sons, and transported in quantities the merchants of the 1800s could never imagine.

The shop-houses were rows of two-story buildings pressed up against each other, following the edge of the river. Shop on bottom, home on top. Many were gone now, lost in a wave of rejuvenation and renewal that seemed to be a constant state on the island. But several remained.

No longer the businesses of old, though. They had been turned into clubs and restaurants, some even extending to the outside, providing dining on the wide path that had been built up many feet above the river water. These reclaimed buildings had been painted in bright colors

258

— blue, pink, yellow, green, orange — as if the brightest would attract the most customers.

'You've got to be kidding me,' Nate said.

Quinn looked back, then followed his apprentice's gaze toward one of the buildings. In bright orange letters above the entrance was a sign that read *Hooters*.

'One of the great American exports,' Quinn said.

Nate smiled. 'Maybe we can stop in for a drink later.'

'Not likely.'

Precise, man-made walls of stone lined both sides of the Singapore River, guiding it in the direction man wanted it to go. The path along the top curved gently with the dictated contour of the waterway. It was kind of a metaphor for Singapore itself — clean, man-manipulated, and tightly controlled.

As they moved west out of Clarke Quay and into Robertson Quay, the shops were replaced by apartments. Nice ones, Quinn noted. Not like some of the government flats they'd passed on their taxi ride into the city. Those had looked like they'd been stuffed full of people. He'd been in buildings like them before on one of his previous trips. Extended families crammed into two-room apartments sometimes not big enough for even one person.

Quinn had also been in buildings like those they were walking by now. Large apartments. Two, maybe even three bedrooms, and none with the feeling that the walls were pushing in on you. Families lived here, too, but seldom more than parents and one or two children. And often they were occupied by only a single person. These were the flats favored by the large ex-pat community. Brits, Aussies, Japanese, Americans, Canadians.

They were the people recruited by the large corporations to come and provide their expertise and to help spur on the continual Singaporean growth. Quinn had known people who'd lived in the area, but was unsure if they were here any longer.

'We're getting close, aren't we?' Nate asked.

Quinn nodded. 'Just like we talked about.'

'No problem.'

The plan was to just do a walk-by, then circle around and return back to Clarke Quay.

They passed a footbridge, its structural design again more than merely utilitarian. Large, curving pipes created the illusion of an oversized cage surrounding the bridge. It was painted in bright colors, like something out of a child's imagination.

But it wasn't the bridge that caught Quinn's attention. It was the building ahead and to his right.

'There it is,' he said.

He pulled a slender box out of his pocket. It looked liked a reduced version of a late-twentieth-century pager. It was a cell phone tracker. Orlando had programmed it earlier to home in on the module Markoff had been pointing them toward. The data on the display indicated they were getting very close.

He slipped the device back in his pocket, then

pulled out his phone and switched it to digital camera mode. 'Let me take a picture of you.'

Nate took several steps ahead. 'Where do you want me?'

'Lean against the railing. I want to get the river in the shot,' Quinn said in a normal tone, smiling like a good tourist. 'It'll be nice. You can show your girlfriend when we get home.'

Nate moved into position. 'How's this?'

'Perfect.' Quinn aimed in Nate's general direction, cheating the lens to the right, and taking in the building that, until a few minutes before, had only been a blue dot on a computerized map.

The structure appeared to be two separate buildings joined in the middle. The first two floors were common to both, but above the second floor, two towers — one at either end — rose up an additional nine floors. The towers didn't take up the whole footprint of the second-floor roof, though. The remaining area appeared to be a large patio. Quinn could make out the tops of several umbrellas near the edge of the roof. Perhaps, Quinn guessed, there was even a pool.

'Got it,' he said, lowering the camera.

'You want me to take one of you?'

'Maybe later.' Quinn pushed a few buttons on the touch screen, e-mailing the picture to Orlando. He traded the phone for the tracking device in his pocket, then pointed at a vehicle bridge that spanned the river just beyond the building. 'Let's stop at that bridge. We can head back then.'

They began walking again. Quinn stayed on the river side so that Nate would be between him and the building. It would make it easier for him to look at the structure without being obvious.

'After dinner, I want to go over the presentation again,' Quinn said, maintaining character. 'I want to make sure we've got it down before tomorrow.'

'Don't worry,' Nate said, falling into the act. 'We'll do fine.'

'And the forecast numbers. We should call New York and make sure those haven't changed.'

'I'll send an e-mail as soon as we're back at the hotel.'

'No,' Quinn said. 'Call them.'

'New York's still sleeping,' Nate said. 'You know that, right?'

As they came level with the building, Quinn first glanced down at the tracker. As he'd expected, it indicated they were even closer now. He then let his eyes stray toward the building. 'Right. Okay, send an e-mail for now. But I want you to call once someone's in the office.'

'Sure. No problem. Anything else?'

A sign was mounted into the wall just below patio level between the two towers. It was a blue rectangle, and written on it in yellow letters was *Quayside Villas*.

'You have the PowerPoint, right?'

'Yes,' Nate said. 'For the millionth time. Why are you so uptight about this? It's a killer presentation.'

'I'm uptight because this could mean a fifty percent increase in our sales,' Quinn said.

Below the sign was an open atrium stretching the height of the first two floors and ending at a glass door about fifty feet in. It was impossible to tell from where they were, but Quinn assumed it was security controlled. That would have been consistent with the other buildings like it he'd seen.

'So what do you want to get for dinner?' Nate asked.

'Are you changing the subject?'

'Absolutely. The presentation's ready. What I'm most worried about is what I'm going to put in my stomach.'

The path forked ahead. To the left, it headed downhill, passing under the bridge, and to the right, it went around the side of the Quayside Villas building to the street. Quinn led them to the right.

Around the lower level were a couple of shops: a bakery, a laundry, a wine shop. Nothing out of the ordinary.

Quinn glanced upward, following the rise of the west tower. There was no way to tell where in the building Markoff's message had been pointing them toward without getting inside. But there was also no doubt the building was where he had placed his beacon.

Around the front was a small two-lane road that passed between the Quayside Villas and a hotel on the left.

'I don't care what we eat,' Quinn said. 'You can choose.'

'A girl in the bar was telling me about a great Japanese place downtown.'

'Japanese? Shouldn't we at least try Chinese while we're here? Or Indian?'

An offshoot of the road curved toward the front door of the Quayside, rejoining the road up ahead. The front door was glass again, leading into a lobby at the base of the west tower. Mounted on the window next to the door was a security pad for a keycard or something similar. There was also a push button that looked like a large, flat light switch. No doorman, though.

But this realization was short-lived. Ahead there was another glass door, this one leading into the east tower. Beside it was a glass-walled room, complete with a bank of television monitors and two security guards.

'I'm ready to head back,' Quinn said. 'How about you?'

23

The phone rang once.

Twice.

Three times.

Four.

Five.

She didn't get the message, Quinn thought.

Six.

Click.

Quinn almost expected to hear the prerecorded Thai voice again, but the line was live.

'Jenny?'

Another breath.

'Jenny. It's Quinn.'

'What happened?' Though the voice was low and rushed, Quinn knew it was her.

'I didn't get your message until too late,' Quinn said. 'The call time you wanted already passed by then.'

'No . . . Steven. What happened?' Her voice was managed, not quite calm, not quite out of control. It was almost as if she was accusing Quinn of killing her boyfriend.

'I don't know exactly. He was . . . he was dead before I even knew he was in trouble.'

'What do you mean?'

Quinn glanced at Orlando and Nate. They were huddled around the small hotel room desk, monitoring the call on the computer.

'A week ago, I was hired to do a job,' Quinn

265

said. He then told her about being shocked that the body he'd been asked to dispose of belonged to his old friend. He didn't fill in all the details, but it was enough, he hoped, to convince her he was telling the truth.

There was a long silence when he was through.

'Whoever sent you the body must have killed him,' she said. 'Who was it?'

'I don't know,' he said.

'Bullshit.'

'Jenny, I don't know. It was an anonymous client. It's how it goes in this business.' He could have given her Albina's name, but he was only the middleman and had nothing to do with it.

She was silent for several seconds, then said in a trembling voice, 'I knew it. When he didn't come back I knew something was wrong. I just thought . . . I hoped . . . Oh, God.'

She could no longer hold it back. Quinn heard a loud sob, then the muffled noise of the phone moving away from her face so she could endure her agony without a witness.

It was half a minute before she came back. When she spoke, her composure had returned. 'Are you really in Singapore?'

'Yes.'

'What are you doing there?'

'Trying to help you.'

'But I'm not in Singapore,' she said.

Quinn looked at Orlando.

Silently she mouthed, 'She's still in KL.'

'No, but Kuala Lumpur isn't far away,' he said into the phone.

'You know where I am.'

'It's okay. We're the only ones who know.'

'What do you mean *we*?'

'There are two others with me,' he said. 'Friends I trust and work with all the time. They're okay.'

'If you know I'm in Kuala Lumpur,' she said, her words sounding more guarded than they had before, 'then what are you doing in Singapore?'

'We're in Singapore because Markoff sent us here.'

'What do you mean?' she blurted out.

'It doesn't matter,' he said. 'Look, I'm going to come get you. I'll take the first flight in the morning. It won't take long. We'll get you out of there and to someplace safe.' The flight between Singapore and Kuala Lumpur was measured in minutes, not hours.

There was dead air for a moment. 'No. I'll come to you.'

'That's not such a good idea,' Quinn said. 'Your boss is flying into town. It would be best if you weren't here.'

'Do you know when he arrives?'

Quinn shot a glance at Orlando.

She whispered, 'Tomorrow, around midnight.'

'Tomorrow,' Quinn repeated for Jenny. 'Late.'

'I'll send you another message when I get there,' Jenny said.

Quinn's grip on the phone tightened. 'No. Stay where you are. It's not safe here.'

But he was only talking to himself. The line had already gone dead.

267

'Kuala Lumpur,' Orlando said. 'But she's moving around the city.'

The tracking software was still up on her computer, and the blue dot blinked above Merdeka Square in the Malaysian capital.

'I should have pushed her harder to stay there and wait for us,' Quinn said. He was near the couch, not quite pacing, not quite standing still.

'How much harder could you have pushed?' Nate asked.

'She seemed anxious to come here,' Orlando said.

'This is the worst place she can be. If Guerrero is here, his men will be here, too.' Quinn came around the end of the sofa. 'When she gets here, we need to find her and get her someplace safe. If Guerrero's men even think she is in the area, they'll hunt her down.'

'I'll keep the tracking software open,' Orlando said. 'If she turns her phone on, I'll know it within seconds.'

'Good,' Quinn said. 'Keep the bulletin board open, too, in case she sends a message. Tomorrow I'll arrange for a place we can take her.'

'Why not here?' Nate asked.

'Too public,' Orlando said.

'Sounds like we're going to have a busy day tomorrow,' Nate said. He pushed himself up out of his chair at the desk. 'I'm going to turn in. See you guys in the morning.'

'Wait,' Quinn said. 'We still have something to do.'

'It's after midnight,' Nate said. 'Isn't it something that can wait until morning?'

Quinn's only answer was a silent stare.

'I know what you're thinking,' Orlando said to Quinn. 'But it's not a good idea.'

Quinn turned to her. 'I don't think we have a choice. Markoff died trying to tell us about it.'

'It might be a trap. You ever think of that?' she said. 'Maybe Markoff didn't write the module ID on the container.'

'But if he did, I can't ignore it.'

'I'm sorry,' Nate said. 'What exactly are we doing?'

'Dark clothes,' Quinn said to his apprentice. 'Then meet me in the lobby in ten minutes.'

★ ★ ★

After Quinn had dressed, he returned to the living room with the backpack full of items he would need. He was happy to see only Orlando remained. She was still at the desk, but didn't look happy.

'We're going to need the communications gear,' Quinn said.

Orlando pointed to her backpack sitting on the floor a few feet away. Inside, Quinn found three boxes of what appeared to be MP3 players. Easily explained as gifts to any prying customs official, they were in fact two-way radios. He grabbed one each for himself and Nate.

'Anything?' he asked, as he glanced over

269

Orlando's shoulder at the computer.

'No. Jenny's phone is still inactive.' She looked around at Quinn. 'Maybe I should come with you.'

'I need you to stay here in case Jenny tries to contact us again.'

'Like that's really likely,' Orlando said.

He glanced at the computer. 'While we're gone, maybe you can try to pin down where the congressman will be staying when he arrives. And LP, someone's gotta know what that means.'

'I've already taken care of the Guerrero part.'

Quinn smiled, not surprised.

'He's got reservations at two different hotels,' she said.

'Someone's a little paranoid. Which ones?'

'The Sheraton and, of course, Raffles.' Raffles was the most famous hotel in Singapore, and one of the most famous in the entire world. Large and luxurious, it had been a mainstay in Singapore for over a century. It was also in one of the Raffles's bars — the Long Bar — that the Singapore Sling had been invented.

'He'll stay at Raffles,' Quinn said.

'That would be my guess, too.' She hit a few more keys, then stopped and looked up at him again. 'You really think it's a good idea going back there tonight?'

'It'll be quiet. Easier to look around.'

'You haven't a clue what you might find. You may not even be able to get all the way to the signal.'

'Markoff pointed us toward the building for a

270

reason. I'll just get the lay of the land.'

She turned back to the screen. 'You really shouldn't go.'

'And you should get some rest,' he said. 'You're getting cranky.'

She scowled but said nothing.

'It's nice of you to offer to wait up for me, though, but it's not necessary,' he said.

'Just don't do anything *über* stupid, okay?'

★ ★ ★

3 a.m.

The streets around the Quayside Villas were all but deserted. In fact, the only person visible was the guard sitting in the glassed-in security office out front. He was alone, but that didn't mean there weren't others. Quinn figured there had to be at least one additional man doing rounds. And to be safe, it was better to assume there were two more, one for each tower.

The lighting in the front of the building had been well planned. It illuminated the façade tastefully, yet left no dark areas someone could use to hide in. And, as Quinn had expected, the front door was particularly well lit.

'This should be fine,' he said.

He and Nate were standing across the street, near the far corner of the neighboring hotel. From their concealed position, they had a great view of the fishbowl security room and the entrances to both towers.

He looked down at the tracking device in his hand.

'Signal's still strong,' he said.

'That's good,' Nate said.

Quinn pulled a small case out of his backpack. It looked like a pair of old, collapsible opera glasses. But while they served a similar purpose, these particular binoculars had a unique feature. Night vision. Not useful for the theater, but perfect for their needs. He handed them to Nate.

'If the security guard moves at all, you let me know.'

'Every time?' Nate asked.

'Every time.'

Quinn had tucked the wire of his radio under his shirt so it wouldn't snag on anything. He picked up the dangling earpiece and put it in his left ear.

'Check, check,' he said, making sure the small microphone jutting out of the earpiece worked.

'I hear you.' Nate's voice came at Quinn both directly and through the earpiece. 'What do you want me to say if you need to get the hell out of there?'

Quinn looked at his apprentice. ''Get the hell out of there' will work fine.'

'Right,' Nate said. 'Good luck.'

Quinn gave him a terse smile, then headed off.

He skirted around the side of the building, returning once again to the walkway along the river. Like out front, the rear of the Quayside Villas was also well lit. Only the coverage wasn't as intensive as it was at the main entrances, and even more importantly there was no permanent security station. There were, however, two cameras covering a large portion of the back,

272

including the central rear entrance.

Lining the walls that led left and right from the entrance were columns about two feet in diameter. They created a narrow portico that was more for decoration than practical use. Above the columns, the second floor was a series of faux windows recessed into the wall and covered with some sort of lattice. And above that, the rooftop patio. That was the key.

Quinn figured it would be the easiest way to get in. Getting there without being seen was the issue. After examining the photos they'd taken earlier in the day, he had located a narrow blind spot in the camera coverage. It was near the southeast corner.

It wasn't perfect, but it would do.

On their way back to the hotel that afternoon, Quinn and Nate had made a stop at a small family-run DIY — do-it-yourself — store near Chinatown. It was crammed full of kitchenware, janitorial supplies, knickknacks, and tools. It was one of those places where if you didn't see what you were looking for, all you had to do was ask. No matter what it was, they'd find it for you.

Without the need of assistance, Quinn had been able to locate a pair of gloves with rubber grips and some sturdy rope. Back at the hotel, he had cut the rope down to twenty feet, then tied a thin piece of cord near one end.

Now as he stood in front of one of the columns at the base of the wall, he attached the free end of the thin cord to one of the belt loops on his pants. It would serve as a safety line for when he had to let go of the rope. The next step was the rope itself. He doubled it up and swung it around the column, then wrapped each end around one of his palms, and pulled tight in unison, checking the strength.

Satisfied, he looked in both directions along the river to be sure he was still alone, then began climbing up the column. The rope held him in place as he moved his feet. Every few seconds, he would lunge upward, scooting his lifeline higher. In less than half a minute, he reached the top of the column. From there, he shimmied his feet back up waist-high, resting them on a lip near the top of the column, his knees against his chest.

The timing of his next move was critical. Simultaneously he dropped the rope, shoved upward with his legs, and reached out and grabbed the bottom ledge of the second-floor window. There was a soft thud as the rope smacked against the column, but it fell no further, the safety cord tied to his pants keeping it from dropping all the way to the ground.

Legs dangling below him, Quinn pulled his body up with his arms. As soon as he was high enough, he swung his right leg like a pendulum, catching the ledge with the heel of his foot.

'Any movement?' Quinn half whispered, half grunted. From the angle of the security cameras, he thought he was still out of range, but there was no way to know for sure.

'No,' Nate said over the radio. 'He's not even looking at the screens.'

Security at the Quayside Villas wasn't a high-risk gig. The mere fact it was right out front and visible to all would have been enough deterrent for most potential troublemakers. The security guards would know that, and no doubt it would make them lazy.

Once Quinn had both feet on the ledge, he maneuvered himself into a crouch. He made a quick scan, assessing his options. The top lip of the wall was about three feet above him. He could make the leap, but if he missed he'd fall backward through the air and land hard on the cement walkway below.

He took a deep breath. Then, without another thought, he thrust upward, his hands reaching for the top of the wall. The lip was curved, and the surface on top had been polished smooth. Quinn's fingertips slipped for a half-second before the rubber grips on the gloves grabbed and held. Knowing he could hold the position for only a few more moments, he quickly swung his right foot upward in the same pendulum move as before, bringing his leg parallel to the ground and catching the lip of the wall with it.

He rolled to his right onto the top of the ledge and took a deep breath.

'You okay?' Nate asked.

Another breath. 'Fine. I'm on the edge of the terrace. What's happening there?'

'Everything's the same.'

'Good.'

Quinn flipped onto his stomach but remained prone. As he had suspected, the roof had been designed as a large deck for the residents. Even in the darkness, it looked like something found at an upscale resort. He was near the east tower.

In front of him was a large swimming pool — wide and long. Lights below the surface gave the water an eerie yet inviting quality. Several lounge chairs were placed around the pool, lined up and ready for the next day.

Beyond the pool, the deck continued toward the other tower, but there were several large potted plants obscuring his view.

Glancing up at the east tower, he noted only two of the apartments had lights on. Both were near the top, and each had their curtains drawn. In fact, most of the east tower windows had coverings over them. During the day, a person looking out from any of the apartments would have easily seen Quinn. But at this hour, no one was interested in the world outside their rooms.

He slipped off the ledge and onto the deck. Bending at the waist to cut down on his profile, he first secured his climbing rope around his midsection, then retrieved the tracking device. The signal was definitely stronger than it had been at street level. Markoff's beacon had to be somewhere in one of the buildings.

Quinn moved along the pool toward the east tower. It took only seconds to find the glass door leading into the building. And, as he had guessed, there was another camera, this one focused on the entry, catching anyone going in or out. Inside, beyond the glass door, he could see entrances to a couple of the apartments, and an elevator on the left.

The signal strength had gone up a few more decimal points, but it had still not reached

1.000. If the beacon was in the east tower, it had to be higher up.

He skirted past the camera and made his way to the other tower.

No pool on the west side. In fact, since the building was much closer to the river here, the available deck space was considerably reduced. The designer had chosen to create small semiprivate spaces for one or two people by using half-walls and planters full of large bushes. Perfect spots for a bit of alone time in the sun.

The west tower itself seemed to be almost a mirror image of its sister. The entrance looked no different. Neither did the camera that was aimed at it. The lobby beyond the door was also identical, but reversed.

There were two notable differences at this end, though. The first was that the apartments on the deck level had small private patios carved out of the main deck, each delineated by a chest-high wall. As far as Quinn could see, there were no cameras on these apartments.

And the second, the signal strength on the tracking device had reached .9900. Its highest level yet.

The west tower looked like it was the winner.

Quinn was about to take a closer look at the patios behind the deck-level apartments when he felt his phone vibrating in his pocket. He pulled it out and looked at the display. Orlando.

'Damn,' Quinn said. Anyone else and he would have just ignored the call.

'What?' Nate asked.

'Nothing. Just keep an eye out. I'm going

off-line for a second.'

He pulled the earpiece out, then flipped his phone open and pressed the Talk button.

'Hold on,' he whispered into his cell.

He moved away from the tower to one of the sitting areas closest to the outer wall. He crouched down so he was completely hidden from view, then returned the phone to his ear.

'Not a good time,' he whispered.

'Are you inside yet?' she asked.

'Working on it.'

'And no one's seen you?'

'The plan is not to be seen.'

'Right. I just thought that since you have no idea what you're looking for, you might have already screwed up.'

'Appreciate the confidence. But I don't really have time for the I'm-smarter-than-you talk right now.'

'Try apartments zero-four dash twenty-one and zero-five dash twenty-one. West tower.'

'What?'

'Zero-four twenty-one or zero-five twenty-one,' she said. 'West tower. Is there a problem with the connection?'

'Why there?'

He could almost hear her smile on the other end. 'Thought it might be easier if you knew where you were going, so I dug a little and found a list of tenants for the Quayside Villas.'

'Why those two?'

'Everything in the building is rented by individuals or corporations. All the owners check out as legitimate. All except the owners of those

278

two apartments. Each is owned by a separate corporation. The funny thing is neither corporation exists. Interesting that out of all the apartments in the building, those two would be one on top of another.'

'That doesn't necessarily mean Markoff meant either one.'

'Have you been able to do a signal check?' she asked.

He paused. 'It's coming from inside the west tower.'

'Well then. My work here is done,' she said.

24

'I'm going in,' Quinn told Nate once he had his earpiece back in.

'Are you sure?'

'Yes,' Quinn said. 'Hold your position and monitor the security station.'

'Got it.'

Quinn moved back through the maze of plants to the main pathway. Just beyond was the private patio of the apartment nearest the tower door. The gray stone wall that enclosed it created an area about twenty feet deep by fifteen wide. A wrought-iron patio table and set of matching chairs sat off to the left. Stuck through a hole in the middle of the table was an opened dark umbrella currently shading the patio furniture from nothing but the stars. Lining one of the walls were several small pots of flowers. At the far end was the sliding glass door entrance to the apartment, the blinds pulled only halfway closed.

Inside, the apartment was dark. Still, Quinn was able to make out what looked to be a couch and an entertainment console. Beyond that, the room plunged into total black.

He was sure he could get in, but there were two problems. The first and most obvious was that someone might be home, while the second was the apartment's proximity to the security camera. Either one was a reason to move on.

He made his way left to the next private patio.

More furniture, this time made of wood. There was even a lounge similar to those on the main deck. But whoever lived in this apartment didn't appear to be a gardener. There were no plants or flowers, just the furniture and a small hibachi grill pulled under the overhang near the door. Again the blinds were not completely closed, but the angle of the building prevented most of the exterior light from shining in, so Quinn could see little beyond the glass. He got the impression, though, that whoever lived there wasn't a big fan of the outdoors and had used their portion of the deck sparingly at best.

Patio number three was similar to the first one. Furniture and plants. Only this time, a curtain was drawn across the glass door.

Quinn glanced back at the second patio, a question on his brow. He walked over to it, looked left and right, then hopped the wall.

He paused for a second, waiting to see if there was any response from inside. Nothing.

'Check,' he said.

'No change,' Nate told him.

Quinn scanned the patio again to make sure there was nothing he had missed, then pulled out his cell phone. He accessed the camera menu and switched it to thermal sensor, maximum strength. The image on the screen went dark. Quinn held his hand up in front of the lens to test, and was greeted with the image of a bright white hand on the screen.

He turned the camera toward the apartment. The screen remained dark. The range on the sensor was spec'd out at one hundred feet, so either the place was a lot bigger than he thought it was, or no one was home.

I'll take door number two, Quinn thought.

★　★　★

'I need a diversion.'

Quinn was inside the apartment, standing next to the front door in the living room. He had replaced his climbing gloves with a pair of latex ones, then had unlocked the door. All he had to do now was pull it open and step through into the common hallway. But he had no idea if there were any cameras in the corridor beyond.

'How long?' Nate asked.

'Fifteen seconds at least. Thirty would be better.'

Quinn could hear Nate's mic rub against something. 'Okay,' Nate said. 'Give me a minute. I'll give you a ready-go.'

Quinn held his position, one hand on the knob and one on the door a few inches higher, holding it closed. If Nate could get the guard's eyes off the screens for a few moments, he should be able to locate the stairs and begin heading up to the fourth floor.

'Ready?' Nate asked.

'Yes.'

There was a pause, then Quinn heard what sounded like a muffled whack.

'Go,' Nate said.

Quinn pulled the door open and raced into the third-floor lobby. He gave himself a safe margin of twelve seconds to find the stairs and disappear inside.

Along the wall across from him were doors to other apartments. To the right, the hallway turned toward the small lobby where the elevator was located.

Where the hell were the stairs?

He looked to the left. Nothing. As he swung back to the right, he spotted a door different from those of the other apartments.

Metal, with no locks.

He ran across the tiled floor and pushed the door open.

He was halfway up to the fourth floor before he allowed himself a moment to relax.

'What's happening?' he asked.

'I think I might have gone just a little overboard,' Nate said.

'What did you do?' Quinn asked. He reached the fourth-floor landing and stopped next to the door.

'I thought I could throw something against the window of the security room. You know, shake them up a little bit?'

Decent enough plan. The room *was* all windows. It wasn't inconceivable some teenagers could be wandering around causing trouble.

'And?'

'I . . . em . . . think I cracked the window,' Nate said. 'By the way, there are three guards. The guy who was in the room nearly fell on the floor when the rock hit the window. He ran outside, then called the other two.'

'Where are they now?'

'They're all outside. They look pretty pissed. Especially the first guy.'

'No one's watching the monitors?'

'Nope.'

Quinn smiled. 'Good job.'

He decided to try 04-21 first. Without opening the door, he pulled out his phone again and scanned the hallway beyond for body heat signatures. The only things he picked up were a series of evenly spaced white blobs. Lights.

He pushed the door to the fourth floor open, then stepped through. The lobby was almost identical to the one on the third floor, only there was no glass door at the other end leading outside. And, as far as he could tell, no security cameras.

He quickly made his way down the hall, then stopped when he reached apartment 04-20. A quick check of the tracking device showed the signal strength had reached .9989, which meant he was within twenty feet of where the signal was coming from.

He allowed himself a quick smirk as he shook his head. Orlando had been right, and chances were, she wasn't going to let him forget it.

From where he stood, the door to 04-21 was another fifteen feet away. To most people, it would have probably looked the same as all the others. But to Quinn's trained eye, he saw one glaring difference.

Not on the door itself, but on the wall opposite. Mounted directly across from the entrance at eye level was a metal sconce with a bouquet of orchids spilling out the top. It fit well with the design of the rest of the building. But while there were similar sconces along the walls of the hallway, they all housed lights. This was the only one containing flowers.

Quinn's mind raced through the possibilities. A sensor, a camera, an alarm. Any one of those could have been hidden inside the wall ornament. He knew it had to be something like that. He wasn't about to believe it was harmless.

There was a quick way he could check, though. He pointed his camera lens toward the sconce. Since it didn't house a light, it should have appeared dark on his screen, or, at the most, there might have been some slight residual heat from the dying flowers.

But while the flowers were all but dark, there was a small gray dot near the base, indicating some kind of power source.

He switched the camera to normal and zoomed in on the base of the ornament. It looked like there was a small hole near the bottom, facing the door to apartment 04-21. His angle was bad, so he couldn't be sure.

Before moving in for a better look, he reengaged the heat sensor and turned the camera toward apartment 04-21. The image was almost completely dark. There was only one grayish hint of heat, about the size of a baseball, but that was it. Perhaps a solitary lamp or some other small electronic device.

He shot off a couple quick pictures in case there was anything his eye wasn't seeing but could be teased out by Orlando on the laptop later, then moved the camera to the left, scanning the rest of the apartment. More darkness, this time complete. No heat signatures anywhere. Odd, he thought. There should have been more. He shot off another photo, then put his camera away.

'Update,' Quinn said.

'Still outside,' Nate said. 'One of them's on the phone.'

'If the police show up, fall back, but stay within radio range.'

'Okay.'

Quinn squeezed himself against the wall and moved toward the ornament. When he was only a few feet away, he lowered himself into a crouch and crept underneath it.

There was definitely a hole near the base. It was a small round recess no bigger than the end of a pencil eraser. It was designed to look like a slot for a screw, but that's not what it was. From his angle, Quinn could just make out a reflection of light on glass.

A lens.

Quinn shoved his hands into his pockets, looking for anything small enough to slip into the recess. A piece of paper would have been perfect. But he had nothing. He took a quick glance along the floor, but it was clean.

As he turned to look at the recess again, his eyes were drawn to the orchids several inches above it. He smiled, then reached up carefully and plucked a couple of petals off the nearest flower.

He hesitated a moment. He'd come to the point of commit or leave. He'd already spent more time in the building than he had planned, but he knew he couldn't leave without seeing what was on the other side of that door. If this was the room Markoff had been pointing to — and the signal seemed to be saying it was — Quinn had to check.

He rolled one of the petals into a cylindrical shape roughly the size of the opening on the sconce, then simply stuck it in the hole and folded the end over to completely cover the lens.

'One of the guards is going back inside,' Nate said.

'The security room?' Quinn asked.

'No. The west tower.'

Quinn frowned. 'Does he seem like he was in a hurry?'

'No. It looks like he's returning to his rounds.'

'All right,' Quinn said. There were eleven floors in the tower. It might be a half hour before he made it to the fourth floor.

Quinn glanced at his watch. Thirty seconds had passed since he'd obscured the camera's lens. Nothing had happened.

He waited an additional thirty, then stepped across the hallway to the door. He scanned the doorjamb top to bottom, looking for any apparent security device, but found nothing.

He next turned his attention to the locks.

There were two: a deadbolt and the lock in the knob. Both looked solid and new. Quinn pulled out his lock picks, then leaned down to get a better look. He moved the pick and tension wrench toward the keyhole of the deadbolt. The wrench slipped into the hole a quarter inch, then stopped. Quinn tried to move it around, but it would go in no further.

'What the hell?' he said.

He set the tools on the floor and retrieved his flashlight, aiming the beam into the deadbolt's keyhole. The problem was the hole wasn't a keyhole at all. It was a fake, made just deep enough to give the appearance it was an actual slot for a key.

Quinn moved the light to the hole on the doorknob. Same story.

'Son of a bitch,' Quinn said.

'What's going on?' Nate asked.

'Not now,' Quinn said as he put his lock picks away.

He placed his palm on the door and gave it a gentle push. Solid. But not wood solid, something more. There was no give in the door at all.

As he started to run the possibilities through his mind, there was a muffled *ding* from his left, around the bend in the hallway. The sound of an elevator car arriving.

He looked to his right. The hallway continued on for another forty feet, then turned again. Perhaps there was another staircase around the corner. There was no way he could make it back to the one he'd used without being seen.

He could hear the elevator door open, then steps as someone exited into the tiled hallway. Whether it was the security guard or not, the last thing Quinn wanted was for someone to see him.

He moved to the right down the corridor as quickly and quietly as he could. When he turned the corner, he saw a doorless opening near the end of the hall.

He reached it in seconds. The room beyond the threshold was unlit, but not totally dark. He could make out a trash chute and a couple of vending machines. With no time to make a more thorough evaluation, he squeezed between one of the machines and the wall. It wasn't a perfect fit, but it was the best he could do.

For several minutes, there was nothing, then the footsteps on tile returned as the security guard neared the utility room. Quinn tensed, preparing himself for action.

Closer and closer, until they were right outside the door. There the steps stopped.

Keep walking, buddy, Quinn thought.

The beam of a flashlight darted into the room. It swept left, right, then left again. Just as quickly, it went out, and the steps began moving back down the hallway again.

★　★　★

Fifteen minutes later, Quinn and Nate met up on the path along the river. On his way out, Quinn had removed the petal he'd stuck over the camera lens in the sconce, leaving no trace that he'd been in the building.

'So what did you find?' Nate asked.

'Trouble, I think,' Quinn said.

'What kind?'

It was a good question. Unfortunately, Quinn didn't have an answer.

25

The night was a short one. Quinn fell into bed just after 5 a.m. Three hours later, his eyes snapped open and his body tensed as someone shook him awake.

'It's just me,' Orlando said. She was sitting on the edge of his bed, a somber look on her face.

'What is it?' he asked as he pushed himself up.

'I have something you'll want to see,' she said.

'What?'

She stood up. 'I've got it up on the computer.'

Quinn watched her walk out of the room, then sighed and pushed himself out of bed. He pulled on a pair of jeans and a T-shirt, then walked barefoot into the other room.

Orlando was sitting at the desk, her computer open in front of her. She was alone. Nate was undoubtedly still asleep in his room.

Quinn walked over to her. 'Okay,' he said. 'Show me.'

She turned the laptop and tilted the screen so he could see it. She had the browser open to a newspaper article from the *Washington Post*.

FORMER CIA OFFICIAL IN CRITICAL CONDITION

Fredericksburg, Virginia — Derek Blackmoore was found unconscious in the entryway of his home outside Fredericksburg, Virginia, yesterday afternoon. Mr. Blackmoore, a former employee of the Central Intelligence Agency, had suffered multiple bruises and fractures when a neighbor discovered him.

'He was beaten severely,' Detective Scott Geist said. 'It appears that he was probably left to die. Mr. Blackmoore was lucky someone found him when they did. He's in bad shape, but he's alive.'

When asked what might have motivated the attack, Geist said, 'We're operating under the theory that it was a robbery at this point, but we're not ruling anything out.'

The article went on to describe the scene in a little more detail. There were no witnesses, and no one heard anything.

'Is this the latest?' Quinn said.

'It's the latest online,' Orlando told him. 'But I made a few calls. He's still alive, but that's it. No one's willing to make a guess if he'll survive or not. I also found out it wasn't a robbery. Nothing was taken from the house.'

'Robbers wouldn't have beat him like that anyway,' Quinn said. 'Killed him, or knocked him out. This was torture.'

She looked up at him. 'Do you think it was the same people who are after Jenny?'

'I don't know,' Quinn said.

There was another question she didn't ask, but Quinn knew all too well. Had he been the one to lead them to Blackmoore?

Orlando was obviously reading his thoughts. 'They could have come at him from all sorts of different ways. You weren't the only one who knew Blackmoore's connection to Markoff. He'd be a logical place for anyone to go.'

'Yeah,' Quinn said. But he couldn't bring himself to believe that.

'Something else,' she said.

'What?'

'LP.'

'You know what it is?'

'I know it has a few people scared. Nobody on our level knew what I was talking about. But a few higher up did. They didn't come out and say it, but I could tell.'

'Did they give you anything?'

She shook her head. 'No. But I was thinking. If these people know, maybe Peter does, too.'

Quinn thought for a moment. 'He might not tell me anything either.'

'Could be worth a try, though,' she said. 'He's probably still at work.'

Quinn looked at his watch: 8:35 a.m. The twelve-hour difference meant it was 8:35 p.m. the previous evening back in New York. From Quinn's experience, Peter seldom went home before 10.

★   ★   ★

'I'm not renegotiating our deal,' Peter said, once he knew it was Quinn on the line.

'I'm not calling to renegotiate,' Quinn told him. 'I have a question.'

'Okay, so ask.'

'Peter, have you ever heard the initials *LP*?'

292

Silence.

'Do you know what LP might mean?' Quinn asked.

'Where did you hear that?' Peter's words were measured and low.

'In a message. But I don't know what it means.'

'You don't need to know — '

'I do,' Quinn said. 'If you can — '

'No,' Peter barked. 'Let it go.'

'I can't. It's important.'

'I'll call you back.'

'Peter, I need — '

'Five minutes.'

The phone went dead.

'What's wrong?' Orlando asked.

'He knows something, but he didn't want to tell me.'

'So he hung up?'

Quinn frowned. 'Said he would call me back in five minutes.'

They looked at each other, neither voicing what they both knew that meant. Instead, they remained silent, waiting as the seconds ticked slowly off the clock.

It was almost five minutes exactly when the phone rang again.

Quinn answered immediately. 'Yes?'

'Where did you hear that?' Peter asked.

The sound over the phone line had changed. Not Peter's voice so much as the ambient sound around him. Before it was hushed, like he was in a box. But now Quinn could hear other sounds in the distance. It confirmed what he and

293

Orlando already knew. Peter had left his office and was probably using his personal secured cell phone for the call.

'I told you, it was in a message,' Quinn said.

'What message?'

'Is that really important?'

'Jesus, Quinn. Just tell me how the hell you heard about LP.'

Quinn hesitated, then said, 'Markoff.'

'Markoff?' Peter paused. 'CIA Markoff?'

'Yes.'

'Why the hell would he mention LP?' Peter asked. 'He's out of the game, isn't he?'

'He's dead.'

That stopped Peter.

'I think this LP, whatever it is, had something to do with it,' Quinn said.

'So what if they did?'

'It's important to me.'

Peter said nothing for a moment, then, 'Why?'

'Because Markoff was a friend of mine. Because I think they may have been the ones who killed him. Because if they are, then they're the ones trying to kill his girlfriend right now. I'm not going to let that happen.'

'You don't want to go up against these guys.'

'Who are they?'

Again silence.

'The straight answer is I don't know exactly,' Peter finally said. 'Let's just say they want things to run their way. And the way they try to do it is from within.'

'What do you mean? Try to run what?'

'Ultimately? Everything.'

294

'So they're some kind of organization?' Quinn asked.

'I guess you could call them that.'

'Who's in charge?'

'That's what no one knows. There's no working list of probable members. They could be anybody.'

'What does it mean? LP?'

'All we know is they go by LP,' Peter said. 'What it means . . . who knows? It probably isn't important anyway.'

Quinn thought for a moment. 'Why did you leave your office to call me back? You think you've been infiltrated?'

He could sense Peter's hesitation. 'I don't think so,' the head of the Office said. 'But no reason to take a chance. Look, Quinn. I've told you more than I probably should have. All I'll say is, if you think LP is involved, it's best if you leave it alone. Trust me on this.'

Quinn started to ask another question, but Peter was no longer there.

Orlando was looking at him as he set the phone down. 'What did he say?' she asked.

'He's almost as scared as Blackmoore,' he said. He then repeated what Peter had told him.

'He could have been a little more helpful,' Orlando said.

'No kidding,' Quinn agreed. 'It's not much. In fact, he was basically telling me to just let it go.'

'Do you want to let it go?'

Quinn frowned at her. 'Since when do I let anything Peter tells me scare me off?'

★ ★ ★

Though Singapore was a place in a constant state of renewal, it had changed little in the eighteen months since Quinn's previous visit. That time, the job he had been hired for had turned into nothing, a situation that occurred about thirty percent of the time. He'd be moved into place before a particular action was to occur, then, if things went wrong, he jumped in to clean up the mess. Sometimes, though, things went right, and he'd get an all-expenses-paid trip plus his fee deposited into his account for what amounted to hanging around.

On his last trip to the island, he'd spent more time at the Kinokuniya Bookstore on Orchard Road than he had discussing the job with his client. And in the end, he was told, 'Thank you very much. We'll call you when we have something else.' Though there was something to be said about making money for doing nothing, Quinn preferred to be in action. It's what he'd been trained for, after all. He hated getting mentally prepped to do something that didn't materialize.

Of course, everything was an opportunity, and while he might have spent a lot of time perusing the shelves at Kinokuniya, he'd also spent time deepening his knowledge of the island and strengthening his relationships with some of the local talent he had gotten to know over the years. You never knew when something like that would pay off.

Like that morning.

Quinn and Nate took a cab from the hotel to the west end of Orchard Road, getting out in front of the OG Orchard Point department store.

Orchard Road was the Champs-Élysées of Singapore. On this street, shopping was the main religion. Department stores, malls, small shops, fancy restaurants, fast food. It all blended together on Orchard. You could find places that catered to the Rodeo Drive mindset across the street from tiny bargain shops that appeased the thriftier customer.

'That way,' Quinn said to Nate, pointing to his right across a small side street at the Orchard Point shopping complex.

It was a multilevel shopping center, with many stores advertising discounts and bargains. At street level, small shops opened directly onto the sidewalk. There were tailors and luggage stores and camera shops and shoe stores. And while prices might not always be negotiable, they weren't out of sight, either. Often the owner or one of the employees stood outside the shop, beckoning potential customers to come in.

Quinn led Nate to a wide set of stairs near the center of the mall, then headed up to the second level. By American standards, the hallways were narrow for a shopping center, maybe five or six people wide. Both sides were lined with stores similar to those outside.

Near where the hall reached the end of the building and made a ninety-degree turn to the right, Quinn found a dress shop. A sign above the entrance identified it as 'Ne Win's Fine Dresses.'

The shop itself was only about twenty feet deep and about the same wide. Racks had been mounted to the walls on both the right and left, double high like clothing bunk beds. There was also a mannequin near the front entrance wearing a beautiful red silk gown.

Before entering, Quinn told Nate, 'Wait here.'

'You looking for something to wear?' Nate said.

Quinn didn't even honor the comment with a dirty look. Instead, he stepped into the store.

Two well-dressed women in their early twenties were talking to an older man, the owner of the shop. One of the girls looked full Chinese, while the other was definitely a blend. Quinn moved over to the side, pretending to look at some of the clothes on the racks.

'And it will be ready by Thursday?' the second girl asked, her accent a mix of British, Australian, and Chinese.

'Of course. No problem,' the man said. His own accent was more pronounced. English was not the language he'd grown up learning.

'And you won't charge her any extra, right?' the second girl said. 'Not like last time.'

The old man smiled, but Quinn could tell he was holding back. 'Of course not. No reason.'

The girls looked at each other, happy. The first girl nodded, then said, 'All right. We'll be back on Thursday.'

As they turned to leave, they noticed Nate standing near the entrance of the shop. Each girl gave him a coy smile, the girl who was full Chinese looking away first while her friend's eyes lingered on Nate a moment longer. From Quinn's angle, it looked like his apprentice's eyes were lingering a bit too long, too.

'Excuse us,' the girl said unnecessarily as she passed Nate.

Quinn smirked to himself, then approached the shop owner. The old man hadn't moved. The same forced smile he'd given the girls while they were in the shop remained on his face as he watched them walk away.

In a quiet, friendly voice, he said toward their receding forms, 'Go fuck yourself, ladies. See you Thursday.' After a moment, he dropped the smile and looked at Quinn. 'Goddamn SPGs,' he said, then headed toward the back of the store.

Quinn couldn't help but smile. SPG, Sarong Party Girl. It referred to that group of young Singaporean women who went out dancing and clubbing, all the time on the lookout for Caucasian husbands. The shop owner had used the term like he was a hip local kid and not the Burmese refugee he really was.

The old man, Ne Win, had escaped his homeland in 1989 when he was suspected of organizing several pro-democracy demonstrations. He once told Quinn if he'd stayed, he'd be nearly twenty years dead by now. That was where he was lucky, he had said. Where he was cursed was with his name.

There was a much more infamous Ne Win, the general who had led the military coup that had taken over Burma in 1962. He was the dictator who had ruled the country for decades, and whose presence was still felt years after his death.

Quinn had known the shop owner Ne Win for a while. It had been Markoff who had introduced them. It had been about five years earlier, during a summit of Asian financial leaders. The connection was one of the reasons Quinn was paying him a visit that morning.

'You hear her tell me not to charge her more?' Ne Win asked.

There was a gray metal cooler against the back wall. The old man opened it and removed two cans of Tiger beer. He tossed one to Quinn.

'Last time her friend order a dress, she come in after I'm almost done, have me change everything. Not my fault. I do exactly what she wants. So she change, I charge her. She mad, but so what? Not mad enough she not come back, eh?'

They opened their beers and knocked them together in a silent toast.

'You want good work, you have to pay for it,' Quinn said, then took a drink.

'Damn straight,' Ne Win said.

Quinn laughed. *That* was a phrase Quinn had taught him.

Ne Win lifted his can to his lips and took a deep drink. 'Your friend want a beer?' he said, nodding his chin toward Nate.

'He's fine,' Quinn said.

'Maybe I have seamstress make the dress a centimeter or two too small. Tell her she must have put on weight since I measure her.'

'You'd do that, wouldn't you?' Quinn asked.

'Hell, yes. Done before. Very funny.'

They both took another sip of their beers.

'How's business?' Quinn asked.

Ne Win shrugged. 'Everyone always wants dress. Just some don't want to pay big store price, huh? My dresses better anyway.'

'That's what I've heard.'

'Who you hear that from?'

'Well . . . actually I heard that from you.'

Ne Win huffed a mock laugh, then brought the can back to his mouth.

'I'm in need of a few items,' Quinn said.

Ne Win continued to hold the beer to his lips, allowing the amber liquid to trickle into his mouth, his expression unchanged. Except for his eyes. They seemed to take in the whole room before focusing on Quinn. The old man lowered the beer, then shook his head once in each direction, the movement all but unnoticeable.

'I don't make men's shirts anymore,' Ne Win said, his voice the same as it had been before. 'I have friend, though. Very good.'

'That would be great,' Quinn replied. 'Is he here in the building?'

'No. No. Down the street.' Ne Win set his can on top of the cooler and turned to Quinn. 'I show you, okay?'

'What about the shop?'

'My daughter watch. She work next door.'

★   ★   ★

Ne Win was silent until they were on the sidewalk walking west along Orchard Road.

301

'Everywhere someone listening, you know?' Ne Win said, voice low. 'Never know when someone put bug in my shop.'

'You don't do a sweep?' Nate asked.

Ne Win narrowed his eyes, giving Nate the up-and-down. 'Stupid question.'

'This is Nate,' Quinn said. 'He's my apprentice.'

'Ah, explains it. Well, Mr. *Apprentice*. Do I check for bugs? Of course. Do you think I'm stupid? Every morning. Every night. I still find them. Couple times a week.'

'Who's putting them there? The police?' Nate asked.

Ne Win blew out a loud, dismissive breath. 'Police don't touch me.'

Nate looked confused.

'Competition. Young guys, you know. Work out of Geylang. Want to find out who my clients are.'

'Why don't you just stop them?' Nate asked.

'That's enough questions,' Quinn said.

The old man smiled. 'Someday when I'm bored, I take care of it.'

It never mattered what day it was, as long as the shops were open, Orchard was crowded. Like a lot of Singapore, it was a mixed crowd — Chinese, Caucasian, Malay, Indian, and all combinations in between. And those were just the residents. There were tourists also — Europeans, Japanese, Australians, and a few Americans — all enjoying a little bit of Asia lite.

They passed two women pushing baby carriages, then stopped at a corner to wait for the streetlight to change.

'The usual?' Ne Win asked.

'To start,' Quinn said, knowing the old man knew about his preference in firearms.

'Something for him, then?' Ne Win's gaze flicked toward Nate. 'You sure you can trust him with weapon?'

Quinn smiled. 'He's all right,' he said. 'There's a few other things I'll need.' He pulled a list out of his pocket and handed it to the old man.

Ne Win looked it over, then nodded. 'Easy, easy.'

The light turned green and they began to cross.

'There's something else,' Quinn said, getting to the other reason for his visit.

Quinn's supplier tensed. It was subtle, but Quinn had seen it.

'What is it?' Ne Win said.

'I'm looking for someone.'

'Good luck. Singapore big city.'

Quinn paused. 'Someone you know.'

'I know lots of people.'

Quinn looked over at the old man. 'It's Steven Markoff.'

Ne Win smiled at a passing woman, but said nothing.

'Have you seen him?'

The old man took a deep breath, then said, 'He not here. Was, but not now.'

'When was this?'

They reached the curb and stepped up onto the sidewalk. 'Don't remember. One week, two weeks, a month? Don't know where he is now.'

'He's dead.'

Ne Win reacted a moment too late. 'Dead?'

'You knew that, didn't you?' Quinn said.

Ne Win looked at Quinn. He didn't appear to be scared, just annoyed. From behind Quinn, there was the sound of footsteps approaching.

'We've got company,' Nate said.

The footsteps stopped only a few feet away. But Quinn didn't turn. Instead, he kept his focus on the old man.

'Tell them everything is okay,' Quinn said, his eyes still on the old man.

Ne Win smiled at Quinn. 'Is everything okay?'

'Did you kill Markoff?'

The old man stared Quinn in the eyes. 'No.'

'Did you have anything to do with killing him?'

'No.'

Neither moved nor spoke for several seconds. Finally Quinn said, 'If that's true, then everything is fine.'

'But you not sure you believe me,' Ne Win said.

Quinn leaned back a few inches and looked away. 'I believe you.'

'Okay, okay,' Ne Win said to whoever was standing behind Quinn. 'Old friend. No problem.'

Nothing at first. Then Quinn could hear the others moving away. He chanced a look back. There were three men, tall and muscular. None were smiling, but they had at least backed away several feet.

'New guards,' Quinn said to Ne Win.

'Nephews. Too lazy to work in corporation.'

Quinn turned back to the old man. 'You don't happen to know Jorge Albina, do you?'

'The name sounds familiar, but I know lots of people.'

'Are you the one who sent him Markoff's body?'

'You the one who told me he was dead,' Ne Win said. 'I see your friend when he here, all right? He was not careful. He looked in wrong places, understand? I tried to tell him to forget, but he didn't listen. Whatever happened to him, that is his business.'

'So he came to you.'

'Everyone come to me if they need some-thing.'

'What did he need?'

'Like you, a little gear.'

'What else?'

Ne Win smiled. 'Like you,' he repeated, 'a little information.'

'You knew he was dead.'

Ne Win said nothing.

'Someone put him in a shipping container to die, then sent the container to the States.'

Ne Win's face grew red. 'You think I kill him? Markoff a client. I don't kill clients. He bring me other business, too. He introduce you to me, remember?'

'Of course I remember,' Quinn said.

'So? You trying to disrespect me?'

'I'm just trying to honor him by finding out what happened.'

Ne Win scoffed. 'Don't try bullshit me.'

'Not bullshit,' Quinn said.

Ne Win eyed Quinn, appraising him. 'Okay. I believe you. Now you believe me. I had nothing to do with his death.'

'Do you know who did?'

Ne Win was silent for several seconds. He then looked past Quinn at his men and said something in Burmese. One of the men pulled out a piece of paper, wrote something on it, then handed it to the old man.

'Go find lunch,' Ne Win said to Quinn, then handed him the piece of paper. 'You and your apprentice go here one hour. You pick up your order then.'

Quinn looked at the paper. On it was written *Le Meridien Hotel, Georges Lounge.*

When Quinn looked up again, Ne Win was already walking away with his bodyguards.

'He had something to do with your friend's death,' Nate said. He, too, was watching Ne Win walk away.

'Absolutely,' Quinn said.

'He's the one who sent the container, isn't he?'

'Most likely.'

'So either he killed Markoff or he knows who did it?'

'He didn't kill Markoff.'

'You believe him?'

Quinn nodded. 'Yes.'

'I don't know,' Nate said. 'I don't trust him. You should have pressed him more.'

'How?' Quinn asked. 'Pulled out a gun and pointed it at his head?'

'I don't know. Something.'

Ne Win had disappeared into the crowd on Orchard Road.

'You might not trust him,' Quinn said. 'But I do.'

26

Two hours later, Quinn and Nate were in a cab on the way back to the Pan Pacific with a satchel full of gear from Ne Win when Quinn's phone vibrated. He looked at the display: Orlando.

'Hey,' he said as he answered. 'We should be there soon.'

'That might not be such a good idea,' Orlando said. 'We're not alone here anymore.'

'What does that mean?'

'I went downstairs to grab a newspaper and get a little fresh air,' she said. 'As I was heading back up, I passed by the reception desk. Two of the men you took pictures of in Houston were there.'

That stopped Quinn.

'Are you sure?' he asked.

'Yes. They were checking in.'

'Hold on,' he said. He pulled the phone away from his ear, then leaned forward toward the cabby. 'Change of plans. Esplanade Park, please.'

The driver grunted in acknowledgment. At the next intersection, the cab veered off its previous course and headed east toward Esplanade Park.

Quinn brought the phone back up to his ear. 'We need to get out of the hotel,' he said.

'Ah, yeah,' she said. 'That was kind of the point of my call.'

'Can you pack up our stuff?'

'Already done.'

Quinn smiled despite the situation. 'Great. Hold tight. I'll call you back soon.'

'Wait,' Orlando said. 'That wasn't the only thing I needed to tell you. Jenny sent another message.'

'She's here?'

'I don't know. She wants you to call her.' There was a pause. 'In eighteen minutes.'

★ ★ ★

Quinn had Nate carry the leather messenger bag with the gear inside as they walked into Esplanade Park. Located at the northwest corner of Marina Bay, the green public space provided a beautiful view of downtown across the water. A main path went west to east through the entire park and continued into the Marina Promenade. It was a favorite of bikers and joggers and those just out for a peaceful stroll. Quinn and Nate walked along the path for a few minutes until they found an empty bench.

Quinn checked his watch. It was three minutes until 4 p.m., the appointed time for the call.

'You realize if the cops catch me with this bag, I could go to jail,' Nate said.

'This is Singapore,' Quinn told him. 'You wouldn't just go to jail. You'd be hanged within months.'

The thought didn't seem to sit too well with Nate. 'Maybe you should carry it.'

'I'm carrying this,' Quinn said, holding up his cell phone.

At exactly 4 p.m., he dialed Jenny's number again.

Two rings this time.

'Quinn?'

'Yes. Where are you?'

'I'll be there tonight. Meet me at the Far East Square. Do you know it?'

'Uh-huh,' Quinn said. It was an outdoor mall in Chinatown.

'The Water Gate entrance. Eight-thirty.'

'All right. Is there — ' He stopped. Apparently, it was becoming everyone's habit to hang up on him.

★ ★ ★

Ne Win looked surprised as Quinn and Nate entered the dress shop. But when he noticed the familiar leather bag hanging from Nate's shoulder, his demeanor changed from surprised to angry.

'What are you doing here?' he whispered to Quinn.

'I need something,' Quinn said.

'I already gave you something.' The old man's eyes couldn't help but glance at the bag.

'I need a place to stay.'

Ne Win held a finger to his lips. He then grabbed Quinn by the arm and ushered him out of the shop, nodding at Nate to follow. He took them down the hallway toward the back of the building. As they passed one of the small shops, Ne Win called out to a woman inside, then pointed back toward his own store.

'Your daughter?' Quinn asked.

'None of your business,' Ne Win said.

Stuck between two of the shops at the end of the hall was a metal door painted the same color as the wall. Using a key from his pocket, Ne Win unlocked it. Beyond was a service corridor, about fifty feet in length, with another door at the far end. The walls were scuffed from being banged against for years.

Ne Win kept moving forward, his pace fast. At the end of the hall, he paused only long enough to pull the door open. He passed through without waiting to see if Quinn and Nate were still following.

The door led outside to a short staircase that descended to a makeshift loading dock at the back of the building. There were trash bins off to the left and several vans parked across the back. Ne Win was already halfway down the staircase. When he reached the bottom, he went from van to van, trying all the doors. He stopped when he finally found one that was open, then climbed inside.

He motioned for Quinn and Nate to join him.

'I apologize,' Quinn said once they were all enclosed within the van's cargo area.

'You don't bring that stuff to my shop,' Ne Win said. 'Police find you in there with that, cause me big trouble.'

'Thought you said the police weren't a problem for you,' Nate said.

'Not problem if I don't have guns in my shop. What you thinking?'

'Things have changed. I need a place to stay.

311

Room enough for several people.'

'I don't run hotel.'

'No, but you can find me something, can't you?' Quinn said. 'I'd prefer an apartment. Something with a private entrance.'

'You want maid and butler service, too?'

'Just the apartment.'

Ne Win's eyes narrowed. 'You going to be a problem for me. I can tell.'

'Maybe,' Quinn said.

★ ★ ★

Ne Win found them a deluxe 'service' apartment in a building frequented by ex-pats. It was across the river, but less than a half-mile from the Quayside Villas. In Singapore, everything was close.

Quinn called Orlando and gave her the address.

'It's going to look kind of odd for me to walk out alone with all these bags,' she said.

'I'll send Nate to help.'

A pause. 'What are you going to do?'

'Jenny said she'd be here in a few hours. We've set up a meet.' There was no need to add he wanted to recon the location first. She'd understand that.

'You shouldn't go alone,' she said.

'Once you get set up at the apartment, send Nate back to help me.'

'What time are you meeting her?'

'Eight-thirty,' he said, then told her where.

He got the sense she wasn't happy with the

arrangement. But the only thing she said was, 'Be careful.'

*   *   *

Four main entrances surrounded the Far East Square, each assigned an element of the earth to 'guard' the complex — water, fire, metal, and wood. Quinn checked out the rendezvous point first.

A large wooden arch framed the entrance. Mounted at the top of the arch was a round sign. The words *Far East Square* were wrapped around a symbolic lion outlined in yellow. Below this hung a smaller sign: *Water Gate*.

A stone path led beneath the arch past four pillars of water, two on either side. The pillars were cylindrical Plexiglas tubes, each about a foot and a half in diameter, with bubbling water enclosed inside. The effect was mesmerizing.

The mall buildings were all painted a uniform golden yellow and were trimmed in white and accented by dark red wooden shutters on the windows. There were clothing stores and jewelry shops and gift stores and restaurants. There were also carts filled with wares set at strategic points along the walkway.

The crowd, like Singapore itself, was a mix of Asians and Caucasians. There were the obvious unrefined tourists with their cameras and loud shirts and constant excitement over things out of their norm. And the equally obvious stealth tourist, acting the part of the uninterested local, but blowing it by acting more uninterested than

313

any local ever would. Then there were the locals themselves, those who worked at the mall, those who were doing a little shopping, and those who'd stopped by for a quick meal.

Quinn noticed them all, and considered each a potential adversary until he felt confident enough to mark them off his list. By a few minutes after eight, he'd eliminated all but a handful as potential problems, and even those he felt were very unlikely to be trouble.

He knew better than to wait right at the gate, and instead took up position inside the mall, sitting at a table outside a small restaurant. On the spare chair, he put the leather bag Nate had been carrying earlier, then ordered a coffee from the waitress and began the waiting. His view of the gate was partially obscured by the shoppers, but he could see well enough.

After fifteen minutes, he glanced at his watch: 8:21. Where the hell was Nate?

Three more minutes passed before his phone rang. Quinn answered without looking at the ID.

'You're late,' he said.

'Jonathan?' It was Tasha.

'I don't have time to talk right now.'

'At least tell me if you've found her?' she asked, her voice hopeful.

He hesitated for a moment, then said, 'Yes.'

'Is she with you now?' Tasha sounded surprised.

'Not yet. Soon.'

'Thank God. Please call me once she's with you. Let me talk to her.'

'If there's time,' he said. There was a beep in

his ear telling him another call was coming through. 'I have to go.'

He disconnected Tasha, then looked at the display before answering the other call. Orlando.

'Where's Nate?' he said once he activated the call.

'Not coming,' she said.

'What?'

'I left him at the apartment.'

'You left . . . Wait. Are you here?'

'I'm outside,' she said. 'Across the street from Water Gate.'

The thought of her nearby ready to help was more than just comforting. 'I'm inside, sitting at — '

'I know where you are,' she said.

Of course she did, Quinn thought. That's why he liked to work with her. She was almost as good as he was. She, of course, would probably say she was better.

'Any sign of Jenny?' he asked.

'No. At least I don't think so,' she said.

'What do you mean?'

'I mean the picture you showed me wasn't exactly in the best of conditions, was it?'

They fell into several seconds of silence. Quinn scanned everyone in view while acting like he was listening to something interesting. He checked the time again: 8:29.

'We've got company,' Orlando said.

'She's here?'

'No. It's one of your Texas friends.'

Quinn tensed. 'Alone?'

Silence. Then, 'I count six.'

315

★ ★ ★

Jenny was walking right into a trap. It didn't matter at the moment how the others had figured out where she was going to be, it just mattered that unless Quinn did something quick, Jenny's freedom was about to be ripped away.

He pushed himself up from his chair and threw some money on the table. 'What are they doing?' he said into the phone.

'They got out of two taxis a half block down from the gate. One of them seems to be in charge. He's signaling two men to go to the left to a mall entrance down the street. Three others are walking toward the gate.'

Quinn was on the move now, heading toward the gate from the inside. 'And the one calling the shots?'

'He's also heading toward the gate, but is hanging back behind his men.'

'Abort and distract,' Quinn said.

'Got it.'

The line went dead.

There was a group of people just inside the gate. They were all Caucasian and looked to be traveling together. Some type of tour group, Quinn guessed. A couple dozen strong.

He swung the leather bag around and slipped his hand inside. He had yet to attach suppressors to any of the pistols, but that was fine for what he needed to do now. He grabbed the first gun his hand touched, then slipped his other hand into the bag, checking to make sure there was a cartridge in the chamber.

Once satisfied, he moved the end of the barrel so that it was just peeking out from under the top flap, and aimed it low at one of the planters along the walkway. He took a calming breath, then pulled the trigger.

The sound of the shot was magnified by the enclosed space of the mall, rolling over all other noise like a sudden avalanche.

For two seconds, the whole world stopped. Silence, no movement. Everyone frozen in place. Everyone but Quinn.

As soon as he pulled the trigger, he began running toward the gate.

'Gun!' he yelled, pointing back the way he'd come.

His voice seemed to break the collective trance. People began screaming, some running with Quinn, some running in the opposite direction.

'Gun!' he yelled again as he neared the group at the gate. Behind him, he heard others taking up the call.

The group of tourists seemed to move en masse, rushing past the pillars of water and through the wooden arch like a stampede. They were joined by more of the terrified shoppers, all wanting nothing more than to get away.

Quinn blended into the back of the group, his head moving side to side, taking in everything and everyone. There were three men, large and dressed in suits, pushing against the tide as they tried to get into the mall. But the swell of humanity exiting through the gate was too much. The more they tried to force their way through,

317

the less progress they made. Quinn saw bulges under each of their jackets. Weapons, no question about it. These had to be the men Orlando had seen.

As Quinn passed under the arch, he looked to the right, down the street, trying to spot the leader. The crowd was thinner in that direction, so it only took a moment for Quinn to pick him out.

But he not only picked him out, he recognized him. He was the last man out of the house in Houston, the blond guy.

Traffic on the street had come to a standstill as people flooded onto the road, becoming obstacles no one seemed interested in hitting. As Quinn watched, Blondie ran up to a taxi, pulled open one of the doors, then jumped up onto the threshold so that he could look over the crowd.

Suddenly he pointed toward the far side of the madness, off to Quinn's left. Quinn whipped his head around. As he did he noticed the suits also following their boss's gesture.

People moved all around Quinn, creating an ever-changing landscape. At first, he couldn't figure out what it was that drew the man's attention. Then the crowd cleared for a split second.

About fifty feet down the street, a woman was running away from the scene. Caucasian, thin, with very short hair. It wasn't until she glanced back over her shoulder that Quinn recognized her.

Jenny.

She had dropped at least twenty pounds since

he'd last seen her, pounds she didn't need to lose. And her shoulder-length brown hair had been chopped short enough so that in the right circumstances, and with the right clothing, she might even be able to pass for a boy. She'd also darkened it until it was almost black.

It was the look of someone on the run, doing what they could to survive.

Quinn began pushing people out of his way as he changed direction. Two of the other men were ahead of him, muscling their way through the crowd. But Jenny was moving faster than all of them, helped by the fact she was in an area momentarily less congested.

Someone grabbed Quinn's arm. He looked over his shoulder. It was the third suit. Only he seemed to just be trying to pass by, and didn't realize who Quinn was.

As the man came abreast, Quinn slammed his elbow into his solar plexus.

The man doubled over in pain and surprise, then fell to the ground as several people plowed into him as they tried to flee.

Quinn began running again. Jenny had almost doubled the distance between them. But the other two men had also made progress and, unlike Quinn, were gaining on her.

Quinn weaved in and out of the mass of people, trying to make some headway. The larger of the two men was also the slower one. Quinn was able to get within a couple feet of him before the man glanced over his shoulder to see whose footsteps were keeping pace with his own.

By then it was too late. Quinn already had the advantage.

He rammed himself into the man's back, concentrating the force of his blow just below the big man's shoulders. The man staggered but remained on his feet. Quinn shoved again, harder. This time the man fell, and Quinn went with him.

The man twisted his shoulders trying to dislodge Quinn, but Quinn held on, kneeing him twice in the kidneys.

'Get the fuck off me!' the man yelled.

He put his hands on the ground and started to push himself up. Quinn's grasp of the man's shirt slipped, and he fell to the side. But even as the man started to stand up, Quinn jumped to his feet.

The big man's hand moved under his jacket, going for his gun.

Quinn didn't have time to pull out one of his own weapons. Instead, he grabbed the leather bag and swung it with as much force as he could generate.

The man's hands started to fly up to block the blow, but Quinn was faster. The bag full of gear smashed into the side of the guy's head, spinning him around and sending him back to the ground.

Quinn was in a full sprint now.

Jenny was almost out of sight, turning left onto China Street. The final pursuer was directly behind her. A second later, she was gone, disappearing behind the bulk of the building at the corner.

As the man following her took the corner, he glanced back toward Quinn. It was the driver from Houston. The look in the man's eyes told Quinn he knew who Quinn was also. Then the driver moved around the corner out of sight.

Quinn ran as fast as he could. He stayed tight to the building as he turned the corner, then came to a dead stop.

Jenny and the driver were gone.

27

Quinn moved down the block, looking left and right, desperate to find Jenny. The crowds were calmer here, as if the near-riot at the Water Gate was a thousand miles away. Several people gave Quinn an odd look as he ran past them.

Somewhere ahead and to the left he heard a muffled cry.

He ran faster than he had in months, looking for the source of the sound. Up ahead, he spotted a break between the buildings. Just before he reached the opening, he stopped, then pressed up against the wall and listened.

Another cry. Female.

He chanced a glance around the edge. The opening was a small service corridor between buildings. There were bins and barrels piled along the side. Just beyond them, Quinn could see the driver's back. If Jenny was with him, she was out of sight, hidden by the stacks of refuse.

Quinn cautiously moved into the small alley, keeping the barrels between himself and the man. Once he was off the street, he removed one of the SIG Sauer pistols from his bag, this time pulling out a suppressor and quietly attaching it to the end of the muzzle.

He crept forward as far as he could without having to expose himself. Then listened again.

'Yeah. Over on China Street,' the driver was saying. 'Hurry up.'

Quinn could hear the beep of a mobile phone being disconnected.

'Our ride will be here in a minute,' the man said. 'You're done. Do you understand? This is over, so you can cut it out!'

Quinn gripped the SIG in both hands, then quickly stepped out of his hiding place and toward the man. He only made it five feet before the driver saw him.

'Stop right there,' the man said. In his hand was a gun pointed at Jenny.

Quinn took a few more steps, his pistol aimed at the man's chest.

'I said fucking stop!'

The gap between them was only ten feet now.

Jenny looked over at Quinn, her eyes dull, almost defeated. After a moment, there was a flicker of recognition, and then the hint of hope on her face.

Quinn took one more step.

'Stop or I'll kill her,' the man said. 'I know you don't want that.'

Quinn knew that wasn't true. They'd want Jenny alive. Whatever it was they were looking for, she was the key.

'Jenny, come here,' Quinn said.

'What the fuck?' the man said. 'Don't you go anywhere!'

'Jenny,' Quinn said. 'It's okay.'

'It's not okay,' the man said. He raised his gun a few inches, changed his aim from her chest to her head.

Quinn was about to call out to Jenny again when a sudden movement from the far end of the alley caught his eye. He barely had time to duck down when he realized it was something flying through the air toward them.

But he needn't have bothered. The man holding the gun on Jenny turned to see what was up instead of following Quinn's lead. His timing couldn't have been worse.

He probably barely registered the spiky oval object before it hit him square in the face.

The force of the blow knocked him backward, but somehow he remained on his feet as he straddled the edge of consciousness.

Quinn immediately closed the gap between them, slamming the man against the wall. This time the man's eyes closed shut, and he slumped down to the ground.

Not wanting to take any chances, Quinn grabbed the asshole's gun just in case. But the man was out cold.

Quinn suddenly heard footsteps following the same basic path as the object that had flown through the air. He whipped both guns around, his fingers on the triggers, ready to fire. But immediately lowered the weapons.

It was Orlando. She was wearing gloves, and in one hand she carried another of the oval objects.

He recognized it now. A durian. It was a regional fruit — green in color, about a foot long and weighing a pound or two. But the most distinctive feature of the durian was the spiky, thorn-covered husk, each point hard and unforgiving. It almost looked like a pumped-up, hard-core version of a pineapple.

Quinn tossed her the SIG with the suppressor,

forcing her to drop the fruit. He nodded to the semiconscious man crumpled against the wall, then knelt down next to Jenny, knowing Orlando would have his back.

'Did he hurt you?'

She shook her head. 'Just grabbed me. What . . . what happened? I heard a gunshot.'

'Later,' he said.

He offered her a hand and pulled her up.

'His friends will be here in a second,' he said. 'You two head down to the end away from the street and wait for me.'

Orlando didn't hesitate. 'Come on,' she said to Jenny, then started running back the way she'd come. Jenny followed a second later.

Quinn knelt down next to the unconscious man and searched him.

He found a phone, wallet, and a set of keys, then put the items in his bag along with the man's gun.

Instead of joining Orlando and Jenny, he headed back toward the street, stopping just before the alley ended at the sidewalk. He eased out enough so that he could look up and down the block.

'Hey!' a voice called from the street.

It was Blondie. He was standing only thirty feet away, and had been looking toward the alley as Quinn had stepped out.

Quinn turned and started running toward Orlando and Jenny.

'Go!' Quinn said.

Neither woman needed to be told what to do twice. They disappeared off to the right.

When Quinn reached the end, he turned right, too. As he did he caught a glimpse of Blondie and two more men entering the alley. One of the men stopped next to their unconscious comrade, but the other two continued the chase.

Then they were out of sight.

Quinn once more found himself in the Far East Square. Only this time it was deserted, the gunfire having driven everyone out. It only took him a second to recognize his location from his earlier recon. There was another exit just ahead.

'To the right!' he called out to Orlando.

She and Jenny had just reached an intersection in the pathway — three directions for shopping, and to the right, an exit.

'To the right!' he repeated.

Orlando nodded, then led Jenny out of the mall. They had just disappeared when Quinn heard Blondie and his friend coming out of the alley behind him.

Quinn ran straight through the intersection, not even looking in the direction Orlando and Jenny had just taken.

There was a dull *thwack*, then a split second later a bullet smashed into a window just to his left. A burglar alarm began to ring.

Another *thwack*.

Quinn could almost feel the bullet whiz by his head. He juked first left, then to his right, then grabbed one of the metallic chairs sitting in front of a bakery. He swung it in a large arc, letting it fly back toward Blondie, but he didn't watch to see what happened.

Thwack. Quinn expected to see the impact of

a bullet nearby, but the only sound was from behind him, the expulsion of air followed by a heavy thud.

He looked over his shoulder. The man who was with Blondie was down.

Blondie himself had moved off to the right, taking cover behind one of the vendor carts lining the walkway.

Beyond, standing in the middle of the intersection, was Orlando.

She was holding the SIG Sauer in her hand. She waited a moment, no doubt hoping Quinn's remaining pursuer would expose himself, but when he didn't, she disappeared back into the exit.

Quinn kept moving. When he reached the next pathway to the street, he took it.

He found himself on the sidewalk along Cross Street. Quickly he scanned the area, trying to locate his friends. It only took him a moment to spot Orlando and Jenny. They were on the other side of the road, at the base of Club Street. Traffic was as much a mess here as it had been outside the Water Gate. No one seemed to be moving anywhere.

At the corner back toward Amoy Street, police lights flashed. Quinn guessed the mall was being surrounded, and that traffic would soon be jammed everywhere. That was a good thing. It meant the only way the others could continue their pursuit would be on foot.

Quinn weaved through the traffic, catching up to Orlando and Jenny as they made their way up Club, away from the chaos.

Unlike the streets bordering the Far East Square, Club was quieter. It was mainly made up of two- and three-story structures that, for the most part, housed private clubs and businesses. The street was not as well lit as Cross Street or the other roads in the shopping district. It was a private place for private people.

'Everyone all right?' he asked.

They each nodded.

'How did they find me?' Jenny said.

'I don't know,' Quinn said.

'Did they follow you?' she asked.

They had either followed Jenny or had followed him. But if they knew where Jenny was, they would have already taken her. So it had to be him. He just didn't know how.

A quick glance from Orlando told him she was thinking the same thing. But to Jenny, he said, 'No one followed me.'

'Are you sure? Maybe they've got you bugged. Maybe they're tracking your phone. Have you been using credit cards? Maybe they tracked you down that way, then tailed you here.'

It was apparent Markoff had given her a pretty good amateur education. 'I don't know how they knew we were meeting you here. But it doesn't matter right now. We need to get you away from here. Get you out of Singapore before they find you again.'

She stopped. 'Wait. I'm not leaving.'

'You realize they want to kill you, right?' Quinn said.

There was the roar of an engine. Not a car, but a motorcycle.

Quinn looked back toward the intersection with Cross. There was a dark bike working its way through the traffic and heading in their direction.

'Stay to the shadows,' Quinn said for Jenny's benefit.

Orlando began running, Jenny only steps behind her.

Quinn, though, remained where he was.

He pulled the other SIG out of the bag and attached the suppressor, then moved as far back from the street as possible, blending into a nook where two buildings met.

The engine gunned as the motorcycle cleared the traffic jam and started moving up the road toward his position. The only question now was whether the driver was trouble or just a civilian.

But that question was soon answered. Dark suit. No helmet. Caucasian.

Trouble.

Quinn waited until the motorcycle was only a few seconds away, then stepped out of his hiding space into the dull light of a distant streetlamp.

The instant the driver saw him, he started to bring the motorcycle to a skidding stop.

Then the flap of the man's jacket flew up, revealing a gun underneath, and a hand reaching for it.

Thwack.

Quinn's bullet knocked the rider off his bike.

Quinn waited only long enough to make sure the man wasn't getting up, then started running after Orlando and Jenny.

Ahead the road curved to the left. Just before

he reached the bend, Quinn checked over his shoulder one last time.

He cursed under his breath. Someone else was coming up the road. This time on foot, and fast. A light in front of one of the houses caught the man's face for a split second. Blondie.

As soon as Quinn took the bend, he stopped worrying about sticking to the shadows and raced up the street, the messenger bag banging painfully against his back.

Orlando and Jenny were nowhere in sight.

Good, he thought. While he acted as the distraction, Orlando would take Jenny someplace safe.

At the next intersection, Quinn turned left, heading up Ann Siang Hill, and followed the road all the way to the park at the end of the street.

Ann Siang Hill Park was not much more than a corridor between the back sides of the buildings lining Ann Siang Road and Amoy Street. Narrow strips of grass and small trees grew on each side of a red tile and concrete path. At intervals there were old-fashioned lampposts providing just enough light so no spot was completely dark.

Quinn slowed as he reached the path, masking the sound of his steps by keeping to the grass. The path wound through the buildings for several hundred feet before opening up into a patiolike area at the top of the hill. At the edge of the patio, there was a spiral staircase leading down to another path running behind the homes on Amoy.

Quinn paused near the top, focusing his attention back the way he had just come.

At first, there was only the distant noise of the city. Then there was something more. Soft but rhythmic. Footfalls. Someone on the path, heading his way.

He stepped on the spiral staircase, padding softly down the steps to the bottom. Then instead of continuing on the lower path, he slipped under the stairs, finding a dark spot beneath the deck, surrounded by vegetation.

He slipped the strap of the leather bag over his head, allowing himself a moment to roll his shoulder back and forth, relieving some of the stiffness. Next he popped the mag out of his gun. He was only down one bullet, but he had been trained never to be satisfied with less when he could have more. From a box of ammo in the bag, he retrieved a new cartridge, reloaded, then returned the mag to its home in the grip of the pistol.

He could hear the person on the path above clearly now. Not quite running, but not walking either. When Blondie reached the patio, his pace slowed, but didn't stop until he stood at the overhang, twenty feet directly above Quinn.

Quinn remained motionless, his breaths long, deep, and silent.

For thirty seconds, there was no sound from above. Blondie shuffled to the left. Five feet, no more. Silence again.

When he moved a second time, it wasn't back the way he had come, as Quinn had hoped, but rather down the spiral staircase.

Quinn took another deep breath, keeping himself loose and ready. Each tread in the spiral staircase was a separate metal triangle connected to a central pole, and beneath was a riser that went halfway down to the next tread, but left a gap of open air. He aimed the SIG through the gap that was level with his eye line.

As Blondie descended into the target zone, Quinn could first see shoes, then a pant leg, then the man's hip, his waist, and, as Blondie neared the bottom, his torso.

As soon as the man set both feet on solid ground, he stopped, his body still.

The guy was good, Quinn thought. Very good. He worked quietly. He had patience. And he'd tracked Quinn up Club Street and into Ann Siang Hill Park.

Quinn moved his finger onto the trigger. Once Blondie moved away from the stairway, he would have a clean shot. Whether he liked it or not, it was a shot he needed to take. A man like this wouldn't stop until he found Jenny, so he had to be removed.

Off to the right down the lower path, a twig snapped. Blondie tensed and took a step back toward the stairs.

There was the murmur of voices. A man and a woman, both speaking in Mandarin. Their conversation was loud and peppered with bouts of laughter. Several seconds later, they staggered into view, the man more drunk than the woman.

Blondie eased out from the stairs again, then started walking down the path. Quinn had him, a ten-foot gimme shot straight into the man's heart. But he couldn't pull the trigger. The civilians were too close. If he didn't kill the man with the first shot, there was a good chance the couple could get caught in the middle of a gunfight.

As his target disappeared down the path, Quinn could only watch, hoping he hadn't just made a fatal mistake.

28

'Where are you?' Quinn asked. He'd worked his way first west, then north back to Boat Quay, until he felt safe enough to make a call.

'I'm on the corner of Church Street and . . . ' Orlando paused. 'Phillip.'

That was only a few blocks from where he was.

'You guys stay where you are and I'll be right there.' He turned and started walking away from the river.

Another pause. 'I'm alone.'

Quinn stopped. 'What?'

'Jenny's not with me.'

'Where is she?'

'I don't know.'

'She *was* with you. Where is she?'

'Goddamn it, I know she was with me. But the only way I could have kept her here is if I'd shot her in the leg. I didn't think you wanted me to do that.'

'Wait there,' Quinn said.

He hung up and flagged down a passing taxi. The ride was short, but it saved him a few minutes.

He saw Orlando as he got out of the cab. She was on the opposite corner, standing away from the street, just out of the light. He waited for a break in traffic, then jogged across the road to join her.

'Please don't yell at me,' she said. 'It's not my fault.'

Of course her nerves were as much on edge as his were. He should have known that. He took a moment to refocus, allowing the calm that usually guided him to reassert itself.

'I believe you,' he said.

'How did they know she was going to be there?' she asked.

'I don't know,' he said.

'That was really screwed up.'

'If you hadn't seen them, who knows what would have gone down.'

'Nice work with the gunshot,' she said. 'It certainly confused things. That was you, right?'

'Yeah.' He gave her a knowing smile. 'I don't think I've ever seen anyone use a durian in a fight before.'

'If you'd have just shot him, I wouldn't have had to throw it.' She looked down at the palm of her right hand. There was a red spot near the base of her index finger. 'The damn thing pricked me.'

'Orlando, where's Jenny? What happened?'

She continued to rub her palm as her mouth tensed. 'I'm sorry.'

'Did they get her?' Quinn asked.

She shook her head.

Thank God, he thought. 'Then where is she?'

Orlando hesitated, then said, 'As soon as we got off the hill, we caught a taxi. I was going to take her back to the apartment, but she didn't want to go.' A breath, then, 'She suddenly told the cab driver to pull over. As soon as he did, she jumped out. I followed her as quickly as I could. When I reached her, I grabbed her arm and stopped her. I told her we were there to help.'

'What did she say?'

'That nobody could help her. People died when they tried to help her. I told her we could get her out of the country and take her someplace safe. But she didn't want that, either. Said she had to stop them.'

'Stop who?'

'I asked, but that's all she said.'

Quinn felt exhausted, the combination of the adrenaline wearing off and Jenny's rejection.

It must have shown in his face, because Orlando said, 'I did get one thing out of her.'

'What?'

'She'll talk to you one more time. I told her she owed you that much.'

'When?' he asked.

She looked at her watch. 'In one hour.'

He tried to smile, but failed. 'That's something. Thanks. Let's go back to the apartment. I can call her from there.'

'No,' Orlando said. 'Not on the phone. In person.'

★ ★ ★

At 11 p.m., Quinn stood at the corner of Upper Pickering Street and South Bridge Road. He was there less than ninety seconds before a taxi pulled up. Quinn leaned down expecting to see Jenny in the back seat, but the only one inside was the driver.

'You called for taxi?' the driver said.

Quinn cocked his head, then smiled business-like and said, 'You know where I need to go?'

'I know where it is. No problem.'

'Then let's go,' Quinn said as he opened the back door.

★ ★ ★

A sliver of a moon had risen in the east, hanging low on the Singaporean sky as the cabby drove Quinn back across the river. There were a few stars out, but most weren't visible through the glow of the city lights.

At first, Quinn thought they might be going somewhere on Orchard Road. There were plenty of clubs, late-night restaurants, and hotels where Jenny could be hiding. But the driver turned before they got there.

To their right were the lights and activity of the city, but to the left was a dark mass of wilderness, a wooded hill rising in the middle of civilization. It took Quinn a moment before he realized what he was looking at. It was Fort Canning Park.

The fort was where the British had built their defenses to watch over the Singapore River in the distant colonial past. Quinn knew many of the buildings were still in place high on the hill, behind the trees and brush, but from his vantage point everything looked black and uninhabited.

The cab first slowed, then pulled to a stop along the left shoulder. The driver turned and looked at Quinn. 'All right?'

Quinn stared out the window for a moment, thinking perhaps Jenny would be joining him in the cab, but no one approached the car.

'This is fine,' Quinn said. He pulled out some cash and held it out.

The driver smiled at the healthy tip. 'The steps are back there,' he said, pointing off to Quinn's left. 'Hard to see in the dark.'

'Thanks,' Quinn said, then got out.

After the cab pulled away, Quinn walked in the direction the driver had indicated. At this time of night, the park was technically closed, so there would be few, if any, people about.

Behind him, he could hear the sounds of the cars on the street, but ahead there was nothing. Silence. Not even the rustle of leaves in the trees. The lack of noise made his feet sound like sledgehammers slamming against the ground with every step.

The stairs were a bit to the right of where the cabby had pointed, but Quinn found them with little extra effort. They were concrete and led up a steep hill. No one seemed to be waiting for him at the base, so he assumed Jenny must be somewhere near the top. Before starting his ascent, he pulled his pistol out of his bag. After what had happened at the Far East Square, he wasn't about to take any chances.

He started up the stairs, keeping his pace steady and tuning out everything but what was immediately surrounding him. He heard something in the distance as he neared the halfway point, something falling from a tree. A branch, perhaps, but too far away to be anything significant.

He continued upward, following the stairs as they curved to the right. Suddenly a bird took flight from a tree beside the path. Quinn paused, wondering if it had been his arrival or the presence of someone else that had set the bird into motion. After thirty seconds of nothing, he returned to the climb.

He could see the top of the stairs now. Though still several dozen steps away, he would reach it soon. He adjusted the strap of the bag, then quickened his pace.

'Quinn?'

He stopped. The voice had come from his left, off the path and behind a group of bushes.

'Jenny?'

'Are you alone?'

'Yes,' he said, though she must have been watching his approach and already knew that.

His eyes scanned darkness, looking for her. At first, there was only the brush and trees, then she moved out from her hiding place, no more than a shadow among other shadows.

'Over here,' she said.

Quinn stepped off the stairs and onto the grass that surrounded the concrete steps. As he did, Jenny disappeared back into the brush. He crossed to the point he'd last seen her, and found a narrow slot through the bushes. He slipped between the branches, then followed the only path he could make out.

He was about to call out to her when he suddenly emerged into a small clearing. It was no more than fifteen feet square, like a room carved out of the faux wilderness.

Jenny was standing at the far edge, her posture rigid. Even in the darkness, Quinn could see there was a look of determination on her face. But there was also exhaustion, like it had been weeks since she had actually slept through the night.

He took a few steps into the clearing, stopping several feet away from her. 'I'm glad to see you're okay,' he said.

'I'm not coming with you,' she said, the words rushing from her mouth. 'Understand?'

'Okay.'

She seemed surprised by his answer. 'I know that's why you came here.'

He shrugged, but didn't answer.

'You're not going to try to convince me?'

'Would that work?' he said.

She shook her head.

'I didn't think it would,' he said.

'You should leave then.'

'Perhaps. But I think we'll stay.'

She held her defiant stance for a second longer, then lowered her head in exhaustion.

'He's really dead?' she asked.

Quinn could only answer with silence.

Jenny's lip trembled. 'How?'

'You don't want to know this.'

'I need to know,' she said. 'When Steven didn't come back, I kept hoping . . . but I knew. Tell me what they did to him. Tell me how you found out.'

It was odd hearing Markoff called by his first

name. 'I don't know if that's a good — '

'What happened?' she demanded.

As much as he wanted to keep the facts from her, he knew he couldn't. 'I got a call about a week ago,' he said, then told her what he knew.

When he finished, more than her lip was trembling. He took a few steps forward, ready in case she collapsed. But she remained standing.

'At least you were the one who buried him,' she said. She looked Quinn in the eyes. 'When this is over, I want you to show me where he is.'

Quinn hesitated, then nodded, knowing that was one promise he didn't want to keep.

'Jenny, I — '

'But what are you doing *here*?' she asked, cutting him off.

'I told you, I'm here to help you.'

'I mean Singapore. You said something about Steven leading you here. What did you mean?'

'Markoff left a message. It led us to the island.'

'What do you mean? Where on the island?'

'It doesn't matter,' he said.

'What if it does?' she said. 'Where on the island? Do you have an address?'

The last thing he wanted was for her to go off on her own and try to find out what was in the apartments at the Quayside Villas. 'The signal was gone by the time we got here,' he lied. 'So we have no idea where exactly he was pointing us.'

She sighed and put a hand to her forehead. 'It could have been the help I needed. It could have proved everything.'

'Proved what?' he asked.

She didn't answer.

'Jenny,' he said. 'I know you feel like you need to finish what you set out to do. And that you won't be safe until then. But maybe I can help you.'

'This isn't about me,' she said, her brow furrowed. 'I don't care about me. Especially now.'

'It's the congressman, isn't it?'

'You know?'

'Not everything,' he said. 'But enough to — '

'Tell me, is he here yet?'

'What?'

'Is he here?' she asked, her voice suddenly anxious. 'Did he come?'

'He was supposed to arrive tonight,' Quinn told her. 'He should be here now.'

'Do you know where?'

Again it was a question Quinn didn't want to answer. 'Does he have something to do with an organization called LP?'

Her head snapped up. 'What?'

'LP. That was part of the message Markoff left. But I'm not sure what it means. Only that it's a group or organization, and that it scares the hell out of a lot of people.'

'I . . . I don't know . . . what that is.' She looked around nervously as if she was seeing the small clearing for the first time. 'I have to go. I have to find him. I have to warn him.'

Quinn reached out and grabbed her arm as she was turning away. 'Hold on,' he said. 'What do you mean 'warn him'? What's going on?'

'You'll die just like Steven did. I can't be

responsible for that.'

She tried to pull herself free, but Quinn wouldn't let her go.

'I don't care what you think,' he said. 'I'm not leaving. I'll find out what's going on with or without your help.' He almost asked her about LP again. She knew something, but like Blackmoore and Peter, the letters had scared her. That wasn't what he wanted to do. Not to Jenny. 'I'll do everything I can to keep you from getting hurt.'

'Please, Quinn. Don't.'

'Let me help you.'

The look on her face was pained and pleading. But he continued to look at her, unwavering. After a moment, she looked down and she pulled a small rectangular box out of her pants pocket.

She held the item up. Even in the low light, Quinn could see it was a micro audiocassette, something that was used less and less in a world of digital recorders.

'I need you to hold on to this,' she said. 'You can help me that way.'

'What is it?' he asked.

She handed it to him.

'The only thing keeping me alive,' she said.

She pulled away again, and this time he let his fingers fall from her arm.

'I'll contact you,' she said.

He knew he couldn't stop her, so he said, 'I'm not going anywhere.'

She gave him a half smile, then disappeared into the brush.

29

The apartment Ne Win had set them up in wasn't quite as luxurious as the ones at the Quayside Villas, but it was clean and it was furnished. There were two bedrooms, a bathroom, a living room/dining room combination, and a walk-through kitchen.

When Quinn arrived, he found Orlando standing near the back window. She'd been looking outside, but had turned toward him as he entered.

'Our little outing at the Far East Square made the news tonight,' she said. She glanced over at the TV. It was on, but the volume was low.

'Are they shutting the city down?' he asked.

Gunfire in Singapore was not a usual occurrence. The authorities' response to even one shot would be something other countries might consider an overreaction.

'They're calling it a prank.'

'Really?'

'They say it was a particularly loud firecracker,' she said. 'I believe that was the newscaster's exact phrasing.'

'What about the body?' Quinn asked. 'The guy I shot up on Club Street?'

'Nothing.'

Quinn thought about it for a moment. A sudden heightened sense of security would probably have forced Guerrero and his fellow congressmen to head out of town, thus lessening the threat against Jenny. So it might have actually been preferable. At least this way, though, he could still move around the city without causing any suspicion.

But what he didn't want was to drag things out any longer than necessary.

'Where's Nate?' he asked.

'Sleeping.'

Quinn walked down the hallway, looking first in the master bedroom, then the smaller room, where he found his apprentice stretched out on the bed, snoring. Quinn walked over and gave Nate a shake.

'Get up,' he said.

Nate's eyes shot open. 'What? What is it?'

'Get up.'

'It can't be morning already.'

'It's not,' Quinn said as he turned for the door. 'Get dressed and come out. I need your help.'

'Ah . . . okay,' Nate said, sleep still heavy in his voice. 'Can you give me a minute?'

'I'll give you two.'

Back in the living room, Quinn quickly filled Orlando in on his meeting with Jenny.

'You're going back, aren't you?' Orlando said when he was finished.

He pulled the cassette Jenny had given him out of his pocket and held it out to Orlando. 'Here,' he said.

'You're changing the subject.'

'Yeah. I am.'

She scowled, then took the cassette from him.

She twirled it around. 'This is an AIT tape.'

'Data tape?' he said.

'Yeah. Sony's version. Similar to an eight-millimeter cassette.'

'She said it was a recording.'

'Could have a sound file on it. Usually we'd just need to de-archive it. But the container looks damaged.'

'I have faith in you.'

'I don't even have anything I can play this on,' she said, obviously annoyed.

'Call Ne Win,' Quinn said. 'I'm sure he can get something sent over.'

'He's not going to have something like this just lying around.'

'He'll find one.'

'Then *you* call him,' she said.

Quinn thought about it for a moment. 'Fine,' he said. There was something he needed to ask the old man to do anyway.

From down the hallway, they could hear Nate shuffle out of his room.

'You taking the Boy Wonder with you?' Orlando asked.

'Thought I might.'

'Maybe I should go with you this time.'

'We really need you to figure out what's on that tape.'

'*If* I can figure it out.'

'If anyone can do it, you can.'

'Gee, thanks, Dad.' Her face turned serious. 'Be careful.'

'Be careful?' Nate said as he entered the living room. 'Be careful of what?'

★ ★ ★

They walked from their apartment to the Quayside Villas. Earlier in the day, Quinn had all but decided to forget about Markoff's message. Whatever was at the Quayside Villas wasn't as important as getting Jenny off the island. But that plan hadn't worked out. In fact, Jenny's feeling that whatever Markoff had found might have helped her had only refocused Quinn's attention on the building. So a return trip seemed the logical thing to do.

On the way, Quinn called Ne Win. He wasn't surprised to find the old man still up.

After Quinn told him what he needed, Ne Win said, 'I'm not convenience store.'

'I never thought you were,' Quinn said.

There was a sigh on the other end. 'Data tape player might take a little while. I'll call when you can pick it up.'

'We need it as soon as you can get it. So instead of calling, have one of your men bring it to the apartment.'

'You are big trouble, you know that?' Ne Win said.

'You should have thought about that before you sent me the container with Markoff's body in it.'

'I never said I sent you container.'

'So you'll get the recorder over to the apartment?' Quinn asked, getting back to business.

'Yes, yes. I take care of it.'

'And the power? You can take care of that, too?'

There was a long pause. 'Take care of that, too. My man call you when they are ready. His name Lok.'

'Okay. We'll be in position in . . . ' Quinn looked at his watch. 'Twenty minutes. It would be great if it could happen right around then.'

'You are big trouble.'

The line went dead.

★   ★   ★

Quinn and Nate stood in the fourth-floor hallway of the Quayside Villas, near the entrance to the stairs. Each had a backpack on his back, and they both wore latex gloves. If someone chose that moment to step out their door and saw them, there would be no mistaking Quinn and Nate as a couple of residents hanging out in the corridor. But like before, the building was quiet, asleep. Their presence had been unobserved.

In Quinn's hand was his phone. It was also silent.

'Maybe your friend couldn't make it happen,' Nate said.

'Patience,' Quinn said.

Another minute passed.

'Perhaps we should go back,' Nate said. 'Do it tomorrow night. You know, give the old guy more time to arrange things.'

This time, Quinn said nothing.

Another minute.

'What if one of the security guards sho — '

The soft hum of Quinn's cell phone vibrating

348

in his hand cut Nate off.

Quinn raised the phone to his ear. 'Yes.'

'Mr. Quinn?'

'Yes. Who is this?'

'Lok.' Ne Win's man. He sounded around the same age as Nate and had a slight British accent. 'We're ready when you are.'

'We're ready now,' Quinn said.

One second. Two. Three.

Suddenly all the lights in the hallway went out. Though there was no window nearby to check, Quinn knew the power outage extended farther than just the corridor, encompassing several blocks on the north side of the river.

'We're dark here,' Quinn said.

'One hour's the most I can guarantee,' Lok said.

'That's plenty.'

Quinn disconnected the call, then switched his phone to thermal camera mode. The faint blue glow from the screen illuminated his face but little else.

'Anything?' Nate asked.

'No,' Quinn said. He closed his phone, then pulled out the small set of night vision binoculars he'd let Nate use on their last visit. 'Wait here.'

Quinn anticipated that one of the residents would come out to check if power was also lost in the hall, but as he made his way toward 04-21 no one had stepped out to join him. Either they were all asleep, or they assumed the entire building was in a blackout.

When he reached room 04-20, he stopped. He

pulled out his phone again and aimed the lens at the wall of room 04-21. Nothing. All was dark. No power and no people, either.

He quickly returned down the hallway where he'd left Nate.

'Empty,' he whispered. 'Let's go up.'

Quinn was working under the assumption that because the door to 04-21 was impassable, there must be another way. And since the room directly above it — 05-21 — was owned by another phony corporation, perhaps that was the way in.

The layout of the fifth floor was exactly the same as the fourth. As was the lack of light.

With Nate's hand on his back, Quinn led the way down the corridor. When the door to 05-21 came into view, he said, 'Same as below. Sconce directly across from the door.' He reactivated his cell phone, then handed it to Nate. 'Check it out.'

Nate accessed the thermal image function, then turned the device toward the ornament.

'I'm picking up two power sources. Probably batteries,' he said.

'Two?' Quinn said.

'One toward the bottom and one near the top.'

Quinn trained the night vision binoculars on the sconce. There was a hole at the bottom just like the one downstairs. So that had to be a camera. But there was no corresponding hole near the top.

Camera first, he thought.

As Nate scanned the apartment, Quinn slipped his backpack off his shoulders and removed a small rectangular box from inside.

'Dark,' Nate said after a moment. 'The apartment's empty.'

'Good,' Quinn said.

He flipped the switch on the side of the box, then a small video screen mounted on the device came to life. He scrolled through a menu until he came to a function labeled SGNL SRCH. He selected it, was presented with another set of options, selected DIG VID, then waited as the device cycled through potential transmission frequencies.

Forty-five seconds later, a dark, murky image filled the monitor. He'd tapped into the feed from the camera in the sconce.

'Here,' Quinn said, handing Nate the monitor.

From his pocket, he pulled out a disk about the diameter of a quarter, and half an inch thick. He removed the protective covering off the sticky rubber base, then crept along the wall until he was only a few feet away from the sconce. He touched a tiny switch on the side of the disk, then pressed the object against the wall. He held his hand underneath for a moment, making sure it wasn't going to fall off.

'That did it,' Nate said. He was looking at the small monitor.

The disk was a jammer. Until it was turned off, the camera would only be generating garbage.

Quinn moved in close to the sconce and pulled out his flashlight.

'Was that other source on this side of the sconce or the other?' he asked.

'The other,' Nate said.

Quinn moved quickly to the opposite side, passing directly in front of the camera lens. He trained his light along the edge of the sconce and worked his way to the top. There was nothing obvious.

Keeping his motion steady and careful, he reached up into the central vase and worked his fingers down along the stems of the flowers. Less than an inch down, he hit a bump. It was about an inch wide, and rounded over the top like a blemish. It was a shape he knew.

He worked his fingers around it and gave it a tug. It resisted for a moment, then pulled free of the wall. It appeared that it had been held in place by a magnetic backing. He could feel it wanting to reattach itself as he moved it up the side of the vase with his fingertips. Once he was free of the sconce, he slipped his prize into his palm.

It was black and no more than half an inch thick at its highest point. It was exactly what he'd expected. But just to confirm, he pulled out the tracking device and held it next to the bump.

1.0000.

They had found the source of Markoff's beacon.

In essence, it was a mobile phone, without the ability to receive or transmit sound. It used the digital airways merely to let others who knew its ID code know it was there. And aided by the fact that the device was basically passive, the specialized battery could last for over a month.

There was no question now. This was where

Markoff had been leading them.

'Do you think he ever got inside?' Nate asked.

'No idea.'

Quinn put the beacon and the box that had tracked it down into his bag. Neither was needed any longer.

Not wanting to waste any more time, he moved quickly to the door and examined its locks. He aimed the beam of his flashlight directly into each slot. Unlike the keyholes on the door to room 04-21, these were not faked.

Quinn held his hand out, and Nate gave him the monitor back. Returning to the main menu, Quinn ran through the options until he'd selected SEC SYS — Security System. He moved the detector along the doorjambs, across the top and the bottom. When he was through, he looked at the display screen. SYS DET — INACT.

'There's something there,' he said. 'But it's not on.'

'So we go in?' Nate asked.

'Yes.'

'Can I do it?'

'Fine,' Quinn said. 'Just be quick.'

From his own backpack, Nate removed a set of lock picks and set to work first on the deadbolt, then on the lock in the handle of the door.

After a moment, he looked up. 'Done,' he said.

Quinn glanced at the detector. The display still read SEC SYS — INACT.

He gave Nate a nod. His apprentice smiled, then turned the handle and pushed on the door until it cleared the jamb.

'I'll go first,' Quinn said.

He returned the monitor to his bag, then pulled out a palm-size flashlight and turned it on. As he entered the room, he swung his flashlight in a wide arc, looking for any type of booby trap.

'Clear,' he said.

Nate entered, then shut the door behind him.

'Check the bedrooms,' Quinn told his apprentice. 'I'll look out here.'

Quinn did a quick sweep of the living room, then moved on to the dining area and the kitchen. The couch, the tables, the chairs, the appliances in the kitchen all spoke of someone who liked to live comfortably. Only it was a sham. A fine layer of dust had settled over everything. In the kitchen, the cabinets were all empty. The same went for the refrigerator.

As Quinn reentered the living room, Nate emerged quickly from the hallway.

'I think I found something,' Nate said.

★ ★ ★

It was in the closet of the smaller bedroom. The only thing that indicated there might be something odd was a metal strip that ran up the center of the back wall.

Nate had already flipped up the tan carpet that had covered the closet floor. Underneath, where Quinn would have expected concrete, there was wood. He tapped the flooring and was greeted with a hollow echo.

'It looks like it flips up here,' Nate said.

354

He slipped his fingers into a groove along the edge closest to them, then began to lift the base of the closet up. It seemed to be hinging along the back wall. As soon as Quinn could get his fingers underneath, he helped Nate to push the floor all the way up.

There was a metal fastener attached to the underside, very near the top. That explained the metal support bar on the back of the closet. Quinn flipped the fastener over the edge of the trapdoor and snapped it into a slot on the bar.

In the void that had been the closet floor, there was a steep metal staircase — almost a ladder — leading down into the darkness.

'Somebody's spent a lot of time and money on this,' Nate said, then looked at Quinn. 'Shall we?'

Quinn moved the flashlight over the makeshift stairwell. It seemed to be exactly what it looked like.

'Keep your eyes open,' he said.

Nate nodded, then stepped onto the staircase and began descending into apartment 04-21. Quinn followed right behind.

As expected, the stairs ended in the closet of another bedroom. But unlike the bedroom upstairs, this one had no furniture inside. Instead, it seemed to be some sort of storage room. There were dozens of cardboard boxes and wooden crates stacked neatly along the wall, filling up nearly half the room.

Quinn ran his flashlight over them, but there were no markings indicating what might be inside. Nate walked over and put a hand on a box at the top of a stack. He pushed, but the box barely moved.

'Heavy,' he said.

Quinn looked at his watch. Only ten minutes had passed. Though plenty of time remained, they still needed to hurry. He wanted to be out of the building and miles away by the time the power came back on.

'Leave them for now,' Quinn said, then pointed toward the main part of the apartment. 'Check for heat signatures again.'

Nate moved the phone in a wide arc, taking in the entire apartment beyond.

'Clear,' Nate said.

They stepped out of the bedroom and into the hallway. Quinn motioned for Nate to wait, then moved to his left to check the master bedroom. More boxes. Bigger than those in the other room, but also unmarked.

He retraced his steps and headed toward the main part of the apartment, this time with Nate following. As they neared the end of the hall, they slowed. The flashlight revealed little of the living room beyond, only the side of some bookcases along the wall.

'Check again,' he said to Nate.

Nate scanned the room ahead of them. 'Still nothing.'

Quinn took a single step into the living room, then moved his flashlight slowly through the space. As the light revealed more and more of the room's contents, the skin at the base of his neck began to tingle.

30

'What the hell is this?' Nate said.

'Don't touch anything,' Quinn ordered.

Despite the fact they were both still wearing their gloves, he didn't want to do a thing until he'd had a moment to process what they'd discovered.

The bookcases they had seen from the hallway weren't bookcases at all. They were display cabinets. *Identical* display cabinets. Five feet wide and enclosed by glass doors allowing the contents to be viewed but not touched. They lined the entire room, filling every inch of wall space, even covering the window at the far end and the spot where the front door should have been.

That explained the phony locks, Quinn thought. The door in the public hallway was just for show.

In the middle of the room were several glass-topped tables. More display cases, Quinn guessed. There was an exception, though. The table near the entrance to the kitchen appeared to be a desk. On top, a small lamp and a laptop computer.

Quinn slowly stepped toward the nearest cabinet. They were made of brushed metal, dulled to a silver gray. Stylish, expensive, and sturdy. Quinn aimed his light through the glass door, examining the contents.

Pistols. Each displayed in profile against black cloth that covered the back of the cabinet. Beside each gun was a small plaque with the make, model number, and other vital statistics of the corresponding piece. There were a dozen in this cabinet alone. A couple of Taurus pistols and nearly the whole Glock family.

Quinn moved on to the next cabinet. More pistols. SIGs this time. A few Smith & Wessons and two Walthers.

'Is this a private museum?' Nate asked.

'No,' Quinn said. 'A showroom.'

'Showroom? You're kidding, right?'

Quinn shook his head.

'You mean they're . . . '

There was no reason for Quinn to finish Nate's sentence. It was obvious what this was — a sample room for an arms dealer. But not the typical street-level variety. Whoever this room belonged to had to be filling some major orders.

'Take pictures of everything. Both wide and detailed. But don't touch,' Quinn said.

'You already told me that.'

'I'm telling you again.'

A little further down the wall, Quinn found cabinets full of rifles: sniper, assault, even a few specialized target weapons. Those short enough were displayed horizontally.

Quinn leaned down to examine the latch on one of the glass doors. It didn't appear to be locked. That made sense. Any customer that was brought into the room would have been accompanied by several of the dealer's security team.

Still, Quinn couldn't help feeling the whole setup felt wrong for some reason. Like it was almost too perfect.

'Check these out,' Nate said.

Quinn turned. His apprentice was standing near one of the display case tables in the center of the room. Quinn walked over.

Knives. Dozens of them, in all shapes and sizes.

'That one's even more interesting,' Nate said, pointing at a table to his right.

Quinn looked over. Detonators, switches, timing devices. All the gear you would need to make a successful bomb, except for the bomb material itself. That wouldn't be on the display-room floor. You'd have to ask for it.

'You get all the cases?' Quinn asked.

'Halfway done.'

'Finish up.' Quinn looked at his watch. Nearly twenty minutes had passed while they checked out the room. 'We need to get out of here.'

'What about the computer?' Nate asked, nodding toward the laptop.

'I'll check it.'

Quinn walked over to the makeshift desk. The computer and the lamp were the only items on top. No papers, no pens, nothing else. There were two drawers built into the table just below its lip, both closed.

Quinn moved his backpack around so he'd have access. From inside, he removed a small screwdriver, then carefully slipped the blade end through the handle of one of the drawers and pulled it open.

There was a pad of paper tucked into the corner of the drawer. Several pages had been torn off, leaving about three-quarters of the pad left. The page on top was blank, though he detected several faint indentations. Whoever had written on the pad last had left a trace of what they'd written behind. Quinn leaned down to see if he could get a better look without touching anything.

It looked like numbers. There was definitely a 5 and, if he squeezed his eyes just right, a couple of 8s. Another looked like either a + or a partial 4. A phone number? He had the feeling it wasn't, but there was really no way to tell.

Quinn stared at the paper for a few more seconds, trying to pull more of the message out, but nothing else came. He frowned. If he took the paper back to the hotel, they would probably be able to figure out what the number was. But would the paper be missed? He wanted this incursion to go undetected. He couldn't risk it, so reluctantly he closed the drawer and opened the one next to it.

This one contained only a few pens and a box of 9mm ammo. He was just about to close it when the beam of his flashlight caught something partially tucked under the box of ammo.

He leaned in for a better look.

It was a hair, dark brown with a gentle curve. Without lifting the box, it was impossible to tell how long it was. Odd that it would be there like that.

He left it untouched, too, and pushed the drawer closed.

Looking over at Nate, he said, 'How much longer?'

'A couple minutes.'

Quinn turned his attention to the laptop computer. Using the handle end of the screwdriver, he unlatched the screen and pushed it up. Suddenly there was a whirring as the hard drive cycled up. A second later, the screen came on, casting a faint blue glow over Quinn and the room behind him. A rectangular box came up in the center of the screen, asking for a password.

'I thought you said not to touch anything,' Nate called out.

Quinn barely heard his apprentice as he did a quick scan of the computer. A power cord was attached to the side, but the machine was obviously running off battery power for the moment.

Why is this on? he wondered. It seemed a little loose and haphazard, unless the users planned to access it from off-site. Of course, since the computer was shut and in sleep mode, that wasn't likely.

Unless, he thought, *someone was using it earlier in the evening and is coming back soon.*

They really needed to get out of there, but he couldn't ignore the potential information on the computer.

'I need the phone,' he said to Nate.

'Hold on. One more.' Nate aimed the phone's camera lens at one of the cabinets. 'That's it.'

He walked quickly over to Quinn and handed

him the phone. Quinn dialed Orlando.

'Please tell me you're on your way back,' she said.

'We're still inside.'

Her voice became serious. 'Are you all right?'

'Yes. We're fine.'

'What did you find?'

'I'll tell you when we get back,' he said. 'Except we did find a computer.'

'You have the bug?' she said.

'I do.' Quinn unconsciously touched his free hand to the strap of his backpack. Inside the front pocket was a wireless computer tap that would allow Orlando to attempt to access any computer within its range. The only problem was, because it had to act as both a bug and a transmitter back to a distant home base, it was bigger than the average tap.

'Then set it up and let's see if I get a signal.'

Quinn handed the phone to Nate, then pulled out the bug. Its shape was similar to that of a saltine cracker, about an inch and a half square. It was all black, and like the signal scrambler he'd used in the hallway upstairs, there was self-stick adhesive on the back side.

The beauty of the bug was that Orlando could power it up and down remotely, so unless someone was doing a sweep while she was using it, there was a good chance it would go undetected. That was as long as he found a good place to hide it.

'Hold this,' he said to Nate, holding out the bug.

Quinn used the screwdriver to pull one of the

drawers open again, then did exactly what he'd told Nate not to do. He grabbed the sides of the drawer with his gloved hands, and pulled the drawer completely out. He set it carefully on the floor.

'Bug,' he said, holding out his hand to his apprentice.

Nate placed the black wafer in Quinn's hand.

Before peeling the protective coated paper off the adhesive tape, Quinn did a visual measurement of the drawer, then looked under the desk to gauge whether the drawer fit snugly against the back of the desk when it was closed, or left a gap.

There was no question. Definitely a gap, at least several inches. More than enough room for what he needed.

He removed the protective paper and attached the computer tap to the outside back of the drawer. The only way anyone would ever see it was if they pulled the drawer out and looked.

Once he'd replaced the drawer, he took the phone back from Nate. 'Try it now,' he said to Orlando.

There was a pause. 'I've got a signal from the tap,' she said.

'What about the computer?'

'Trying to access now,' she said. Quinn could hear her breathing faintly on the other end. 'There. Yes, got it. Log-in screen.'

'See if you can log in before we get back,' he said.

'Is this a race? Because if it is, I guarantee you I'll be in before you've even gotten out of the building.'

'Wait,' he said. 'What about the screen?'

'What about it?'

'The top was closed on the laptop when we came in, and it was asleep.'

'That's fine,' she said. 'Close it. I can still wake it up. As soon as I log in, depending on how much is on the machine, I'll only need ten minutes or so to download everything.'

Quinn shut the computer. 'It's closed,' he said. 'We'll see you in a bit.'

He hung up and put the phone in his pocket.

'Everything the way we found it?' he asked Nate.

'I didn't touch anything. You're the only one who was moving stuff around.'

'Fine, then let's — '

Quinn's phone began vibrating in his pocket. He pulled it out. It was the same number Lok had called him from earlier.

'What's up?' Quinn asked.

'Whatever you're doing in there, you may want to get out now,' Lok said.

Quinn looked at his watch. There was still over ten minutes left in the hour that had been promised him. 'What's going on?'

'Someone pulled a few strings. The power will be back on in less than five minutes.'

'Dammit,' Quinn said to himself.

'That's not all,' Lok said. 'My boss also put someone outside the Quayside Villas to keep an eye on things.'

Quinn's eyes narrowed. He hadn't asked Ne Win to do that.

'A car just pulled up in front,' Lok went on. 'Two people. One got out to talk to the security guards. A Caucasian. The other's still in the car. Another guy. Younger.'

'Great,' Quinn said, mainly to himself. 'All right. Thanks.' He hung up and looked at Nate. 'Time to go.'

They raced up the staircase, replaced the false floor in the closet, then sped through apartment 05-21 to the front door.

Quinn pulled the door open and rushed gun-first into the corridor, the night vision binoculars held to his eyes.

'Clear,' he whispered, then turned on his flashlight.

Nate joined him, shutting the door behind them. Quinn crossed over to the interference disk they'd left next to the sconce and removed it from the wall.

'Stairs,' he whispered to Nate. 'Hurry.'

They moved quickly down the hall, trying to remain as quiet as possible. When they reached the door to the stairwell, Quinn put a hand on it and started to push it open, but stopped.

There were footsteps coming up from below.

Quinn motioned for Nate to follow him, then headed further down the corridor. There was just enough curve left in the hallway that if they went to the end and hugged the right corner, they would be out of sight of the stairwell door.

As soon as they took up position, Quinn doused his flashlight and replaced it with his

SIG. He aimed his pistol through the black void toward the corner.

Seven seconds later, the stairwell burst open. There was light, not a lot, but enough to send a gentle glow around the corner toward them. Quinn stood motionless, counting footsteps and waiting for the moment one of them decided to check around the corner.

But no one did. And within seconds, he could hear the two people moving down the hallway toward apartment 05-21.

A door opened, then closed again. Suddenly the hall was plunged back into darkness.

'What about the bug?' Nate asked.

'What?' Quinn whispered.

'The bug? Isn't Orlando trying to get onto the computer right now?'

Nate was right. Quinn should have thought of it, too. He quickly dug out his phone and called Orlando.

'Don't tell me you're still — ' she started to say.

'Someone's going inside. Shut it down now!' he said, then hung up. He put a hand on Nate's shoulder. 'Let's get out of here.'

★ ★ ★

Nate went straight to bed when they returned to their new base, with instructions to wake everyone up by noon the next day. But Quinn stayed with Orlando, giving her a more detailed description of what had happened.

'I've never seen anything like it,' he said when

he was through. 'It's set up like a very high-end operation.'

'But?' she said, obviously sensing his hesitation.

'But . . . ' He thought for a moment, then said, 'It seemed off.'

'You're going to have to give me a little more than that. What do you mean by 'off'?' There was an underlying irritation in her voice. But it was easy to see why. Her eyes were bloodshot from working on the computer, and her cheeks were taut with fatigue.

'It was like something wasn't right,' he said, trying to clarify. 'Everything seemed too well put together. Too perfect. Like the indentations on the pad of paper.'

'That wasn't perfect,' she said.

'No. That was sloppy. Someone in this kind of operation shouldn't do something like that.' Like Quinn and Orlando, they would have been trained to place individual sheets of paper on a hard surface before writing, never on something that would record their words.

'Maybe you should have brought it back with you,' she said.

He shook his head. 'I got the feeling it was left there on purpose. If I took it, it would have been noticed.'

He then told her about the hair. How it also seemed out of place, and that he had seen no others anywhere.

'That's really odd,' she said. 'Tucked under the box? No others?'

'No others,' he said. 'In fact, the rest of the

367

apartment was pristine. No fingerprints or anything else.'

'I think maybe leaving them there was the right move,' she said. 'It *does* feel off.'

'It just didn't make sense.' He began to yawn. 'Why don't you take the other bedroom,' he told her. 'I'll take the couch.'

'I've got too much to do,' she said, turning back to her laptop. Sitting next to it on the table was a rectangular metal box about two inches thick. It was cream colored and whirred in a similar fashion to the arms dealer's computer, only louder.

'You'll probably do better with a little rest,' he said.

When she looked back at him, he realized he'd said the wrong thing. 'Look. What do you want? Do you want to know what's on the tape Jenny gave you? Because it was pretty fucked up and it's going to take me time to get any information off it. And what about the computer from tonight? Do you want me to analyze what's on it or not? Not to mention finding out something about the unknown LP. Or do you want me to just get some sleep and let all this sit until then? I'm willing to do that if that's what you want, because God knows I'm tired. But I was under the impression we needed to figure this stuff out sooner rather than later. Was I wrong?'

She stared at Quinn, defying him to say anything.

'Okay,' he said, keeping his voice calm. 'I'll stay up and help you.'

'Oh, that's a brilliant idea,' she said, rolling her

eyes upward. 'And just what exactly do you expect to do? Maybe we can take turns typing every other letter.'

'I was thinking more I'd keep you company,' he said softly.

She looked at him again, her eyes unblinking. Then after several seconds, she closed them and took a deep breath.

'I'm sorry,' she said, though there was still an edge to her words. 'I'll do better if I can just concentrate on my own. You go. You need the sleep as much as I do, and one of us should be fresh.'

As much as he wanted to argue the point with her, her logic was sound. Things had been moving fast since Markoff's body had shown up.

'If there is something you need me for, anything,' he said, 'wake me up.'

She smiled, acknowledging his offer but not exactly accepting it.

As he started to walk out, she said, 'Quinn?'

He stopped at the entrance to the hallway and looked back.

'I'm sorry.'

This time her annoyance was gone.

★ ★ ★

In his dream, he was on a sailboat not unlike the one Markoff had rented in San Diego. Only it wasn't Markoff he was sailing with, it was Peter and Nate. The waves gently rolled the boat. Peter said something about pulling in the fish being Quinn's job. But Nate was talking about sail length, and rudder speed, and —

'Scoot over.'

Quinn's eyes fluttered open. Though the light was off, there was enough sunlight seeping in around the edge of the curtains for Quinn to see her. Orlando was standing next to the bed, wearing only a white tank top and matching underwear.

'Come on. I'm tired,' she said.

As Quinn moved more toward the center of the bed, part of his mind thought maybe he was still dreaming.

Orlando lifted the blanket and slipped underneath.

He didn't move. He didn't know what to do.

Perhaps she just didn't want to be alone. He could understand that. Hell, despite what most people thought, he didn't want to be alone either.

She rolled so she was facing away from him, then inched her way back until she was pressed up against his body — her back against his chest, her legs against his legs. Without even realizing what he was doing, Quinn moved his arm over her, hugging her around the waist.

Her hand slipped down in response, her fingers entwining in his. He closed his eyes and moved his head forward, burying his nose in her hair.

He could both hear and feel her take in a deep breath. He thought for a moment that she had fallen asleep. Then her head turned, and his lips brushed her ear. Then her cheek.

Then her lips were on his. Tentative at first,

their kiss light, almost chaste. Then she turned her whole body to him, and his hand moved from her stomach to the small of her back.

As he pulled her close, her lips parted, their tongues touching, searching, caressing.

For a fleeting moment, the image of Durrie appeared in his mind, a reminder that his old mentor had once said Orlando belonged to him and no one else.

'I made you promise, Johnny,' Durrie's voice seemed to say to him. 'I made you promise never to move in on her. Remember?'

For so long, Quinn had done as Durrie had requested.

But for the first time, Quinn realized the promise meant nothing anymore.

So he didn't stop.

And neither did Orlando.

31

The door to the bedroom opened.

'Rise and shine,' Nate said. 'It's noon.'

Quinn's first thought was that now Nate knew what had happened between him and Orlando. But as he opened his eyes, he realized he was alone in the bed.

He rolled onto his back and peered across the room. Nate was standing in the doorway.

'You wanted me to wake you up, remember?'

'I remember.'

'Orlando told me that I should let you sleep a little longer. But I figured since you said noon, it was going to be noon.'

'Thanks,' Quinn said, not sure if he meant it. 'Where is she?'

'Where else?' Nate said. 'At the computer.' He stepped into the hallway, then leaned back into the room. 'Coffee's ready, too.'

Orlando couldn't have been gone too long, Quinn thought. He remembered holding her while he slept, and waking every once in a while because he wanted to know she was really there.

As he got up, he could smell her on the pillow, the distinct scent of her body: tangy and sweet and inviting.

A quick hot shower cleared the fog from his mind and helped him to focus on the here and now. Once he was dressed, he went straight for the kitchen, grabbed a cup of coffee, then returned to the living room.

'Hey,' he said as he approached the table where Orlando was working.

'Hey,' she replied.

The silence wasn't exactly awkward, but it wasn't normal either.

'Did you sleep all right?' Quinn asked.

She glanced up at him, the barest of smiles on her lips. 'I slept fine.'

'Good,' he said, then added a little too quickly, 'So did I.'

Another lull.

'If anyone's wondering, I slept pretty good, too,' Nate said.

Usually Quinn would have said something like 'Nobody's wondering' or 'I really don't care,' but instead he said, 'Excellent.'

'Well, it wasn't *that* good.'

'Get anywhere?' Quinn asked Orlando.

She nodded. 'I was able to download everything on the hard drive of the computer at the Quayside.'

Quinn pulled out a chair and sat down next to her. 'See, I told you you could do it.'

'I never thought I couldn't.'

'Anything worth noting?'

She smiled. 'Stuff you'd expect, mainly. Office-type software and a few document files. There's also a whole PDF catalog of everything they're selling. You might find this interesting.' She clicked on a file, and a spreadsheet opened up. 'Price list.'

The document listed items and their individual price followed by lower and lower discount prices depending on the volume of weapons purchased.

'Anything on who these guys are?'

'Nothing,' she said. 'Even the software and the computer are registered to a generic name. A. Lee. No company.' She paused. 'Something else interesting, though. I went into the system and got the serial number on the machine. Turns out it's less than a month old. Sold two weeks ago right here in Singapore.'

'You know where?'

'Mail order to an address just off Orchard Road. And, yes, I checked it out. No such address.'

'Wonderful,' Quinn said. 'What about clients? Was there anything on the drive about them?'

'There is a client folder, but it's empty.'

The look on her face told him there was more. 'But?' he said.

'I dug around the hard drive and retrieved any deleted files I could. There weren't many. Either everything else has been written over, or they just don't use the computer that much.'

'But there was something?'

'Yes. Several files were spreadsheets. Strictly numbers, so I have no idea what they mean. There was a copy of the catalog, some temp files the computer generated, and a text document.'

She opened the text document.

A Kamarudin
SR-98

'Kamarudin. Sounds like a name,' Nate said.

'It is,' Orlando said. 'But I didn't get any unusual hits on it.'

'Could be an alias,' Quinn told them. 'It's the 'SR-98' that's interesting to me.' He had heard the numbers before. He knew they denoted a weapon, but he was having a hard time bringing up an image of it. 'Rifle,' he said, half remembering.

'Sniper rifle,' she corrected. 'British. Used by the military in the UK, Australia . . . ' She paused and looked up at Quinn. 'And even Singapore.'

'So it would be easy to obtain.'

'That would be my guess,' she said. 'But it's weird, you know? Why would this one file still be retrievable? It would seem to me this would be something they'd do a secure dump on, make sure it was written over. There are no other deleted files like it.'

'Maybe they just missed it,' Nate offered.

'It's a possibility,' she said, then glanced at Quinn. 'But even more than before, I think you're right. It's just too perfect.'

'Like a setup,' Quinn said.

'Yes. Only for what?'

Quinn leaned back in his chair and ran a hand through his still-damp hair. 'I don't like it. I don't like any of this.' He took in a quick, deep breath, then forced the air out of his lungs. 'I don't care what Jenny wants. We're going to find her, and we're going to get her the hell out of here. End of story.'

'But we don't know where she is,' Nate said.

For a moment, it seemed as if Quinn was just

as tired as he had been when he had fallen asleep a few hours before. He closed his eyes and tried to think of an option, some way to get Jenny to agree to give up whatever mission she thought she was on and go someplace safe. But he knew if he just contacted her, there would be no way he could talk her into coming with him. She had already made that clear enough.

'I think I might know what we can do,' Orlando said.

Quinn opened his eyes and looked at her.

'We know she's interested in Congressman Guerrero, and given the chance, she'll try to contact him.'

'Why would she do that?' Nate asked. 'He's trying to kill her.'

'That's not what she believes. She said she had to warn him. She wouldn't warn someone she thought was trying to kill her,' Quinn said.

'Right,' Orlando said. 'So I was thinking we could use that to our advantage.' She looked down at her computer and pulled up a file that had been open but hidden. 'I was able to get a copy of the congressman's itinerary. Most of the time, he's scheduled to be in private meetings. But he does have a couple of public appearances. Tomorrow he's scheduled to visit a hawker center in the afternoon' — the Singapore version of an outdoor food court — 'and then spend some time shopping before leaving to go back to the States in the evening. But tonight there's a reception for the American congressional committee at a restaurant on Orchard Road called Rivera's. Technically, the party isn't open to the public, but the restaurant is in a shopping center.'

'Easy access,' Quinn said, starting to see where she was going with this.

She nodded. 'I was thinking you could contact her on the Sandy Side message board and tell her about the reception. Maybe even tell her where a good place to spot the congressman might be.'

'Isn't that defeating the purpose?' Nate said. 'I thought we were trying to keep her away from Guerrero.'

'He's just the bait,' Orlando told him. 'We have to lure her out of wherever she is. But then we get to her before she has a chance to approach the congressman.'

'Sounds risky,' Nate said.

'You have a better idea?' Quinn asked.

Both Quinn and Orlando looked at Nate, waiting.

'No,' Nate finally said.

Unfortunately, neither did Quinn.

★ ★ ★

Rivera's was part of a new upscale shopping complex on Orchard Road. It was located on the second-floor atrium and took up the majority of the east side of the building. The location was no doubt highly desirable. Quinn guessed rent for that much space would have to be considerable.

If it had been located in Los Angeles, it would have been one of those restaurants celebrities dined at to be seen. Upscale, expensive, and trendy. It would have also probably been hot for a year, then just as suddenly forgotten as newer and even trendier places opened up. But this was Singapore, not L.A. Perhaps here it would have a fighting chance to survive.

Quinn and Nate were dressed in dark suits, both to conceal the weapons they were carrying and, if necessary, to blend into the crowd at the reception later. They arrived at the restaurant early so they could eat a late lunch and do a little recon. As they were being seated, the waiter told them the restaurant would be closing in an hour, his tone friendly but firm. Without actually saying it, his meaning was clear. Be done or leave without finishing.

There was a bar near the entrance, and to the right the main seating area. Beyond the dining room were the kitchen and restrooms. With the exception of the decor — dark but warm — it wasn't much different than any other restaurant. The same basic rules applied.

In truth, Quinn hoped they'd get to Jenny before she ever reached the restaurant. If she got inside, where the congressman would undoubtedly have his men with him, it could get really messy. That was the last thing Quinn wanted. But being prepared was ingrained in him. So familiarizing himself with the location only made sense.

Not long after their food was brought to them, two women and a man entered the restaurant. The man wore a gray business suit, while the women were in dresses suitable for a party. The man carried a clipboard in one hand and a thick package in the other. The older of the two women seemed to be in charge. She was the only one doing the talking, while the other two simply nodded.

After a couple of minutes, they separated, the man and the younger woman staying near the front door, while their boss headed for the kitchen.

'I'll be right back,' Quinn said to Nate.

He got up and headed toward the two near the front. They were standing near a small table just off to the side of the entrance. The man had opened the package and was pulling out several items.

'Excuse me,' Quinn said as he reached them. 'My name is Tim Foster, I was supposed to meet with someone who's organizing tonight's reception. You don't know where I might find them, do you?'

The woman smiled. 'You've found us. I'm Darla Wong, and this is my associate Dean Gaboury. How can we help you?'

'Oh, this is great. I'm sorry. I thought you worked for the restaurant,' he said. 'I'm part of Congressman Guerrero's advance team. I just want to make sure everything's okay. We never actually received any hard-copy invitations.'

'Everyone is on the list,' the woman said. 'No invitations necessary.'

'Great. And you've got all of us, right? I believe there are eleven people in the congressman's group.'

'Let me check. Dean, can I have the list please?'

Gaboury handed the clipboard to his colleague. 'We updated the list this morning,' the man said. He had a slight Australian accent. 'I'm sure everyone's there.'

As Darla began looking at the list, Quinn moved around so he could glance over her shoulder. The name of the attendees were in a column on the left. In the column next to it was the name of the group, if any, they were with. And finally, there was a column with either a *C* or a *T* in it.

'What does the letter at the end denote?' Quinn asked.

Darla glanced up, surprised that Quinn had moved in so close. 'Ah . . . *C* is for 'confirmed,' and *T* is for 'tentative.''

'Of course,' Quinn said.

The woman went quickly through the list, obviously uncomfortable with Quinn's gaze, but apparently too polite to tell him to back away.

'I count nine people,' Darla said.

'Nine? Are you sure?'

'Yes,' she said. 'I'm sorry.'

'That's okay. Not your problem. I just have to get ahold of my boss and see what the deal is. Thank you.'

'No problem.'

Quinn turned back toward his table, the names of five women who were listed as only tentative to attend etched in his mind.

★   ★   ★

After they finished their meal, they spent several hours scoping out the shopping center both inside and out. They met up with Orlando a block down from the shopping center's entrance thirty minutes before the party was to begin.

'Are you set?' he asked her.

She nodded. 'Third place I called. Wendy Hsiao. She's apparently in Sydney on business.'

'ID?'

Orlando pulled a blue card out of her small purse. It was a Singapore National Registration Identity Card — NRIC. It had Orlando's picture and Wendy Hsiao's name. 'Ne Win's source cranked it out in an hour and a half. Don't think it'll pass any computer checking, but it should do nicely as a visual ID.'

'Good, once the guests start arriving, you and I will move inside the mall,' Quinn said, looking at Orlando. 'Nate, I want you out here on the street. Jenny doesn't know what you look like, so you won't scare her off.'

'Sure,' Nate said.

'I want you to get inside the party right away,' Quinn said to Orlando. 'You'll be backup in case Jenny gets past us.'

Per Quinn's instructions, she'd come dressed for the reception. She was wearing a sleeveless black ankle-length dress with lavender highlights, a mandarin collar, and a back that dipped three quarters of the way down her spine. She was beyond beautiful.

'Got it,' she said.

'Where will you be?' Nate asked.

'Outside the restaurant, at the other end of the

atrium,' Quinn said. 'Everyone got their comm gear?'

They both nodded.

'Good. Let's go.'

★ ★ ★

By 7 p.m., the party inside Rivera's was filling up. But as at the gallery show in Georgetown, the congressman hadn't arrived yet.

Several times a minute, Quinn glanced toward the elevator at the back side of the center. He knew from their recon earlier it led down to a subterranean parking garage. Since several of Guerrero's House colleagues who were also on this trip had arrived that way, it was a pretty fair guess the congressman would be doing the same.

Quinn's gaze moved to the restaurant. Orlando had disappeared inside fifteen minutes earlier, her ID working perfectly.

'Anything?' Quinn said.

'Clear here,' Nate reported.

'Same. No sign.' Orlando's voice was barely a whisper, the noise of the party around her nearly drowning her out.

Movement to his right drew Quinn's attention back toward the elevator. A new group had arrived. Three men. They exited the elevator, but stopped only a few feet away, waiting.

'A couple of our friends from the Far East Square are here,' Quinn said.

He recognized two of the men from the chase the night before.

'Heading my way?' Orlando asked.

'Not yet.'

The elevator door opened again, and out stepped Blondie, followed almost immediately by Congressman Guerrero and his wife. The three who had been waiting suddenly became alert. Two fell in behind the congressman and his wife, while the other joined Blondie in front as the group began walking toward the restaurant.

'Shit,' Nate said.

'What?' Quinn asked.

'I think she just passed me.'

'Jenny? You were supposed to stop her.'

'I'm not one hundred percent sure. I think it's her. If it is, she's wearing a wig.'

'Where is she?'

'She just entered the complex. Hold on.'

Quinn could hear Nate moving quickly up the front stairs into the shopping center.

'I see her,' Nate said. 'She's heading toward the escalators. Blue dress. Brown wig, hair below her shoulders.'

Quinn stood up and moved around the atrium balcony toward the escalator that would bring the woman up to the second floor.

'What do you want me to do?' Nate asked.

Quinn said, 'Stay down there in case this isn't her.'

The escalator let out on the south side of the floor. There were over a dozen people riding up it as Quinn neared. Most were dressed in suits and fashionable dresses, ready for a party.

He leaned over the atrium railing just enough to take in the entire escalator. The woman Nate had seen was only a quarter of the way up.

Unfortunately, she was turned away, looking toward the restaurant and not at Quinn. Her height was right, and so was her build, but that wasn't enough for a positive ID.

Quinn pulled back.

'Is it her?' Orlando asked, her voice a whisper in his ear.

'Don't know,' he said.

He'd seen enough of the escalator to get the timing right. Just before it was the woman's turn to exit, he moved forward, his head down. As she stepped onto the second-floor balcony, Quinn bumped into her, putting a hand on her arm.

'I'm sorry,' he said. 'Wasn't watching.'

'Don't worry about it,' she said, her voice familiar.

Jenny didn't even look at him. Her attention was focused on the restaurant. Quinn started to tighten his grip on her arm, but she pulled away from him and began moving quickly across the tiled patio floor.

Ahead, the congressman and his party had just reached the entrance to the restaurant. Jenny must have noticed this also and was making a beeline for Guerrero.

'She's heading for the restaurant,' Quinn said. 'Front door.'

'On my way,' Orlando said.

Several people had gotten in between Quinn and Jenny. He wanted to sprint after her, but that would attract too much attention. The last thing they needed was to alert Guerrero's security.

'Orlando, where are you?' Quinn asked.

'Almost there.'

'She's going to get to the door before I can reach her,' he said.

There was a man standing behind a podium near the front door, checking guest names on a list. Jenny must have caught his attention as she quickly approached the entrance. He snapped a small walkie-talkie off a clip on his belt and started to say something into it.

Suddenly he lurched forward, bending over the podium and losing his grip on his radio. As he straightened back up, Orlando moved around him, her hand on her mouth as if she was extremely embarrassed. She said a few words to him, her eyes conveying her apologies.

Jenny was only a dozen feet away now. But she had spotted Orlando and had stopped.

She took a few steps back, and walked right into Quinn.

As she turned around, he put a hand on each of her arms, holding her tight.

'Quinn?' she said, surprised.

'We have to get you out of here,' he said.

'No,' she said. 'Let me go. I have to see the congressman.'

'You do that and you're dead.'

She shook her head. 'You're wrong. I have to see him.'

She tried to pull away, but he held on tight.

'You realize that some of those men with him were the same guys who were trying to grab you yesterday at the Far East Square?'

'He wouldn't hurt me.'

'He wouldn't have to,' Quinn said. 'They'd do it for him.'

'Not once I talk to him. He won't let that happen.'

Orlando came up behind Jenny. 'We really need to leave now,' she said.

Quinn looked toward the restaurant entrance. While almost everyone was moving into the reception, there was one man coming out.

Blondie.

He had a pack of cigarettes in one hand and was shaking one of the sticks out. Quinn tried to move to the side so that Jenny and Orlando were between him and Blondie, but it was too late. The man spotted them.

'Come on!' Quinn said as he began pulling Jenny and accelerating toward the escalator.

She ran beside him, no longer resisting.

A group was just exiting the up escalator. Quinn maneuvered Jenny around them, then all but shoved her onto the down escalator.

'Run,' he said to her. He grabbed his collar and held it out so that his transmitter was only inches from his mouth. 'We need a ride. Now!'

Nate answered over the radio immediately. 'I'm on it.'

'To the right,' Quinn said to Jenny as she reached the bottom.

When he hit the last step, he took off after her, chancing a quick look over his shoulder as he did.

Orlando was getting off the escalator, while Blondie was just starting down at the top.

The pack of cigarettes was gone, but while he tried to conceal it, his hand wasn't empty.

'Armed!' Quinn said, just loud enough for Orlando to hear.

But it was the wrong thing to say. Jenny heard it, too, and looked back toward the escalator.

'Keep moving,' Quinn said.

There was the spit of a suppressor behind him. Jenny fell to the ground.

There were only a few people in the first-floor courtyard of the shopping center. All their eyes were on Quinn and Jenny, and had not seen the gun in Blondie's hand go off. The only thing they'd seen was Jenny fall down.

One couple started toward her to see if they could help, but Quinn raced over ahead and got there first.

There was another spit, then a bullet flew past Quinn's hip, slamming into the tile floor. The woman who had been approaching suddenly screamed. Quinn pulled out his gun, swiveled, and pointed it in Blondie's direction.

He started to squeeze his trigger, but stopped. The man had crouched down behind the metal railing of the escalator. There were several innocents nearby, suddenly aware of the danger and trying to get away. A shot would be too risky.

Quinn spotted Orlando crouched near where the escalator let off, less than ten feet from Guerrero's man. She waved for him to keep moving. But he leaned down, put his gun on the floor, and slid it across to her.

As she reached out to grab it, Blondie stood up, his gun coming around to aim past Quinn at Jenny.

Quinn dove toward her, not so much to shield her body as to get her moving.

'Up, up,' he said as he lifted her to her feet.

Thwack.

Quinn braced himself, expecting to be hit, but he was untouched.

He got Jenny on her feet and pulled her forward, his arm around her waist. He didn't look back until they reached the exit.

Orlando was running toward him. Behind her, lying at the base of the escalator, was Blondie. His face was twisted in pain as he cradled a bloody hand against his chest. But they weren't out of trouble yet. Two of his friends had just rushed onto the escalator from the second floor.

'Are you all right?' Quinn asked Orlando.

'Fine,' she said.

Outside at the curb, Nate was standing next to a taxi. The back door was flung wide open.

Quinn pushed Jenny in first, then climbed in after her, with Orlando getting in last. Nate took the passenger seat up front.

'Drive!' Nate said to the taxi driver.

'I don't want trouble,' the driver said, apparently sensing something was up.

Orlando pointed her gun at him. 'Then get the hell out.'

The driver obviously thought this was a good idea, as he threw open his door and jumped out of the car.

Nate was already climbing into the driver's vacated seat, knowing it was his job now to get them out of there.

He dropped the car into drive and pressed the pedal all the way to the floor. He didn't even bother shutting the driver side door. It did it on its own as they sped away.

Finally feeling momentarily safe, Quinn leaned over to take a better look at Jenny.

'Are you hit?' he asked. He hadn't spotted any blood, but she'd gone down right after Blondie had shot at them.

'I . . . I don't think so,' she said. 'I heard something next to my head, then I fell.'

Quinn patted her legs, then her side. She winced when he reached her left shoulder.

'I think . . . I think I dislocated it,' she said.

He pushed on it a little harder, and she yelled out.

'Phone's in my pocket,' Quinn said to Orlando. 'Call Ne Win. We need a doctor.'

32

Quinn and Orlando got Jenny into the apartment, while Nate drove away in the taxi, with orders to abandon it as far from their location as possible.

They took her into the master bedroom and sat her on the bed.

'How is it?' Quinn asked Jenny.

'It hurts,' she said. 'But I'll be fine. You should have let me go. You should have let me talk to him.'

'Just relax. Let's not worry about that right now.'

From down the hall they could hear the front door open.

'Quinn?' It was Ne Win.

'Back here,' Quinn yelled.

The old man appeared at the bedroom door, trailed a second later by a younger man holding what looked like a medical bag. Ne Win was also carrying a bag, though it was more of a canvas shopping bag.

'You're the doctor?' Quinn asked.

Though the man looked scared, he nodded.

'Then get the hell over here,' Quinn said.

Ne Win pushed the doctor through the door. 'Don't worry. Dr. Han good doctor. He just not have to make house call in a while.'

Dr. Han quickly scanned his new patient. 'What's the problem?'

'Shoulder,' Quinn said. 'Dislocated, I think.'

'Right or left?' Dr. Han asked Jenny.

'Left,' Quinn said.

The doctor glanced at Quinn, then bent down to get a better look at Jenny's shoulder. As he began probing with his fingers, Jenny gritted her teeth, barely holding in whatever cry of pain she wanted to let out.

'I'll need you to remove your dress,' Dr. Han said.

Jenny looked at Quinn, then Ne Win.

'Maybe you two can go make some coffee,' Orlando said.

Quinn didn't want to leave. He felt responsible. But he nodded and turned for the door.

'Quinn?' Jenny said.

He stopped.

'I know you were only trying to help, and that maybe you were right, maybe I shouldn't have gone there.'

'You're all right now,' Quinn said. 'Everything's going to be fine.'

'No, it's not,' she said, with more force than any of them expected. 'You don't understand. Steven died trying to help me stop it.'

'Stop what?'

Her eyes grew intense, flickering wide open for a moment, then half closing again as if she'd spent whatever energy she'd had left. 'If you really want to help me, you'll get me to the congressman. We're his only chance.'

'*His* only chance?' Quinn said.

'You listened to the tape, right? So you know,' she said. 'Guerrero. We have to save him.'

'Can I have a few minutes alone with my patient, please?' the doctor said.

Reluctantly Quinn nodded. He wanted to hear more, but it could wait until after the doctor had left.

★   ★   ★

'Nothing to worry about,' Ne Win said to Quinn. They were both sitting in the living room while Dr. Han worked on Jenny. 'Dr. Han is okay. He does a lot of work for me.'

'He'll keep quiet?'

'Very quiet. He know if he doesn't, he is not doctor for long.'

They fell into silence. At one point, Ne Win held out the canvas bag to Quinn.

'The data player.'

Quinn took it, then set it on the floor beside his feet. 'Thanks.'

The old man rose and headed toward the kitchen. 'You want something to drink?'

Quinn shook his head.

For twenty minutes, neither of them spoke. Ne Win slowly sipped his glass of water, while Quinn tried to make sense of everything. Why would she want to *save* Guerrero? He was the one after her. It was one of his men that had shot at her. It was his men that had undoubtedly killed her boyfriend.

Quinn looked over at Ne Win. 'Why did you send Markoff to me?'

The old man looked at him. For nearly half a minute, neither of them even moved.

'I only did what he told me to do,' Ne Win said.

'What?' Quinn asked, not sure he'd heard the old man correctly.

But Ne Win remained silent.

'Are you saying Markoff told you to send his body to me?'

It seemed as though Ne Win was still not going to say anything, then he leaned forward. 'He told me if anything happened to him, I should get word to you.'

It was almost as if the air had suddenly gained weight. It pressed down on him as if trying to collapse him.

Markoff.

He was the one who had wanted Quinn involved. It wasn't just chance, or someone thinking Quinn should have been the one to bury his old friend. It had been Markoff from the beginning.

'Tell me what happened,' Quinn said.

Ne Win thought for a moment, then began to speak. 'He came to me, much like you did this week. Need my help. I think okay. Markoff always fair with me. No problem help.'

'What kind of help?'

'A little equipment,' Ne Win said, then added, 'and some manpower.'

'Manpower?'

'One guy. Markoff doing surveillance. Needed someone to help him.'

'The Quayside Villas,' Quinn said.

'He did not tell me where.'

'But your man did.'

'My man is dead. Like Markoff.'

Quinn paused. 'I'm sorry.'

Ne Win leaned back in his chair. 'Something happened and they caught Markoff. My man trail them, trying to see where they take him. He call me on the phone and tell me what was happening. I say to him to call me back when he knows where they go. While I wait, I get my other men together. But no call back.'

Quinn looked at the old man, letting Ne Win go at his own pace.

'For four days, nothing. I know they dead, but I keep looking, asking people who might have seen something. Most give me nothing. Finally one woman tell me about activity down at a storage facility for shipping containers. We go have a look.'

'That's where you found Markoff,' Quinn said.

'Yes,' Ne Win said. 'He already dead, two, three days.'

'What about your man?'

'He not there. One day later, his body wash up on beach.'

Silence.

'The message in the container,' Quinn said. 'Was that there when you found Markoff, or did you write it?'

'Message already there.'

'Did you know what it meant?'

'No. But I figure it important.'

'That's why you sent me the whole crate,' Quinn said.

A slight smile touched Ne Win's lips. 'Many

times Markoff say how much he trust you. You his good friend.'

'Yes, he was.'

'When you and I work together, I see what he mean. You good at what you do. You reliable, and you trust but with eyes open.'

'I try,' Quinn said.

'Whatever Markoff was doing he didn't tell me, okay? I know nothing about the Quayside. I know nothing about anything. I could do only what he ask me to do. So I send him to you.'

'Great. Thanks,' Quinn said.

'It worked, yes?' Ne Win said. 'You find Jenny. You save her. Now you get her out.'

Quinn smiled weakly. Jenny's words came back to him. *We're his only chance. We have to save him.* Getting her away didn't look quite as simple as it had a few hours earlier.

'I may need your help,' he said.

'Sure. I can get you out of country.'

Quinn shook his head. 'No. That's not what I mean.'

The look in Ne Win's eyes became guarded. 'I give lot of help already.'

'You have,' Quinn agreed. 'But I may need more.'

He told the old man about what he'd found in the fourth-floor apartment at the Quayside Villas.

'Not possible,' Ne Win said. 'Anyone running weapons here I know about. No one in Quayside. You're wrong. It's something else.'

'I agree. It is something else. It's only supposed to look like it belongs to an arms dealer. What will the Singapore police think when they go in there? Or even the FBI or CIA?'

Ne Win tilted his head back as he sucked in a breath through his nose. 'They will believe what they want to believe.'

'Right,' Quinn said. 'Depending on how and why they find it.'

The old man seemed to think about Quinn's words for a moment. 'Yes. Depending on how and why. So you think it's fake.'

'You said it yourself. Anyone running weapons in Singapore you'd know about, and you didn't know about this. So, yes. I think someone has set it up to be found. Under the right conditions.'

'And what are those conditions?' Ne Win asked.

'That's where I might need your help.'

'You want me to find out?' Ne Win asked, his tone doubtful.

'I want you to keep your ears open, sure,' Quinn said. 'But no. I'll try to find out what's up. It's what we do about it after where you might come in.'

Ne Win looked at Quinn for several seconds, neither of them moving nor saying a word.

Finally the old man nodded once. 'Okay.'

Dr. Han and Orlando appeared at the end of the hallway a few minutes later.

'I think it was a temporary dislocation when she fell. Without an X-ray, I can't tell for sure. It hasn't really swollen up yet, but it should soon.'

'Thanks, Doctor,' Quinn said. He stood up and started walking toward the hallway.

'Hold on,' the doctor said. 'You can't talk to her right now.'

'Why not?' Quinn asked.

'I gave her something for the pain. Knocked her out a few minutes ago. Sleep is what she really needs anyway.'

'Wonderful,' Quinn said. He was anxious to talk to her, but he also knew the doctor was right. Sleep was what she needed. Sleep was what they all needed.

'I should probably come back in the morning,' Dr. Han said.

'We'll call you first,' Quinn said. He wanted to stay flexible.

'Whatever you'd like.'

As the doctor headed for the door, Ne Win stood and started to follow.

'Call me as soon as you know,' Ne Win said to Quinn as he stood in the open door. 'This is my island. I don't like surprises like this.'

As soon as Ne Win and Dr. Han had left, Orlando said, 'What was that all about?'

'He's going to help us.'

'Help us what?' she asked.

Quinn told her about his conversation with Ne Win.

'So Markoff meant for you to be involved all along,' she said.

'Looks that way.'

'If he was alive right now, I'd kill him,' Orlando said.

'Why?' Quinn asked. 'He's only been trying to help Jenny.'

She let out a soft, derisive snort. 'Have you

397

stopped to take a look at yourself lately? Have you seen what this has done to you? His death has consumed you.'

'Then why did you come with me?' he asked.

Anger flashed in her eyes, and she opened her mouth but stopped herself before any word escaped. After a moment, she said, 'You know why. You're just not letting yourself see it.'

He rubbed his hands over his face. 'I'm sorry,' he said. Then, as if he was unsure if the words had actually escaped his lips, he said again, 'I'm sorry.'

He felt her fingertips on his arm, moving slowly up and down, their very presence calming him. Then she moved to him, wrapping her arms around him and laying her head against his shoulder.

'I go anywhere you need me. It doesn't matter why,' she said.

He placed his hands on her back and held her. For the first time he could remember, he was no longer alone.

They stood like that for several minutes, then finally Orlando leaned back.

'You should get some sleep,' she said.

'We both should,' he said.

She picked up the canvas bag with the data cassette player inside and carried it over to her computer on the table. 'I need to get the tape going first. Make sure everything is running correctly.'

Once everything was connected, she turned on the computer, typed her password, then accessed a software application. Quinn wasn't familiar with it, but it was easy to see it had something to do with audio.

'Since the tape is so damaged, I want to make sure we get it the first time. This will take a little longer than normal,' Orlando said. 'But it'll interpolate the damaged audio, then filter out any extraneous noise.'

'How long?' Quinn asked.

'No way to tell for sure. I don't know how much is on this tape. But no more than ten hours. Should be done in the morning.' She yawned.

'Sleep time, I think,' Quinn said. 'Which room do you want?'

'Quinn,' she said. The look on her face wasn't a happy one.

'What?'

'What the hell's wrong with you?'

She grabbed his hand and began pulling him toward the hallway.

33

The sun was shining brightly beyond the windows of the bedroom when Quinn opened his eyes. His back ached, but that wasn't surprising. He'd spent the night sleeping on the floor of the master bedroom so that he would be close if Jenny needed anything.

Orlando was beside him, tucked against his side, her head on his chest. It was nearly the identical position they'd been in when they'd fallen asleep hours before. They had been too exhausted to do anything more than hold each other.

He could hear Jenny breathing evenly on the bed. She had stirred only once during the night, but had not come fully awake — a bad dream, no doubt, probably heightened by Dr. Han's pain medication.

Quinn tried to slip his arm out from under Orlando without waking her, but she stirred, then suddenly stretched. Her eyes opened just enough to look at him through her intertwined lashes.

'What time is it?' she whispered.

He looked at his watch. 'Ten-forty,' he said, surprised. It was the longest night of sleep he'd had since Markoff had turned up dead.

He pushed himself up, then pulled on his jeans and a black polo shirt. 'I'll make coffee.'

★ ★ ★

The pot was almost done when he heard Orlando come down the hall. He waited until the coffee was finished, then filled two cups and carried them into the living room.

Orlando had changed clothes and had pulled her hair back into a ponytail. It looked like she'd run some water over her face, too. She looked refreshed and ready to go.

She was sitting at the table with her laptop open again. Quinn set one of the cups down beside the computer.

'Did it finish processing?' he said.

'Looks like it.'

'And?'

'Hold on,' she said.

The folder on the screen displayed a single file. She opened it.

'Is that coffee?'

They both looked up. Nate walked into the living room looking only half awake.

'In the kitchen,' Quinn said.

With a grunt of thanks, Nate shuffled across the room and out of sight.

'Let's hear it,' Quinn said to Orlando.

She hit the Play button, but no sound came out of the speakers.

Orlando stopped the playback, then moved the cursor to the middle of the file timeline and started it again. Again there was nothing.

'What's wrong?' Quinn asked.

'Hold on.'

She tried a couple different spots on the

timeline with the same result.

'What's going on?' Nate asked as he emerged from the kitchen with a cup of coffee.

'Not now,' Quinn said.

Orlando had opened the conversion software she'd been using and was examining the log. After a moment, she shook her head and closed the program.

'What is it?' Quinn asked.

'I don't know,' she said. 'It should play. The log says it converted fine.'

She tried the file again. Dead air.

She leaned back and stared at the screen.

'There was something on the tape,' Quinn said. 'Right?'

'Yes, there was something on the tape,' she snapped. 'Please, just . . . give me a few minutes to figure this out.'

'Sure,' Quinn said. He touched her shoulder. 'It's okay.'

'It's not okay,' she said, glaring up at him. 'There should be something here. We should be hearing it.'

Quinn went into the kitchen to refresh his coffee and to give Orlando a little space. When he returned, her mood seemed to have gotten worse.

'It should be there,' she said. 'There's no reason why it's not.'

'Then run it again,' he said.

'That'll take another day.'

'Okay, so it takes another day. We've got nothing now.'

'Another day will be too late,' Jenny said. She

was standing near the entrance to the hall, her good shoulder propping her up against the wall. 'Can I get some water?'

Quinn shot Nate a look, then nodded toward the kitchen.

'I'll get it,' Nate said.

Quinn walked over to Jenny. He put an arm around her waist and guided her into the living room.

'Sit down,' he said when they reached the couch.

She didn't need to be told twice.

'How's the shoulder?' he asked.

'Not too bad if I don't move it.'

Nate came back in carrying a glass of water. He handed it to Jenny, and they all watched while she took a drink.

'What did you mean?' Quinn asked after she set the glass down. 'Why too late?'

'It was on the tape,' she said. 'If you'd been able to listen to it, you'd have understood.'

'We don't have that option right now,' Quinn told her. 'You're going to have to tell us what was there.'

She looked down at the glass in her hand and sighed. 'They're going to kill him,' she said. 'Today.'

'Kill who?' Orlando asked. She'd turned in her chair so she was facing everyone.

'Guerrero?' Quinn asked.

'Yes,' Jenny said.

'Who's going to kill him?' Quinn said.

'I don't know exactly who. Someone was hired to do it. That was what was on the tape. A conversation between the killer and . . . '

'And who?' Orlando asked.

Jenny didn't look up. 'The congressman's wife.'

'What?' Quinn said.

'I know. I didn't believe it at first either. But then Gerry gave me the tape. He worked with the congressman's wife. He was Ms. Goodman's personal assistant.'

'*Was?*' Orlando said.

'He's dead,' Jenny told them. 'A day after he gave this to me, they killed him. That's why I had to run. I didn't want to die, too. But once I heard what was on there, I knew I couldn't ignore it. I tried getting in touch with the congressman, but others were keeping me from him. I came here because I knew this would be the only chance I had.'

'Hold on,' Quinn said. 'The congressman's men have been after you.'

'Not the congressman's men, his wife's.' She paused. 'When his campaign started getting serious this past summer, she told him she would hire a security team for him. She comes from money, you know that, right? Very politically active. He didn't think it was necessary, but she insisted. But I think the people she hired really work for the person who's going to kill her husband. She sent them after me because she knows I have this tape. That I can ruin all of her plans.'

Jenny took another drink of the water.

'But why kill her husband?' Orlando asked.

Jenny looked briefly at Orlando and then

Quinn before glancing away, saying nothing.

'Jenny, why?' Quinn asked.

'At . . . at first I thought it had something to do with their marriage. Maybe she caught him cheating on her and wanted to avoid any potential embarrassment. I don't know. Could have been a million reasons. Spouses kill spouses all the time.'

'You said 'at first,'' Quinn reminded her after she'd fallen silent for several seconds. 'You don't think that now.'

She shook her head. 'No. I don't.'

Again she looked away, seeming reluctant to elaborate.

Quinn knelt down directly in front of her. 'What is it?' he asked. 'Why would she want to kill him?'

'Steven figured it out,' she finally said.

'Markoff?'

She nodded. 'I'm sure that's why he's dead.'

'Jenny, what did he figure out? You've got to tell us.'

This time when she looked at him, she didn't look away. 'Steven said there's this group . . . this organization that tries to . . . manipulate things to benefit its members,' she said.

'LP?' Quinn asked.

'Yes.'

'Manipulate what?' Orlando said.

'Policies. Laws. Whatever it takes. That's what Steven told me, anyway.' She paused. 'He said they've been building up over time, moving members into key positions in every department and branch of the government.'

'A shadow government,' Orlando said.

Jenny looked over at her. 'That's exactly what Steven said. 'They're a shadow government lying in wait.''

'So Guerrero's wife? She's what? A member?' Quinn asked.

Another nod. 'Exactly.'

'But I still don't understand why LP would want her husband dead.'

'Some administrations are more open to the ideas fronted by LP than others. The current administration is not one of those. The way things are looking right now, the President is going to win reelection easily. No one in the congressman's party will be able to catch him. Not the way things stand now. Steven said LP couldn't sit still for that.'

'So they kill Guerrero? Someone from the same party they want in power?' The plan did make sense to him, though as he started to ask the question, an inkling of what they had in mind began to form.

'He was a military hero. A Marine,' Jenny said. 'He was involved in the Panamanian invasion in the late eighties. Saved a few of his men. When he got out, moving into politics came naturally to him. But though the congressman is loyal to the party, he's not a yes man. He votes what his conscience tells him, which puts him at odds with almost everyone at some point or another. But the public likes his independent spirit. That's why he's seeking the presidency. He feels he provides an alternative to the status quo.'

'Man of the people,' Orlando said.

'Yes,' Jenny said. 'Exactly right.' She took a second, then continued. 'But Steven said that despite the fact the congressman's wife is in the LP, the organization has no control over him. But they have found a use for him.'

'So they're going to kill him because they can't control him? Why not just create a scandal? Force him to leave office?' Nate asked.

'Let me ask you something,' she said, glancing at Nate. 'What would happen if a U.S. presidential candidate was assassinated in a foreign country?'

'It wouldn't be good,' Nate said.

'And what if the evidence pointed at the killer working for Islamic extremists?'

Nate's eyes widened. 'We'd . . . go right back to the mindset the country had after September eleventh.'

'Perhaps not to that extent, but definitely on the way there,' she said.

Jenny was about to say something else, but Quinn stopped her.

'They're changing the dynamic,' he said, not a question, but in his mind a fact. 'The more we draw back within ourselves as a country, the harder time the President's going to have getting reelected.'

'You're missing one thing,' Jenny said.

'What?'

'Once Congressman Guerrero is dead, his wife is going to take his place in the election.'

No one said a word for several seconds.

'Oh my God. She's playing Corazon Aquino,' Orlando said. 'I mean, Aquino wasn't the one who killed her husband, and he wasn't running for office at the time, but in effect her political career was launched because of his death.'

'I don't think the congressman's wife is in the same league as Corazon Aquino,' Quinn said.

'Maybe not,' Orlando said. 'But she's a white woman . . . a white *widow* of a man who will have been assassinated by the enemy. She's well known. Her views are ones that will play well with the changed national psyche. And if her friends at LP arrange any more incidents, perhaps ones embarrassing to the President? She wins in a landslide.'

Quinn tried to picture Jody Goodman as the next President of the United States. It was hard, but not impossible.

'The assassination is supposed to happen here in Singapore, isn't it?' Quinn asked.

'Yes,' Jenny said. 'That's why I've been trying to talk to him, to tell him.'

'He leaves for the States tonight,' Orlando said.

'And that's why there's no time to wait for the tape to be fixed,' Jenny said. 'All I know is that it's supposed to be at some sort of public place. Something on his itinerary.'

Orlando moved quickly back to her computer. After a moment, she looked up. 'The Maxwell Food Centre,' she said. 'It's the only public outing he has left on his schedule. He's supposed to be there at 1 p.m.'

Quinn looked at his watch. It was 11:10 a.m. 'Where is he now?' he asked.

Orlando looked back at the computer. 'He

should be finishing up a meeting at the U.S. embassy. Then he heads to another meeting at the Von Feldt Building near Chinatown before heading over to Maxwell.'

'He's at the embassy right now?' Quinn asked.

'Yes.'

'Nate,' Quinn said. 'Get dressed, then get us a car. Orlando, gather up the gear.' He looked at Jenny.

'I'm coming with you,' she said.

As much as he would have liked to leave her in the apartment, she might be the only one who could convince the congressman if it came to that.

'Ask Nate for one of his clean T-shirts.'

★ ★ ★

While everyone was getting ready, Quinn made a phone call to the embassy.

'Kenneth Murray, please,' he said once his call was answered.

He was put on hold for a few seconds, then the line began ringing again.

'Kenneth Murray's office.' It was a woman's voice, soft and young. If Quinn knew Murray, her looks would match her voice.

'I need to speak to Mr. Murray,' Quinn said.

'I'm sorry,' she said. 'He's on a conference call. Can I take a message?'

'I need him now,' Quinn said.

'I'm sorry, sir. But he's unavail — '

'Tell him it's Quinn.'

'That won't change anything.'

'Do it. Please.'

He could hear her exhale an angry breath. 'One moment.'

While he was on hold, Nate reentered the living room dressed in a dark blue T-shirt and jeans.

'Hurry,' Quinn said.

Nate nodded, then left the apartment. Stress was the great focuser for Quinn's apprentice. It would be one of his major strengths in a few years when he went out on his own.

There was a click on the line. Then a voice, very tentative, said, 'This . . . is Murray.'

'Kenneth, I need your help now.'

'Oh hell. It *is* you.'

'I don't have any time for bullshit. I need you to listen to me.'

'Quinn, I don't work for you. So — '

'Shut up and listen. Congressman James Guerrero is somewhere in your building. You need to keep him there. Don't let him leave.'

'What?' Murray said, confused. 'Why?'

'Because if you let him out, he's going to be killed.'

'I don't know if I can — '

'I'm not screwing with you. Do it!'

'Just a minute.'

Murray's reluctance to help was understandable. Beyond the fact that he had somehow developed the idea that Quinn was an assassin who might kill him at any moment, he had almost lost his job and gone to jail the previous winter in Berlin for helping Quinn. But none of that had happened. Quinn had made sure of it.

In fact, Quinn had been the one instrumental in getting Murray transferred halfway around the world to his current cushy job in Southeast Asia.

Jenny came back into the living room wearing the same pants she'd been wearing the night before, and a blue T-shirt.

Only seconds behind her was Orlando. She had a black backpack hanging from her shoulders and had another in her hand. Each looked full and heavy.

'Who are you talking to?' Jenny asked.

'The embassy,' he said.

She looked surprised. 'Have . . . have they been able to stop him?'

Before he could answer her, Murray came back on the line. 'He's already gone.'

Quinn closed his eyes. 'When did he leave?'

'Twenty minutes ago.'

'Twenty minutes?' Quinn said, looking over at Orlando.

'His schedule says he shouldn't be leaving for another ten,' Orlando said.

'You have to send someone after him,' Quinn said to Murray. 'Get him someplace safe.'

'I can't just do that for no reason.'

'I've told you the reason!' Quinn yelled.

'I need *proof*, Quinn,' Murray said. 'I can't just say 'I heard someone's going to try to kill the congressman.''

'Hell yes, you can!' Quinn said. 'Look, the congressman is scheduled to visit the Maxwell Food Centre at 1 p.m. He won't leave there alive. You need to stop him before he even gets there.'

'I don't know if I can. I mean, if you'd just give me a little — '

'Do it, goddamn it! Just do it!' Quinn hung up the phone, then looked over at Orlando and Jenny. 'Let's go.'

34

They headed toward the Von Feldt building in a Mercedes Nate appropriated a couple blocks away from the apartment. Nate was at the wheel, with Quinn in the front passenger seat. Jenny and Orlando sat in the back.

'Where did the tape come from?' Quinn asked.

'Gerry got it. I don't know how, but he figured out what was going on. He told me he began recording Ms. Goodman's conversations.'

'So she was the contact person for the assassin?'

'Yes.'

'And she didn't find out about the recordings?' Orlando said.

'She must have,' Jenny said. 'That's why Gerry's dead. I think he probably believed she was onto him, and that's why he gave me the tape.'

'Why you?' Quinn asked.

'We were friendly. We occasionally had to work together to coordinate the congressman's and his wife's schedules. I guess he thought I could get it to my boss.'

'But you didn't,' Quinn said.

'Congressman Guerrero was out of town for a couple of days when Gerry gave it to me. I was going to talk to him the minute he got back.' She paused. 'But Gerry was killed the next day. That's why I actually listened to the tape. As

413

soon as I heard it, I knew that was the reason he was dead. I also knew I had to get out of there, or I'd be dead, too. I made an excuse, told the office I had a family emergency and needed to take a leave of absence. Then I disappeared.'

'Turn left,' Orlando said to Nate.

'Are you sure?' Nate asked.

'Yes. Left.'

Nate whipped the car to the left, barely making the light.

'Gerry said there were other tapes, too,' Jenny went on. 'He had them stored someplace safe. He said he was going to get them and bring them to me.'

'He should have just called the police,' Nate said.

'I said the same thing to him,' she told him. 'But he said he couldn't. That there were others, and they could be anywhere. After Steven told me about LP, I realized that's what Gerry meant.'

No one said anything for a moment.

'Did Gerry tell you anything else? Anything at all that might be helpful?'

Her eyes grew distant for a moment. 'Only that Ms. Goodman talked to her one more time after the call on the tape he gave me. He'd taped that one, too, but had left it someplace safe. He said he was going to bring it to me the next day. But he never did.'

'Wait,' Quinn said. 'Did you say 'talked to *her*'?'

'Since you couldn't listen to the tape, you don't know,' Jenny said, realizing what he was

414

asking. 'The killer Ms. Goodman hired is a woman.'

Suddenly, missing pieces began to fall into place in Quinn's mind.

'What is it?' Orlando asked. She was staring at him, her brow knitted in concern.

'Tasha,' Quinn said.

'Who's Tasha?' Jenny asked.

'Tasha Douglas?'

Jenny looked back at him, her face blank. 'I don't know anyone by that name.'

Quinn had been played. Deceived from the very beginning. Tasha had been using him to find Jenny. It was only because of his own wariness that he hadn't led her all the way to her target.

'Hold on. Does that mean — ' Nate began.

'Yes.' Quinn cut him off.

'Who are you talking about?' Jenny asked.

'Not now,' Quinn said.

He was running everything through his mind, playing it back and forth, and analyzing and reanalyzing. Tasha would have stayed behind in Houston to see if he would show up again. She had played the innocent, the friend desperate to find out where Jenny was. All the while, she was trying to figure out Quinn's involvement and, once she did, trying to get him to lead her to Markoff's girlfriend. It was no coincidence she'd been watching him when he had investigated Jenny's apartment. She had never lost sight of him, he was sure of that now. She had wanted him to see her. It was just another step in building her alternate identity. And again, when he had found her waiting for him outside

Guerrero's office building, it had all been planned.

There had been no call from her brother about someone breaking into her home back in Texas. The trashed hotel room in D.C. had been faked. She could have easily had her men stage the room while Quinn was in talking with Blackmoore. And then, of course, there was Blackmoore himself. She would have also had her men play the old spy runner a visit to find out what he knew.

And finally, after they had left her in California, she had continued to call him. Somehow she must have worked out a way to trace his signal — a signal that was supposed to be untraceable.

Quinn's jaw tensed as he remembered answering her call right before he was to meet up with Jenny at the Far East Square. He had even told Tasha he was about to see her 'friend.' Her men must have been shadowing him, and with a word from their boss, they had moved in.

'There it is,' Nate said.

Though Quinn had been looking out the front window, he had seen nothing. Now, with his eyes refocused, he spotted the Von Feldt Building half a block away on the left.

'Where do you want me to go?' Nate asked.

There were no obvious diplomatic vehicles parked in front of the building.

'Pull over there,' Quinn said, pointing to an open spot just past the building.

Once the car was parked at the curb, Quinn opened his door. 'I'm going to look around.'

416

'I'll go with you,' Orlando said, already opening her door.

'What about us?' Jenny asked.

'Wait here. We won't be long.'

Orlando and Quinn walked down the sidewalk toward the high-rise.

'There's got to be VIP parking, some kind of garage or something around here,' Quinn said.

'Quinn,' Orlando said, 'Tasha is obviously a professional. She's as good at what she does as you or I are at what we do. You didn't expect to run into someone like her.'

'I should have never let that happen,' he said.

'But Tasha hasn't gotten to Jenny. You've done okay.'

'I should have left her in D.C.'

'It worked out all right. We know about her now. We know what she is.'

He frowned. 'It was a mistake.'

Before she could say anything more, he stopped and pulled out his phone. He punched in Ne Win's number and hit Send.

'I was expecting your call,' Ne Win said. 'You are still here, aren't you?'

'Yes.'

'So what is it you need?'

'I know what the dealer setup at the Quayside is for,' Quinn said.

'Really?'

'It's a diversion,' Quinn said. He gave Ne Win a quick version of Jenny's story about the upcoming assassination attempt on her boss. 'Here's what I think. Somewhere not too far from the Maxwell Food Centre, there's going to be a dead body. The person will be ID'd as the man who killed the congressman. It won't have been him, of course, but that won't matter. The evidence will all point to him. There'll be something on the body, something that links the man to the weapons showroom at the Quayside Villas.' Quinn paused. 'The hair.'

'What hair?'

'I found one hair in a desk drawer at the showroom. I'll bet you anything it belongs to the fall guy.' Quinn took a breath. 'That can be checked later. Once the police find the showroom, there'll be something there that will eventually lead them to an extremist group, probably Islamic.'

'Assassination of an American official in Singapore would be bad for business. Especially if it looks like one of us did it.'

'I agree. If they put everything together, they'll have a full-fledged jihadist conspiracy on their hands.' He paused. 'But if there's no body to find, there's no link to the apartment.'

'And no link to any organization.'

'Exactly right.'

'So you want me to find the body,' Ne Win said.

'Yes.' Quinn looked at his watch. 'If they're playing it smart, the body won't be moved into place for at least another thirty minutes.'

'If they are playing it smart,' Ne Win said, 'the body is still alive right now.'

The old man was right. To make it seem realistic, the red herring had to die in relatively the same time period as he would have if he were the real assassin.

'Can you find it?' Quinn asked.

'It won't be easy,' Ne Win said. 'But we will try.'

'If you do, be sure to remove all the evidence.'

'Interesting. I seem to be doing your job today.'

'Trust me, I wish it was the other way around.'

There was a beep on the line, another call coming through. Quinn moved the handset out far enough so he could see the display. A Singapore number.

'Let me know if you find anything,' he said to Ne Win, then switched the calls. 'Hello?'

'Is this Mr. Quinn?' The voice was vaguely familiar, female.

'Who is this?' Quinn asked.

'Brianne Solomon. I work at the embassy. I'm Mr. Murray's assistant.'

'Okay. Why are you calling me?'

'This is Mr. Quinn, correct?'

'Yes,' he said, his patience slipping rapidly. 'What is it?'

Orlando had been scanning the neighborhood, looking for the kind of car Guerrero might have arrived in. But she looked back at Quinn and shook her head.

'Mr. Murray would like it if you would call him on his mobile phone.' She read off a number. 'Do you need me to repeat it?'

'No. I got it.'

He disconnected the call, then punched in Murray's number and hit Send.

'Quinn?' Murray's voice came over the line the moment the connection was made.

'What is it, Kenneth?'

'You're a son of a bitch, you know that? You got me in it again.' Murray sounded like he was outside somewhere. Quinn could hear traffic and distant voices. Murray, apparently concerned he might be overheard, was keeping his voice low.

'What happened?' Quinn asked.

'I took your *warning* to the appropriate person at the embassy.' Quinn assumed that was either the CIA resident or, more frequently in these post-9/11 days when they'd been given more international responsibilities, an agent from the FBI. 'I played it off like I'd received an anonymous tip. Good thing, too. *They* said they'd received a similar warning. *They* said they'd checked it out. *They* said it was nothing.'

'They said they looked into it?' Quinn asked.

'I think the direct quote was, 'There was nothing there, Mr. Murray. But thanks for bringing it to our attention.''

'They're lying,' Quinn said.

'Dammit, Quinn . . . Yeah, I know they're lying,' Murray said. He sounded pissed off. 'Normally they wouldn't just dismiss something I told them like that. But if Homeland Security isn't going to do anything about it, what the hell am I going to do?'

'Call the congressman directly. Stop him. He'll listen to you.'

'I am able to figure a few things out on my own,' Murray said. 'I already tried that. I called the Raffles Hotel, talked to one of his staff. Turns out the congressman's schedule has changed quite a bit. The meeting at the Von Feldt Building has been moved someplace else, but the guy I talked to had no idea where. Said if I wanted to get ahold of him, then the next possibility would be the 1 p.m. stop at the Maxwell Food Centre.'

'Son of a bitch.' Quinn looked at Orlando. 'Come on. He's not here.'

They started running back toward the car.

'I asked the aide if he'd give me the congressman's mobile number, but he wouldn't,' Murray said. 'Said he'd be happy to pass along any message.'

'Did you tell him it was an emergency?' Quinn asked.

'Of course I did.'

They reached the car and got in quickly.

'He's not here,' Quinn told Nate.

Nate gave him a single nod, then pulled the car away from the curb and headed down the street. There was no need for Quinn to tell him where to go next.

But Murray was a different story. 'You need to go to the Maxwell Food Centre,' Quinn said.

'What? Why?'

'You need to be there. You're a representative of the U.S. government. I need you to cover my ass, and make sure that the right story gets out.'

'What do you mean 'the right story gets out'?'

'The one you're going to have to take on faith. But I promise you're going to come out of this smelling good.'

'Like last time?' Murray asked.

'I'd say it worked out pretty well for you.'

'Fine,' Murray said.

Quinn disconnected the call.

'So what are we doing now?' Jenny asked.

Quinn looked back at her. 'Now we try to keep your boss from getting killed.'

35

Hawker centers were born from the desire to clean up Singapore. At one time, food carts were everywhere, lining the streets and roads of the city. Then someone got the idea to move them into centralized locations where there would be community seating and a clean water source.

Maxwell Food Centre was just one of many, but more popular than most because of its location near Chinatown. Tiny walk-up food stands made of cinder blocks were jammed together side-by-side-by-side under a giant corrugated tin roof. The restaurants were aligned in rows back-to-back, creating wide aisles full of tables for the hungry to enjoy their meals with a few hundred of their closest friends. And while the roof covered the entire complex, there were no walls on the outside of the center, just support columns and open air.

Quinn directed Nate to park the Mercedes a block away.

'Everyone radio up,' Quinn said. 'Orlando and Nate, I want you to take up positions inside. Look for anything unusual. I'll hang out near the street and try to stop Guerrero from getting out of his car.' Quinn looked at Jenny. 'We'll give you a radio, but you'll stay here. If we need you, I'll let you know.'

She looked like she wanted to protest, but

didn't, her damaged shoulder no doubt reminding her what happened when she got directly involved.

Orlando passed out the communications gear. Once they were all outfitted, she gave Quinn and Nate each a 9mm SIG Sauer P226 and matching suppressors. For her own use, she pulled out a Glock.

'Here.' Orlando handed both of them a miniature version of the messenger bag Ne Win had given Quinn a couple of days before. Then, for Nate's benefit, she said, 'Keep your gun in the bag unless you absolutely have to pull it out.'

Quinn checked the chamber to make sure a round was already loaded, then popped out the magazine to confirm that it was maxed. After he'd attached the suppressor, he put the gun in his bag in a way that would make it easy to reach in, aim, and fire without ever pulling the pistol out.

'What about Jenny?' Orlando asked.

Quinn looked at Markoff's girlfriend. He still couldn't get used to her short hair or the lack of a smile on her face. But most of all, he couldn't get used to the sense of controlled anger she exuded.

'Do you know how to use a gun?' Quinn asked her.

She nodded, hesitantly. 'Markoff showed me.'

'Leave the big bag where she can get to it,' Quinn said to Orlando. To Jenny, he said, 'There are a couple guns inside, and some other things you won't need. But don't pull anything out unless it's an absolute emergency.'

Jenny nodded.

Nate and Orlando left first. Once they crossed the street, they separated and entered the food center from different directions.

While Quinn waited for a moment, he said to Jenny, 'Why didn't you get help? Isn't that what your friend wanted you to do?'

She took a second before answering. 'There wasn't time. When he was killed, it scared the shit out of me, you know? I didn't want any of this, but I couldn't ignore it. I tried to call Steven, but he was out of town and didn't pick up. I didn't know what else to do, so I went back to Houston, to my home there. Steven showed up the next morning. I told him everything and then played the tape. It was his idea to get out of the country. We were on a flight for Europe within hours.'

'Then why was Markoff in Singapore?'

'He wanted to get more proof. Something to go along with the tape. He thought he could find it here.' She looked at Quinn. 'Maybe he did find it, only like you told me, his signal didn't last long enough for you to locate it.'

Quinn nodded. Markoff had done exactly the same thing Quinn would have done: get Jenny as far away as possible, then try to find another way to prove what was going on so that Jenny's life would no longer be in jeopardy. He did it all because he loved her. Even in his last moments of life, when he knew they would never be together again, he had pointed toward a clue that could possibly set her free.

It was time for Quinn to go.

'If you see anything or hear anything you think I might need to know about, just start talking,' Quinn said. 'Otherwise, unless we ask you a direct question, it would be best for you to just listen.'

'Okay,' she said.

Quinn got out of the car.

★　★　★

Quinn purchased a pork bao and a soft drink from one of the vendors nearest the edge of the hawker center, then found a seat in front of the Zhen Zhen Porridge booth.

Unless you were with a large group, there was no such thing as getting your own table. At Quinn's table there was an older couple, each with a bowl of porridge. They smiled at Quinn as he sat down, then returned to their meal.

'Check,' Quinn said, voice low.

'Check,' Orlando said. 'I'm on the northwest side. Nothing here.'

'Nate?' Quinn asked.

'Check,' Nate said. 'Center aisle. But nothing out of the ordinary here, either.'

The old couple gave Quinn an odd look, so he took a bite of the bao and smiled.

'Quinn. Quinn!' It was Jenny.

He stood up and began walking toward the street. 'What's wrong?'

'A woman just walked by,' Jenny said. 'I've seen her before. She was with the congressman's wife once back in D.C. She's not alone. She's with some of the men I've seen protecting

426

Congressman Guerrero. My God, do you think she's the killer?'

'Where is she?' Quinn asked. He was moving quickly through the crowd toward the street.

'She got out of a car about half a block away from me. She's walking across the street now.'

Quinn dodged past a group of teenagers and craned his head, looking in the direction Jenny had indicated. There was a group of five coming across the street. All but one of them were male. One of the four men was a guy Quinn had seen in Houston and again in D.C. He was sure of it.

The hit squad, he thought.

He checked his watch: 12:30. They'd arrived early so they could be in position by the time the congressman got there.

As Quinn looked back at the group, the men began moving off in different directions. For the first time, Quinn was able to get a look at the woman.

Even though he'd already prepared himself for it, he still stopped in his tracks. He could feel anger beginning to swell inside him again, only instead of clouding his judgment, it focused him.

'Tasha,' he said.

'God, I was hoping you were wrong,' Nate said.

'Me, too,' Quinn said, teeth clenched.

He stared at Tasha for a moment longer, then tore himself away.

'Orlando, two of them are heading in your direction. They're not going to be hard to miss. White guys in suits. Tall, short hair. Nate, move

427

to the south. See if you can keep tabs on the other two.'

'Check,' Nate said.

'Be careful,' Orlando said. 'She's a lot more dangerous than you thought she was.'

Quinn grunted a response. No matter how dangerous she was now, he was pissed and she was going to pay.

He moved to his right, keeping a layer of people between himself and the road as he got closer to Tasha's position. She had none of the helpless look he'd seen in her before. She was all business, her face hard and determined.

As she scanned the food center, Quinn knelt down as if he'd dropped something. From the lower angle, he could see her continuing her examination. Her gaze passed right by his position, not even noticing him.

'We've got another problem,' Orlando said over the radio.

'We don't need another problem.'

'Well, tell that to the congressman. His car just pulled up.'

Before Quinn could say anything, Nate jumped in. 'I've got movement over here. The two I'm watching are headed north now.'

Quinn stood up. Tasha was moving, too, heading in the same direction as the others. They were all converging on the congressman's position.

'Orlando, we're all coming to you,' Quinn said.

'Check,' she said.

Tasha stayed to the street, so Quinn paralleled

428

her from his position inside.

'The congressman is getting out of the car,' Orlando said. 'His wife is with him. So is your blond friend from last night. He's got a nice big bandage around his hand.'

'Keep your eyes open,' Quinn said. 'The shot can come from anywhere.' Just because Tasha was in charge didn't mean she'd necessarily be the one to pull the trigger. It could come from any of her team — not only those who'd arrived with her, but also the men supposedly guarding the congressman.

They all worked for Tasha.

'My guys have stopped in the crowd and are just watching, not moving in,' Orlando said.

'Mine, too,' Nate said. 'We're a little bit south of you.'

As Tasha neared the corner, she turned in, passed beneath the metal roof, and entered the food center. She kept scanning the crowd as if she expected to find someone, but she never stopped moving forward.

Quinn had at first thought she was going to take the most direct route to the congressman, but instead she headed a little to the south, aiming for a break between the permanent food stands that would take her into the central aisle.

Quinn circled around so she was in front of him, then followed her, keeping about fifteen feet between them. If she were to turn around, she'd see him, but her focus seemed to be on what was ahead of her, not behind.

'Status,' Quinn whispered.

'Holding position here,' Nate said.

'Same,' Orlando said. 'The congressman's party is starting to move down the central aisle. He seems a little tired. His wife is tense, though.'

'Go figure,' Quinn said.

'The blond guy stayed back at the car,' she said. 'But two of the security men are with them. They've also got someone who looks local with them. Chinese, I think. He seems to be giving the congressman a tour.'

Ahead, Tasha moved into the ten-foot-wide passageway. Because of the angle, she passed out of his sight for a moment, hidden by one of the cinder-block restaurants.

Quinn quickened his pace, but when he reached the gap, she wasn't there.

She must have turned either right or left immediately on the other end of the short corridor; those were the only options. Quinn ran to the other end, slowing just as he reached the central aisle so as not to attract undue attention.

He looked right.

Then left.

But she wasn't there.

He turned around to look behind him, thinking maybe she *had* spotted him and had just tricked him into passing by her. But she wasn't behind him either, and there was no place in the passage she could be hiding.

Again he scanned the central aisle. But the result was the same.

Off to his left, near where the rows of restaurants began, he could see the congressman and his party. Their guide had led them to one of the stalls and was explaining something to them.

'Quinn?'

Quinn whipped around, his hand slipping into the opening of the bag on his shoulder. But it wasn't Tasha or one of her team. It was Kenneth Murray.

'I saw you, but I wasn't sure,' Murray said. He was an average-sized man, with an average-looking face. The kind of guy who would be hard to describe later, if you even remembered him. 'I mean, I thought it was you, but . . . well, I guess I was right.' He paused. 'What is it you wanted me to see?'

'Kenneth, I nearly killed you just now,' Quinn said.

'Wh . . . what?' Murray stammered.

Quinn could see the white all the way around Murray's irises.

'Rule number one for you, never sneak up on me.'

'Okay, sure. No problem.' He took a step back. 'Maybe actually I shouldn't be here. I'm just in the way.'

Quinn grabbed Murray by the arm and turned him so he was facing the north end of the food center.

'There,' Quinn said. 'You see him?'

Murray glanced nervously over his shoulder at Quinn, then looked down the central aisle of the hawker center. 'What am I looking for?'

'That group of people down near the end. The man in the dark suit, that's the congressman.'

'Okay. Yeah, I see him.'

'I need you to go down there and get him out of here.'

'Whoa. Wait. You just said you wanted me to see something. You didn't say you needed me to *do* something.'

'If you don't do it, he's going to die. But you have to be careful. Those security men with him, they aren't the good guys.'

Murray started to pull away. 'No. You do it.'

'I can't,' Quinn said. He knew if he did and Tasha saw him, she'd move in before he could get to the congressman. Murray had a much better chance. 'You've got to go now!'

'Dammit, dammit, dammit, dammit, dammit,' Murray said. 'I swear to God you'd better be right.'

36

There were people everywhere. The lunch crowd jammed itself into the hawker center like it was the only place to eat within miles. Lines in front of the most popular stalls were growing by the second.

Quinn moved out into the central aisle, his eyes darting back and forth as he tried to find any sign of Tasha.

'Status,' he said.

'My guys are still holding back,' Orlando said.

'Ditto,' Nate said.

'Does anyone see Tasha?'

'You lost her?' Nate asked.

'Is that a no, then?' Quinn said.

'Sorry,' Nate said. 'Yes, it's a . . . no. I mean, you know. No, haven't seen her.'

'Neither have I,' Orlando said.

Quinn looked to his left. Murray was fighting his way through the hungry mob toward the food stall the congressman had stopped at. The only problem was, the congressman and his party weren't there anymore. They had moved back to the middle of the aisle and were making their way deeper into the hawker center, moving toward Quinn's position.

'Dammit,' Quinn said under his breath.

He had to find Tasha. He had to stop her.

He started weaving through the crowd, heading in the direction of the congressman.

'I have movement,' Nate said. 'My guys are closing in.'

'Mine are holding back,' Orlando said.

Mop-up duty, Quinn thought. In case things didn't go well for the first team.

There were still at least forty feet and nearly a hundred people between Quinn and the congressman. As he started to skirt around a couple of teenage girls, someone bumped into him, and almost immediately he could feel a cool liquid dripping down his shirt. It had the sweet, fruity smell of fresh juice.

'Oh, sorry,' a male voice said.

Quinn's instincts told him to duck. Unfortunately, they came a half-second too late.

A fist smashed into his back right above one of his kidneys.

Pain shot through Quinn's torso as he fell forward. He tried to twist on his descent, but was only partially successful in landing faceup.

The people closest to him pulled back, forming a small hole in the sea of customers. They looked down at Quinn in surprise and confusion. All, that was, except the blond man who was standing directly behind where Quinn had been a few seconds before.

Blondie's damaged hand was held loosely against his stomach. But it was the good hand that was the problem. It was reaching for something under his jacket.

Quinn didn't wait to see what it was. He pressed his hands against the dirty concrete floor and pushed himself up and out, aiming his feet at the man's knees. He missed the left, but solidly connected with the right.

Quinn could feel the man's kneecap slide to the right, dislocating from the socket.

Blondie cried out and quickly joined Quinn on the ground.

Whatever he'd been reaching for had been forgotten as he reflexively grabbed his kneecap and tried to push the bone back into place.

Quinn knew he had no more time to waste. He got to his feet, then stepped on Blondie's bad hand.

With all of Blondie's attention on the pain no doubt shooting through his body, Quinn reached under the man's jacket. He was definitely armed, but pulling the gun out would cause instant panic.

Quinn moved his shoulder bag down so that he could maneuver the opening under the man's jacket. He then slipped the gun inside with his own and stood back up.

'Quinn! She's moving in!' It was Orlando.

Quinn whipped around until he was looking in the direction of the congressman. It seemed Quinn's run-in with Blondie had attracted only local attention. The crowd at large appeared oblivious to what had gone on.

As Quinn pushed his way through, he spotted Guerrero. The congressman's wife was no longer with him. She had moved off toward one of the stalls with a member of Guerrero's security team — getting out of the way, perhaps, and creating a legitimate reason why Guerrero would have only one guard at his side.

What he couldn't see was Tasha.

'Where is she?' he asked.

'She's about fifteen feet in front of me, coming in from the north,' Orlando said.

She must have circled around, Quinn thought.

'Take her out!' Quinn said.

'What do you think I'm trying to do?'

'Nate, do you see her?'

'No,' Nate said.

Quinn no longer cared about maintaining secrecy. He began shoving people out of his way. He could hear angry voices behind him, but no one took their protest further.

He closed to within twenty feet of the congressman and shouted out a warning. But his words were swallowed by the noise of the crowd.

'Bad guy coming up on your right,' Nate said.

'You have visual on me?' Quinn asked.

'Yes. I'm not far behind him.'

Quinn looked to his right and immediately spotted one of Tasha's men.

'Keep him away from me,' Quinn said. 'I don't have time.'

'Check,' Nate said.

The congressman was only ten feet away when someone tugged at Quinn's arm. Quinn pulled back, ready to lash out at his new attacker, but it was Murray.

'I . . . I lost him before,' Murray said. 'I'm sorry. Do you still want me to talk to him?'

Quinn grabbed Murray by the back of the shirt and started pushing him toward the congressman. 'Get in there and get him on the ground! Now!'

He gave Murray a powerful shove, sending

him racing through the crowd.

Quinn looked past Guerrero, in the direction Orlando said Tasha would be coming from.

And there she was. Only five feet behind the congressman. She was reaching into the large purse that hung over her shoulder.

Quinn threw the man who was standing in front of him to the side.

'No!' he screamed as he rushed forward.

Everyone looked up — Tasha, the congressman, his remaining bodyguard. They were all looking toward Quinn, so none of them saw Murray rushing up to the congressman. Without a word, Murray tackled Guerrero to the ground.

Then all hell broke loose.

Guerrero shouted out in surprise. Then the crowd itself seemed to realize something bad was going on.

Everyone began yelling and shoving, and trying to run. Some wanted to see what was happening, while others wanted to get away. No order. Only chaos.

Guerrero's bodyguard pulled at Murray, trying to get him off. But Murray was hanging on tight.

Tasha had rushed forward, too, a gun now in her hand. She was bending down to get next to the congressman. The frenzy had actually played into her hands, covering her actions. Not only that, but Murray was holding the congressman still for her, unintentionally aiding her efforts.

Quinn had no time to get to his weapon. He took two quick steps, then dove at her.

She saw him at the last second, and tried to

get out of the way but couldn't. He slammed into her right shoulder, and they both tumbled backward onto the ground.

Quinn grabbed for the gun in her hand. He tried to twist it out of her grasp, but she held on tight, displaying a strength she had hidden when she had been with him last.

She tried hitting him in the face, but he deflected the blow.

They began struggling, each trying to get control of the other as they tumbled first one way, then another across the ground.

Suddenly they knocked up against one of the permanent tables. Quinn angled Tasha's arm up, hitting it into one of the chairs. But she wasn't letting go of her gun.

'Where is she?' Tasha demanded.

Quinn hit her hand against the chair again.

'Is she with you? Is she here?'

She pushed against Quinn, rolling them both away from the table. As they did, her arm got caught momentarily by the support bar under the seat. Her fingers, already bloody from hitting the chair, could no longer hold on to the pistol. It clattered to the ground as they both rolled several feet away.

They let go of each other and both dove for the gun. Quinn got his fingers on it first, but Tasha got there a second later and shoved at it, sending the weapon sliding across the floor under another table ten feet away.

She sent an elbow into Quinn's chest, rolling him onto his back, then jumped to her feet and began running for her weapon.

Quinn quickly got to his feet, reaching for his own gun as he did.

'Stop!' he yelled at her.

Tasha looked over her shoulder and saw the gun in his hand. Instead of going for her weapon, she changed direction and jumped over the counter into one of the tiny restaurants.

Quinn knew he should pursue, but first he turned back to the congressman.

Murray was still on him, but Nate was there now, too. The bodyguard that had been his responsibility lay unconscious on the ground next to him.

'Get them out of here,' Quinn said to Nate. 'Take them back to the apartment.'

'Got it,' Nate said.

'What's going on?' It was the congressman. He sounded both pissed and scared.

'Go,' Quinn said to Nate.

Quinn ran over to the restaurant Tasha had disappeared into. Even from beyond the counter, he could see the entire space. She wasn't there.

'Orlando,' he said, 'where are you?'

'I was following the wife,' she said. 'Her bodyguard took her and the tour guide back to the car. Once he got them inside, he waited around for a few seconds, like he was hoping some of his friends would show up. But then they took off.'

'Rendezvous back at the car,' Quinn said. 'Nate's taking the congressman and Murray to the apartment. Don't wait for me. Get to the apartment. I'll meet you there.'

'Got it,' she said.

Quinn figured Tasha must have climbed over the wall at the back of the stall into the restaurant on the next row over.

There was another corridor between the stalls off to his left. He ran over, then through it to the next aisle.

The intense crowds that had been filling the hawker center were gone. It was like a movie set, all the props in place, but the extras had yet to arrive. Only, he realized after a second, it wasn't completely empty.

Quinn saw about a half dozen pairs of eyes peeking over counters at several of the restaurants — shop owners afraid of being ripped off. There was no sign of Tasha, though.

As Quinn ran over to one of the booths, the man who had been peeking from it slipped below the counter, trying to hide. Quinn leaned into the restaurant so the man would know he'd been found out.

'No money, lah. Go now,' the man said.

'The woman, did you see her?' Quinn asked.

'Take food, but I have no money. All gone.'

'I don't want your money. There was a woman, Caucasian. She must have run through here a minute ago. Did you see her?'

'No. I no see.'

Quinn reached over and grabbed the man's shirt.

'That way. That way,' the man said, pointing down the aisle to Quinn's right.

Quinn let go and began running down the aisle.

There was another seating area at the end of

the row, and beyond it was the street. For a second, he wondered if she might have hidden in one of the restaurants he'd run past, but then he spotted her. She was sprinting across the street.

He slipped his gun back into his bag but kept his hand on it as he ran out from under the food center roof. There were more people on the street, refugees from the food center, halfheartedly hiding behind cars and each other. They eyed Quinn suspiciously as he emerged from the deserted center.

'What the hell?' It was Nate's voice over Quinn's radio. 'What are you doing? Hey!'

Though the digital receiver didn't pick up the full effect, Quinn heard the sound of a suppressor.

'Nate?' he asked.

There was no response.

'Nate?'

Ahead, Tasha dodged between two cars parked at the curb, then started running along the sidewalk. Quinn increased his speed.

'Orlando, where are you?'

'I'm heading for the car,' she said.

'Nate's not answering.'

'Yeah, I know.'

'Be careful,' Quinn said.

'Where are you?'

Quinn cut through an opening onto the sidewalk. 'Tasha's just ahead. I can't let her go.'

'All right. You be careful, too.'

There was another street up ahead. Tasha turned down it, moving momentarily out of sight.

Quinn increased his speed, not wanting to lose her. But as he turned the corner something smacked him in the chest.

He doubled over, the wind all but knocked out of him.

As he rolled on his side, he saw Tasha standing a few feet away against the building, the foot that had kicked him back on the ground. Before he could do anything but suck in a breath, she came at him again, this time throwing a punch at his head. Quinn lifted his shoulder in defense, and the blow hit him in the back. But now he had an opening, and whipped his elbow into her side.

She groaned in pain but swung the fist at him again.

This time he was able to pull back just enough so she hit nothing but air.

Before she could bring her arm back around, he pulled his gun out and pointed it at her.

'Stop,' he said. 'It's done. You're through. It's over.'

'Where is she?' Tasha asked.

'I'm not going to let you hurt her,' Quinn said. 'Your plan is done. You're finished.'

'I should have had you put in jail when I first met you,' Tasha said.

Quinn's eyes narrowed. 'Don't even try it,' he said. 'Once the authorities get ahold of you, you'll be the one rotting in jail.'

'Don't you get it?' she said. 'I *am* the authorities!'

Orlando's voice came over his receiver. 'Holy Christ. Quinn, you've got to get over here.'

'What is it?'

'Nate's down. It's bad.'

'What about the congressman?'

'There's no one else here.'

'Jenny?'

'She's gone, too. And Murray, and the car.'

Quinn looked at Tasha, but before he could say anything, she said, 'Where's the congressman?'

'You tell me. Because if he dies because your men took him, it's going to be even worse for you.'

'I'm not the one trying to kill him,' she said. 'I'm the one trying to stop it.'

'Bullshit,' Quinn said.

A look of dawning realization spread on Tasha's face. 'You really think I want to harm the congressman, don't you? You think what you've been trying to do is stop them.'

Quinn said nothing.

'Don't you see?' Tasha said. 'I'm not the assassin. Jenny is.'

37

Quinn grabbed Tasha by the arm and led her half a block away where a cab was parked at the curb. He pulled open the driver's door.

'Out,' he said to the cabby, showing him his gun.

There was no protest.

Quinn shoved Tasha through the open door and told her to crawl across to the passenger seat. Once she was clear, he got in and started the car.

'Orlando, what's your position?' he said.

'We're over near where we parked the Mercedes.'

'I've got a car, we'll be there in a second.'

'Hurry.'

Quinn whipped the car around in a U-turn and for a moment headed away from the hawker center. It would be quicker and easier to get to Orlando if he avoided the streets in front of Maxwell. He kept a hand on his gun and had the barrel pointed in Tasha's direction.

'If she's got the congressman, you're right, it is over,' Tasha said.

Quinn kept quiet.

Before anyone else spoke, a voice came over Quinn's receiver. 'She's right, you know.'

Quinn held up a hand so Tasha wouldn't say anything else. The voice was Jenny's.

'Steven had no idea. Not until the end.'

'Where are you?' Quinn asked.

'Sorry, that I won't be telling you.'

Tasha looked at Quinn, a question in her eyes. By way of answer, he moved the barrel of the gun a few inches to the side, so it was no longer pointed directly at her.

'Do you have the congressman?'

'Yes. And your friend Mr. Murray.'

'There's no reason to kill anyone now. You're not going to be able to blame it on anyone else. We found the weapons cache at the Quayside Villas.'

'Unfortunate, but that doesn't change any-thing,' Jenny said. 'The story will be spun the way we want it. That you can't do anything about.'

'By who? The LP?'

She let out a short laugh.

'The story you told me about the congress-man's wife, most of that was true, wasn't it? Only you're the killer.'

'You know how it is, Quinn.'

The best lies are those hidden in truth. How many times had he heard that over the years? Not just from Durrie, but from almost everyone in the business.

'I'll bet his wife doesn't have anything to do with it at all, does she? Somebody else would have stepped up to take advantage of his death.'

'*Will* step up. But that's not my part of the operation,' Jenny said. 'Good luck convincing anyone of that.' She paused. 'Thank you for helping expose those who were following me. Oh, and delivering me the congressman. That was extra special.'

'Wait,' Quinn said. 'Tell me. Did you enjoy killing the man who loved you?'

'The man who loved me was going to expose me. I couldn't let that happen. Goodbye, Quinn.'

'Jenny?' he said.

Nothing.

She had either removed her gear or just wasn't talking. Quinn let go of the gun, and pulled his own microphone off his collar and crushed it between his fingers.

'Believe me now?' Tasha said.

'What are you?' he asked.

'CIA,' she said.

'Your presence is too small. You should have people swarming all over the place on this.'

She looked over at him. 'I'm off the books. Deep. There was . . . a concern they would know we were onto them.'

'They?' Quinn said. 'LP again?'

She nodded.

There was no time to ask another question as Quinn spotted Orlando at the curb. He quickly pulled over and jumped out of the car.

Nate was lying on the ground, unconscious. His shoulder was soaked in blood, but it didn't look life threatening. So had Orlando reacted like it was —

Then he saw it.

His face paled and he could feel the bile moving up his throat. It wasn't that he hadn't seen gruesome in the past. His life was full of images that would make most people sick for weeks.

This was different. This was his apprentice.

Nate's foot was crushed and twisted 180 degrees backward. The shin was also pulverized up to the point where the remaining bone had ripped through his apprentice's skin.

There was blood, too. A lot of it.

'He was still conscious when I got here,' Orlando said. 'Barely. I think they rammed into him. Crushed him against this car.'

The side of the vehicle next to Nate was smashed in. Quinn imagined Nate trying to jump out of the way, but not being able to completely clear the oncoming car's path.

Without another word, he and Orlando picked Nate up and carried him to the taxi. Tasha had gotten out and had opened the rear door.

Once Nate was settled, Quinn handed Orlando his phone. 'Call Ne Win. He'll tell you where to take Nate. Then tell him to have a couple men meet me at Esplanade Park.'

'You're going after her?' Orlando asked.

'I have to,' Quinn said.

'I know. God, I'm sorry. I . . . I — '

'Just go. Nate needs help.'

'But how are you going to find her?' Orlando asked.

Quinn glanced for a second at Tasha, then looked back at Orlando. 'Markoff's message.'

* * *

'I should be putting you in jail,' Tasha said.

They were in a Toyota Crown Quinn had hot-wired. Quinn was driving again, while Tasha sat next to him. They were heading toward a rendezvous with one of her people. Tasha had called ahead, asking for the device Quinn had told her they needed. Now, though, it sounded like she was having second thoughts.

'You've injured several of my men. Federal officers. You've hindered a terrorist investigation, which pretty much means you're dead. So why shouldn't I arrest you?'

He said nothing. She already knew the answer. Without Quinn's help, the congressman was as good as dead, and Jenny would have disappeared.

After several seconds, Tasha asked, 'Are you sure this is going to work?'

'No,' he told her.

'That's just great.'

A few minutes later, they approached the corner of River Valley Road and Clemenceau Avenue.

'There,' Tasha said, pointing at two men standing off to the side.

'No games,' Quinn said. 'And no following, either. If they do, I'll know.'

Quinn pulled the car to the side of the road but kept rolling slowly forward, never bringing the vehicle to a complete stop. He dropped a hand down to his lap where his SIG lay waiting. 'Roll down your window. Have them toss it inside.'

Tasha did as he asked. The two men started

walking with the car, keeping pace.

'Are you all right?' one of the men asked.

'Fine,' she said. 'Just give it to me.'

The other man leaned down to get a better look at Quinn. 'I thought he was one of the — '

'He's okay,' Tasha said. 'He was working undercover. NSA.'

'He's not coercing you?'

'No.'

The first man handed her something through the window.

'I'll check in soon,' she said.

As they drove off, Quinn kept an eye on the rearview mirror in case anyone was following. But they seemed to have gotten away cleanly.

Tasha held up the device she'd been handed. 'What are we looking for?'

'Cell phone ID.'

'You really think her cell phone's traceable on one of these?' The tracer they'd just picked up would never work on a scrambled signal.

'Not her phone,' Quinn said.

He gave her the same ID number Markoff had scrawled on the inside of the container he'd died in. The transmitter Quinn had taken out of the vase at the Quayside was sitting in his bag in the car Jenny had stolen from him. As long as she hadn't switched vehicles or dumped the bag, they'd find her.

'I've got a signal,' she said. 'It's east of here. At least a couple of miles.'

That was good. It was the same direction they needed to head in to meet up with Ne Win.

'Tell me again why you're here,' Quinn said.

'I told you, I'm running an off-the-books op. Protection for the congressman.'

'Protection? Or are you using him as bait?'

She had no answer for that.

'Who's your handler?'

'I . . . I'm working directly for the DDNI,' she said. The Deputy Director of National Intelligence. 'No one else in the chain. Just him, then me.'

'What about the Director?'

She shook her head.

'Does the Deputy Director suspect the Director's part of the LP?'

'There's no way to know,' she said. 'It's safer not to involve him at this point. Like I said, no one else knows what I'm doing.'

'What about the men you're working with? The men working protection for the congressman? That family in Jenny's house in Houston?'

'I was given the okay to tap a few CIA resources, but only ones I trusted completely. It limited what I could do.'

'Why destroy Jenny's homes?'

'We searched them thoroughly, thinking there might be something we could use to lead us to her LP contacts. Something that would help us crack into the organization. But there was nothing. My boss wanted to send them a signal. Let them know they were being hunted.' She paused. 'When you showed up, I thought you were one of them. That's why I waited. I knew you'd come back.'

'But you destroyed the house.'

'The incendiary device was on a timer. But

there was a backup trigger on the window.'

'In case I returned,' Quinn said.

'Yes.'

'So you were just going to let your explosives take care of me, is that it?'

'That was the plan,' she said matter-of-factly. 'But then I wondered if maybe we could use you. Maybe you knew something more that might get us closer to her.'

Quinn's mind went back to that moment in Houston, right before the house was destroyed. 'You moved. Right as I was starting to open the window.' He shot a quick glance at her. 'You tried to distract me. Get me to move away from the house.'

'And it worked.'

⋆   ⋆   ⋆

When they got to Esplanade Park, Quinn spotted Ne Win and his men standing on the curb.

'We're switching cars here,' Quinn told Tasha.

'Who are these guys?' she asked, once they were parked behind Ne Win's car.

'Friends.'

'I could have brought my men.'

'Well, I brought mine,' Quinn said. 'Come on.'

Tasha wasn't the only one who didn't seem pleased with the arrangement. Quinn could tell as soon as Ne Win saw her he wasn't happy either. But unlike Tasha, he kept his thoughts to himself.

They squeezed into Ne Win's sedan. Then got

onto the East Coast Parkway heading toward the airport.

'Did you find the body?' Quinn asked.

Ne Win swiveled around to look back from his seat up front. He eyed Tasha for a moment, then shook his head. 'No. But,' he said, then paused, 'we did find where the body was supposed to be.'

'What do you mean?'

'Gun there. Spent cartridge. A few other items. Everything looking perfect. Only no body. No blood.'

Of course. Jenny had abandoned her original plan. She'd prepared the site, but the need to kill the faux assassin had gone away as she'd adapted to her new plan.

They drove for another five minutes, leaving the main part of the city behind them.

'We're getting close,' Tasha said, looking at the device in her hand. Then, a mile later, 'There.' She looked toward the right side of the road, then back at the signal tracker. 'I think we just passed it.'

There was a turnoff ahead. 'Take that exit,' Quinn said.

While they were pulling off the parkway, the driver said something to Ne Win in Mandarin.

Ne Win said something back, then looked at Quinn.

'What?' Quinn asked.

The look on Ne Win's face was somber. 'I know where they go.'

'Where?'

But Ne Win just shook his head and turned back toward the front.

Once they were on the side road, there was a strong scent of ocean in the air. The sea was close now, a strip of land separating it from the road they were on. Quinn noticed several large compounds on the strip, most filled with dozens and dozens of shipping containers, stacked and protected by fences topped with razor wire.

Quinn could feel the skin at the base of his neck tingle. He realized he, too, had a pretty good idea where Jenny had taken her hostages.

After several minutes, Ne Win told the driver to pull the car to the side of the road and park as close to the brush as possible. As soon as the car was stopped, the old man looked back at Quinn and Tasha.

'We're almost on top of the signal,' Tasha said. She looked up from the tracker at the old man. 'How did you know?'

Ne Win didn't even smile in response. 'We walk from here.'

* * *

The sign in front of the compound read *Kwan Shipping*. But instead of entering through the front gate, the man who had been driving — Ne Win said his name was Lian — led them through the brush along the east side.

The day had gone gray, the clouds over the island now dark and heavy with rain. Quinn could feel the moisture beginning to gather in the air in anticipation of the regularly scheduled afternoon rain.

'Our first priority is freeing the hostages,'

453

Tasha whispered to Quinn. 'Then we take Jenny. I want her alive.'

Quinn kept his eyes on the path ahead of them, and his mouth shut.

'She's the link to LP. We need to know who her contact is,' she said. 'Understand?'

He glanced over. 'Sure. I understand what you want.'

He looked away, then sped up a little so they were no longer walking abreast.

About one hundred and fifty feet away from the road, Lian led them out of the bushes and up to the fence that surrounded the compound. There was a place where the barrier had been cut apart and then pulled back together and held in place with several thick wires. The other man began untwisting them.

'You went in this way last time?' Quinn asked.

Ne Win nodded.

As soon as the last of the wires came off, Ne Win's men pulled the fence apart so everyone could pass through.

The compound was dense with shipping containers. Some had names on the side, some had none. Quinn even saw a few marked BARON & BARON LTD., like the one Markoff had been in.

Ne Win tapped one of his men on the shoulder and motioned for him to scout ahead, but Quinn stopped the man before he left.

'I'll do it,' he whispered.

'I'll go with you,' Tasha said.

Quinn shrugged, then left the others behind and entered the metal maze. He could hear

Tasha behind him, stepping lightly on the sandy ground.

Ahead and a little to his right, he heard a voice. He couldn't make out what was being said, only that the speaker was male, and the words sounded like English.

Quinn looked at Tasha and held a finger to his lips. The glare she gave him back told him there was no need to emphasize the obvious.

He took the next aisle right, then zigzagged toward where the sound had come from. Again Tasha followed.

Ahead a car door slammed shut.

Quinn could see an open area beyond the final stack. The noise had come from there.

He eased forward until he was only a few feet from the end. He could feel Tasha peering over his shoulder.

He turned his head. 'Wait back there,' he said, the words barely audible. He nodded in the direction they'd just come.

'Uh-uh,' she murmured.

'Now,' Quinn said.

Her jaw tensed, but a few seconds later she pulled back and retreated to the end of the row.

Quinn returned his attention to the clearing. It looked to be about fifty feet wide and was lined on all four sides by more of the metal boxes. There were narrow passageways between each row, with only one wider break. It was off to Quinn's right and was large enough for a truck to pass through. The front gate, Quinn assumed.

He moved right to the edge, tilting his head so he could see around the corner of the container.

The Mercedes sedan that he and the others had taken to the Maxwell Food Centre was parked in the middle of the clearing.

There were four people near the car. Two were on their knees, their hands clasped behind their heads. There was no mistaking them.

It was Congressman Guerrero and Kenneth Murray.

Jenny was standing in front of them, a gun in her hand. Behind them was a man Quinn had never seen before. But he was willing to bet it was the same man who'd showed up at the Quayside during the blackout. There had been two people then. One had been young and was sitting in the car when Ne Win's man had spotted them. With her short hair and slight form, Quinn was also willing to bet the young man had been Jenny.

Quinn took a deep, silent breath. For over a week, he'd been trying to help Markoff's girlfriend and discover who had left Markoff to die. But the person he was after was also the person he'd been trying to help. Jenny had never cared about Markoff. She'd only been using him. And when that usefulness had run its course, she'd disposed of him.

And now she had played Quinn like she'd played Markoff.

Only Quinn wasn't going to be played anymore.

Jenny said something to her partner, then started walking toward the stacks that lined the rear of the compound.

Quinn pulled back until he reached Tasha.

Further down the aisle, he could see Ne Win and his two men waiting. Quinn held up one finger, then motioned for someone to come to him.

Ne Win tapped Lian on the shoulder.

'Take my position here and keep an eye on them,' Quinn whispered directly into Lian's ear as soon as he got there. 'If it looks like they're going to kill one of the hostages, take the shooter out.'

Lian nodded.

Quinn reluctantly motioned for Tasha to follow him, then began moving off to his right. Within moments, they reached an intersection of a path that ran along the back side of the compound. It led toward the section Jenny had entered moments earlier.

Quinn leaned around the edge of a container. He could hear footsteps in the distance, down one of the intersecting aisles. At this distance, he couldn't tell exactly which direction they were going in.

'Wait here,' he said to Tasha.

'No,' she replied.

'I don't need you getting in my way.'

'I don't give a shit what you need,' she said. 'I'm the one who'll be bringing her in.'

He knew whatever he said she wasn't going to listen, so he made his best guess which aisle Jenny had gone down, and began running toward it.

He stopped when he reached his target aisle, got as close to the edge as possible, then listened. It was quiet, no steps at all. *Did she hear us?* he wondered.

He looked over his shoulder past Tasha, half expecting to see Jenny standing there waiting for him to notice her. But there was no one there.

There was the crunch of sand under a shoe, then again. The steps had returned. They were at least fifty feet down the new path and moving away from Quinn's position. Then the feet stopped again and were followed almost immediately by the sound of metal on metal.

He'd heard the sound before, recently, though it seemed like years ago. It was the sound of the doors of a container opening.

After about ten seconds, the doors shut again, and the footsteps returned. Apparently, Jenny was looking for something specific. Not cargo; these containers would all be empty.

No, she was looking for the perfect tomb, he realized. An unfitting resting place for a presidential candidate.

Instead of following her, he turned in the other direction and led Tasha toward the clearing.

Nothing had changed. Guerrero and Murray were still kneeling on the dirt, and Jenny's man was standing watch behind them.

Nothing had changed, that is, except Quinn's angle. He was now behind the watcher.

He listened and was immediately rewarded with the sound of Jenny's footsteps still far away.

'This time you stay,' he said to Tasha. 'Watch my back in case she returns.'

'What are you going to do?'

'Our first priority,' he said, repeating her words. 'Freeing the hostages.'

'You can't do it alone.'

'Just stay here.'

The nod she gave him was so slight, it barely even registered. But it was enough.

Carefully he moved out from between the containers. He measured each step, rolling from the balls of his feet to his toes, then pushing off again. He didn't let his heels touch the ground until he was standing two feet behind the man.

Quinn wanted to shoot him, but while the sound of a suppressor was by design minimal, it was still distinctive, especially to those who were familiar with it. Quinn had no doubt it was a sound Jenny knew well.

He flipped his SIG around so that he was holding it by the barrel, then whipped it against the man's temple. There was the slap of metal against skin, but that was it. The man didn't even have the opportunity to yell out in pain before he lost consciousness.

Quinn caught him as he fell to the ground, minimizing the additional noise.

He stepped over the body, then leaned forward and touched the congressman on the shoulder. Guerrero reluctantly looked over his shoulder, then his eyes grew wide when he saw who it was.

Quinn was holding a finger to his lips. The congressman seemed to understand and remained silent.

Quinn then tapped Murray.

'You son of a — '

Quinn put his hand over Murray's mouth. Once he was sure Murray was going to keep quiet, he pointed at each of them, then at a break in the stacks off to the right. Lian was standing just in view, having moved out in response to Quinn's actions.

The congressman nodded, then rose into a crouch and began running toward Lian. Murray seemed to quickly realize the merit of the idea, and followed closely behind Guerrero.

As Quinn waited for them to disappear between the containers, rain began to fall. It went from nothing to downpour without any warning. The deluge pounded against the tops of the containers in a thunderous staccato.

Quinn turned and ran back over to where he had left Tasha. He no longer worried about masking his footsteps, as the rain effectively negated all other sound.

But before he even reached the metal maze, he brought himself to an abrupt stop, slipping nearly a foot on the new mud, but not falling down.

Tasha was no longer standing near the containers. She was lying on the ground, writhing in pain.

Standing where she had been was Jenny.

38

Jenny brought her pistol up to fire at Quinn. Without even thinking, he aimed his SIG in her direction, and pulled the trigger as he dove to the right.

He hit the ground hard. Mud and water splashed up onto his face and clothes. He fired again, but Jenny was gone.

In an instant, he was on his feet and running. Staying in the clearing only meant death. When he reached Tasha, he knelt down. It didn't look like she'd been shot, but there was a large gash on the side of her head.

'Can you hear me?' he said.

'Yes.' Her voice was infused with pain. 'I'll be fine. Just go find her.'

Quinn looked back to the clearing and saw Lian heading in their direction. The man pointed at Tasha, then at himself. The message was clear: he'd take care of her, Quinn could go.

Instead of heading for the aisle he'd last seen Jenny in, Quinn veered to the right, taking the next path over.

He was soaked, but he barely noticed as he raced between the containers. He tried to listen for her steps, but he was again defeated by the storm.

He came to a small opening between the containers. It was not quite a path, but was wide enough for him to squeeze through. As he

461

worked his way between the metal boxes, he realized there were thousands of places she could be hiding. He might never find her before she found him. This was the advantage the hunted had over the hunter, especially when the hunted was armed and deadly.

When he reached the next aisle, he paused for a second. There was no sound but the rain from beyond. Slow and deliberate, he moved out into the aisle just enough so that he could get a look in either direction.

To the left was the way back to the clearing. It was empty. And to the right, more metal containers. And rain.

And movement.

Jenny.

The rain had cut down visibility so he had almost missed her. But there she was, about seventy-five feet away, and headed deeper into the compound, toward the back fence.

Quinn moved into the aisle and began running after her. He stayed to the left, hugging the containers and using what little camouflage they could provide him.

She was moving fast, and he had to sprint to gain even a few feet on her. He was in serious danger of losing her again.

Without stopping, he brought his gun up and aimed in her direction. He knew as he pulled the trigger there was very little chance he would hit her. And he was right. There was no sign she had even noticed the bullet.

He took aim again and fired.

Another miss, but this time she reacted,

jumping to her right as if she was getting out of the way. She glanced over her shoulder, then cut to her left and disappeared around the end of a stack.

The rain was still continuing its relentless assault as if it were trying to erase all signs of man from the island. Quinn almost felt like he needed a machete to hack through it as he took the first opening to the left, down a parallel path to the one Tasha was on. The aisle at the next intersection was empty.

He continued on.

Another empty aisle.

But when he reached intersection number four, he caught a glimpse of her on the parallel path at the far end of the stack. Then she disappeared again.

He turned to his right, intending to move in behind her, but his movement had been too abrupt, and he slipped on the mud and slammed into the side of a box marked EVERGREEN.

His gun was knocked loose from his hand and landed in a dirty puddle a few feet away.

Quinn wiped the excess water from his forehead, then pushed himself onto his feet. His left shoulder pulsed with searing pain, and the arm below it felt like someone was randomly applying electroshock through his elbow.

He pushed the pain as far back in his mind as he could, then stumbled over and retrieved his gun. It was wet and covered in mud. He checked the end of the suppressor and wasn't surprised to find it full of crud. He detached it and threw it to the ground. There was no time to clean it, but at least the actual barrel of the gun was clean.

He forced himself back into a run. Pain shot out from his shoulder with every step, but it was just one more thing to ignore. Ahead was the path Jenny had been on, but he knew there was little chance she'd still be in sight.

He took the corner fast, hoping he was wrong. It turned out he was.

He barely made it halfway through the turn when a fist smashed into his cheek, sending him to the ground. Before he could even move, a foot landed on the gun in his hand.

'You're an annoying son of a bitch, aren't you?' Jenny said. Her gun was aimed at his head. 'Now you're going to be a dead one.'

Quinn let go of his own gun, then thrust his hand forward, grabbing the back of her calf and pulling her leg out from under her. She stumbled but caught herself, using her gun hand against the container.

Quinn lunged at her, his good shoulder leading him, and knocked her hard against the container.

He twisted her body as she started to bring the gun around, knocking the barrel against the metal box. Her grip slipped, but not enough for the gun to fall out of her hand.

He rammed her against the container again, but still she held on.

As he attempted to do it once more, she swung her leg up and back, pressing her foot against the container so that her knee was jutting out toward him. When he slammed into her again, her knee caught him square in the stomach and nearly knocked the air out of him.

She began to turn her gun on him as he staggered back a few feet. He had only one option. He whipped his SIG upward, knocking it into her pistol a second before she pulled the trigger. His gun raked against her thumb and cut a groove across her knuckle.

'Fuck!' she said.

Quinn hit her hand again. This time she reflexively opened it and let her gun tumble to the ground.

Her eyes grew wide with anger as she realized she had no chance to pick it up before Quinn would shoot her. So she kicked Quinn hard in the stomach, then took off running as he stumbled backward.

Quinn fell against the container, then pushed himself off and continued the pursuit.

Jenny was weaving in and out of the containers, making it impossible for him to get off a clean shot. Less than a hundred feet ahead, the stacks of containers came to a sudden end against a chain-link fence. Beyond the fence were bushes.

As they neared the end of the aisle, the rain began to lessen.

Jenny turned right, moving out of sight again. Quinn accelerated, taking the corner only seconds later. Only she wasn't there.

He raced ahead to the next aisle. No one.

As he glanced back the way he had come, he saw her. Not in one of the aisles, but on top of one of the container stacks. They were only two boxes high along the back of the compound.

Quinn realized from there someone could easily jump over the fence.

He found a stack he thought he could climb, then made his way up as quick as he could with one good arm. When he reached the top, he could see Jenny at the far end, getting ready to jump.

'Don't!' Quinn said.

He pointed his SIG at her, but she looked at him, laughed, then jumped over the fence.

Quinn cursed under his breath as he ran across the top of the stack to where she'd been. The rain was finally stopping, but there was still a distant rhythmic rumble. Quinn barely noticed, his concentration completely on Jenny.

He took three seconds to examine the other side of the fence, found a landing spot as good as any, then launched himself into the air.

The dirt was soft, loose, and wet. But it wasn't enough to keep his shoulder from yelling at him again. He clenched his teeth together to fight the pain as he quickly regained his feet.

Jenny was nowhere in sight, but the rain had turned the soft sand into a more than passable tracking system. Her footprints led south through the vegetation.

Quinn followed them, cautious and alert. The rumble he had heard from the top of the containers grew louder the further he got into the brush.

The tracks kept moving him forward. Then suddenly the bushes receded, and the source of the noise became evident. Across a small strip of sand was the Singapore Strait, its waves ending in mellow crashes onto the beach.

Out on the water, dozens of vessels, mostly container ships, moved through the strait. And beyond, he could see Indonesia. No rain there. Only blue sky.

Quinn looked left and right down the beach. If there had been anyone out enjoying an afternoon in the sun, the rain had chased them way.

But the beach wasn't completely empty. Jenny was standing near the water. She was looking at him, her back to the sea. Her hands hung at her sides, empty.

Quinn walked slowly toward her. He held his gun in front of him and kept it trained on her torso.

When only ten feet separated them, he stopped.

They stared at each other for nearly a minute, neither blinking nor moving.

Finally Quinn asked, 'Did you ever love him?'

'That's a stupid question,' she said. 'You're a professional, or at least you pretend to be. What do you think?'

'I think you used him right from the beginning. I think you talked him into helping you get a job with the congressman. I think it was all part of the plan your friends at LP came up with.'

She smiled, but didn't answer.

Behind him, he could hear footsteps on the wet sand, but kept looking at Jenny.

'So are you just a role player? Or are you on the permanent roster?'

'We don't use role players like you.' There was

a hint of superiority in her tone. 'But if you're interested in joining, I can put in a good word for you.'

'I think I have enough work for the moment.'

The steps behind Quinn suddenly stopped a few feet away.

'Who's your contact?' It was Tasha.

Quinn sensed her stop next to him, but there was no way he was going to take his eyes off of Jenny.

'Sorry. I don't know who you're talking about,' Jenny said.

'At LP, who do you report to?' Tasha asked.

That only garnered a laugh.

'Are there others like you planted out there?' Tasha said.

Still no response.

Tasha took a step forward. From the corner of Quinn's eye, he could see blood on her face. 'The only thing that's going to help you now is if you talk to us.'

'Hmm, really? I guess I'm not going to get any help, then, am I?'

'Don't think any of your *friends* are going to be able to get you out of this. You'll talk to us eventually.'

But the smile on Jenny's face led Quinn to believe Tasha was mistaken.

He asked, 'If you wanted to kill Guerrero, why did you leave D.C. early instead of traveling with him to Singapore?'

She took a step toward him.

'No,' he said, taking a step back. 'You're fine where you are.'

She laughed to herself, then looked at Tasha. 'Ask her.'

'We were getting too close,' Tasha said. 'You knew we'd get you before you had a chance. So running was your best option.'

'Something like that,' Jenny said.

'And Markoff?' Quinn asked.

'My wonderful boyfriend was beginning to suspect me. Not at first. At first he believed my story. The same one I told you, remember? You believed it, too.' She smiled. 'He never said anything to me. Tried to act all calm and cool. But I knew. I always know. That's why I'm good at what I do. No one ever deceives me. My only mistake was waiting too long before I disposed of him. I should have taken care of him before I left Washington.'

'You think that's the only mistake you've made?' Quinn said. He could feel every micrometer of the trigger's surface. A simple twitch would move it. Just a twitch.

Jenny didn't answer.

'Who is your contact?' Tasha asked for the third time. 'Give us names and we can work a deal.'

'You mean because you think you've caught me?' she asked. 'So I do a little jail time, that was always a risk. But I bet you'll be surprised how little time I actually end up spending there.'

'Not really. I know exactly how much time you'll spend in jail,' Quinn said. There was only one way this could play out, but he had to wait until Tasha realized it, too.

'What? You're going to kill me, Quinn? I don't believe that.'

Tasha took a step forward. 'Who. Is. Your. Contact?'

For over a minute, no one spoke, then Quinn slowly shook his head. 'Whatever information she has, you will never get it.'

Tasha's shoulders rose and then fell again as she took a deep breath.

'You already must realize it,' he went on. 'The minute it gets reported that you have her in custody, her friends in the LP will know.'

She hesitated a moment, then nodded.

'And I'm guessing they'll have the power to get her out.'

No nod this time, but she didn't argue the point.

'She killed Markoff,' he said. 'He was one of yours once.'

Finally she looked at Quinn. 'Eye for an eye?'

'I owe him.'

Tasha looked back at Jenny, saying nothing.

'So?' he asked.

'Give us a name,' Tasha said to Jenny. 'Something to go on.'

Jenny looked at Quinn, then back at Tasha. 'Did you guys work this routine out ahead of time? Think it might scare something out of me? Take me in, and let's get this over with. I'm getting hungry.'

'Give us a name,' Tasha repeated.

'Mother Teresa,' Jenny replied, smiling.

'Okay,' Tasha said. She looked at Quinn. 'I'm done.'

Without another word, she turned and started walking back toward the compound.

Quinn raised the gun another inch. His mind flashed on a memory of a fishing trip out of Cabo San Lucas. He and Markoff downing Coronas and paying very little attention to their lines. Jenny kissing her boyfriend before stretching out on the cabin roof to get a little sun.

Jenny laughed. 'You're not going to kill me, so just arrest me and take me in.'

Athens, where separate jobs had brought Markoff and Quinn to the city at the same time. A bottle of nasty ouzo, a night that went later than either had planned, and a conversation about dreams and desires that could only happen under the combination of the liquor and the hour.

'You're just a cleaner. A janitor,' Jenny said. 'You know how to remove the bodies. You don't know how to kill them. Quit playing around.'

San Diego, on the sailboat later in the day. Quinn watching Markoff as Markoff watched Jenny. The care and growing love in the older man's eyes genuine. But for what?

'I'm not playing,' Quinn said.

Jenny was still smiling when the bullet hit her in her chest.

It hadn't been a perfect shot, but it was more than adequate.

Quinn walked over to where she had fallen backward on the sand. He could hear her sucking in the last bits of air her lungs would ever absorb. The look on her face was one of surprise and shock.

'Your last mistake was underestimating me.'

471

39

Quinn stood over Jenny, waiting until he was sure she was dead. He then picked her up, put her over his good shoulder, and began walking back toward the compound.

Tasha was waiting for him at the edge of the bushes.

'You would have never gotten anything out of her,' he said.

'I know.'

'And what I said about her friends being able to get her out, that was the truth, wasn't it?'

'I can't know for sure, but my guess would be yes.'

'Who are they?'

'That's what we're trying to find out.'

Quinn nodded. This was no longer his fight. Markoff's killer was dead. That's all that mattered for the moment.

'My boss isn't going to be happy,' Tasha said as they trudged through the brush. 'But he'll understand. I'm . . . uh . . . I'm going to tell him she was killed during a pursuit.'

Quinn shrugged. 'Whatever works.'

As he neared the chain-link fence, Lian jumped down from the top of the container on the other side.

'Let me,' Lian said, motioning to Jenny's lifeless body.

'I'll do it,' Quinn said.

Lian nodded, then by a silent agreement Ne Win's man led Quinn and Tasha around the outside of the compound. When they reached the opening in the fence, Lian held it open while Quinn carried the body through.

Ne Win was waiting for him on the other side.

'The congressman and my friend?' Quinn asked.

'In the car,' Ne Win said. 'They are fine.'

'What about the man I knocked out?'

Ne Win shrugged. 'What man?'

'Thanks,' Quinn said. He turned to Tasha. 'I assume you don't need the body.'

'No.'

Without another word, he turned and started walking silently between the stacks of containers. This time only Ne Win and Lian followed.

It took Quinn nearly ten minutes before he found what he wanted.

The container was dark blue, and on the side in large white letters were the words BARON & BARON LTD. He looked at Lian, then pointed at it.

'That one,' he said.

After Lian opened the container door, Quinn carried the body inside, then dropped it on the floor. He didn't pause or even look back as he exited.

Once Quinn was back outside, Lian closed the doors.

'It would be good if that one went out to sea soon,' Quinn said to Ne Win. 'And it'll be a shame when it falls off the deck in the middle of nowhere.'

'Yes,' Ne Win said. 'A shame.'

★　★　★

'Exactly when did you tell me there was a chance I might be killed?' Murray demanded as Quinn opened the door of Ne Win's car.

'Not now, Kenneth,' Quinn said.

Quinn and Tasha climbed into the back with Murray and the congressman. It was a tight squeeze, but they made it work. Murray was obviously agitated, but the congressman was quiet, staring down at the floor, not looking at anyone.

In front, Lian switched places with Ne Win's other man in the driver's seat, while Ne Win climbed into his customary spot. There wasn't room for everyone, so the other man had to wait for someone to come back and pick him up.

As they started to drive away, Guerrero finally looked up. 'She worked for me for a year,' he said like he couldn't believe his own words. 'I had her to my house for parties and meetings. I saw her at the office almost every day.' He turned to Tasha. 'When you told me she was there to kill me, I . . . I couldn't believe it. Why? Why would she do that?'

Quinn looked out the side window. 'Because that was what she was told to do.'

The congressman sat quietly for a moment, his breaths deep and even. Finally he looked from Tasha to Quinn. 'Perhaps you should tell me everything. And Mr. Drake, you can start by giving me your real name.'

Quinn thought for a moment. There was no way they were going to tell the congressman

474

everything, but they could tell him enough.

'I'm Jonathan Quinn,' he said, starting off with a lie.

Like Richard Drake, Jonathan Quinn wasn't his real name, either.

★   ★   ★

Nate was in surgery until almost midnight. He was in a small private hospital west of downtown. Dr. Han — not a surgeon himself — had seen to it that Nate got the best help possible. And Quinn, through Ne Win, had promised substantial reimbursement for everyone's silence.

Quinn and Orlando waited in a small windowless room. Ne Win was there, too. But he kept getting phone calls, so he'd excuse himself and walk outside to take them.

'Lots of stuff on news tonight,' Ne Win said during one of his lulls between interruptions. 'Everyone talking about gunfight at Maxwell. Think there are some dangerous people in town.'

'There were,' Quinn said.

'Congressman go on CNN International, too. He say he in wrong place at wrong time. He say some helpful locals get him to safety. No one mentioned assassination attempt.'

Quinn grunted. That was good. But in truth, he didn't really care what happened at this point. He didn't care much about anything except Nate and Orlando.

He had left Los Angeles because he was worried his dead friend's girlfriend was in trouble. Now she was dead, and he was the one who had pulled the trigger. He tried not to think about it, but he was doing a lousy job of it.

Orlando seemed to sense what he was going through. She put a hand on his back and slowly rubbed the base of his neck. She said nothing, which was just another testament to how well she knew him. If he needed to talk, she'd be there. He knew that.

It was another thirty minutes before Dr. Han came into the waiting room.

'He's in his room now,' the doctor said. 'He's a tough one. That was a lot of blood he lost, but he never stopped fighting to stay alive. He'll be okay. Well . . . considering . . . '

The doctor led them to Nate's room.

'He won't stir until the morning,' Dr. Han said.

'We won't stay long,' Quinn said.

The doctor looked at Quinn, then at Orlando, and finally at Ne Win. 'I think you could all use some sleep also,' he said, then left.

Quinn stood next to his apprentice's bed. There were wires and tubes everywhere, making Nate look like an unused marionette waiting for his puppet master to wake him up.

His face looked serene and unscathed. Quinn could almost believe that Nate was fine, that all would be back to normal soon. But then he allowed his gaze to move away from Nate's face, first to the shoulder that was covered in bandages, then toward the end of the bed.

There was a little bump jutting up from the sheets where Nate's left foot was. But where his right should have been, there was nothing. The amputation was from just above where the break had occurred near the midpoint of his shin.

The foot could have stayed, but it would have never been useful. Nate would have been forever crippled. Of course, he was forever crippled now, Quinn knew, but at least he had the chance at the appearance of normality.

Prosthetics had come a long way. At least that's what Orlando had said when Quinn had been forced to make the decision of whether to keep Nate's foot or not.

★   ★   ★

Quinn saw Tasha one more time. They met at one of the shop-house restaurants along Clarke Quay. Tasha had gotten there first and was sitting at an outside table next to the river.

'We found the patsy,' she said, once the waitress had taken their drink order. 'His name was Ahmad Kamarudin. We found him tied up and unconscious in a government flat east of downtown. Well, we didn't find him. Your friend did.'

She was talking about Ne Win. By mutual consent, he had continued his search for Jenny's red herring.

'The hair at the Quayside apartment was his. Just like you said.'

Quinn nodded. There was nothing for him to say.

'We've also been able to backtrack Jenny's movements. There might be some stuff there we can use to find out more about . . . the people she worked for.'

'You may want to check the wife,' Quinn said.

'Guerrero's wife? Do you think she's one of them?'

'No,' he said. 'But I'm just wondering if maybe she's been targeted for recruitment, perhaps with the intention of bringing her in after her husband was killed. They could have been planning to use her just the way Jenny said they would. My guess is if that was the case, she's probably already had some casual contact with the LP and doesn't even know it. Perhaps even someone in the policy think tank she belongs to.'

Tasha thought a moment. 'It's possible. I'll try to check it out. Thanks.'

Quinn's eyes were drawn to a river taxi passing slowly by. When he looked back at Tasha, he asked, 'Why are you being so open with me about this?'

'Because — ' Tasha stopped herself as the waitress appeared and set their drinks on the table — a Tiger beer for Quinn and a gin and tonic for Tasha.

Once she was gone, Tasha started again. 'Because I want you to come work for me. You know at least a little about what's going on, and there are only a few people I can trust.'

Quinn took a drink of his beer, then set the glass back down. 'I don't do exclusives.'

'You're an excellent tracker. You found Jenny when we couldn't. You're smart, and you adapt quickly.'

Quinn took another drink, then stood up. 'I'm not a tracker. I'm a cleaner. Sorry.'

She looked him in the eyes. 'I need you. This is more important than any rules you think you might have.'

Quinn said nothing for several seconds. Finally, 'If I'm available, we can talk.'

As he started to walk away, she said, 'So that's not a no?'

He didn't turn back.

★ ★ ★

Orlando stayed for nearly a week, going with Quinn to the clinic during the day, making love with him at night. In many ways, they were the best few days of Quinn's life, and in many ways, when it came to Nate, they were the worst.

One night at dinner, Orlando said, 'I have to go.'

Quinn knew it was coming. Her son needed her. 'I understand,' he said.

'Do you?' she asked. 'Do you know how hard it is for me to leave you now?'

Just as hard as it will be for me to see you go, he thought. But he only nodded.

'Maybe . . . maybe I can bring Garrett to L.A.,' she said.

'No. Don't. I'll come to you. I just . . . I need to get a few things settled first.'

She leaned across the table and touched his face with her hand. 'We'll be waiting.'

★ ★ ★

It was another two weeks before Quinn and Nate were able to leave the island.

'I've lined up some appointments for you back home,' Quinn said to Nate as they flew back to Los Angeles.

'What kind of appointments?' his apprentice asked.

'With a doctor, and a prosthetic clinic.'

'Oh.' Nate turned back to the magazine he was looking at. Five minutes later, he said, 'This doesn't change anything. I can still do this job.'

It was still too early to have this conversation, and it was definitely the wrong place. 'Let's see what they say,' Quinn said.

'I know what you're thinking,' Nate said. 'But I'll prove it to you.'

'Okay.'

'Is that an 'okay shut up'? Or an 'okay you'll give me a fair chance'?'

'It's an 'okay we'll see.''

The answer didn't seem to satisfy his apprentice, but he let it drop.

★ ★ ★

Early October was already cold in southern Wisconsin. Not mid-winter cold; there was no snow on the ground. But at night, water would freeze, and in the morning, grass would crunch underfoot.

Quinn usually hated the cold. But for this trip, it seemed appropriate.

The graveyard was a small one just on the outskirts of Madison. The plot Quinn had purchased was in the back, near a stand of trees. Out of the way. Inconspicuous. Perfect.

The hole was already dug, and the casket was suspended above it when Quinn arrived. He asked the two cemetery workers standing nearby if they wouldn't mind giving him a few minutes alone. They nodded in understanding and walked toward the small chapel at the front of the facility.

Two days after Quinn and Nate arrived in Los Angeles, Quinn had taken another drive out into the desert. Finding Markoff's temporary resting place had not been difficult. Neither had digging up the remains.

Now he was in Markoff's home state, giving his friend the burial he should have had from the very beginning. Nate had offered to come, but Quinn had left him in Los Angeles. When Quinn had called Derek Blackmoore, the old spy runner had also wanted to attend, but his recovery from the severe beating he'd had was slow and painful. So Quinn was alone. Somehow, though, that felt right.

Quinn closed his eyes and recited the Lord's Prayer. He didn't know if it was even the right prayer to say, but it was all he knew, and even then, he didn't know it well.

When he was through, he looked at the box again, then took a step back. 'I guess this'll have to make us even,' he said. He turned and began walking back to his car.

As he drove toward the Dane County Regional Airport, he pulled out his cell phone.

'Are you asleep?' he asked when she answered.

481

'No,' she said.

Though it was the middle of the night in Vietnam, Orlando had known what he was doing today, and had insisted he call her when he was through.

'How did it go?' she asked.

'Fine,' he said. 'Quiet. It's a beautiful area, not like where he was.'

'How are you?'

Quinn thought for a moment before answering. 'I'm okay. Better now, I guess.'

'Good,' she said.

The air between Middle America and Southeast Asia went silent for several seconds. But it wasn't an awkward silence. It was as if each knew the other was there and that was enough.

'When do you go back to L.A.?' she asked.

'Tonight. Nate's got an appointment with a doctor tomorrow afternoon.'

'Tell him I'm thinking about him.'

'I will.'

'Quinn?'

'Yes?'

A pause.

'When are you coming to me?'

ACKNOWLEDGMENTS

First and foremost, a special thank-you to my editor Danielle Perez for her insights and dedication; to Nita Taublib for her enthusiasm and support; to Irwyn Applebaum for everything he does for writers and publishing; and to Chris Artis, Sharon Swados, and the rest of the Bantam Dell team for their tireless efforts. In addition, thank you to my wonderful agent Anne Hawkins, who has always been there for me.

I'd also like to acknowledge a group of people who have helped me in various ways — from research to reading drafts to just being there as I threw out ideas. They include, but are not limited to: Bruce, Suzie, Brooke and Jessica Lambert, Darren Battles, Richard Weideman, Catherine White, Rick Von Feldt, Tammy Sparks, Kathy Karner, Theresa Imbach, Jon Rivera, Dawn Butler, James and Barbara Battles, Derek Rogers, Brian Perry, Donna Kuyper, Stephen Blackmoore, Spike Koplansky, Alison Perkins, James Vandersea, Bobby McCue, Linda Brown, Phil Hawley Jr., Bill Cameron, Sean Chercover, Tasha Alexander, John Ramsey Miller, John Gilstrap, and Robert Gregory Browne.

As always, any errors can be attributable to only one person. When I find out who that is, I'll let you know.

We do hope that you have enjoyed reading this large print book.

Did you know that all of our titles are available for purchase?

We publish a wide range of high quality large print books including:
Romances, Mysteries, Classics
General Fiction
Non Fiction and Westerns

Special interest titles available in large print are:
The Little Oxford Dictionary
Music Book
Song Book
Hymn Book
Service Book

Also available from us courtesy of Oxford University Press:
Young Readers' Dictionary
(large print edition)
Young Readers' Thesaurus
(large print edition)

For further information or a free brochure, please contact us at:
Ulverscroft Large Print Books Ltd.,
The Green, Bradgate Road, Anstey,
Leicester, LE7 7FU, England.
Tel: (00 44) 0116 236 4325
Fax: (00 44) 0116 234 0205

THE CLEANER

Brett Battles

Jonathan Quinn is a freelance espionage operative with a take-no-prisoners style and the heart of a loner. His job? Professional 'cleaner'. Nothing too violent, just disposing of bodies, doing a little erasing of uncomfortable evidence if necessary. When Quinn has to investigate a suspicious case of arson, it seems simple enough. But when a dead body turns up where it doesn't belong — and Quinn's handlers at 'the Office' fall strangely silent — he knows he's in over his head. With only a handful of clues, Quinn dives for cover, struggling to find out why someone wants him dead — and if it's linked to a larger attempt to wipe out the Office.

BEAT THE REAPER

Josh Bazell

Peter Brown is a young Manhattan emergency room doctor with an unusual past. His real name Pietro Brnwa, and he is on the FBI's protection programme. After finding his grandparents dead, murdered by the Mafia, he's become proficient in Martial Arts and using a handgun. His goal: to find and despatch those who committed the crime. He fortuitously befriends, and is assisted by, a Mafia lawyer, who discovers their identities. But when he reveals them to Pietro, is there an ulterior motive? Then a new patient visits Peter who knows him from his other life, when he had a different name and a very different job. Now, whatever it takes, he must keep his patient alive so he can buy some time . . . and beat the reaper.

THE REAPERS

John Connolly

They are the reapers. The elite among killers. Men so terrifying that their names are mentioned only in whispers. The assassin Louis is one of them. But now Louis, and his partner, Angel, are themselves targets. And there is no shortage of suspects. A wealthy recluse sends them north to a town that no longer exists on any map. A town ruled by a man with very personal reasons for wanting Louis' blood spilt. There they find themselves trapped, isolated, and at the mercy of a killer feared above all others: the assassin of assassins, Bliss. There's only one man who can help. Charlie Parker.

THE DARKER SIDE

Cody Mcfadyen

FBI Agent Smoky Barrett and her team are called in by the Director himself to investigate a murder committed on a flight from Texas to Virginia. They find that they are dealing with a serial killer who has already struck a truly horrific number of times. He kills people with the deepest, darkest secrets and is using them to target and destroy his victims. The case is about to go public, with all the accelerated power of the internet behind it and public hysteria is not far behind. Smoky is under intense pressure to get results, yet the team has never been faced with such an apparently insoluble problem. Who will the next victim be? Everyone in the world has secrets. Even Smoky.